A
CROWN
OF
WISHES

ALSO BY ROSHANI CHOKSHI

The Star-Touched Queen

A
CROWN
OF
WISHES

ROSHANI CHOKSHI

St. Martin's Griffin
New York

A CROWN OF WISHES. Copyright © 2017 by Roshani Chokshi. All rights reserved. Printed in the United States of America. For information, address St. Martin's Press, 175 Fifth Avenue, New York, N.Y. 10010.

www.stmartins.com

The Library of Congress Cataloging-in-Publication Data is available upon request.

ISBN 978-1-250-08549-8 (hardcover)
ISBN 978-1-250-15609-9 (international, sold outside the
U.S., subject to rights availability)
ISBN 978-1-250-08550-4 (e-book)

Our books may be purchased in bulk for promotional, educational, or business use. Please contact your local bookseller or the Macmillan Corporate and Premium Sales Department at 1-800-221-7945, extension 5442, or by e-mail at MacmillanSpecialMarkets@macmillan.com.

First U.S. Edition: March 2017

First International Edition: March 2017

10   9   8   7   6   5   4   3   2   1

For my siblings, Monica and Jayesh.

And for all siblings who refuse to be secondary characters in anyone's tale.

You are legends in the making.

ACKNOWLEDGMENTS

Second books are hard. I realize how trite that sounds. Writing is hard. Getting out of bed on Mondays is hard. But second books are a unique form of pain because they are ruthless in their demands. It's like *If You Give a Mouse a Cookie* but throw in cesspits of despair, an ego ravaged by debut year and the sheer panic of not knowing "how to book." But this book emerged tough and hungry, and it wouldn't have been possible without the help of so many resplendent individuals.

To my critique partner, Lyra Selene: You read this in awful draft form and loved it first! Thanks for the feedback and crying Claire Danes gifs. I am so glad to call you a friend. To JJ: Let the record show that you claimed Vikram first. Thanks for letting me ramble over drinks and then ramble because of drinks. You are an Oracle. To Stephanie Garber: Thanks for being an imitable cheerleader and fellow Regency romance reader. Our hours-long phone chats bring me the best kind of joy. To Tristina Wright, Sona Charaipotra, Ayesha Patel, Annie Kirke,

ACKNOWLEDGMENTS

Amanda Foody: Thank you for beta reading with kind eyes and an open heart. To Sarah J. Maas: Thank you for lending your invaluable warrior queen insight on this draft, for Barrons (because *swoon*) and for taking the time to listen and advise with kindness and humor. To Jessie Sima: Thanks for the beautiful art and fangirling over PYNCH with me. To Kat Howard, Kavitha Nallathambhi and Sohum Chokshi: I am always indebted to your wisdom and friendship, and grateful for your insight. To the Ladies of Tall Tree Lane (Leah Bobet, Ryan Graudin, E. K. Johnston, Lindsay Smith and Emma Higginbotham): Thanks for the liquor and laughter and vanquishing of dock spiders. "It was a good death." To Sabaa Tahir, Renee Ahdieh, Beth Revis and Jodi Meadows: Thank you for your kindness, generosity and brilliance throughout the year. I am so grateful.

I can't thank the booktube and blogging community enough for shouting about *The Star-Touched Queen* and inspiring me every day. Special thanks to Rachel Simon, Brittany at Brittany's Book Rambles, Alexandra at Lit Legionnaire, Summer at Butter My Books, Rachel at YA Perfectionist, Samantha at Thoughts on Tomes and Melissa Lee at Live Love Read YA. Shoutout to Viktoria (@seelieknight) and Andrea (@ashryvur) whose playlists got me through revisions and coaxed out the words.

To my St. Martin's Press family: Thank you so much for your support, guidance and for giving a loving home to my stories. Eileen, you see the bones of a story when all I see is purple prose and nonsense. Thank you for believing in me, and for wearing a thousand hats: cheerleader, romance novel recommender, life guru. To the fabulous marketing and publicity team (Brittoni, Karen and DJ): Giving each of you a crown of wishes would still be inadequate thanks. To the library team (Talia and

Annie): Thank you for all that you've done! Talia, I'm working on your vampire story.

A thousand and one thanks to my brilliant agent Thao Le. I am so humbled to have someone as hardworking and creative as you on my team. To my family at Sandra Dijkstra Literary Agency, especially Jessica Watterson and Jennifer Kim. Thanks for all your help and support. To Andrea Cavallaro: Thank you for taking *The Star-Touched Queen* overseas and giving it a home abroad.

To my friends, without whom I would be a codfish. Victoria G.: Thanks for switching shoes with me that fateful day in kindergarten. Niv S.: Thank you for the tea and fairy tales. Bismah R.: Thank you for Swedish Fish and quasi-French lessons. Chelsey B.: Thank you for agreeing that poisonous courtesans are always a yes.

To the Chokshi, Gandhi, Negrosa, de Leon clans: your support and love is my foundation. Forever indebted to Momo, Dodo, Cookie, Poggi and Panda Bear: Thanks for not batting an eyelash when I run through the house, leaving glasses everywhere, donning horns, consulting with the forces of evil and never quite explaining my writing projects. To Shraya, Pallavi Auntie and Sanjay Uncle: Thank you for letting me into your lives and your kitchen. Thanks for the support, love, rat gasps, and pizza. To Aman: Thank you for the laughter and pecan pie, for keeping promises and banishing nightmares, for reminding me how to human and always challenging me. Most importantly, thank you for coaxing out the magic in the world when I've forgotten how to see it.

And last, to my readers. I adore you to pieces. You inspire me every day and humble me beyond measure. Thank you for the fan art, playlists, letters, encouragement and love. Thank you for giving me the chance to tell these stories.

A

CROWN

OF

WISHES

THE INVITATION

Vikram had spent enough time with bitterness that he knew how to twist and numb the feeling. Tonight, he didn't draw on his years of experience. Instead he let the acidic, snapping teeth of it chew at his heart. As he walked to the network of wooden huts that formed the ashram, the echo of laughter hung in the air. He stood in the dark, an outsider to a joke everyone knew.

Since he was eight years old, he had spent part of every year at the ashram, learning alongside other nobility. Everyone else resented the part of the year where they returned to their kingdoms and endured having to put their lessons to use. Not Vikram. Every time he returned to Ujijain, he was reminded that his education was a formality. Not a foundation. He preferred that. No expectations meant learning without fear of being limited and growing opinions without fear of voicing them. His thoughts preferred the fertile ground of silence. Silence sharpened shrewdness, which only made him embrace the title his father's empire had, albeit grudgingly, given him: Fox Prince.

But shrewd or not, the moment he entered the ashram, he wouldn't be able to ignore the celebrations of another prince called home to rule. Soon, Ujijain would summon him home. And then what? The days would bleed together. The hope would shrivel. It would be harder to outwit the council. Harder to speak. He tightened his fists. That bitterness turned taunting. How many years had he spent believing that he was meant for more? Sometimes he thought his head was a snarl of myth and folktales, where magic coaxed ignored princes out of the shadows and gave them a crown and a legend to live in. He used to wait for the moment when magic would drape a new world over his eyes. But time turned his hopes dull and lightless. The Council of Ujijain had seen to that.

Near the entrance of the ashram, a sage sat beside the dying flames of a ceremonial fire. What was a sage doing here at this hour? Around his neck, the sage wore the pelt of a golden mongoose. *Not a pelt.* A real mongoose. The creature was napping.

"There you are," said the sage, opening his eyes. "I've been waiting for you for quite some time, Fox Prince."

Vikram stilled, suspicion prickling in his spine. No one waited for him. No one looked for him. The mongoose around the sage's neck yawned. Something tumbled out of the creature's mouth. Vikram reached for it, his heart racing as his hand closed around something cold and hard: a ruby. The ruby shone with unnatural light.

The mongoose yawned . . . jewels?

"Show-off," said the sage, bopping the mongoose on its nose.

The creature's ears flattened in reproach. Its fur shimmered in the dark. Bright as true gold. Bright as . . . magic. When he was a child, Vikram thought enchantment would save him. He even tried to trap it. Once he laid out a net to catch a wish-bestowing *yaksha* and ended up with a very outraged peacock. When he got older, he stopped trying. But he couldn't give up hoping. Hope was the only thing that lay between him and a throne that would only be his in name. He clutched the ruby tighter. It pulsed, shuddering as an image danced in its face—an image of *him*. Sitting on the throne. Powerful. Freed.

Vikram nearly dropped the ruby. Magic clung to his body. Starlight raced through his veins, and the sage grinned.

"Can't speak? There, there, little Fox Prince. Perhaps all the words are knocking against your head and you simply can't reach out and snatch the right one. But I am kind. Well, perhaps not. Kindness is a rather squishy thing. But I do love to lend assistance. Here is what you should say: 'Why are you here?'"

Shocked, all Vikram could do was nod.

The sage smiled. Sometimes a smile was little more than a sliver of teeth. And sometimes a smile was a knife cutting the world in two: before and after. The sage's smile belonged to the latter. And Vikram, who had never been anxious, felt as if his whole world was about to be rearranged by that grin.

"I am here because you summoned me, princeling. I am here to extend an invitation for a game that takes place when the century has grown old. I am here to tell you that the Lord of Wealth and Treasures caught a whiff of your dreams and followed it until he found your hungry heart and cunning smile."

The ruby in Vikram's palm quivered and shook. Crimson light broke in front of his eyes and he saw that the ruby was not a ruby, but an invitation in the shape of a jewel. It shook itself out . . . unfurling into gold parchment that read:

THE LORD OF WEALTH AND TREASURES CORDIALLY INVITES YOU TO *THE TOURNAMENT OF WISHES.*

Please present the ruby and a secret truth to the gate guardians by the new moon.

This ruby is good for two living entries.

The winner will be granted their heart's wish.
But know now that desire is a poisonous thing.

Vikram stared up from the parchment. Distantly, he knew he should be frightened. But fright paled compared to the hope knifing through him. That shadowed part of him that had craved for something *more* was no childhood fantasy gone twisted with age. Perhaps it had always been a premonition. Like knowledge buried in the soul and not the sight. True but hidden things.

The sage nodded to the ruby. "Look and see what awaits you."

He looked, but saw nothing.

"Try singing! The ruby wants to feel loved. Seduced."

"I wouldn't call my singing voice seduction," said Vikram, finding his voice. "More like sacrilege, honestly."

"It's not the sound of your song that coaxes out truth. It's the sincerity. Like this—"

The sage sung no song, but a story. Vikram's story. An image burned in the ruby. Vikram clutching the Emperor with one hand and tightly holding a bundle of blue flowers in the other. Voices slipped out of the gem: muffled displeasure, the title "heir of Ujijain" spoken around a laugh. He saw the future Ujijain promised him—a useless life of luxury wearing the face of power. He saw the nightmare of a long life, day upon day of stillness. His chest tightened. He'd rather die. The sage's voice had no tone. But it had texture, like a scattering of gold coins.

> "If you want a throne, you'll have to play
> The Lord of Treasures loves his games and tales
> A wanting heart will make his day
> Or you can waste your life recounting fails
> But say it, little prince, say you'll play this game
> If you and a partner play, never will you be the same."

The ashram huts loomed closer and the fires crackled like topaz. The idea took root in Vikram's mind. He'd built his life on wanting the impossible—true power, recognition, a future—and now magic had found him the moment he stopped looking. It breathed life into all those old dreams, filling him with that most terrible of questions: *What if . . .*

But even as his heart leapt to believe it, the sage's words made him pause.

"Why did you say partner?"

"It is required of your invitation."

Vikram frowned. The princes in the ashram had never inspired his faith in teams.

"Find the one who glows, with blood on the lips and fangs in the heart."

"Sounds as though they would be hard to miss."

"For you, doubly so," said the sage. His voice expanded. Not quite human. The sound rose from everywhere, dripping from the sky, growing out of the dirt. "Say you will play. Play the game and you may yet win your empire, not just the husk of its name. You only get one chance to accept."

The sage sliced his hand across the flames. Images spilled out like jewels:

A palace of ivory and gold, riven with black streams where caught stars wriggled and gave up their light. There were prophecies etched on doorframes, and the sky above was nothing but undulating ocean where discarded legends knifed through the water. A thousand *yakshas* and *yakshinis* trailed frost, forest brambles, pond swill and cloudy coronets. They were preparing for something. Vikram felt as if he'd tasted his dreams and starved for more.

Magic plucked at his bones, begging him to leave this version of himself behind. He leaned forward, his heart racing to keep up with the present.

"Yes," he breathed.

As if he could say anything else.

The moment split. Silently, the world fell back on itself.

"Excellent!" said the sage. "We will see you in Alaka at the new moon."

"Alaka? But that's, I mean, I *thought* it was myth."

"Oh dear boy, getting there is half the game." The sage winked. "Good for two living entries!"

"What about two living exits?"

"I like you," laughed the sage.

In a blink, he disappeared.

PART ONE

THE GIRL

1

TO BE A MONSTER

GAURI

Death stood on the other side of the chamber doors. Today I would meet it not in my usual armor of leather and chain mail, but in the armor of silk and cosmetics. One might think one armor was stronger than the other, but a red lip was its own scimitar and a kohl-darkened eye could aim true as a steel-tipped arrow.

Death might be waiting, but I was going to be a queen. I would have my throne if I had to carve a path of blood and bone to get it back.

Death could wait.

The bath was scalding, but after six months in a dungeon, it felt luxurious. Gauzy columns of fragrance spun slowly through the bath chambers, filling my lungs with an attar of roses. For a moment, thoughts of home choked me. Home, with the pockets of wildflowers and sandstone temples cut into the hills, with the people whose names I had come to murmur in my prayers before sleep. Home, where Nalini would have been waiting with a wry and inappropriate joke, her heart full of trust that I hadn't deserved. But that home was gone. Skanda, my brother, would have made sure by now that no hearth in Bharata would welcome me.

The Ujijain attendant who was supposed to prepare me for my first—and probably last—meeting with the Prince of Ujijain didn't speak. Then again, what do you say to those who are about to be sentenced to death? I knew what was coming. I'd gathered that much from the guards outside my dungeon. I wanted intelligence, so I faked whimpering nightmares. I'd practiced a limp. I'd let them think that my reputation was nothing more than rumor. I'd even let one of them touch my hair and tell me that perhaps he could be convinced to get me better food. I'm still proud that I sobbed instead of ripping out his throat with my teeth. It was worth it. People have a tendency to want to comfort small, broken-looking things. They told me they'd keep my death quick if I'd only smile for them one more time. I hated being told to smile. But now I knew the rotation of the guards' schedule. I knew which ones nursed battle wounds and how they entered the palace. I knew that no sentinels guarded the eastern gate. I knew which soldiers grinned despite their bad knee. I knew how to escape.

My hair hung in wet ropes against my back as I slid into the silken robes. No coarse linens for the Princess of Bharata. Royalty has the strangest advantages. Silently, the attendant led me to an adjoining chamber where the silver walls formed gigantic polished mirrors.

Slender glass alembics filled with fragrant oils, tiny cruets of kohl and silk purses of pearl and carmine powder crowded a low table. Brushes of reeds and hewn ivory shaped like writing implements caught the light. Homesickness slashed through me. I had to clasp my hands together to stop from reaching out over the familiar cosmetics. The harem mothers had taught me how to use these. Under my mothers' tutelage, I learned that beauty could be conjured. And under my and Nalini's instruction, my mothers learned that death could hide in beauty.

In Bharata, Nalini had commissioned slim daggers that could be folded into jeweled hairpins. Together, we'd taught the mothers how to defend themselves. Before Nalini, I used to steal shears and sneak into the forge so the blacksmith could teach me about the balance of a sword. My father allowed me to learn alongside the soldiers, telling me that if I was bent on maiming something, then it might as well be the enemies of Bharata. When he died, Bharata's training grounds became a refuge from Skanda. There, I was safe from him. And not just safe, but not *hurting* anyone. Being a soldier was the only way that I could keep safe the people I loved.

It was my way of making amends for what Skanda made me do.

The attendant yanked my chin. She took a tool—the wrong one, I noticed—and scraped the red pigment onto my lips.

"Allow me—" I started, but she shut me up.

"If you speak, I will make sure that my hand slips when I use that sharp tool around your eyes."

Princess or not, I was still the enemy. I respected her fury. Her loyalty. But if she messed up my cosmetics, that was a different story. I closed my eyes, trying not to flinch under the attendant's ministrations. I tried to picture myself anywhere but here, and memory mercifully plucked me from my own thoughts and took me back to when I was ten years old, sobbing because my sister, Maya, had left Bharata.

Mother Dhina had dried my tears, scooped me onto her lap and let me watch as she applied her cosmetics for the day.

This is how we protect ourselves, beti. *Whatever insults or hurts are thrown at our face, these are our barriers. No matter how broken we feel, it is only the paint that aches.*

We can always wash it away.

A soft brush swept across my cheek, scattering a fine dust of pulverized pearls across my skin. I knew, from the harem mothers, that the powder could make skin look as incandescent as a thousand mornings. I also knew that if the powder got in your eyes, the grit would make you weep and temporarily rob you of sight.

The scent of the powder fell over me like a worn and familiar cloak. I inhaled deeply, and I was sixteen again, preparing for the palace's monsoon celebration. Arjun said I looked like a lantern and I'd stuck my tongue out at him. Nalini was there too, defiantly wearing the garb of her own people: a red patterned sash around a silk-spun *salwar kameez* sewn with thousands of moon-shaped mirrors.

A year later, when Arjun became the general, I told him I meant to take the throne from Skanda. I had protected my people as much as I could from his reign. But I couldn't stand by the edges. Not anymore. Without questioning, Arjun pledged his life and his soldiers to my cause. Six months after that, I made my move to take the throne from my brother. My brother was cunning, but he would protect his life before his reign. I thought that with Arjun and his forces supporting my bid for the throne, I could ensure a bloodless transfer of power.

I was wrong.

The night I tried to take the throne, I wore my best armor: blood red lips for the blood I wouldn't shed and night-dark kohl for the secrecy I had gathered. I remembered the fear, how I had cursed under my breath, waiting with a handful of my best soldiers beneath a damp stone archway. I remembered the pale bloom of mushrooms tucked into the creases of stone, white as pearls and corpse skin. They were the only things I could see in the dark. I remembered emerging into the throne room. I had practiced my speech so many times that when I realized what had happened, I could summon no other words. But I remembered the bodies on the ground, the lightning breaking the night sky like an egg. I remembered Arjun's face beside my brother: calm. He had known.

"Done," said the attendant, holding a mirror to my face.

My eyes fluttered open. I grimaced at my reflection. The red pigment had crossed the boundaries of my lips, making them look thick and bloodstained. The kohl had been unevenly smudged. I looked bruised.

"It suits you, Princess," said the attendant in a mockingly pandering voice. "Now smile and show me the famous dimpled smile of the Jewel of Bharata."

Few knew that my "famous dimpled smile" was a scar. When I was nine, I had cut myself with a blunt pair of shears after pretending that the wooden sculpture of a *raksha* was real and that he meant to eat me. *Fate smiles upon you, child. Even your scars are lovely,* said Mother Dhina. As I got older, the scar reminded me of what people would choose to see if you let them. So I smiled at the attendant, and hoped that she saw a dimpled grin, and not the scar from a girl who started training with very sharp things from a very young age.

The attendant's eyes traveled from my face to the sapphire necklace at the hollow of my throat. Instinctively, I clutched it.

She held out her palm. "The Prince will not like that you are wearing something he has not personally bestowed."

"I'll take my chances."

It was the only thing I had from my sister, Maya. I would not part with it.

My sister's necklace was more than a jewel. The day Maya returned to Bharata, I hadn't recognized her. My sister had changed. As if she had torn off the filmy reality of one world and glimpsed something greater beneath it. And then she had disappeared, darting between the space of a moonbeam and a shadow. The necklace was a reminder to live for myself the way Maya had. But it was also a reminder of loss. Vast and unwieldy magic had stolen away my sister, and every time I looked at the pendant, I remembered not to place faith in things I couldn't control. The necklace told me to place my faith in myself. Nothing and no one else. I didn't just want to believe in everything the necklace meant. I needed those reminders. And I would die before I parted with it.

"I rather like the look of it myself. Maybe I'll keep it," said the attendant. "Give it. Now."

The attendant grabbed at the necklace. Even though her arms were thin, her fingers were strong. She pinched my skin, scrabbling at the clasp.

"Give. It. To. Me," she hissed. She aimed a bony elbow at my neck, but I blocked the jab.

"I don't want to hurt you."

"You can't hurt me. The guards told me how weak you truly are. Besides, you are no one here," said the attendant. Her eyes were bright, as if touched with fever. "Give me the necklace. What does it matter to you? After all you took? Isn't that the least I can take away from you, one damned necklace?"

Her words stung. I took no pleasure in killing. But I had never hesitated to choose my life over another's.

"My apologies," I said hoarsely, knocking her hand away from my neck. I had been gentle before, careful not to harm the skinny and heartbroken thing standing in front of me. This time she lurched back, shock and fury lighting up her face.

Maybe the girl had lost her lover, or her betrothed, or her father or brother. I couldn't *let* myself care. I'd learned that lesson young. Once,

I had freed the birds in the harem menagerie. When Skanda found out, he covered my floor with ripped wings and told me the cage was the safest place for foolish birds. Another time, Skanda had punished Mother Dhina and forbade the palace cooks from sending her any dinner. I gave her half of mine. He starved me for a week. Those were just the instances where I was the only person hurt. My brother had taught me many things, but nothing more important than one: Selfishness meant survival.

Caring had cost my future. Caring had trapped me under Skanda's thumb and forced my hand. Caring had robbed my throne and damned all I had held dear. That was all that mattered.

The attendant lunged forward, and I reacted. Hooking my foot behind her calf, I tugged. I swung out with my right fist—harder than I should have, harder than I needed to—until my hand connected with her face. She fell back with a hurt yelp, knocking over a slim golden table. A cloud of perfume burst in the air. In that moment, the world tasted like sugar and roses and blood. I stepped back, my chest heaving. I waited for her to stand and fight, but she didn't. She sat there with her legs crossed beneath her, arms wrapped around her thin rib cage. She was sobbing.

"You took my brother. He was not yours to take. He was mine," said the girl. Her voice sounded muddled. *Young.* Tears streaked her cheeks.

"You're a monster," she said.

I secured the necklace.

"We all have to be something."

2

BURNING ROSES
GAURI

The guards unbound my wrists and shoved me into a red room. I waited for them to go before pulling out a small silk bag of pearl dust I had swiped from the cosmetics table. I repeated the flimsy plan in my head: *Throw the dust in his eyes, gag him, steal his weapons.* If the Prince made a sound, I'd hold the dagger to his throat and hold him ransom. If he didn't make a sound, I'd make him free me for his own life. I knew I couldn't get far on my own, but most people could be bribed, and if bribery didn't work, threats always did.

I was glad they hadn't taken me to a throne room. The last time I was in a throne room, Skanda had ripped away my hopes for the kingdom and destroyed my future.

Arjun did not meet my eyes. And he refused to look up when his new bride and my best friend was hauled into the room. Nalini sank to her knees. Her gaze was frantic: leaping back and forth from me to Arjun and the dead on the ground.

Skanda's knife was pressed to her throat, sharp and close enough that beads of blood welled onto her skin.

"I know what you want," said Skanda.

I closed my eyes, shuttering the memory. I looked around the room, wondering which corner was the best position for attacking. At one end, a trellis of roses covered the wall. My chest tightened. I used to grow roses. One trellis for every victory. I had loved watching the blood red petals unfurl around thorns. Looking at them reminded me of my people's love: red as life. A month before Skanda had me thrown over the Ujijain border, he had set them on fire in a drunken stupor. By the time I got there, it was too late. Every petal had curled and blackened.

"You think these flowers are tokens of Bharata's love for you," he had slurred. "I want you to see, little sister. I want you to see just how easy it is for everything you plan and love and tend to go up in flames."

I'll never forget what burning roses look like. All those scarlet petals turning incandescent and furious. Like the last flare of the sun before an eclipse swallows it from the sky.

"You think they love you now, but it doesn't last. You're the rose. Not them. They are the flames. And you'll never see how quickly you'll catch fire until you're engulfed. One step out of the line I draw, and they will set you on fire."

I turned my back on the roses.

I chose a corner of the room, and then sank my teeth into the insides of my cheek. It was a habit I'd picked up on the eve of my first battle. Nerves had set my teeth chattering, so I brought out a mirror and glowered at myself. The glowering didn't help, but I liked the way my face looked. The small movements made my cheekbones look as sharp as scimitars. And when I tightened my lips, I felt *dangerous*, as if

I were hiding knives behind my teeth. Biting my cheeks became a battle tradition. Today I went into battle.

A door in the distance creaked. I ran through what I knew about the Prince of Ujijain. They called him the Fox Prince. And given the way some of the soldiers had jealously said his name, it didn't seem like a name given because his face had animal features. He spent part of every year at an ashram where all the nobility sent their sons. Reputedly brilliant. *Not good.* Weak with weapons. *Excellent.* The guards were fond of retelling the story of his trial with the council. Prince Vikram had to submit to three tasks in order to be named heir of Ujijain—give the dead new life, hold a flame that never burns, and deliver the strongest weapon in the world. For the first task, he whittled a piece of bark into a knife, proving that even discarded things could be given new life in purpose. For the second task, he released a thousand jars of fireflies and held the small insects in his hand, proving that he could hold a flame that never burned. And for the last task, he said that he had poisoned the council. Desperate for the antidote, the council named him heir. The Fox Prince then revealed that he had lied and proved how belief itself was the strongest weapon in the world.

I rolled my eyes every time I heard the tale. It sounded like something that villagers with a restless imagination would spin beside a fire. I'd heard another rumor about him. Something about his parentage. That he was an orphan who'd moved the Emperor to pity. But I doubted the vicious Emperor would be moved in such a way. The guards told me that the Emperor kept great beasts at his side that could tear the throat out of anyone who dared to cross him.

Footsteps shuffled down the hall. I clutched the silk bag of pearl dust. The Prince might be clever and eloquent, but you can't talk your way out of death and I wasn't going to give him a chance to speak. All my intelligence told me that he was no match for me. I'd have him on his knees and begging for his life in a matter of moments.

A final door opened.

The Fox Prince was here.

·》 3 《·

WINTER BLACK
VIKRAM

The past two days blurred behind Vikram's eyes. At the ashram, a messenger from Ujijain had been waiting to take him back to the palace. He barely heard what the messenger said. Something about diplomatic urgency. Vikram ignored him. His thoughts were elsewhere, caught inside the ruby. Even now, his skin felt too tight, as if his bones had soaked up the promise of magic and he could hardly fit inside himself. Standing outside the Ujijain throne room, he darted a glance out the window. A new future called to him. His body felt restless. Hungry. The doors opened. Birdsong, ruffled feathers and scraping claws filled his ears:

"His Majesty will see you now, Prince Vikramaditya."

Over the past decade, his father had turned the throne room into a menagerie. The ceiling soared out of reach and warm sunlight puddled through the glass windows. Bird droppings splattered the tapestries. Huge tracts of the rugs had been gouged out by the claws of various animals.

"Son!" said the Emperor Pururavas.

Vikram smiled. His father, portly and close to losing his sight, toddled forward. On one of his shoulders sat a one-eyed golden monkey. A great leopard strode at his side. One of its paws was missing, but the animal looked more regal than half the court. It stood protectively at his side, leaning on the old Emperor as if to prop him up against the heavy hand of Time.

Vikram eyed the animals. "I see you have not lost your hobby of collecting the weak and defenseless."

The Emperor harrumphed. "I do not see them complaining."

"Why would they? They are grateful. As am I."

He flushed. "You are not some broken thing I rescued."

Wasn't he though? Eleven years ago, the Emperor found him crouched over the lip of a cliff. His limbs and skin were intact, but the pieces of his heart had shattered and cut him from the inside. Vikram never knew what the Emperor saw in him that day. He could have tossed him some coins and left. But he didn't. He brought him to a palace, filled the hollow in his heart and gave him a crown for his head.

"Are they feeding you at that ashram?" asked Pururavas. He prodded Vikram in the ribs. "Stop spending your time running. You look bonier."

"You mean leaner."

"And you're as wiry as a *moringa*!"

"You mean taller."

He laughed. "You always had a way with words. You'd make a fine ruler."

"You mean puppet," Vikram said, before he could stop himself.

The Emperor's face fell. "Not again, my boy. Perhaps over time you may convince the council to defer to your judgment. You are as clever as any trueborn prince."

Vikram choked at the thought of convincing the council. He'd already tried that when they placed the Royal Trials before him. He'd shown them new life, a flame that never burned and the strongest weapon with nothing but a piece of wood, a bright insect and a lie. But all his success—or performance as some still called it—had earned him was a nickname and a reputation.

"What did you bring me here for, Father?" he asked. "Your messenger said it was a matter of diplomatic urgency. Is the leopard fighting with the monkey?"

The leopard, whose muzzle rested on its paw, huffed indignantly.

"It's a curious situation. Bharata is willing to enter peace negotiations with us. But only if we publicly execute a prisoner who was sent to us. The prisoner, however, is the Princess Gauri."

Vikram's eyebrows shot up.

"... the Jewel of Bharata?" he scoffed. It was a ridiculous title. And then he remembered that his own people compared him to a sharp-toothed, fluffy-tailed animal and stopped smiling. "I thought she was in line to take the throne after the Raja Skanda. I doubt he's sired a child after all this time. Why would they want her dead?"

"They will not say."

When he first heard of the Princess, a pang of envy had stabbed him. What had she done to earn the throne other than be born in the right place? She had a reputation as a warrior, but reputations were slippery. So often they were little more than threads of rumors strung together. Unlike him, she probably never had to fight for anything.

"And the Council of Ujijain is willing to consider this? It could be a trap. Nothing is more war-inducing than a beloved princess turned martyr. We'd all be slaughtered."

"The council wants you to announce the execution. It would be your first royal decree, and it would be the start of a treaty with Ujijain."

"I would've thought they'd try a bloodless alliance first."

Another lesson of ruling he'd gathered was this: If you cannot win against them, marry them. The Emperor flushed.

"We offered that, but . . . they'd prefer her dead."

"That's one version of mercy, I suppose."

The words took hold. *It would be your first royal decree.* His heart sank. Only his father and the council knew he was not the biological son of Pururavas. Everyone else in the kingdom believed that he had been a sickly child, too weak for royal events until he was seven years old. His father believed that blood made no difference. But the council believed otherwise. To them, he would always be an illusion of power, with the real strings held tightly in meetings he was not allowed to attend.

"You want *me* to announce the execution of the Princess as my first royal edict. But what about you?"

"I will take a more advisory role."

"No. You will be the reinforcement should things sour."

"Vikram, I—"

"The council is unsure of this decision so they will have a new face announce the plan. And if the plan is not well met, they can formally renounce my claim to the throne and reinstate you as sovereign."

"That is a worst-case scenario, my child," he said. To his credit, he did not lie. Still, a light tremor shook his voice.

"Careful, Father. Someone might hear you claim me as your own," said Vikram coolly. "But how can this play out in a way they want? The council does not want war."

And then the idea made sense.

Vikram waited for rage to grip his heart, but he felt nothing. For a moment, the world constricted to the menagerie and there was nothing in it but ruined silk, crippled beasts and bird droppings.

"Of course," he said softly. "The council does not want war. They just seek to rid themselves of two errors at once. Remove Bharata's folk heroine, and accept the outrage if Bharata falls through on its promises. As a show of goodwill, they will force me out of 'power' and probably make me live in an ashram for the rest of my life. And if all goes as planned, Bharata's folk heroine is still removed and I will remain on the throne as a puppet king. Clever. I am almost tempted to congratulate them."

Pururavas's shoulders fell, and Vikram softened. His father could coax a wild leopard to rest its head on his lap, but he could never persuade the council to make Vikram a true king. Decades of complacency had sucked the marrow from the Emperor's voice. The throne room should have been a seat of power, but in his father's reign, it had become a playpen of wounded animals.

"I received the council's word that you would always be well provided for, and that you would receive a pardon within the next year should things sour," he said, his voice wavering. "You would maintain status, be granted land. And I hoped that perhaps we might take advantage of your role as king to find an advantageous marriage—"

"No."

Vikram's hand fell to his side, hitting his pant leg. Something sharp met his palm. The ruby. *Play the game and you may yet win your kingdom, not just the husk of its name.* He'd stayed here long enough. Fire ran through his veins. He could change this life.

"I will do as you ask, Father."

Pururavas raised an eyebrow. "What do you want in exchange?"

"Am I so predictable? Do I never give without getting?" asked Vikram, grinning. "Now that you mention what I'd like, that does remind me that I would like to leave for a month before taking the throne. In the empire's history, it is customary for the heir to spend a month away in meditation. You did the same yourself, Father. Puppet king or no, the council should at least want me to maintain an illusion of decorum."

His father eyed him shrewdly, and then he sighed.

"For someone so decidedly against tradition, what has brought this on?"

"Patriotism?" tried Vikram.

Pururavas folded his arms. "Patriotism is *not* the reason. Where will you go?"

"I know where to go. I need to figure out how to get there."

"You speak in riddles."

"I always did have a way with words."

"One month," said the Emperor, his eyes glassy with tears. "I cannot buy you more time than that. But tell the Princess. The council needs to know you spoke with her."

Vikram grimaced. "On the eve before I leave, you want me to condemn a girl to death?"

"You wish to be a king, do you not?"

Vikram left his father's menagerie. The guards led him down a hall painted a bright and vivid red. He twisted his hands. The last thing he wanted before he left was some inconsolable princess begging for her life. He'd never met her. What would he say? "A pleasure to meet you. Also, my kingdom is going to execute you at dawn. Goodbye."

He bit back a groan, swung open the door and plopped into the first chair. The Princess Gauri stood near the windows, her body blocking out the light. She was tall. Nearly as tall as a man. But it was her eyes that stopped him. They were as black as winter nights. Black as sleep. For a second, they transfixed him.

Before he could speak, she ran toward him. Her mouth was smeared blood-like. And if she looked like a dream, it was only to distract his mind from realizing that she was a nightmare.

Something glittered dangerously in her hands. Vikram rolled out of the chair. Behind him, he heard a series of curses and then a snapping sound. The Jewel of Bharata had broken the chair leg and was now holding it over her head. He looked up, ready to reason with this mad princess, and his breath caught. Glittering motes clung to the air around her. She glowed.

Find the one who glows, with blood on the lips and fangs in the heart.

And then she spoke:

"Come near me, and I will kill you so swiftly you will have no time to cry for help."

4

THE FOX PRINCE

GAURI

My plan with the pearl dust hadn't worked. Never mind. I had something sharp in my hands, and that's all that mattered. I cast a quick glance over the Prince. No weapons belt. Only a person who'd never supped at the table of fear would refuse to carry a knife. Coddled, pampered prince. He'd probably never fought for anything in his life. I cast a quick glance at the door. No sounds. No one was coming for him. If I needed to, I could end him right now and still slip out of the halls before the drunk guard woke up from the end of his shift. But the Prince might still have something useful on his person, maybe an heirloom of a brooch or decorative scabbard that I could sell in a market for at least a dozen mercenaries.

Candlelight shone behind him, sending his features into an inscrutable blur. He was a gathering of lean limbs. Young, beardless, broadshouldered and slender. He didn't even bother rising to his feet after he'd rolled out of his chair. Instead he sat up, leaned forward and steepled his fingers. His fingers were long and slim, tapered and clean. He had the hands of a scholar. Not a soldier.

"This is quite possibly the most exciting meeting I've ever had. Do continue."

My shoulders dropped. "What?"

"You have demands, I imagine. Let's hear them. I entered the room resigned, and now I stand intrigued."

"You're sitting."

Brilliant observation, Gauri.

He glanced down. "Too true. My intrigue is entirely supine. But I'd hate to make a liar of you. May I stand?"

I lowered the broken chair leg to his throat. "Go ahead. But if you try to scream, I promise it won't even leave your throat."

He stood. To his credit, he didn't blink or tremble. Maybe he was brave. Or criminally stupid. He angled his body to the light and I studied his features. He couldn't be much older than me. Dark hair fell over his brow. Golden brown eyes latched on to mine. He was handsome in a way that made me want to kick him on principle. And then he tilted his head. Fox-like. There was something of the trickster in his expression—wry mouth, pensive eyes.

"Thank you, Princess." He bowed gingerly, mindful of the chair leg. "Obviously you want something or you would have killed me on the spot. Or perhaps you couldn't. I heard rumors that you're a rather accomplished soldier, but between you and me, we both know that the reputations of royals are largely falsehoods."

Annoyance prickled across my skin. My life was filled with princes like him. Sometimes I'd even dispatched their marriage proposals with a single glare. I forgot how long it had been since I'd had a formal meeting. When they kept me prisoner, all I could do was shout my demands—

water, clean linens, more food—and now I'd practically forgotten this dance of veiled threats and gilded words.

"I want to get out of Ujijain," I blurted.

Subtle.

He should have balked and flatly refused. Instead, he lifted one eyebrow as if to say: *Is that all?*

"How uninspired. You were supposed to be the heir to the throne of Bharata," he mused, "and now you have nothing. Yet all you ask from me is safe passage? Don't you want more?"

Of course I wanted more. I wanted my throne and my people's safety. I wanted freedom from Skanda.

"They sent me here to tell you that you will be executed," he said quietly.

I wasn't shocked. Skanda had told me as much when he caught me: "Think of it this way, sister. Your death might even be useful. We may have a new ally if they do as I demand." And then they had me gagged, bound, tossed into the back of a chariot and dumped over the border, where an Ujijain search party found me at dawn.

The Prince was staring at me strangely. No man had looked at me that way. Men had looked at me in admiration, in fear, in lust. They'd looked at me with disbelief at who I was. He looked at me with disbelief at who I could be.

"I want you—" he started.

I glowered, pressing the chair leg into his neck. "I would *die* before I let you touch me."

"What an improvement. First it was me who would die. Now it is you who offers to die before touching me," he said. "Another man might be insulted. Now, if you would allow me to finish—"

I glared.

"—I will give you your freedom and *more* in exchange for your aid as partner . . . in a game."

Molten longing lit up his gaze. I could see straight down to the scrabbling, hungry wish in his eyes. It ignited me. Because I saw it in myself.

"What kind of game?"

He hesitated. He turned something in his fingers, a rather large ruby that shone with its own light.

"A magical game." He tossed the ruby into the air and I caught it.

"What is it?"

"Proof. Of magic. If you're convinced by it, then I hope you will join me," he said matter-of-factly. "Like you, I have everything to gain and nothing left to lose."

Madman.

This was foolish. I had half a mind to knock him over the head with the chair leg and escape while I could. The ruby in my palm quivered, casting a scarlet light that swallowed my gaze. It was as if someone had hooked a thread through my spine and pulled *up.* I was out of myself. Out of this room. Out of, it seemed, time itself.

The ruby held a promise. I saw myself on the throne, Nalini standing beside me with her head held high. I saw a world without my brother and traitorous Arjun. This magic felt like I had glanced at my destiny sideways, as if I had never seen it for what it was and now the hope of what I wanted most loomed bright and lurid in the corners of my heart. I had glimpsed enough of magic when Maya disappeared to know what it should feel like—a whisper and a roar, a wonder fusing into the bones, forcing you to believe that you could never live without it. When the light released me, I felt boneless with want.

Prince Vikram plucked the ruby from my hand, eyeing me wordlessly. I dropped the chair leg. My breath was thin and cold, rattling in my chest. I had believed in magic ever since I saw the impossible: my sister returning from the graveyard of Bharata's memories and disappearing into the Chakara Forest. But recognizing enchantment and feeling it surge within me was different. The ruby felt like a summoning. A seam twisting open inside my heart, taunting me with all that could happen if I only dared to seize it. And yet . . . terror cut through those imaginings. That . . . that *thing* had reached into my heart and held up my hopes to the light as if they were nothing more than pieces of colored glass.

Ever since I lost Maya in the forest, I hated magic. It swallowed people whole the way it swallowed my sister. Instead of leaving me a body to mourn, the Otherworld had left me with a chest full of caution and a string of nightmares.

Even if enchantment could help me, I wanted nothing to do with it. I would forge my own victory. No magic necessary.

"Well?" asked the Prince.

I eyed the large ruby. I could sell it for gold to buy an entire crew of mercenaries. And if I killed the heir of Ujijain, our two countries would enter enough turmoil that I could slip into Bharata unnoticed, free Nalini and leverage the chaos. Skanda wouldn't know the first thing about warfare. Only I would be able to keep them safe. But first I had to get out, which meant that I needed this fool of a prince to free me under whatever pretense was necessary.

"Tell me about this game."

He smirked, thinking he had won.

"It's called the Tournament of Wishes. The winners get a wish. Isn't that more tempting than just freedom from Ujijain? If I freed you,

you'd have as much luck as a beggar during a famine. But imagine what you could do with a wish? You could have your throne back, Princess. I am guessing you lost it since your own people want you dead."

My throat felt dry. A wish. In that second, I felt my sister's hand reach through time to grasp my fingers. Her storytelling voice, like dusk and honey, poured through my thoughts:

. . . they say the Lord of Treasures hosts a tournament for the very best and the very worst, the dreamers and the broken. He'll play a game with you unlike any tournament you have ever played. You might have to find your true name in a castle of stars, or wrestle your voice from a demon, or sip poison and eat fear . . .

My sister had spun me that tale when I was seven. I'd never forgotten it. But I forced down the desire to entertain it. I wouldn't place my life at the mercy of magic. I'd spent enough of my life under Skanda's control. I wouldn't trade one tyrant for another.

"The Tournament itself is held in a city of immeasurable treasure and wealth. I doubt many have heard about—"

"Alaka," I whispered. Only when I heard my voice did I realize I'd spoken the name aloud. My hand moved to my necklace.

Vikram looked at me sharply. "How do you know that?"

"Does it matter?" I snapped, dropping my fingers. "I know it's a kingdom in the Otherworld. The palace of *yakshas* and *yakshinis*. They're said to be the guardians of treasure found in trees, rivers and caves."

He blinked.

"It's also the home of Kubera, the Lord of Treasures and the guardian of the North," I muttered.

"So you are a scholar and a soldier. How unusual for a princess."

I laughed. "The women of Bharata are singers, artists, soldiers and academics. I'm no different from them."

"How do you know those stories?"

"I have ears," I said. He didn't get to know about Maya. "You've told me what I'll get out of this wish, but what about you? You're the heir, what more could you want?"

For a moment his expression clouded before he shrugged gracefully. "I want everything."

I recognized a deflection when I heard one, but his secrets meant nothing to me. Turning the ruby in my palms, I found a small engraving on the jewel that had not appeared until now. It was the outline of a man crawling on his hands and knees.

"It's a ticket. For two living entries into the game."

"Not two living exits?"

I cursed inwardly. Why was I even asking? I had no desire to play this game.

He grinned. "I asked the same question. Perhaps winning is the only way to leave. So. Princess Gauri, Jewel of Bharata and former heir to the throne. Will you be my partner?"

Absolutely not. I glanced at the ruby in my hand. The moment we were out of Ujijain, I would kill him and take the jewel. I eyed his rich clothes. Those would fetch a good price too. And if I stole his clothes and cut his throat, his death would look as if a robber had gotten to him. No blame on Bharata. I smiled.

"How long do we have to get there?" I asked.

His smile was all victory: "New moon."

"That's in three days."

"Admittedly, I am not quite sure how to get there," said the Prince, steepling his fingers.

"Did you ask the ruby?"

His eyes widened. "Princess, you have depths of genius untold! I would have never thought to do *the most obvious thing.* Go ahead and ask it how to get to Alaka. See what answer *you* get."

I was well and truly going to maim him. I muttered the question at the ruby. The jewel spun and a length of parchment erupted from the crystal:

Alaka is past the place where memories devour
and the held-breath place to put an end to cowards.

I may have wanted nothing to do with magic, but it still *did* something to me. The words of the parchment wrapped around my heart. When I blinked, I heard Maya's voice in the dark, spinning tales of grand adventures that would always find their way into my dreams later. But the memory of her collapsed into shards of nightmare. I would never know what happened to her.

"Helpful," I said, trying to keep from wavering.

"I've been thinking about it nonstop. We need an entryway into a place of magic. At first I considered entering through cremation grounds, but I have no desire to end up in Naraka—"

"Do you know where to go or not?" I asked impatiently.

"Can we truly know anything?"

I rolled my eyes. "How soon can we leave?"

"Not so fast, Princess. I want you to be my partner, but I need a demonstration that your reputation is more than rumor. I can't defend both of us and I have no problem admitting I'd let you die."

"At last, we've found common ground," I said sweetly. "I feel the same about you."

He stood up, bracing his legs in what I assumed he thought was a fighting stance. But his balance was off center and his legs were not bent far enough to withstand an impact. His posture was nothing but posture. "Disarm me."

"I do not prey on the weak."

"That's not what I hear."

Wrong thing to say. I feinted left. He fell for it. Naturally. He was not much of a fighter or strategist. In seconds, he was on his back.

"That does not count," he wheezed. "I was disarmed by your beauty."

"You were disarmed by a swift kick."

"That too."

He moved to stand, and I placed my foot on his chest. "I will not perform for you or anyone. Never ask me to do something like that again."

He stared at me. "Are you done?"

"Yes."

"May I get up?"

"No."

"I see you like your men with their egos gutted."

"Only when I'm feeling generous."

He laughed. "My apologies."

"We leave by nightfall," I said. "And I want my weapons and clothes back."

He tucked his hands behind his head like a pillow before glancing at the ceiling.

"Fine. Now can you kindly remove your foot from my chest?"

5

A GOLDEN APPLE

GAURI

The Fox kept only half his word. When I got back to my prison cell, my clothes had been discreetly tucked beneath a loose wooden tile. I still didn't have my knives, not that I blamed the Prince. It was, perhaps, the first intelligent thing he'd done. Now all I had to do was wait until nightfall when he would—allegedly—spring me from this prison and we would escape.

For the first time in months, I let my mind wander toward the hope of returning to Bharata. When I returned, there would be no question of who the throne belonged to. My brother would either sink to his knees or fall to them in pieces. Nalini would be free.

Almost six months had passed since Arjun's betrayal. One more cycle of the moon and it would mark the anniversary of Nalini's arrival in Bharata and my Age Day. I still remembered the harem preparing for her arrival. Nalini was the daughter of an important tribe leader on the outskirts of Bharata, and her upbringing at court was a promise of peace. She would be raised as a princess of Bharata and married into the nobility. In exchange, her kinsmen would keep the borders safe.

Nalini arrived the day I turned thirteen years old. Immediately upon arriving, she tried to set fire to the harem and escape. Her name was on everyone's lips, which meant that everyone forgot about me. I disliked her instantly.

The week after, I tried to get my revenge. Skanda was holding a celebration along the waterfront. The women walked in pairs, shielded by an ivory screen that broke our view of the world outside the harem. Nalini defiantly walked by the water's edge, her chin held high and gaze fixed ahead. I stuck my foot out when she walked past. She stumbled, lost her balance and fell with a loud splash into the water. It was meant to be a prank. But when she didn't come up for air, I panicked. And so, amid all the shouting of Bharata's citizens and the thin screams of the harem wives—and in full view of Skanda—I leapt in after her and pulled her back to the surface.

"I thought you could swim," I gasped, coughing up water.

Nalini hissed a stream of curses, but no one heard over the villagers' loud proclamations:

"The Princess Gauri is a hero!"

"Praise her! Praise her!"

"See how she saved the savage princess's life!"

Eventually, Nalini and I would become as close as sisters, but it would be years before I realized how that day became the beginning of a story that would trap me for the rest of my life. Skanda was the one who made sure everyone called me a hero. He retold the story of how I dove in after Nalini so often that it muddled people's memories, until it became a different tale altogether. Being called a savior shamed me. I had done something petty and had been rewarded for it. It wasn't right. I should have told the truth. Maybe things would have been different.

A muffled sound caught my attention. I stood, flattening myself against the wall. A quiet shuffling sound followed. Someone fumbling with keys. The door swung open gently and the Prince stood over the threshold.

"Ready?" he asked.

I nodded, stepping outside and over the sleeping forms of the drugged guards. The moment I left the room behind, I felt as though the world had been waiting. The air pinched and shifted around us. Agitated and restless. Midnight had divested itself of stars. Not a single light fell on us as we ran through stone archways to the warm musk of the stables. Not a single sound rustled in our shadows as we untethered two horses and clattered out of the palace. Not a single echo of breath lit up our escape. It was as if we'd slid into the lost moment before sleep.

We rode until dawn smudged scorched clouds across the world. The horses shone with sweat. By then, whatever magic had let us escape into the night had lifted. Birds screeched. A thousand insect wings stabbed the air. My stomach groaned. Being a palace prisoner was more coddling than I thought. At least I was fed on time.

I eyed the Fox. He was almost irritatingly vulnerable. He still wore no weapons belt. And yet he held himself as if he were invincibility made flesh. Before we left Ujijain, I'd checked the pack slung across my horse and found a pair of knives. They weren't my customized weapons, but I'd still hidden one of them in the sleeves of my tunic. The Fox wore the ruby openly. It glinted from a shallow pocket on his tunic, ripe as fruit and begging to be plucked. So much for clever. Killing someone on a horse wasn't difficult, but I didn't want to spook the horse. Besides—

"What do I call you?" he asked, turning to me. I froze. "The 'Jewel of Bharata' just seems too modest, don't you think?"

I hated that nickname. Skanda had ordered that the title be spoken at every festival.

"Call me Gauri."

"How intimate."

I glared. "Enjoy it, because that's as intimate as this will ever get, Fox Prince." *Consider it a courtesy before I end you.*

"I prefer Vikram," he said, smiling as if I'd given away a secret.

We were still too close to Ujijain for me to kill him. Besides, I wanted to lead him closer to Bharata.

"Where are we going? You said we'd need access to a magical place first."

"Ah. Yes." He patted the pocket with the ruby, but didn't bring it out. "I imagined the ruby would become something like a compass."

"And?"

"My theory was incorrect."

"So . . . you don't know where we're going?"

"I didn't say that," he said. "We're going to the Chakara Forest. The legends always said that the Otherworlds were linked. If we find one entrance, we find the bridge to all of them."

The words snipped at my heart. The Chakara Forest was the last place where I'd seen Maya. The night she disappeared, enchantment had cinched the world tight, drawing down the heavens and tempting me to grab a fistful of stars straight out of the sky. I pushed out the memory of Maya and focused on the advantage. The Chakara Forest was close to Bharata. I could kill him and sell the ruby in the markets by tomorrow.

I dug my heels into my horse. "Then let's go. We can't lose the light."

The day wore on. I kept looking over my shoulder, waiting for a search party, but none followed. I wasn't arrogant enough to assume that our departure was so stealthy and intelligent that it had stumped an entire kingdom. Some force of the Otherworld had snapped common sense and logic. It . . . wanted us. I snuck a glance above me, as if I'd see the soft underbelly of magic crouched over us like a beast closing in on its prey.

By evening, we had reached the outskirts of the forest. Even on the fringes, it seemed like a place touched by magic. The trees didn't stay in one place. A silver pool spilled over inky roots that had slumbered in earth only a moment ago. Cold fingers slid down my spine. I felt the shadow of the forest like something that would cleave my life. If I stepped inside, the magic I was trying to avoid would swallow me whole.

Which meant I had to kill the Prince right here.

"We should get off the horses," I said. "They might spook in the dark."

He raised an eyebrow, but jumped off without comment. Soldier or no, there was something too shrewd in his gaze. I had to catch him off guard.

"I'll secure the area first," I said, moving away from him.

"Without a weapon?" he asked, leaning against a tree.

I stilled. I couldn't give away that I already had one. I fake-rummaged through the pack and lifted the other knife. On closer inspection, I'd never seen a blade like this—it was sharp with a fine enough balance, but there was a strange bump on the hilt.

Poorly designed.

The Prince grinned, waving me away. I made a great show of moving into the forest, but I kept to the shadowy edges. I bided my time, waiting for the growing dark before I stalked him. I kept one arm over my mouth to hide my breathing and kept my steps to the soft, silent grass. The Prince had his back to me.

I lunged.

I grabbed him around the collar, pressing the knife to his throat right as he fell to his knees. I placed my heel at the instep of his foot, pinning him into place.

"Aren't you going to ask if I have any last words?" he gasped.

"You just uttered them. Toss out the ruby."

But he only smirked. "Anything for you, fair princess."

He reached into his pocket and threw out . . . a piece of colored glass. A decoy.

"Where is the real ruby?"

He shrugged. "Must have dropped it."

"It must be on your person. Give it."

"Go ahead and search every inch of my body," he said, winking. "In fact, keep me alive for that."

I pressed the blade harder and a thin line of blood seeped from the metal. The Prince winced and then smiled.

"Try," he said.

I was done with this. I pressed the blade harder and felt a slight give in the hilt. Like a sigh. One half-push later and the blade snapped off, falling into the grass. The Prince snatched the blade, rolled away from me and shook the dirt from his hair.

"Clever, isn't it?" he said, tossing it behind him. "My own design.

Took me about a year to perfect the mechanics. Any killing pressure breaks the blade."

I stared at the useless hilt in my hand. "You gave me a fake blade?"

"And showed you a fake ruby," he added. His eyes met mine and he grinned. "What were you going to do, Princess, kill me and sell the ruby? Raise an army on your own?"

My mouth fell open.

"Trust me, I have no desire to work with you, but the ruby led me to you and you fit the description. Think of what we could do *together*," he said. "We could use magic. But you'd rather close your eyes to all that in exchange for a couple of mercenaries?"

I growled, stalking toward him. "A blade would have been a more merciful death for you."

Hesitancy flashed in his eyes. He took one step backward into the Chakara Forest. I followed, ignoring how magic soaked the air, reaching for me, whispering *yes, yes, yes.*

Vikram held up his hands. "Consider the possibilities—"

A flash of gold glinted in the trees. Air rushed past me. Vikram paused. I snapped my head in the direction of whatever sailed toward us. I squinted. A ball? A rock? I ducked out of the way just in time to catch the thing in my palm.

A golden apple sat in my hand. Its rind was as burnished as a miniature sun. Not just golden.

It was pure gold.

Vikram stared. "Is that—"

The branches overhead snapped. Sharp monkey laughter split the air, cawing and cackling. A hundred apricots, cherries and split guavas rained from the sky. Through the veil of fruit, I caught the shape of three creatures. I scanned the trees. Nothing else joined them. I thought monkeys traveled in huge packs, but these three were acting as a hunting group. Or a band of soldiers.

I tried dropping the golden apple and reaching for a stick on the ground to scare them off, but it clung to my palm as if it had grown tiny burs. Honey seeped from the rind.

The fruit stopped falling. Vikram moved to my side just as the three monkeys approached us. Dread gripped my heart in a fist of cold. Magic clung to the air, pushing the air out of my chest. When I blinked, something shimmered behind the trees. A ghostly outline of cities. Nocturnal eyes blinking open. The Otherworld felt like a body in the dark, a presence hiding its true face.

I didn't need a ruby to tell me that these creatures were connected to the Otherworld. They walked like men, wore gold jodhpurs and one even had a helmet. The tallest—black-furred with a silver scar down his forehead—eyed us, a bright sword gleaming in his hands. I tensed. I knew I couldn't fight with one hand, but I wasn't entirely useless. Magical or not, everything bled.

A pile of dirt and fruit peels caught my eye. I kicked it hard, aiming straight at the monkey's eyes.

"Run!" I shouted at Vikram.

My aim was true. The monkey screamed, dropping the sword. Just as I reached for the blade, something sharp grazed my throat. Knives floated in the air. Poised to kill. One of the monkeys had forced Vikram to his knees. Three enchanted knives formed a collar at his throat.

"Get these things away from us, monkey—"

"Not monkeys," hissed Vikram. "*Vanaras.*"

Vanaras. Real *vanaras.* I ran through what I knew about them from Maya's stories. Cunning. Ruled over by the legendary Queen Tara in the cold kingdom of Kishkinda. I couldn't use any of that information, though. Maya's stories had failed to mention that they weren't short, talking monkeys but tall beings that looked as strong as Bharata's best soldiers. Worse, they knew magic. And they showed no hesitation in wielding it to kill.

"You!" screeched a *vanara*, jerking his head at Vikram. "We came for you! A thief always returns to the spot of plunder."

Vikram's eyes widened. Sweat gleamed on his brow.

Is this what you wanted out of magic?

"I didn't steal anything."

"You can't fool us," said a *vanara* with a yellow ruff of fur. He took out a knife and cut a slash in the air.

A thin ray of light stretched where the air had been cut, widening into an image of a man running through an orchard of bone trees. He reached into the bark, pulling out a golden apple. There was no mistaking the man: It was Vikram. In the image, he ran away with the apple before hurling it through the branches.

Then the image disappeared.

"See?" said the *vanara*. "We've waited for you for a hundred years."

"I've always hoped to age with grace, but a hundred years? That's impossible. Look at me. That can't be me," protested Vikram. "I've never seen an orchard like that."

But the *vanaras* paid him no attention. The yellow *vanara* smiled slowly. "I know what thievsies and beasties gets."

"A trial!" shouted another.

"But the Queen is not here," said the gray one. "She left us. More than a thousand moons have since guarded the sky and not one has seen her."

"What the Queen does not sees, the Queen does not scolds."

"Then why not just behead them and be done with it?" said the yellow one. "I like their horses."

I couldn't fight like this, so I reached for a second tactic: bargaining.

"If you want the fruit, then just take it back!" I shouted, holding out my hand where the fruit refused to budge. "You can take it and keep him. I don't care."

"The fruit has claimed you, girl," said the gray *vanara*. "It is useless to us now. But if you wish to see even the hope of a new day, I would not eat it."

New tactic: lie.

"If you behead me, you'll have to answer to the army of Bharata," I said, trying to hold my head high. "And they won't hesitate to slaughter beasts. I—"

The *vanaras* stilled. "What did you call us?"

The largest one stepped forward. "You would reduce our proud and ancient race to *beasts?*"

Cold twisted my heart. The knives dug into my throat, on the threshold of blood and flesh. This was it. I wanted nothing to do with magic and now it was going to kill me—

"What if we're spies?" called Vikram.

The knives faltered.

"Spies?" repeated the *vanaras*.

"Yes. Spies. If you behead us first, you'll never know what kind of intelligence we may have. Why, if it was so easy for me to steal this . . . apple . . . what if it becomes easier for other people to steal it too? We could tell you where your guarding went wrong and teach you how to prevent it from happening again."

The *vanaras'* tails flicked.

"If it was a trial," continued Vikram, "then we could talk reasonably. As civilized folk do. And then you can behead us."

"Leave me out of this," I said under my breath.

"Not a chance," said Vikram.

The *vanaras* huddled together, tails whipping the air. The decision was on their faces.

"You will come with us and await judgment by our laws," said the yellow one.

The knives disappeared. A second later, metal weighed down my neck and arms. Chains. Once more, I tried to shake the fruit from my bound hands. It wouldn't leave. Worse, I felt as if I could *taste* it in my own blood. Vikram was thrown to my side, equally chained.

"I can't believe you didn't have a real weapon on hand," I said.

"I have my mind," he said. "You should thank me."

I raised my chained hands. "I am bursting with gratitude."

"We're alive, aren't we? And now I've found us an entry into the Otherworld," he shot back. "No thanks to you."

Resentment flickered inside me. Much as I hated to admit it, he had saved us. Then again, he'd also used the moment to get us into the Otherworld, which was the last place I wanted to visit. The *vanaras* tugged us forward and we fell into step, marching through the Chakara Forest.

"Did you steal that fruit?" I asked.

"Of course. I want nothing more than to steal apples. I've also always manifested the ability to travel through time, and at night I turn into a beast and only your kiss can break the—"

"I get it. That's a no. But then where did that image come from?"

His brow furrowed. "I have no idea."

The *vanaras* led us like cattle down a path of trees.

"Ignoring the indescribable stupidity of not bringing any useful weapons, you did keep us alive. Now just keep quiet."

"Brilliant advice, Princess. Right up there with 'Breathing is rather useful if you want to live.'"

"You should listen to me, Fox. Who's the one with more experience at surviving as a prisoner?"

"And who's the one who was never stupid enough to become a prisoner in the first place? At the moment, I'd say one of our opinions is more useful than the other."

I glared. "If they don't behead you, I will."

"Where will this trial be held?" asked Vikram, ignoring me.

"At home," grunted the largest *vanara*. "Must run some errands though. The Queen won't want to return to an empty palace."

"If she ever returns," sighed one of them.

"She'll come back! Curses aren't made to be permanent. They like to be broken or they become resentful that everyone's forgotten about them," said another.

"I thought Kishkinda was in the Kalidas Mountains," said Vikram.

"It is."

Vikram frowned. Light stained the end of the tunnel, trailing silver ribbons across the compacted dirt floor. The Kalidas Mountains were more than a day's trek from them.

"Mirror pools," whispered the yellow *vanara*, turning over his shoulder. "Left behind by the war."

"What war?" I asked.

But they didn't answer. The *vanaras* led us through a cavern hidden behind a veil of twisted vines. Light flared from creases of rock. I squinted against the brightness until we emerged from the cavern and into a valley that sprawled vast as a kingdom. My heart stopped. Day and night tore the sky in two, each half grabbing greedy fistfuls of clouds from the other. Stars glistened above.

My breath caught. "We're in the Night Bazaar."

6

DREAM SEEDLINGS

VIKRAM

The ashram might have taught the princes numbers and letters, philosophy and diction, but Vikram knew something far more useful. He was raised on a bellyful of want—always kept at a distance, always in sight of everything he wanted and could never sink his teeth into—which only made him that much more attuned to seeing through words and straight to the desires. Know the value of the desire and the value of the deficiency. That was how he lived around his own wants.

First, he knew the apple was valuable to the *vanaras*. Yet the *vanaras* refused to hear anything about taking it back and letting them go on their way. And they refused to let it out of their sight. Vikram had tried bribing them. At one point, he offered Gauri's hand in marriage, which earned him two sharp jabs in the ribs. For equality's sake, he offered his own hand in marriage, but that ended all bargaining negotiations on the spot. Then again, even if the *vanaras* had agreed, it would have made no difference. The apple refused to leave Gauri's hand.

Second, the *vanaras* had given away their greatest weakness without even realizing it: They felt adrift. Their queen had left them and they wanted her return. What if he combined them—the apple and the missing queen? If he spun the right tale, maybe it would be enough to bargain their freedom.

But the moment he stepped inside the Night Bazaar he forgot everything he knew.

Wonder sharpened his senses. The Night Bazaar was the pith of stories murmured in the dark, the seedling of dreams and the haunt of nightmares. And he was *in* it. He drank in the scent of the Night Bazaar. On the side of star-touched night, a plume of winter hung in the air—cold pears and banked embers, polished gems and *kefir* cream. On the side of rain-kissed day, a lace of fire spiraled through the air—overripe plums and ripped flowers, dusky berries and cold honey.

Seeing the Night Bazaar was a *victory*. All his life, Ujjain had treated him as an afterthought. A glorified case of pity. Stories were his solace, the one place where someone like him could become someone else. And now, staring at the Night Bazaar, he felt that his whole life had aligned. He breathed deeply, out of breath from the trek through the caverns. His legs ached from hours on horseback, and the heavy chains had already cut into his neck.

Beside him, Gauri looked distraught. Chivalry demanded that he should inquire after the Princess's well-being. Then again, when the princess in question had tried to kill him and probably would try again the next chance she got, perhaps chivalry should be ignored. She caught him looking at her and frowned:

"You're heaving like a water buffalo in its death throes."

Never mind.

The *vanaras* dragged them through both sides of the Night Bazaar. No one paid them much attention. Vikram shuddered. Was it that normal to drag humans into the Otherworld?

"Can you imagine what they sell here?" he asked, venturing a glance at Gauri.

"Dreams," she said hoarsely, not looking at him. "Or so I was told. At least, I hope it's true."

Her chin tilted up and her black eyes filled with the sky. For a moment, she looked as if she were made of light. Vikram caught himself staring and turned from her sharply. The Otherworld was playing tricks on his sight.

The Lord of Treasures must have a foul sense of humor to have set him up with the enemy princess. He thought the promise of a wish would keep her from killing him, but she wanted nothing to do with magic. Even now, she was looking for a way to get out, scanning the Night Bazaar like a predator stowing away information for later. If Bharata wanted her dead, then why did she want her throne? The callous part of him thought she simply wanted a toy she no longer had. Another part of him suspected there was more to her. Who was this girl who softened beneath a sky full of magic and hoped that the city she'd stepped inside traded on dreams? Vikram straightened his shoulders. *Forget it.* He didn't need her life story. He needed her partnership in the game or else he couldn't get into the Tournament of Wishes. She *had* to be it. He'd felt it the moment he'd thrown the ruby to her, like a thread snapped into place. But how could he make her want to play?

As they walked, tents leapt in front of them, shaking their wares: golden fruit that grinned, splitting down its middle like a smile ("for when your speech must be comely even when your heart is a rotten thing"); a chain of star fragments, each one humming with celestial song ("for temporary wisdom and brilliance"); the *ghungroo* ankle bells of an *apsara* dancer ("guaranteed to bring the wearer beauty . . . seller-shall-not-be-responsible-for-mistaken-affections-from-less-compelling-potential-lovers"); a tray of teeth taken from a *makara* ("aphrodisiacs for the lover seeking a bit more fight and bite in the bedroom!"); and more.

The *vanaras* first purchased a jar of heartbeats from a woman with no eyes. Gauri fidgeted. The apple still hadn't left her hand. She was staring at the path they'd walked down, as if plotting an escape.

"Very useful in battle," murmured the yellow one. "Pour it down your throat and you may get a mouthful of last words."

"How do you harvest heartbeats?" asked Gauri.

"You snip them from the chest while a child loses his footing, or a new bride hears the footsteps of her husband outside the threshold of their bedroom. Humans waste their heartbeats," said the woman. "Why, girl, do you wish to make a trade?"

She opened her mouth to speak but the *vanaras* pulled their lips back from their teeth and hissed: "No. She does not."

Next, they marched them through a tent full of thousands of bolts of silk. Vikram strained against his manacled wrists to touch them. There were silks crafted of apple blossoms and a golden net of whirring honeybees, bolts of river water where fish bones drifted through the waves and threads of birdsong hanging in the corner. The *vanaras* haggled viciously over a cloth sewn of shadows.

"I'll give you the shadow cloth and throw in a cursed brooch if you'll give me the handsome human boy," smiled a thin young woman with needles for teeth.

Vikram froze.

"Do I want a brooch?" asked the yellow *vanara* to the gray one.

Please say no. . . .

"You do not want a brooch."

Vikram sagged against the chains, relieved. The woman shrugged and handed over the cloth. As they walked away from the tent, they crossed a booth of strange-looking weapons carved from crystal. Gauri tensed. When the *vanaras* pulled them, she sucked in her cheeks, feet planted. Was she going to try to topple into a table of weapons? He watched her expression narrow. Yes, Yes, she was.

The moment she sprang up, the *vanara* in front of them snapped his fingers. Gauri froze in midair.

"Bad beast," he snarled, yanking her out of the air and pulling her chains until she stood upright. "Walk. Or I'll cut off your feet."

She walked.

Last, the *vanaras* dragged them to a platform in the night section of the Night Bazaar. Twelve women stood on the dais. Blue stars shone on their throats, and impossibly bright flowers covered the stage. One by one they withdrew their veils. The twelve women were so beautiful that every single person in the audience sighed. Even Gauri raised a disbelieving eyebrow. The women looked like temple carvings, distant and perfect. Some had the silky complexion of burnished gold. Some had skin the deep blue of a peacock's throat, and some had no skin at all but *scales.* The only thing the women shared was the blue imprint of a star at their throats. Gauri's eyes widened. Vikram stared at them . . . a word danced at the tip of his thoughts. Something that made him step away from the women. Gauri drew in a sharp breath.

"*Vishakanyas,*" she whispered.

That was the word he remembered. Vikram shuddered. Most of Ujjain treated them as rumor, but his father had told him that his uncle had been felled by the touch of a poisonous courtesan. She had been sent as a gift by an enemy kingdom. One day later, the uncle was dead and the courtesan had disappeared. A single touch would kill a man.

"You recognize them?" asked the yellow *vanara*, impressed. "That makes sense that you would recognize your own. They started out human."

Gauri looked horrified. "They used to be *human*? Do those women even want to be *vishakanyas*?"

Vikram stared at Gauri. Most of Ujjain's court treated women like fashionable baubles, easily traded and replaced. His mother, a former palace singer, had been one of those discarded fashions. The moment the court discovered she was with child, she was sent away. He'd known only a few royals who considered the lives of those outside their courts.

Gauri opened her mouth to speak, but the shrieking cheers of the audience drowned out her words. A *vishakanya* had selected someone from the crowd. A handsome musician ascended the platform and sat before her.

"Are they going to kill him?" asked Vikram.

"They can't kill *us*," said the *vanara*. He nodded at them. "Well, you, certainly. And her. There is no better food to a *vishakanya* than human desires. And don't look at me like that, rude girl. You won't meet your end with them. We'd rather save the pleasure of killing you for ourselves."

"Then why did you bring us here?" she spat.

"To witness their last performance!" shouted the other *vanara*. "Tomorrow they will disappear for the Tournament of Wishes—"

Vikram's expression brightened. What if they could follow the courtesans to Alaka? But his expression must have given something away because the yellow *vanara* started laughing.

"You're not the only man who wishes to be spirited away with them, boy. But you cannot fool their magic into taking you."

Gauri raised her head sharply, her gaze flying to Vikram. His gut twisted. Poisonous courtesans would be at the Tournament?

"While they're away, no one will be able to send them to the human realm and end the life of a foul or unpleasant king, and that means no demonstrations," sighed the yellow *vanara*. "No pleasure."

On the stage, the *vishakanya* sang and stroked the musician's neck.

"*This* is why we will miss them when they go," whispered the *vanara*.

At her touch, a strange whorl of smoke appeared in front of the musician. It took life and shape from the *vishakanya*'s touches and whispers, becoming a man made of smoke. The smoke being beckoned to the musician, and his face constricted in want. The moment the *vishakanya* lifted her hand, the smoke being vanished. The musician stood up, a thin line of blood dribbling from his lips. He wiped it away and stared at the *vishakanya* hungrily. Like an addict. Violent applause burst through the crowd. Vikram's stomach turned.

The yellow *vanara* turned to them, his pupils dilated to the point where they had nearly eaten away the whites of his eyes.

"You sees?" he asked. "They can show you what you want the most. You can drown in it."

The gray *vanara* laughed. "Ah, desire. Such a poisonous thing."

Vikram frowned. Where had he heard that? But the thought faded as they were once more dragged through the Otherworld. For all its beauty, there was something unfinished about the Otherworld. Many stalls were in the middle of construction. An orchard with silver saplings lay enclosed by a pearl fence. Even the sky looked sewn together; pieces of the night sky wore strange white scars that were neither clouds nor stars, but thread. Vikram recognized the looks of the place. The city bore the aftermath of war, as if it had grown harder and more wary.

"Who won the war?" asked Gauri. "You said there was a war here."

"Oh yesses," said the *vanara*. "The Dread Queen and her Cold Consort soothed Chaos to sleep, muddled the stars, broke the thread, ate the dark and spits it up!"

Vikram rolled his eyes. Their captors were insane. Which didn't bode well for whatever would happen next. He steadied his nerves. He had knowledge about a weakness, and that was the greatest weapon he could demand. He'd talked his way from tight spots before and if he had to sell his soul to get them free and take them to the Tournament, he would.

At the bottom of a sloping valley lay a glowing number of pools. The land looked like the earth after thunderstorms, divots of silver puddles lighting up the world. The gray *vanara* expertly picked his way through the pools. Vikram peered into the pools, and what he saw stole his breath. He saw a forest of glass birds. A hundred suns. A thousand moons. As the reins tugged him forward, he caught a glimpse of the gray *vanara*. His hands were gripping something glittering. A shining ruby. For a panicked second, Vikram thought the *vanara* had stolen from him. But then he felt his own ruby grazing his chest from the concealed pocket in his jacket. What was a *vanara* doing with a ticket to Alaka? His thoughts went no further. The *vanaras* jumped into a pool. His feet skidded over the edge. A rush of hollow terror filled his stomach and he shut his eyes, bracing for the fall.

7

A BITE OF VENGEANCE

GAURI

I was dying.

I had to be. Hunger like this was impossible. Hunger started threading through my body when we were in the Night Bazaar. It was as if the apple *wanted* me to bite it. Only the *vanaras'* threats kept me from sinking my teeth into the rind. When we jumped through the mirror portal, the hunger became impossible to ignore. Hunger smeared my vision. I hardly saw the ghost city we were led through. Low fires burned in faraway embankments but the streets were empty. Vaguely, I could just make out tattered pennants hanging from lopsided turrets. In the distance, the crooked teeth of a mountain ridge grinned and widened, as if preparing to snap the world in half.

"Home," sang the yellow *vanara*. Even through the haze of hunger, I could hear the hurt in his voice. "One day, Queen Tara will return. One day, her penance will be enough."

I couldn't remember being shuffled from one place to the next. It was only when I heard dungeon doors clanging shut behind me that I realized we'd been locked inside.

"The trial will be held at first light," called the gray *vanara* through the door.

A dank, fetid smell wafted through the room. I bit back the urge to retch. Slabs of wet, gray stone formed the walls. In one corner, an iron tree sprang up to brush the ceiling. It was too thick to break apart the pieces and try to lever the stone slabs apart. Besides, I could hardly stand. Something hung from the iron branches, a bulky cloak probably left behind by some former doomed inmate.

Now that the chains had been removed, I rubbed my neck with one hand, wincing at the swollen and bruised skin. Vikram leaned against a wall, murmuring to himself.

"I think if we can fool them into thinking that we have some ties to the Queen, we can sneak out. You can still fight, can't you?"

My face must have given away my answer, because he groaned.

"Show me that apple."

I was too tired to fight, so I held out my hand. The apple's golden rind had begun to wrinkle like day-old fruit. It looked molten in the stingy light.

"Strange," he said.

"Is there no end to your wisdom?"

He ignored me. "How do you feel?"

"Like I will die if I don't eat this apple."

He considered this. "Then why don't you bite it? See what happens."

"Are you mad?"

"I prefer curious."

"It could kill me!"

"I don't think so," he said. "The *vanaras* kept a tight leash on your throat. You couldn't have possibly eaten anything with it on. . . . What if it was to prevent you from eating it?"

"No."

I couldn't put into words what terrified me about the apple. I felt as if it were capable of devastating consequences. It had to be, if a group of people was willing to guard it with no hope of its return for almost a hundred years.

"They warned me against eating it."

"And you trust them?"

"No," I said. "But I trust eating this fruit even less."

Vikram stalked off, muttering things that sounded a lot like "stubborn" and "why me" under his breath. I tried to will away the pangs of hunger, but they only seemed to grow louder and more insistent. My gaze fell on Vikram. Exhaustion had stamped bruises beneath his eyes. His face—severe and sharp—drank up what little light filled the dungeon. His body was less skinny than I'd first thought. He was muscular, but trim, with the lean angles of a runner. Nothing in excess. And it made me . . .

Hungry.

Maybe if I ate him, I'd have the sustenance to fight my way out of here.

Maybe if I ate him, I'd survive.

What was *wrong* with me? Horrified, I stepped back. But whatever demon possessed me demanded a voice. I croaked out:

"You'd be more use to me dead than alive."

Vikram's head snapped up in the same instant that another voice chortled and hissed from the corner of the room:

"I agree entirely."

I jumped. Cold sweat ran down my back. I looked up to the iron tree standing flush against the cold wall. I thought I'd seen a former prisoner's cloak hanging from its limbs. But it wasn't a cloak. It was a corpse. Pale. With only a handful of flesh left to stretch over its bones.

"Only a corpse," I breathed.

"A *corpse*? What a common thing!" huffed the body. "Have you never seen a *vetala*?"

Vikram stared, his jaw slack. "Those are only supposed to exist in cremation grounds."

"Very good!" croaked the creature. "Cremation grounds are the best place to steal bodies. As one does when one is just incorporeal evil."

I knew very little of *vetalas*. Maya refused to share stories about them, for fear of giving me nightmares. I knew they stole bodies and fed on souls, but nothing else.

The *vetala* swung upside down from the tree, pale and decaying knees locked to the branches. Behind him, folded and what I'd first mistaken as a cloak, were a great pair of wings.

"Admiring them, are you?" he asked, twisting his neck all the way around. "Pity they are nothing more than ornamentation. But I couldn't bear to be parted from them. They add style to decay. What afterlife is worth living without some beauty, wouldn't you agree?"

The *vetala* looked me up and down, and sniffed. "Perhaps you wouldn't."

Vikram moved closer to me. Which didn't seem wise, given my last thought.

"What do you want, creature?" he demanded.

"A body with more cartilage would be nice," exclaimed the creature. "Would you be willing to give me yours?"

"No," said Vikram.

"Perhaps I might have your wife's instead?"

"I am not his wife."

"Unmarried? Perhaps you might like to be *my* wife? Mine was most unfortunately beheaded by villagers. No one quite understood her humor." The *vetala* sighed. "Ah, Putana . . . your breasts may have been filled with poison, but they were delightfully plump."

Vikram crossed his arms. "Have you been sent here to spy on us?"

"Why would I waste immortality on you?" laughed the *vetala*. "I only decided to speak up to offer some advice. Best give that non-wife of yours a bite of your arm. That's *rakshasi* fruit in her hand. The want alone will devour you. But she'll be fine. It's all temporary. Like any rage. Difficult to avoid the temptation though. I'm surprised she has not eaten you yet. She *was* musing about it."

"Wait, what?" said Vikram.

"*Rakshasi* fruit?" I said. "As in . . . demon fruit?"

"Did you actually want to eat me?"

"Calm down, I wasn't going to follow through with it."

He raised an eyebrow, as if to say: *You tried to kill me earlier today.*

"The ashram archives said there was nothing left of demon fruit. That it had simply stopped growing in the human world."

"Pah. Sages are fools," said the *vetala*.

Vikram peered a little closer at the demon fruit stuck to my hand. "I never imagined it would look so—"

"—beautiful? Burnished? Bright as hope? Golden as first love?" trilled the *vetala*. "You boy things are all the same. You think a demoness fruit will be horned and bloody, with a rind of thorns and flesh like iron nibs. Have you never been in love? Ah, love! Never has hell and heaven produced such a fine fruit. All demon in its soul. So gilded in its form. Like a woman at her ripest."

"What does it do?" I asked.

"For a short time, it grants the eater demon-like powers. Increased size, strength, that kind of thing," said Vikram. "But it doesn't explain why the *vanaras* think I could've stolen it. It's impossible for me to use the fruit. It only answers to women. Some say it was grown from the willing heart of a demoness."

"The boy is leaving something out," sang the *vetala*.

"What is it?"

Vikram didn't meet my eyes. "If *rakshasi* fruit is eaten at the wrong place and wrong time, the woman who eats it could possibly . . . eateveryonearoundher."

"Is that so? At least I'd be rid of you."

His eyes widened. "You choose *now* to make a joke? You are joking. Right? Gauri?"

I said nothing. The *vetala* cackled. Vikram took a small step away from me.

"Why would the *vanaras* be growing this?" he asked. "They don't have a queen anymore to lead an army. And from what I saw of the city, it's been abandoned ever since Queen Tara disappeared."

"That's not why they keep the fruit," trilled the *vetala*. "They're just tending their ghosts. What you hold in your hand, dear girl, is Queen Tara's curse. And that is why, dear boy, your plan to spin the *vanaras* a tale of lies and win your freedom will never work. Not now! Not ever! We can spend the rest of eternity together. What fun."

"Stay silent or I will cut out your tongue," I hissed at the creature.

"Not my tongue!" said the *vetala*. "What fun would I be? And besides, if I had no tongue, who would tell you how to escape? I'm the only one who knows."

"You know how to get back to the human world?"

The *vetala* swayed. "*Human* world? You can't go back there if you eat the demon fruit. Wherever it is eaten, that is the world you are stuck in for at least one turn of the moon."

The choice loomed before me: Eat the fruit, stay in the Otherworld and potentially die here, or don't eat the fruit and certainly die here.

I hesitated. "You're lying."

"My dear, I am showing myself down to my bones! For you, I have bared my heart. Or what's left of it, rather." He swayed in his tree, flashing a mouthful of blood-claggy teeth. "There is nothing of me which you do not see."

"Why are you even in this cell?"

"A little monkey wandered into my cremation ground. And I ate him! Pity he turned out not to be a monkey. Oh, but I was fed for days upon days upon days."

Vikram crossed his arms. "What did you mean that the demon fruit is Queen Tara's curse?"

The *vetala* eyed us slyly. "That is what she grew from loving too much. She loved her consort and he loved her. But a group of courtesans slew him and two other kings. Instead of letting her love become a phantom ache, she clung to it until it grew a thick and impenetrable hide. It is said that one of the kings had grievously injured the sister of the courtesans. But the king was innocent! Then again, who cares? No one ever mourns the innocently killed! What does your realm call them? Ah, yes. *Casualties.* As if taking a life is an informal thing. Like a yawn or a laugh." The *vetala* swayed and laughed. "No one would avenge her husband. No one cared. So she grew her own vengeance. Cut out her heart to nourish it, stole bones to prop it up against the elements, coaxed it to bear fruit with her tears. And she forced it upon others, to eat of her fruit and partake of her vengeance. And to bring down all the kingdoms who denied her justice. Ah, but how much blood must you guzzle before time breaks you of your sorrow? Bad queen. Bad bad bad. For her greed, she is cursed until a kiss falls upon her stony brow."

"How much of that is true?"

"Who cares if a story is true or not so long as it is told? Either way, your *vanaras* will not accept the fruit that damned and stole their queen."

What a ridiculous curse. If I could have taken down kingdoms with demon fruit, I would've grown it too. The *vetala* fixed its hollow eyes on me. "Careful, girl. The Queen wanted too much too. Her story was vengeance. Do that, and your life's tale will be nothing but another's ending."

That still didn't answer the question. Had Queen Tara's crime only been to lead an army of women? What was the crime in making yourself invincible? Skanda's grinning face flashed in my memory. If I had the choice of invincibility, I would've taken it too.

"So, let's assume that you eat this fruit and don't eat everyone around you," Vikram said. "Could you smash through the walls of this place and free us?"

"You could do that," said the *vetala*, butting into our conversation once more. "But how will you get out?"

"The way we came," I said.

"And then what?" said Vikram. "That doesn't leave us with many clues. And we only have two days before—"

"Don't!" I shouted.

"—Kubera's tournament," finished Vikram.

Panic thrummed through my chest.

"What did you say?" said the *vetala*. His voice was deathly quiet. I pushed myself off the wall despite the impossible pain and hunger setting me on fire.

"Maybe I should follow my instincts and eat you just for being plain stupid," I snarled.

Vikram stepped backward, his eyes widening.

"It astounds me that Ujjain has any plans to make you ruler. Did they teach you nothing?" I gritted out, just out of earshot from the *vetala*. "Never reveal where you are going. Never reveal what you *need*. You just gave away two of those things by, once more, loudly observing all the ways in which we are in dire need of help."

"I didn't mean—" started Vikram.

"I don't care what you mean. I care about what you've done. That *thing*—" I said, flailing an arm in the *vetala*'s direction. "—will sweet-talk you into giving away your own soul just to get to where you want to go."

"What if it is telling us the truth?" he countered. "Are you the only person capable of being correct? What is so impossible about taking a leap of faith and *trying*? Besides, it wants something from us. And until it helps us, it won't get it."

"You're assuming I'll even follow you to this Tournament. I might as well hide out in the Otherworld until a cycle of the moon passes and go back to the human world."

"Are you that frightened of magic?"

I narrowed my eyes. "If you were half as clever as they say, you would be frightened too."

"So you'll waste a month of your life instead of grabbing the best opportunity?"

I opened my mouth. Closed it. Doubt dug into my thoughts. Before, I didn't want any part of magic. But if we survived, I couldn't waste a month of my life. Where would I go? What would I do? I remembered the promise tucked inside the enchanted ruby . . . the lull and temptation of everything I wanted folded neatly into a wish.

"I know how to get out and I know how to get to the Tournament of Wishes," trilled the *vetala*. "Did you know they call Alaka the Kingdom of Desire? It is just north of Naraka. So quaint, is it not? Death and desire are almost always hand in hand. You will not even leave this kingdom without me. This is the kingdom of the *vanaras*, you short-lived fools. They are wiser, stronger. Their tunnels and insies and outsies are not like your straightforward forts with their hidden passageways. But I can't break the walls. The girl would have to do that."

"What do you want, *vetala*?" I asked.

"I want a body."

"We will not give you ours."

"How about only one of you dies?"

"No."

"Well, if you shall not part with your bodies, then I suppose I must settle for your shoulders," said the *vetala*. "I cannot walk. Or fly. I wish for the crematory grounds, and not this damn solitary confinement with a single stinking iron tree and not a dead body around me for miles."

Vikram turned to me. "So will you try it or not? That demon fruit is all we have. I can distract them with a tale, but that won't be enough to get us out. I need you. Not just to get out, but for this Tournament. Think about what you could do with a little bit of magic."

The choice knotted my stomach. Vikram reached out for my hand, cradling it with a strange tenderness that for a moment drowned out the loud call of the demon fruit. I didn't jerk it away.

"This is our *life*," he said. "Our wish is on that line. We can't lose it."

I pulled back my hand. "And I won't lose myself. What skin are you putting into this game, fox? Your eloquence? What a sacrifice."

"It's my life too," he said tightly.

"Your life makes no difference to that girl," laughed the *vetala*.

"Maybe someday. But today is not that day. Beast of a girl, I think in another life you would eat it. But bravery needs a bite. And you have lost it somewhere. Broken heart, perhaps?"

Vikram looked at me sharply.

"Know this," he said. "I will not die with you. I will compete in the Tournament."

The *vetala* laughed. "Compete? Dear boy, the game does not start when Kubera's players arrive in his kingdom. It begins as soon as he chooses the players."

8

DEEPEST, DARKEST SELVES
GAURI

In the months after I pulled Nalini from the water, the city and villages had rejoiced so much that Skanda allowed me to become a representative of sorts. I was allowed to attend council meetings. Sometimes, Nalini and I played alongside the sons and daughters of village leaders. Bharata began to know my name and slowly I began to love my country and its people, its customs and its history. I thought I was lucky. I thought my brother's heart had changed. But when I was fourteen, I realized why he had let my face and name become so closely entwined with Bharata.

Skanda called me inside the throne room. I suspected he was angry with me. Yesterday I had disagreed with him in front of the council on whether or not to build a temple in a drought-ravaged village.

"Prayers are good, but what sustenance are words compared to water?" I had said. Nalini had thought of that line, and I smiled after catching looks of both admiration and shock on the council members' faces. When I entered Skanda's

throne room, he was grinning broadly. Half the council stood in the shadows, watching our exchange.

Skanda lifted an ornate box that I had never seen.

"Thank you for this generous gift, dear sister."

I frowned. "What gift?"

Skanda opened the box: milky white snakes twisted and writhed. The council gasped, but Skanda merely raised his hand and laughed. "Water snakes? Don't worry, councilors. It is a private joke between my sister and me."

With one hand, he dismissed them. The room emptied within seconds, but not before I'd caught several suspicious and disgusted glances.

"I never gave you that," I said, horrified. "Why would I ever give you poisonous snakes?"

"So innocent, little sister," he said, laughing. "And you're wrong. It's not their bite that's venomous. It's their touch. If they fall into a well of drinking water, they can wipe out a village in a day."

The threat took shape between his words. The drinking well that I had advocated for before the council could become a death trap. And the poison could be linked back to me all because he had said before a group of people that the snakes were from me.

"You lied."

He laughed. "Lies! Everyone tells tales, sister. I may not have the public's ardor and attention the way you do, but I do have the ear of very convincing people."

"What do you want, Skanda?"

"I'm glad you asked," he said. "I'll allow this drinking well to be built. But in return, I want you to convince half of the village's militia to join Bharata's forces."

"That village has suffered enough unrest. They need a strong militia to keep their own people in check. Bharata's forces are well trained."

Skanda kicked the closed box of snakes and a furious hissing welled from inside the wood.

"They need what I say they need. And I need our eastern territory secured."

Fury rose inside me. "And if I don't agree, you'll poison an entire village and let my future die alongside them?"

"Do you doubt it?"

"Don't you care?"

He didn't hesitate: "No. Caring will make you careless. Caring always ends in a cut throat. So no. I don't care if they die. I care about my palace. I care about staying on my throne. I care about living."

"You cannot break me with a tale, brother."

"You're happy, aren't you? You're loved. You love others. I think people are convinced that if you asked the sun not to rise, it would stand down for you. But there's only one story that people like better than a rise to fame—a fall from grace. And I can make it swift. And I can take all this away. You see, a story is not just a thing told to a child before sleep. A story is control."

I never forgot his threat. After that, I was careful not to give anyone power over me. And for the next three years, I played my brother's political games.

Outside, the sky looked wounded. Gashes of crimson ripped apart the night. Soon, the *vanaras* would come. I had a choice. My life could end either way. If I ate the fruit and we escaped, what then? Trusting magic was like trying to harness a thunderstorm. But I couldn't hide out in the Otherworld for a month knowing Nalini could die any day. I set my jaw. If I survived the fruit, I would fight in this Tournament. I would treat magic the way it should be treated: not like a gift, but a weapon. Something to be wielded with wariness. Not wonder.

"*Vetala,*" I called, whispering so that Vikram would not hear. "What will I become if I eat the fruit?"

The creature grinned and swayed. "Nothing but yourself, maiden.

Nothing but your very self. What is more frightening than our deepest, darkest selves?"

Footsteps clattered on the stone. I bit down on my cheeks, steadying myself. I would either die by my hand or by theirs. And I would not let that be decided for me. The fruit sang, juice spilling down my palm. I walked to Vikram and kicked his foot.

"What?" he bit out. Red ringed his eyes.

"I need you to distract them."

He sat up. "And after that?"

I took a deep breath. "If we survive, I'll . . . I'll be your partner in the Tournament."

"And you won't make any more attempts on my life?"

"Let's not be rash."

He grinned. "I'll take it."

"If I—" I hesitated. "If I cannot seem to regain myself. Don't let me live—"

"What would you wish for right now?" asked Vikram, cutting me off.

Fists beat the door.

It was nearly time.

He stood up, blocking out the light and throwing his face into darkness. He bent down to my ear, his voice low and urgent: "I know you're scared of losing yourself but think only of what you want. Sometimes that's all it takes to keep us from losing sight of ourselves.

"So tell me, Gauri," he said. "What would you wish for?"

I thought of Nalini trapped in her cell. Of Skanda sitting on his throne and seeping lies.

"Freedom," I breathed. "I'd wish for freedom."

His brow furrowed. As if he had expected any answer but that one. The door clanged open. Screeching iron drowned out the stillness.

"Timesies has come!" squealed the yellow *vanara*. "Hoppity trot, fruit stealers. Time for your beheading."

The *vetala* yawned and unfurled his tattered parchment wings. "I'll be the one languishing in the corner should you decide to live."

"Distract them. When the time comes, I'll break down the walls. We'll get the *vetala*. We'll escape."

He nodded. Neither of us mentioned how all our plans hinged on one thing:

Could I hold on to myself?

"Are you ready?" asked the *vanara*.

Vikram darted one last look at me. He didn't look at me with an unspoken farewell in his gaze. He looked at me with understanding. For a moment, I felt as if fire braided the space between us. It was charged and alive, lit by a shared dream: to wish.

A practiced smirk slid into place as he turned to face our captors. The moment he turned, I brought the golden fruit to my lips. My reflection distorted on the metallic rind. I sank my teeth into it, expecting them to cut on the demon fruit. But the rind yielded like silk. A strange taste flooded my mouth—iron and cold.

Like blood and snow.

THE BEAST PRINCESS

VIKRAM

The moment he turned, panic dug into his skin.

This was it.

He'd practiced calm before, but nothing like this. Three *vanaras* stood in the doorway with arrows notched and bows drawn.

"Before you cart us away to certain death, I'd like to hear a recitation of what we've done wrong."

"Read the list of the prisoners' crimes."

The yellow *vanara* cleared his throat. "Taking our fruit!"

The gray *vanara* nodded. "And?"

"And?" repeated the yellow one, frowning. "What do you mean *and?* What else did they do?"

Vikram stole one more glance at Gauri. She was hunched over in the shadows of the cell. Swinging her head like an animal, she stared at him. Bright gold juice glistened on her lips and dribbled down her chin. The black of her pupils had spilled out of its rings. She was moving her hands. Trying to tell him something. And then he saw it:

Claws. Claws erupting and curling from her palms. Her thighs were bent strangely. Like haunches. Talons sliced out of her sandals. Gauri was not hunched over because she was in pain. She was crouching because soon she would be a demoness unleashed. Her gaze was livid.

She mouthed a command:

Use me.

"No more of this!" shouted the gray *vanara*. "You will come with us now—"

"Would your queen take so kindly to this corrupt trial?" said Vikram. "I think she'd be ashamed that this is how you uphold her legacy."

The yellow *vanara* made a hurt and wounded sound before turning to the one beside him. "Would she really, brother?"

Behind him, Gauri pawed the ground. Panic frosted his thoughts. If she turned on them, would he be the first victim? As the *vanaras* argued, he glanced behind him. Her eyes were the same despite resting in a face that had the tufted ears of a leopard, and strange glittering antlers uncurling from her forehead. She tossed her head, lips pulled back from her teeth as she snarled and mouthed: *Use. Me.*

Right before his eyes . . . she *grew*. The tunic split down the middle, but it didn't matter, because gold fur grew where skin once stretched. She stood, taller than a horse, back as broad as a bear's. And then she roared. The *vetala* laughed even as the rumbling sound shook him from the iron tree and sent him tumbling to the floor.

The *vanaras* gasped. "She took it!"

"No—" screamed the gray one.

Vikram turned and grinned.

Too late.

Nothing human remained in her aspect except those glittering eyes. A snow leopard's tail lashed from behind her.

Now, said her eyes.

Vikram sprang toward her, grabbing the *vetala* as he jumped onto her back. Somewhere in the shadows of the Kishkinda kingdom, he thought he heard the barest trace of delighted laughter. The *vanaras* loosed their arrows, but Gauri broke them in her teeth.

"*Vetala!*" he yelled. "We've kept our word. Now honor yours."

The *vetala* shuddered. "Honor? There should always be better motivation than honor. Try something more appealing. Like half-clothed women or a vat of goat blood."

"Tell us where to go!"

"Pretty monster," said the *vetala*, patting Gauri's massive head. She hissed. "Bad cat."

The *vetala* licked his hand and held it to the windless air. "Into the wall."

"Are you insane?" asked Vikram.

"Yes?"

"Straight into a stone wall?"

An arrow sliced through the air. Gauri brought down a massive paw and snapped it in half. Vikram thought he heard a laugh rumble in her stomach.

"Get out of the way or die," he said to the *vanaras*.

Gauri began to gallop, her body stretching for the stones just before them.

One.

Vikram's gut wrenched. He didn't want to die slammed by a wall of stone. He didn't want to die *at all.*

Two.

The air smelled sour. He could imagine the sound of Gauri's beautiful antlers shattering.

Three.

Her fur glinted, light rippling over her body. Vikram held tight, bracing himself for a thud . . .

That never came.

10

A BOWL OF LUSH MEMORIES

GAURI

I didn't know hurt. Or fear.

When my skin gave way to fur and my nails bent into claws, I knew what it meant to be stripped down to your barest self. It meant seeing the world for what it was. I took off my skin and released the thing that had always lurked, crept and slept within me: A beast. A monster. A myth. A girl. What was the difference?

My last thought before I turned was the wish I would've made. For freedom. True freedom. And even though I couldn't speak it aloud, I could feel the weight of that wish filling me from the inside, pressing against my teeth. I felt that wish like a line of light, a boundary that my mind wouldn't cross lest I lose myself forever.

We ran and I reveled. I could see and smell and taste. I licked starlight out of the air. Saw midnight cresting over a mountain. I thought I'd lost Vikram as we jumped through that wall, but then his scent caught me. He smelled of wanting and bottled-up dreams. And in some dimmed human part of me, heat flared.

The *vetala* stroked my head. "Run toward the scent of death, pretty monster. The Grotto of the Undead will be the first boundary to Kubera's kingdom."

It was not a difficult scent to follow. The smells of death lit up the world already, but finding where the scent rang strongest was painstaking. I pawed the ground, turning up the earth and trying to find that smudgy scent of stale death—mushroom pale, a crease of shadow in a skein of light, flattened sounds that trembled in my ears like the blunted teeth of echoes.

When I found it, I chased it. I didn't know how long I ran. I ran until there were no more animal sounds. No more scents. This was death: the absence of all. I was still a beast when we finally reached the Undead Grotto. But my claws had receded. An antler had snapped off sometime earlier. The effects of the demon fruit were fading fast.

I shrugged off the *vetala* and Vikram like an itchy cloak. They tumbled to the ground. The *vetala* let out a stream of curses, but Vikram only stood and straightened his tunic. Whatever brief understanding we'd shared before I turned had disappeared. Once more, his eyes sparked as sly as a fox's.

"Since you can't respond yet and since you have no claws left, I will take this moment to remind you that you thought eating the demon fruit would be a bad idea. It was not. To which I say—" He drew a deep breath. "—*I told you so.*"

"Fool," muttered the *vetala*.

I snarled and with one last burst of strength, swiped my paw behind Vikram's knees and sent him tumbling. He gasped.

"I will," he wheezed, rolling onto his stomach, "take your silence as a form of agreement."

Vikram sat on the ground, tugging one dark curl around his ear. Even with dirt smudged across his ears and nose, he looked regal. His long legs were crossed in front of him, and he reclined against the rock outcropping as if the earth had put it there just for him.

I turned to the Undead Grotto, which was a desert-like basin between two cliffs. Bone white trees rose from the uneven ground like spindly fingers. Lichen and greasy-looking flowers splashed over vermillion rocks. The moon was nowhere to be found. Even looking at the place made my fur stand on end. The Grotto was a place not quite out of myth. Scouts had sometimes returned to Bharata carrying tales about the place. How the wind taunted members of the scouting party. Those who wandered into that land refused to leave or were never found. Even those forcibly brought back were never the same. That much was clear from the landscape alone. Piles of abandoned armor. Even some weaponry. I padded through the refuse, pawing aside the rusted bits until I found a blunt knife. It was better than nothing. I picked it up in my mouth, carrying it back to Vikram and the *vetala*.

Vikram kept his gaze on the Grotto. "How much longer until the demon fruit stops working?"

"She is already turning." The *vetala* huffed. "Don't look so disappointed. I know what you're trying to do, tall fox. You think the Grotto is a place you can fight through with the help of some demon fruit. But it's not about fighting. It's about *seeing*," said the *vetala*. "Alaka has two doors before it opens its golden ones: the Grotto and the Crossroads."

I remembered the rhyme from the ruby: *Alaka is past the place where memories devour and the held-breath place to put an end to cowards.* Which one would the Grotto be?

A cold wind shuddered through me. I felt my mind unspooling, my body shrinking. Those powerful demoness muscles were now draped onto a smaller set of shoulders, a thinner set of bones. The world dimmed and receded.

Oh, I thought, at the same time I heard my voice rasp:

"Oh."

And then:

"Oh no."

The only thing that had stayed on my skin since the moment I turned was Maya's necklace and my sandals. My tunic hung off me in strips. At this moment, Vikram was pretending that there was a spot of great interest just beyond my shoulder. The *vetala* had squeaked and drawn up his tattered wings over his face.

"Give me your jacket," I demanded.

Vikram—who was now pretending that his life depended on looking at the spot right beyond my shoulder—grumbled, "When you ask so kindly, you're impossible to resist."

He threw the jacket to me. Shrugging out of my tunic, I kept my eyes trained on his face. Gratefulness flooded through me. Most men wouldn't have thought twice about looking. Some would have pressed it further than a look. To so many men in Bharata, your body wasn't yours. It infuriated me. But the one time I tried to do anything about it, I only hurt someone. Once, I had a soldier whipped for what he tried to do after cornering a serving girl. Luckily, Arjun had gotten there in time to pull the man off and let the girl escape.

The whole time he was whipped, the soldier had screamed in defense: "The Raja Skanda doesn't care!"

"Do I look like my brother?" I had sneered.

That day, I felt proud. As if I could protect people. Skanda found out what I said and had the girl brought to his chambers that night. I only found out the next morning, when the girl stopped me on my way to the barracks. Her eyes glistened with tears: "Spare me your mercy next time, Princess."

It haunted me thinking about how many people I had harmed just for trying to protect them. For one moment, I squeezed my eyes shut. Then I tightened the jacket.

"How's the view?" I asked, turning.

Vikram blinked, not looking at me. "Excellent. Best I've ever had."

"Good for you, Vikram. Because it might be your last."

I picked up the blunt dagger and walked past him to where the *vetala* hummed and drew circles and stars into the dirt.

"Keep your word, creature. Get us to Alaka."

"There now," said the *vetala*, crawling toward us. "Did I not say that it is a matter of perspective? And am I not an honorable corpse thing? Lean close. Lean close. I shall tell you things."

Vikram's shadow fell over me as we both crouched before the *vetala*. The creature drew up its ragged knees. It opened its mouth as if to speak. And then . . . it *spat* into our eyes.

I jerked back, dragging my arm across my stinging eye.

"I don't need my knives to kill you, *vetala*," I bit out.

"I better not go blind," groaned Vikram, rubbing his fist into his eye.

I tried to jab him with my elbow, missed and lost my balance.

"You are most welcome," said the *vetala* silkily.

I touched my left eye—the one he had spat into—and found it strangely cool to the touch. Vikram met my gaze.

Where both of his eyes had once been brown, one of them was now bright green. I glanced over the rest of his face, noticing things that had been invisible mere moments ago. The dying light tugged his sharp chin, cut jaw and hooded gaze from Otherworldly to beautiful. When I looked into his eyes, my breath caught. I saw *things* and *people* swimming in his sight—a woman with gray streaked in her temples, a fistful of blue flowers, a stout king with a one-winged bird on his shoulder. Empty cradles and darkened halls. And a boy. A boy who held himself as if there were a storm gathering bolts of light within him. Vikram, too, looked disturbed. His brows were pressed together, and when his gaze fell to Maya's necklace, his lips parted in wonder.

What had my eyes betrayed?

He turned suddenly, and his eyes widened.

"Gods," he breathed.

I followed his line of sight and horror gripped me.

Before, the Grotto had seemed a lifeless, barren thing. Now shapes twisted before us. Creatures clung to the bone white trees. Creatures who were not resting in the branches or frozen in death, but awake and skittering.

And staring straight at us.

"Hurry, hurry," whined the *vetala*. "This isn't just about the two of you fools, you know."

I covered the eye the *vetala* had spat into and looked out onto the Grotto. Nothing but bone white trees met my eye. But when I covered the other eye and looked out, bodies teemed and writhed, gnashing their teeth.

"One eye to see the illusion . . . another to see through it . . ." said Vikram softly.

"But then why were we able to—" I stopped.

Vikram caught my gaze and quickly looked away. Why had we been able to see through one another, as if we were nothing more than panes of colored glass?

"The body is its own illusion. Now you can see through it," said the *vetala*. "Rather like fleshy thuribles. They're just keepers of things. What's inside you is the thing those beasties like the most. You are, basically, a bowl full of lush memories. They want to scoop them out, sink their teeth into them, drown themselves in the imprints of living moments."

"How do those monsters tease out our memories?" asked Vikram.

The *vetala* smiled and ice poured down my spine.

"They can sniff the shapes of memories rising off your skin like steam. They will tug on them. And you, like a drowsy fat bumblebee lulled by the blue throat of an intoxicating blossom, will fall into the arms of whatever illusion they craft."

I sucked in my cheeks and patted the jacket. I was ready. Vikram looked more hesitant. The color had drained from his face and he was staring at the Grotto as if he knew exactly which nightmare was waiting for him.

"If you die, you die. Do not feel bad. I died. And I am quite fine," said the *vetala*. "If you do, however, manage to be killed—and by the looks of you, I would not be surprised so much as irritated—please try to keep your heads. You're no use to me decapitated."

Since I'd already transported us to the Grotto, Vikram agreed to let the *vetala* climb onto his back. The *vetala* smoothed Vikram's hair, crooning: "Nice donkey." At the end of the sloping cliff, I checked once more to make sure that the enchanted eye worked. Vikram let out his breath to speak, and I prepared to hear formal, solemn words like "death comes for all of us anyway." What I heard, instead, was:

"Race you to the end?"

It was such a bizarre thing to say that I . . . started laughing. I was shocked that I had a laugh left inside me and even more startled that it chose to announce itself moments before a battle where death had victory pinched between its thumb and forefinger. Once freed from my belly, the laugh warmed my bones. Maybe that's why the best laughs tend to break free on the edge of lightless horror. Only then can they give wings to a drooping spirit. I needed that. And whether or not Vikram knew what he had done, I felt grateful.

The *vetala* groaned. "You are bound to die."

All it took was one step for the Grotto to transform. The wind picked up my hair. One moment, I could see the slit of light at the end of the Grotto. A cave opening. At the back of my head, I heard Maya's voice: *The Lord of Wealth once ruled Lanka, a city of gold. Gold everywhere. Gold in the trees, in the rivers, in the air.* Perhaps it was gold. Gold just on the other side. All I had to do was reach it.

But in the next moment, the world transformed. Thick clouds of mist rolled in front of us, hiding the light. I felt Vikram at my side, but I couldn't see him. I held my breath. *Who will the Grotto taunt me with first?*

I didn't have to wait long. Out of one eye, I saw a dark hand stretch toward me. Faded blue tattoos flecked her arms like dull stars. Nalini's beautiful face twisted in hurt:

"You left me there to die."

11

A POISONED SPOON

GAURI

I kept moving.

You're not real.

"Vikram!" I called out.

Nothing.

"You were supposed to keep me safe. I trusted you," she said. "I did *everything* you asked. All I asked was for hope. Don't you remember? I came to you. I begged you. And what did you do?"

Shuddering, I moved forward. One step. Two. The mist grew heavier, blanketing my feet. My heart sped. The ends of the *sherwani* jacket got caught around my legs. I tried to look through the enchanted eye, but it could see only through the spirits of the Undead Grotto. Not the mist. Beneath me, the ground turned craggy. I was used to fighting on uneven surfaces, but usually I had boots and both eyes open. Here, I was walking on threadbare sandals, one hand clasped over my eye and my sense of space and depth faltering. My toe caught. I fell, flinging out my arms for support.

A voice too close to my ear whispered:

"Answer me, Gauri. We were closer than sisters." My head rang. I scrambled to stand, my eyes drifting up without asking permission from my mind. Nalini stared down at me, hazel eyes bright with accusations. "How could you?"

My voice broke. "I was trying to keep you safe. I thought there was a spy, Nalini. It wasn't what it sounded like."

It was the day before the rebellion. I had stopped eating; anxiety chewed at my core. We had one chance to do this right. Months of planning had built up to this day. But I could feel Skanda's eyes tracking me. Maybe someone had spied on our meetings. Or someone had sold me out. I started keeping information to myself. Refusing to meet people. Even Arjun and Nalini. That night, Nalini visited me in the gardens, and I could have sworn that the nocturnal eyes blinking open in the jungle belonged to Skanda's spies.

"Gauri," she said. "What's happened to you?"

I said nothing, my eyes fixed on the jungle.

"What are you hiding?" she demanded. "You haven't even visited Arjun since he came back—"

"You mean since I rescued him?" I returned angrily.

A week ago, I had brought Arjun home. It was all thanks to Maya. The day she staged a fire in the harem, I'd been able to escape Bharata and rescue Arjun. Ever since, he had been trying to talk to me, but I couldn't jeopardize our operation by allowing us to be seen together. Skanda was still furious with me for going against his direct orders and saving Arjun.

"Do you know what horrors he faced? Do you even care? What happened to the promises you made me?"

The darkness rustled. Skanda had spies everywhere. Were they watching us?

"There is nothing to hide, Nalini," I said, my voice cold and distant. "Arjun is a soldier. When I found him, he was wounded. I saved his life. I don't owe him more than that, and I certainly owe you nothing."

If I had told her the truth, would she have escaped imprisonment? When I walked into the jungle after, the rustling had been nothing more than a hare trapped beneath a tree root. Not a spy. I could have apologized to Nalini. But paranoia is a house full of locked doors. So I withdrew.

Nalini reached out, brushing her fingers against my arm. I shuddered. She felt so cold.

"You were never meant to get hurt," I said fiercely. "You were the reason I fought for the throne."

Nalini had saved my life. The day she knocked a poisoned spoon from my hand was the day I stopped hiding and started hunting. It was the first time Skanda had tried to kill me. Until he was removed from power, Nalini's life was at risk. Before then, I hadn't been willing to risk everything. If I failed, I wouldn't be able to protect the few that I could. But if Skanda was trying to kill me, it meant that he never intended to keep his promise of naming me his heir.

"I deserved better," said Nalini.

My heart snapped. "I know."

"I'll forgive you, sister. Embrace me as you once did. Let us start anew."

I moved to her, the grass blades cutting into my feet. Blood beaded on my skin. I looked down, frowning. Grass shouldn't cut.

"Come to me, Gauri," said Nalini. Her voice bordered on desperation. "Don't I deserve an apology and embrace after what you did to me?"

"What did I do to you?"

Nalini said nothing. But the skin on her arms flickered from her usual lacquered brown to an unusual oily black. I stepped back.

"*What did I do to you?*" I asked loudly.

The question yielded the answer:

I had put her in prison. She was supposed to be lying somewhere in a cell in Bharata.

"Why aren't you in prison?"

She tilted her head. Cold spread in my chest. The gesture was wrong. Inhuman. I was forgetting something. I stared at my hands: They were dirty. Bloodstained. I shouldn't be dressed in a man's *sherwani*. Slowly, I lifted my hand to my eye, the movement guided by some knowledge that glinted at the edge of my thoughts. Nalini hissed, her jaw snapped open in a gruesome grin.

And then I saw her for what she was:

A monster of smoke and teeth. It clicked its teeth. Wet talons reached for me. I stumbled back, breaking the wall of mist. This *thing* had used my best friend's voice.

"Gauri?" it called sweetly, its belly scraping along the ground as it started crawling.

I picked up my knife, flinging it straight at one of its arms and pinning it to the ground. It let out a shrill and icy scream. A small boulder nudged my foot. I lifted it, not looking at the thing as I heaved it over my head and smashed it into the creature's body. The screaming stopped. I covered my eye, plucked my dagger from the inky arm and started running.

The cave at the end of the Grotto shone with light. I ran. I ran past a vision of Maya sprawled out with her throat cut. I dodged a vision of Mother Dhina rocking back and forth, blood running down her wrists. Vikram passed me. I chased his lean shadow, and the ground disappeared beneath me. My memories loomed dark and lurid until a crease of light caught my eye. *The cave.* I was nearly there. As the mist sulked and spun, a dark blot scuttled toward me on ragged wrists and knees. The *vetala.* His hand wrapped around my foot.

"The boy thing is dead," he huffed. "Pick me up."

12

THREADBARE HEART

VIKRAM

As a rule, Vikram ran only when he was furious. As it so happened, he was almost always furious. Every day he treaded the threadbare line between livid and lucent. There was horror in knowing that he was only ever meant to be a puppet king. And there was hope in knowing that he was capable of so much more. When he ran, those sticky intangibles—title, birth, expectations and resentments—couldn't cling to him.

He was simply moving too fast.

The *vetala* cackled, roping bony arms around his neck.

"Faster, donkey! Faster!" he screeched.

Vikram knew what the Grotto would show, which memories it would pluck from his mind and spin into spiteful sylphs. It took years of practiced charm to erase the boy that the Ujjijain Empire grudgingly accepted. Only his father remembered the day he was found. No one remembered the wilting blue flowers in his hand, or the way he had clung to the brittle, colorless blossoms until they crumbled to dust. No one chose to see. It was the way of royalty.

He was nearly at the cave, dry winds burning in his lungs, when he heard it:

"*Beta?*"

I knew you would come for me.

The *vetala* cackled and whispered in his ear: "Protect the head, protect the head."

Vikram clapped one hand over his eye, but a tug in his heart stalled his feet. He had steeled his heart against seeing her. But *hearing* her? He hadn't trained his heart against the longing to curl around the sound of her voice. Whenever his mother spoke or sang, the sky brightened. Even the stars would drift a little closer to catch the silver of her voice.

"My child, have you forgotten me? I waited a long time for you to come back," said his mother. "You wanted to surprise me. Remember?"

"Yes," he said, hoarsely.

"I forgive you, for what you did to me. Won't you embrace me, my son?"

Vikram looked up from his feet, and found himself at the edge of a dusty cliff. He stumbled back, his nose filling with the sharp scent of pine. A net of tree limbs danced above him like laced fingers.

"*Beta,*" breathed his mother. "Come to me."

He wanted to. Gods, he wanted to. But something stayed his hand. *Hand.* His mother stood with her arms folded across her chest. A burst of blue caught his eye. Blue blossoms. It was the blue tingeing her neck at the bottom of a cliff, her mouth full to the teeth with rocks. He frowned. *Impossible.*

The image burst.

He stumbled out of the mist, his head ringing as the *vetala* screamed:

"—fool of a boy!" He started running again, heart racing, to get to the other side. With only one eye open, he turned and found the thing from the Undead Grotto stumbling after him.

"Come back, Vikram!" it called in his mother's voice.

He ran blindly into the mist, dodging thin tree limbs. But his foot slipped just as a boulder draped in mist lurched into sight. The last thing he saw was the gravelly dirt rising to meet him.

Vikram woke to being dragged across the uneven ground of a darkened cave. Small threads of light stitched their way across the rock, casting a thin and stingy illumination. The *vetala* squatted on his chest, and cackled when Vikram tried—and failed—to shove him off.

Gauri's silhouette caught the dim light. Dirt streaked her arms, but she carried herself like a queen reclaiming her country. She was also, to his infinite loathing, hauling him around like a sack of fruit.

He groaned. *Do I make you laugh, Universe?* Once, when he was ten, he attempted to fly by attaching silk scarves to his arms and leaping from a tree. It did not work. When he was fifteen, he dressed like a courtesan to sneak into the harem. He ended up appearing too convincing to a palace guard and was forced to throw off his silks and punch the man. All things considered, this was not the most shameful thing he had endured.

But it was certainly one of them.

"Wakey! Wakey!" shouted the *vetala*, slapping his face. "I jumped off because I thought you were a husk of a thing. But the pretty monster came back for you."

He wanted to strangle the creature. It would have been far better to feign unconsciousness and just allow himself to be dragged across the cave. Maybe the Universe would have smiled down at him and knocked his head against a rock. He twisted out of Gauri's unnervingly strong grip. She dropped his leg with little ceremony.

"Get up," she said.

"I appreciate your concern and my mind is perfectly intact. Thank you for inquiring."

He wobbled to a stand and snuck a glance into her eyes before breathing a sigh of relief. The *vetala's* enchantment had worn off. Their memories had retreated back into their skin. Still, he wondered what she had seen in that Undead Grotto. Her face looked pinched in the cave light, her lips pressed tight. Now that her hands were free, her fingers twisted protectively around her necklace. When he looked at her under the enchantment, he had seen a girl who wore a hundred faces and never smiled in any of them. He'd glimpsed a memory of a princess who hid a sparrow with a broken wing in her room. He'd seen her clutch her blue necklace tight to her throat and drop her shoulders when no one was looking. Who was she?

The *vetala* raised his arms like the most grotesque infant. "Pick me up."

Grumbling, Vikram swung the creature onto his back. The *vetala* promptly rested his chin on Vikram's head with a delighted sigh. There was nothing else to do but follow the light. As they walked, Vikram sensed the enchantment of the Otherworld buried in the cave silt. It was subtle. Like moonlight soaking fruit trees, storm clouds crouching over palace spires and watchful eyes blinking open in the dusk. And it stirred him awake and wide-eyed.

"Thank you," he said, partially to break the silence, but mostly because he truly meant the words. "You went back for me."

"We need two to participate in the Tournament. And the *vetala*"—she jerked a disdainful nod at the creature—"would be of little use. So don't thank me. I did it for myself."

The *vetala* brought his head to Vikram's ear. "I heard her heart leap from its cage of bones when I said you were dead."

His own heart did a strange flip. They'd crossed through a Grotto where their own memories had been treacherous, but all he remembered was the sound of her laugh when he asked if they should race. Her laugh was low and throaty, as if rusty with disuse. He hadn't been able to shake it from his mind.

"Vikram!" shouted Gauri.

His head snapped up. A moment from his toes, a massive rip in the cave floor reared to meet them. He ground his heels into the floor, his stomach turning as if he had fallen through the hole. *Smack.* The *vetala* brought his bony elbow down sharply on Vikram's head. His body jerked forward, just as the *vetala* shoved Gauri.

"Jump! This way, cowards!" the *vetala* shouted.

Vikram's heels slipped. He kicked uselessly, his arms spinning. Gauri tumbled alongside him. A furious, near-inhuman roar ripped from her throat. Vikram let himself fall, bringing out his arms as if he could fly. This would not be his death.

He hollered, an impossible grin stretching on his face. The dark slid over his thoughts. He reached into the shadows for Gauri. And found her.

13

THE TRUTH OF FIRST LIGHT

GAURI

A warm hand brushed against my forehead. Without thinking, I had leaned into the embrace when a voice splintered that stolen calm:

"If the girl thing does not awaken by dawn, I claim her body, yes?"

Then followed the thumping sound of someone smartly smacking another person. I blinked. Vikram stared down at me, his lips pressed in a tight line. This close, I could see that his eyes weren't quite as dark as I'd thought. Lines of gold shot through the deep brown. Like stars breaking through the night. Or sunlight threading through branches. I sat up quickly—

"I wouldn't do that—" Vikram started.

As if in response, a dull ache throbbed behind my eyes. My vision went black before sight returned. Once more, I was on the ground. Only this time, Vikram's arms were not around me.

"You hit your head," he said.

I glared. "That can happen when you're pushed into a hole in the ground."

"You're welcome," said the *vetala* brightly.

When I'd given my body a chance to adjust, I looked around the silk tent, which was half-opened to reveal part of the land and sky. Everything was familiar and unfamiliar. I recognized the citrus and sweet-almond trees to my right. They were identical to the ones in Bharata's gardens. A wave of homesickness rushed over me, so strong and unyielding that I couldn't breathe. Beside the trees, the silk pennants of Ujijain fluttered in the windless air. But what stole my breath was the sky dusted with stars. Silvery stairs rose and dwindled into the night sky and I wondered what impossible kingdom they climbed toward.

I looked down and found that I was sitting on a rich rug. Two cotton beds sat low to the ground, downy pillows and warm blankets spread across them.

And the feast.

Split guavas sprinkled with cane sugar filled a crystal bowl. Saffron rice, buttery naan, savory onion and potato dishes, cold yogurt studded with pomegranate seeds like rubies and silver cups of spicy dal waited for us. My vision filled with desserts: crystallized pistachio slivers, dusky almond chews and creamy *ras malai* sprinkled with rose petals. My favorite—golden, syrupy *gulab jamun*—called to me. My mouth watered.

As far as I could tell, there was no one here but us. I checked the makeshift belt I had made from part of Vikram's jacket, and found my dagger resting warmly against my hip. Aside from the slight headache and the scratch along Vikram's forearm, we were unscathed from the tumble and the Grotto. Physically, at least.

"Where are we?"

"The Crossroads," said the *vetala*, singing.

I thought back to the rhyme from the ruby. We'd already crossed the Grotto, which fit *the place where memories shall devour*. Did that mean we were in *the held-breath place to put an end to cowards?*

"Well. A feast calls, and I shall answer." Vikram stood up, dusting his torn tunic.

"Have you gone mad?" I shouted. "We need to think through this!"

This place was clearly enchanted. It didn't matter that no one else was around us. Magic hid its knives behind a closed-mouth grin. I wasn't taking any chances.

"I believe he was mad before this," mused the *vetala*. "Or maybe it's the effect of the Crossroads. It likes to unspool things of comfort."

So that explained the bits of Bharata springing up in this strange place. I paced in the tent. "But how do we get out?"

Vikram heaped food onto his plate and offered me a dish. I hesitated. Ever since the poisoning attempt, I didn't like eating food that I hadn't seen prepared. Besides, Maya had always warned me about eating the food of the Otherworld. One bite of the demon fruit had been enough to prove that.

"Do you think I'm trying to poison you?" asked Vikram, raising an eyebrow.

"Are you?"

"You saved my life," said Vikram. "I would not try to poison you after that. I owe you."

"Don't eat that!" I said, making a grab for his plate. But Vikram moved faster, holding the plate aloft. "Do you intend to reward me by dying?"

"Not at all," he said, turning back to his food and defiantly heaping even more rice onto his plate. "I could marry you, if you'd like. That seems to be a popular reward back home."

"I prefer the poisoned food."

"You may be rewarded yet," he said. He popped a handful of pomegranate seeds in his mouth.

He froze, some of the juice spilling from his lips.

"Oh no," he breathed, clutching his chest.

"Vikram!" I screamed.

He held up his hand. "I meant to start with mangos."

I stopped short of scrambling toward him, cold flushing my body as he laughed. Fiend. I left him to his cackling and poked the *vetala* in the side.

"How will we get to Alaka from here?"

The *vetala* grumbled and cracked open one eye. "Are you daft? Follow the directions, of course!"

Directions?

I pushed back the silk curtain and walked to the back of the tent where eight statues loomed far above us. Even from a distance, the statues were as tall as elephants. The cardinal directions were inscribed beneath the statues, which depicted the directions' respective guardians. Kubera, the Lord of Alaka and guardian of the North, carried a mace in one hand, a necklace of gold on his stone chest. Northeast: Ishana, the Lord of Destruction, with his matted hair and fearsome trident. Northwest: Vayu, the Lord of the Winds, waving a flag in one hand. East: Indra, the Lord of the Heavens, gripping a thunderbolt in one hand. West: Varuna, the Lord of the Waters, holding a lasso. Southeast: Agni, the Lord of Fire, carrying his spear of fire. Southwest: Nritti, the Lady of Chaos, with a scimitar in a lovely hand. South: the Dharma Raja carrying his staff and noose.

Beyond the spinning dais of directions stood eight identical doors.

Nothing distinguished them from each other. Neither the height nor width, the color nor cut. A yawning, impassable ditch separated us from the doors. The only thing that might fit in that space was the spinning dais of statues. But if the dais was supposed to be a bridge, we couldn't use it until it fell to the ground and stopped moving. Statues and illusions enclosed us. We needed to start planning how to leave. I turned around to see Vikram drinking deeply from a goblet.

"What?" he asked. "Did you change your mind about my marriage proposal?"

"I didn't hit my head that hard," I said. "Did you realize we were closed inside these walls? The *vetala* must have tricked us into following a dead end."

"Me?" screeched the creature. "All I wanted was a body. Now I am left to the mercy of your wits. I suspect I am doomed."

"I did realize," said Vikram. "You seem to forget that you were unconscious. I already checked the parameters of the place. We are certainly trapped for the night."

"Only a night?"

Vikram reached behind him for a slip of parchment that was embossed with golden ink and handed it to me:

Weary traveler, take your heart's delight
You have come to the final crossroads of fate
Thank the Ushas for the truth of first light
Until then, feast and drink for your heart to sate
But know these walls will forever bend
And when they are through, no bones can you mend
Take care of the direction you choose
Thousands will come here and thousands will lose

I read the words slowly. Trapped until first light. Only at first light could we choose which direction to travel in? But how would we know which was true? I glanced up at the palace of night so out of reach. *Thank the Ushas for the truth of first light.* The Ushas was the goddess of dawn.

"Is there a reason you didn't share this with me until now?"

"And miss the opportunity to see you fly into a rage?" he asked. "There is plenty of time to contemplate our inevitable doom. We have much less time to sate our stomachs. Besides, I wanted to ensure I'd have a head start on eating the desserts."

"Ever the optimist."

"I am optimistic," said Vikram, waving around a plate of food, "about not starving."

My stomach growled. Vikram didn't seem any different from eating the food, so it was likely safe. I crouched beside him, taking the *halwa* for myself, and then sat facing the corner of the square room that resembled the view outside my bedroom window.

"Your home?" asked Vikram.

I nodded. "And the corner with the view of Ujijain . . . is it yours?"

"Yes."

It was a strange view. Vikram's view of Ujijain was the realm itself. It was cold. Proprietary.

"You love Bharata," said Vikram. A statement of fact.

"I do."

"What made you decide to play in the Tournament? You could've just waited for one cycle of the moon and rushed back to your beloved Bharata."

I bit my lip. If I waited that long without a hope of a plan, Nalini was as good as dead. It wasn't as if I could stroll into Bharata at the end of the moon cycle. If I set one foot on Bharata's soil, Skanda would

execute Nalini and then pin the blame on me. All the games, manipulation, losses and secrets would be for nothing. Worse, it would plunge Bharata into warfare if we lost the support of Nalini's tribal home.

"Circumstances," I said tightly.

Vikram watched me. "What did you do to make your own kingdom want you dead?"

I clenched my hand. "Let's just say that politics in Bharata forced me to play a game of power I thought I could win. I did not win. Hence the death order."

Vikram rolled his eyes and clapped slowly. "Did princess study include theatrics? Do you also run around the city as a hooded vigilante?"

"You don't know anything about my life or what it was like for me," I said angrily. "All you princes are the same. You've never worked for anything so you wouldn't know the first thing about another person's struggle."

His gaze sharpened. "In that, Princess, you are mistaken."

I let out a breath and pressed my temples. "Now that we've eaten and argued, what about the riddle?"

"We know the way to Alaka is to follow true north. The statue bearing Kubera's image says as much. But the statues are set on a spinning wheel—"

"And they may not be accurate directions when they settle."

Vikram drew his brows together. Setting down his goblet, he drew an image in the dirt: a dais and eight doors. He studied it, steepling his long fingers. I groaned. Enough was enough.

"Why do you do that?"

"Do what?"

"That." I mimicked his hands, flattened my brows and tried to make my eyes look somewhat insane.

"I will have you know that it is my meditative pose."

"I will have you know that you look ridiculous."

"What about you?" he asked. He sucked in his cheeks and glowered, pointing at his face and then pointing at me. "What kind of meditative pose is that?"

"It's not a meditative pose at all," I shot back.

"My apologies. Is it your bellicose-let-me-drain-your-blood face? Could you not master an expression that looked less like an outraged cat?"

"Better than steepling my hands and looking like an overgrown spider."

"An overgrown spider who is rarely wrong."

"My bellicose-let-me-drain-your-blood face has saved your life."

"And this overgrown-spider pose is about to save yours."

He rested his chin on the edge of his palm, his head tilted just so. Pale light slid over the carved planes of his face, from his narrow nose and sharp jaw to infernal lips that always danced on the edge of a laugh. Vikram caught me looking at his lips and smirked. I bit back some choice curses.

"When the Ushas leave their home, that would be the equivalent of dawn. So it would be first light. I think the spinning wheel of statues will freeze," he said. "I think it will come down to where we can cross the dais and access those eight doors. We should monitor it throughout the night and see if it begins to fall."

"If that happens, we only have until first light to choose which statue to follow through which door," I said. "We don't know how long the dais will remain in place. Any idea?"

He tapped his fingers together. "I believe we should follow Kubera's statue in the direction of true north."

"That's far too simple." I held up the invitation of the Crossroads and read aloud: "'Thousands will come here and thousands will lose.' I am sure many of those thousands tried the simplest route."

"It's not about the simplest or most direct path though," said Vikram. "Magic is a test of faith . . . why else would we have escaped Ujijain, eaten a demon fruit and allowed ourselves to be tortured by our pasts if we didn't believe in what the Tournament offered?"

It was the first time he had mentioned what he had seen in the Undead Grotto. Pain flashed in his eyes, so brief it might have been mistaken for the light glimmering above us. But I caught it.

"You speak with conviction that relies on feelings, not facts," I said. "Following true north is too easy. It sounds like a trap."

"But that's half the guile of this place. How many times have answers been so simple and yet someone is determined to take the path of thorns instead of roses?"

"It's not earned."

"That's a very human thing to say."

"An inclination I can't help."

"It's not about things that are earned, but just things as they are. Magic chose us for a reason. Did you believe in the Otherworld before you saw it with your own eyes?"

I nodded.

"Magic is like that," he said. "It's like faith."

He spoke so earnestly I almost believed him. But Vikram had something I didn't. Innocence. Maybe the world would break for him because he believed it would. But it wouldn't do the same for me. To me, the Otherworld and the human world were the same because of one thing: Neither world coddled or cared.

"I need to think."

"Fair enough," he said. "Consider the options yourself. But don't think that just because you saved my life, I will follow you to the ends of the earth and through any door."

"Thank the gods. That would be the last reward I'd demand for saving your life."

Vikram stood up and stretched. "Do as you will."

He crossed the small tent. I studied his gait. You could tell a lot about a person from the way they occupied space. Skanda walked as if he expected a knife around every corner. Vikram held himself as if the world had whittled this moment for him alone and he was not simply going to live it, but rule it. He was so sure of everything that it made me envious.

He reached for one of the water basins and started scrubbing his face. I sat half frozen on the ground. Was I supposed to get up and leave? But then I frowned. Why should I leave? *If he doesn't want me to look, he should go.*

He didn't go.

He shrugged out of his tunic, and then he was down to his trousers. His back was partially turned, but I could still see the outline of corded muscles gracing his shoulders and the sinewy length of his arms.

Once, I had tried to squeeze myself into an outfit that wouldn't fit because I'd had one too many helpings of dessert that day. The room felt like that. Like a whole body puckered and determined, too tight and too conscious of every contour and shape within it. I had to leave.

"Stop admiring the view," he said.

"Critiquing it," I lied, standing and scooping up my plate of *halwa*.

"What do you find lacking?"

"Honor."

Not exactly a lie.

"Alas. I must have misplaced it."

"Is there a reason why you seek every opportunity to annoy me?"

"It's fun. Your scar flashes when you frown. It almost looks like a dimple," said Vikram. "I'm still waiting for your face to turn red with anger. It might make you look like you're blushing. Or perhaps I am making you blush?"

I froze. No one except Mother Dhina and Nalini had recognized the small scar for what it was.

"I trained alongside male soldiers for years and have seen, and probably smelled, far more than I should have. Or wanted to," I said. "You will never make me blush."

"If we leave this place alive, I am determined to prove you wrong."

The *vetala* cackled from the other side of the tent.

"I would choose a more achievable quest, boy. Perhaps you could apply yourself to make the girl snarl at you. That seems far more likely. Or rip out your throat. Also more likely," huffed the *vetala*. "Mind the head, though, girl. And that jacket you took from him. I grew fond of it during our travels."

14

A SCAFFOLD OF SILENCE

GAURI

People always think killing requires a force: a cup of poison tipped into a mouth, a knife parting flesh from bone, a fist brought down repeatedly.

Wrong.

Here's how you kill: You stay silent, you make bargains that peel the layers off your soul one by one, you build a scaffolding of flimsy excuses and live your life on them. I may have killed to save, but I killed all the same.

Two years ago, Skanda had fallen in lust with the daughter of a prominent noble. The nobleman loved his daughter and didn't want her wasting away in Skanda's harem. So he had her betrothed immediately to someone else. Skanda got angry. The girl's betrothed was brought to his personal chambers, where the girl's wedding sari, stolen by a spy, had been placed. One look at it was enough to convince the man that his betrothed had been unfaithful. He broke off the engage-ment. Two days later, the girl took her life to spare her family shame.

I had seen the girl's betrothed when he left Skanda's chambers. I had seen confusion and fury warring in his face. But I needed more recruits for the army, medicines for the village children, and I wanted Skanda to start apportioning funds for Nalini's dowry before her wedding to Arjun.

So I stayed silent.

Maybe if I had been braver, I would have spoken up. But at what cost? I hadn't forgotten the serving girl I tried defending. My voice was one of the only things I could control—when to unleash it, when to tamp it down like a burning ember, when to grow it in secret.

All my life, control and power had worn the same face.

I believed in gods, but the only faith I truly practiced was control. Nothing in excess. Nothing that placed my life in the hands of another. And yet for the second time, I was considering giving myself wholly to a magic I could neither wield nor know.

"I was right," said Vikram, pointing above us.

The rotating dais of directions had begun its descent in the night. Now it spun faster and faster, counting down to the moment where I would have to make a choice.

"I say we choose the north and follow Kubera," said Vikram. "Are you with me or not?"

"But what if it's a trap? What if we go with south instead and choose the Dharma Raja?"

"We might find ourselves in Naraka then, and I have no intention of dying so soon."

Above us, the neighing of horses lit up what was left of night. A silver chariot creaked out of an unseen hall, ready to pull the moon out of the sky and usher in the new day.

"*Vetala!*" called Vikram.

"Seeing as I've already died, this part is not terribly exciting," shouted the *vetala*. "Go on then. This was most entertaining."

Vikram threw up his hands. "If you don't come now, we're not turning back to get you."

"I know," said the *vetala* softly. "I know."

A screeching sound ripped through the cave. We stood a short distance from the ditch, ready to jump onto the dais the moment it fell into place. With a ripping sound, the dais fell out of the air, crashing into the ditch just as the sky seamed with light.

Eight doors glowed in the gloaming.

Eight doors that held no promise of where they would lead.

One chance to choose the right path.

First light was about to fall. Together, we raced and leapt onto the dais. I nearly lost my footing reaching for that stone. Wind blurred the world. The eight statues stared down at us with vacant eyes and knowing grins.

Choose.

"*Vetala!* This is no time to play!" called Vikram once more.

He crouched, as if ready to retrieve the creature, when I yanked on his arm.

"We only have until first light. It's survival or sympathy," I said. My voice was stone. "He told us to go on. It's your choice to find him. But I'm not waiting."

He paused for only a moment before he stepped to my side. Maybe the *vetala* had abandoned us because it realized we were bound to die. The sky lightened. Dawn had roused the horses. They clambered through the air, soaking up what was left of the darkness so that they gradually turned from white to smoky, then gray to deepest plum. Vikram gripped the page of instructions tightly.

Around us, sheaves of dirt slid in fat waves . . . swallowing the gossamer tent where we had eaten, lapping up the false groves that had been our heart's desires. I watched the ground drag down the only place I could call home.

Step by step, we crossed the dais. Slowly, slowly, it screeched its halt. At once, the eight doors glowed, each door opening barely more than an inch. Behind each one: light unending. Vikram halted in front of the door marked by Kubera's statue.

"Well? Will you follow me from one world to the next or not?"

Determination blazed in his eyes. There was no doubt in his mind that he was right. His belief felt like heat that crinkles and greases the air. The force of it pressed and needled the world, as if it could summon kingdoms out of sheer force. His conviction set me alight.

I grasped his hand.

Vikram touched the statue of Kubera. Every door slammed shut but the one to true north. Stone gears smacked together like pressed lips. Huge waves of earth rolled to us, pushing us through the door. Golden light washed over my eyes, and dry heat crackled against my skin.

The door slammed shut, dissolving into nothing.

I slammed against Vikram, knocking him to the ground. It took a few blinks before I could see in front of me. We were sprawled on top of a lush green hill. A path of thorns and moonstones wound through small valleys and between sparkling lakes before ending at a red gate that encircled the golden kingdom. The kingdom sat in the cupped hollow of a violet mountain range. The palace loomed so large that its great golden spires looked as if they had unraveled from the sky. A thousand turrets bearing pennants of gem-encrusted silk fluttered into the day. I could make out the silhouette of handsome lawns teeming with glittering fountains, fragrant fruit orchards, feast tables piled high with sweets and savories and a large crowd of people who wandered aimlessly through the grounds.

"We're here. We made it to Alaka."

Vikram took in the view, his eyes widening.

"It's beautiful." He turned to me, mischief glinting in his eyes. "How do they celebrate good fortune in Bharata? In Ujijain, we kiss."

I let go of his hand. "Look elsewhere."

"Are you sure? You spend an awful amount of time looking at my lips."

"That's only because I'm horrified at the sheer idiocy of the words leaping out of them."

"Such tales," he tutted. "If you're curious, I'm willing to indulge you."

"Go kiss a rock."

"I will," he said with a gallant bow. "Rocks are kinder and softer than you anyway."

He turned around, walked over to an outcropping of rocks and promptly kissed a boulder.

"There," he said brightly. "That one even looks like a woman."

I peered at the rock he'd kissed. He was right. A lonely lemon tree grew beside the handful of rocks, but the boulder he'd kissed was as tall as a woman, with worn carvings that might even resemble the outline of hair and lips, breasts and a whittled waist.

"You're certain that *rakshasi* fruit is out of your system?" asked Vikram.

"Yes?"

"Good." He took a deep breath. "Because, once more, I told you so."

"You do realize that I don't need the enhancements of demon fruit to knock you to the ground?"

"I do. But I concede that some bodily harm from you is inevitable. I'm just trying to minimize the damage."

"How very wise," I said, rolling my eyes.

Vikram grinned. "You saved my life, now I have saved yours."

"We're no longer in each other's debt then," I said, walking past him.

"No reward, fair maiden?" he asked, jogging to keep up with me. It was at least an hour's walk to the front doors of Alaka. "If you remember, I very generously offered you my hand in marriage."

"And I rejected it. Consider that your reward."

Vikram stopped, turning to the spot where the door had opened in the air and dropped us into Alaka.

"Silly as it sounds, I'm almost concerned for the *vetala*."

I understood that. Even I almost liked the *vetala*. But he'd made his choice. We'd offered help. The creature rejected it. I didn't waste time mourning.

"I wish he had come with us."

I swatted Vikram.

"Ow! What was that for?"

"We're in Alaka now. I wouldn't start off any sentence with 'I wish.' Save it for when you win."

Vikram pulled the ruby from his pocket, tossing it into the air so that the gem caught the light.

I looked ahead of us to the outline of the palace, appraising it as I would any enemy on the battlefield. Maya's stories ran through my head. This was a place where dreams and nightmares borrowed each other's faces. Somewhere, folded among all that dark gold and all those bright jewels, was my wish. A new reign in Bharata. Nalini's safety.

Skanda's legacy scrubbed out of history. I saw a promise of freedom so close I could snatch it out of the sky. But I also saw Maya swallowed whole by the dark of the forest. I saw every night I had spent wondering where she was, what had happened. What waited for us wasn't just a tournament, but a new future. And I would fight for it with my eyes wide open.

I looked at Vikram and caught the same hungry gleam in his eyes.

"Race you to the end?" I said.

He grinned. "What does the winner get?"

"A chance to risk life and death at an impossible game."

His smile fell away. "That's a solemn victory."

I shrugged. "Most victories are."

"What about the loser?"

"The loser gets no chance at all."

Vikram eyed the palace. "Then we better start running."

15

THE TASTE OF BREAD

AASHA

T he blue star at her throat burned.

"What's wrong?" asked one of her sisters.

"Nothing," said Aasha, covering the star with her hand.

"You're hungry," said another. "You need your strength, my dear. If you don't drink down some desire . . ."

Aasha sighed, shutting out her sister's words. She knew already what would happen. She'd heard the threat her whole life. Without devouring desires, no *vishakanya* would be able to fend off the poison in her veins. She'd die. She should eat. She *would* eat. But in the meantime, she dreamed of what it would be like to eat something *other* than desire.

When they had set up their tent yesterday, she could smell the feast from the palace of Alaka. All roasted vegetables and golden bread, crackled rice and glistening sweets. But *vishakanyas* could not digest such things. Aasha had nearly tripped on her silks because she couldn't tear her eyes from the wispy spirals of the cooking fires. Her mouth watered.

She knew the words "spice," "sugar," "salt" and "sour." But they were little more than phantom words. She had no experience to bring them to life.

"We are the entertainment after all," continued her sister, "so—"

"Is that all we are? Just entertainment?" asked Aasha.

"Technically anyone in Alaka during the Tournament of Wishes is a contestant, but it's not like the human players who get rules and trials."

"So we could win a wish?"

Her sister laughed. "What would you want with a wish? You came to us so young that hardship never had the chance to look your way. There aren't enough wishes in the world to make you any luckier, Aasha."

Aasha twisted her silk scarf into a knot. She didn't want luck. She wanted something she had never been given, not since the day the sisters had bought her from her birth family at four years old. The *vishakanyas* said they had rescued her. They took her home, opened their veins and poured their bitter blood past her lips until a blue star bloomed on her throat and magic coursed through her. They had taught her their trade: of dancing and music, poetry and philosophy, singing and seduction.

They called their powers—to slay with a touch and feed off desires—the Blessing.

When she was younger, Aasha loved the story of how her sisters inherited the Blessing. They said a warrior queen was called into the fray of battle, but didn't want to leave her sisters defenseless. So the goddess gave the sisters some of her own blood, and their touch grew venomous and deadly. Every hundred years, the goddess would decide if they were worthy enough to keep the Blessing. For the past three hundred years, they had been worthy.

Most of the sisters joined the *vishakanya* harem after losing or leaving a husband, running away from cruel families or simply stumbling into the Otherworld and seeking employment and freedom. Aasha was the only one who had never lived outside the harem. She was the only one who never made the choice between the taste of bread and the taste of desire.

The first time she was sent to the bedchamber of a crooked human prince, her sisters had told her of the man's misdeeds. They told her how he had found a woman of the Otherworld and seduced her only to abandon her when she quickened with child. They told her how he defiled the sacred spaces of the rivers and how all his people wished him dead. They told her how he deserved it.

Not one of her sisters mentioned what she deserved.

The taunt of that unlived human life started as a seedling of curiosity. It grew in the dark of her thoughts, gaining shape and strength when she wasn't looking—a home somewhere with a thatched roof and no silk in sight, an orchard where the trees groaned with fruit, an expanse of skin free of a blue star. Now, it ate up the space around her heart. A living nightmare that snapped her joy. What was that life she had been denied? Maybe it would have been short, but at least it would be hers. But no one cared that she desperately wanted to touch someone and feel their pulse rising to her fingertips and not their life withering at her touch. And no one noticed when she returned home from that first mission, sick and shivering, the human king's sticky desires glommed to her skin. Her sisters called that first mission a mark of freedom.

In the end, no one cared that her freedom didn't look like the freedom of her sisters.

16

THE GATE OF SECRET TRUTHS

GAURI

Even from a distance, the red gate looked wrong. It was dull, with a jagged texture, like uneven chips of garnet that didn't reflect the light but guzzled it greedily. When we stood before it, I realized what crafted the strange gates of Alaka.

Not gems, the way folklore would have a child believe . . .

Tongues.

Thousands of tongues. Red and bloated, severed at the root and piled like stones until they towered above us. A metallic tang hung in the air. Like iron. Or blood.

Vikram paled. "That's not supposed to be there."

"Where did you read that?" I grimaced.

"Wouldn't the stories say that the entrance to Alaka is surrounded by . . . by *that?*"

I was going to answer him, but the gate lurched to life. A hundred

red tongues wagging. Instinctively, I shoved Vikram behind me and brought out the dagger.

"What are you going to do?" asked Vikram lazily, pushing past me. "Threaten to cut out their tongues?"

I glared. All at once, the wagging tongues fell still. The gate grumbled. Shuffled. A deep voice echoed from within:

"Stories are slices—"

"—dices—"

"—pretty slivers of—"

"—not so pretty things—"

"—clever prince and—"

"—fierce princess."

Vikram stood up a little straighter. The tongues had begun to move once more. Speaking to us.

"Have you come to play the Lord of Treasures' game? Do you wish—"

"—to win a wish? Then give us—"

"—the secret truth lodged in the crease of your first heartbreak—"

"—and we will let you pass."

"What are you?" Vikram demanded.

Even though the gate was nothing but tongues, I thought I could feel the air tugging into a sly smile.

"We are the toll paid by those who came before and left Alaka—"

"—and those who came before and—"

"—didn't."

"You see, a truth parted with has its own way of becoming a tale. It is told so often that it stumbles in the telling, little bits flaking off, little bits sticking on, and then years accrete and they—"

"—tend to warp the truth, press it into something it was not at the beginning—"

"—not a lie, but a—"

"—tale. It's easier to see the truth when you disguise it."

Vikram cleared his throat. "I'll go first."

I prepared to leave. His secrets were his own business. But the gate huffed.

"You play together. You break—"

"—together. That is the rule."

I shot Vikram a questioning glance, but he didn't look at me. He seemed to be looking some distance ahead. He breathed deeply, tapping his fingers together.

"I am not the Emperor's true son. If I take the throne, it will be in little more than name."

"That—"

"—is only a part of the truth—"

"Tell us—"

"—what happened to her?"

Vikram's face paled. "She died. From a rockslide. That's where the Emperor found me."

"That—"

"—is not all."

Vikram's jaw tightened. And then he said hoarsely, "She was looking for me over that rock edge. I left my sandal there to play a joke on her. I wanted to make her laugh." He swallowed. "I was going to jump out from behind the trees and surprise her with the flowers. But the moment she stepped onto the rock, she fell."

The gate stilled, as if letting that secret truth sit on its tongue like a candy.

I didn't meet Vikram's eyes, but I felt his burning gaze. My whole body felt numb. It wasn't a skin-tight feel of disgust, but that plummeting humiliation. I knew what he felt. I knew that loss and guilt, that cold twist where a single moment might have made all the difference.

"Your turn—"

"—Princess."

My throat felt dry.

"I tried to overthrow my brother. If I return, he will unleash a state of terror in Bharata and kill my best friend."

I knew what the gate would say even before I heard the wet words on the tongues.

"That—"

"—is not all."

The words pushed out of my throat, sharp and cutting. I remembered the girl's sari in my brother's room, the serving girl Skanda punished when I had the soldier whipped. All those times I had pushed Nalini and Arjun away before that failed rebellion. I was trying to keep them safe.

"I did my best to play my brother's games," I said, keeping my eyes fixed on the ground. "But the choices I made and the silences I kept were just as deadly."

I looked up. What I saw in Vikram's gaze rooted me to the spot: understanding. Those secrets had coaxed a shadowed part of us to step into the light. Understanding felt like a hand reached for and found in the dark. No one had ever looked at me that way because no one, until now, could.

"Now you have our secrets," I said, turning from him quickly. "Let us through."

"—we wish you—"

"—a tale—"

"—worth telling."

"Not luck?" asked Vikram.

The gate heaved with wet laughter.

"—what good is—"

"—such a thing."

The gate parted and we entered Alaka. Vikram cleared his throat and started pointing to the places and people. Some of the stories I remembered from Maya. Others I had no recollection of, and treated the tales as I would any gathered intelligence before a battlefield. It was all something to wield for later. But even as he spoke, I felt the weight of what we'd seen and said, that tendril of understanding that I didn't know how to hold on to.

At the end of one path, a garden unfurled at our feet, studded with pillars of diamonds. Vikram pulled me back before my feet could touch the grass.

"*Nandana*," breathed Vikram, bending to touch the grass. "This is part of the courts of the King of Heavens."

All the Otherworlds are linked.

The gods were watching. He gestured for us to slip off our sandals as a sign of respect. Only after our feet were bare did we step into the grass. The land hummed.

One test passed.

In this labyrinth, the beautiful and savage walked with their faces tilted toward a sky where stars drifted in a black ocean. Wave upon wave of comets and clouds, eclipses and nebulae rolled above us.

"The audience chambers of the King of Heavens hosts all the stars," said Vikram. "That must be where we are."

Out of habit, I glanced above me, searching for Maya's and my constellation. It wasn't here. *No matter where we are, we'll always share the same sky.* My throat tightened. Maya had lied. There were places where one sky ended and a universe unfolded. Places where I couldn't follow her. What sky was my sister looking at?

The Nandana gardens flowed seamlessly into a hall of ice. Ghostly lotuses floated in the air. From their cut stems dripped a sweet and fragrant liquid that drew a small crowd. *Yakshinis* with glass wings or the jeweled tails of peacocks, took turns drinking the liquid and singing.

"This is their city," said Vikram, pointing at the beautiful men and women.

I knew that much from Maya's tales. *Yakshas* and *yakshinis* were the guardians of treasure hidden in streams, forests, seas and caves. Around us, music filled the hall of ice. The songs had no words but gusted images through my head—a lace of ice across a palm, winter blooming on a mountain, the pinched and sallow feel of a sky empty of rain.

"What else?" I muttered back. "Any weaknesses? Strategies in case we need to fight them?"

Vikram frowned. "The stories always said they don't like reminders of the mortal realm."

"How helpful," I said, rolling my eyes.

I tried to move us quickly through the hall, but one of the women saw us. Or rather, saw Vikram. She smiled widely. One blink later, and three of them were standing before us.

"Would you drink with us, Prince?" asked one *yakshini.*

At her throat lay a crystal necklace where a miniature dawn and dusk warred for sovereignty. Across the silk of her sari, a thousand rose-gold mornings bloomed and retracted.

"Drink with us, sweet prince," said another *yakshini*. She was feral and beautiful, as savage as a fire raging through the woods. "And if you find the drink not to your liking, perhaps you will find the company sweeter."

"Yes, do," said a third. This one had blue skin, and ice trailed across her wrists. "You look so tired. So thirsty."

The *yakshinis* laughed. My irritation slid to fury. Where *Vikram* was offered a nice, cooling drink and possibly more, I was standing here parched and forgotten. On top of that: I was starving, dressed in a men's jacket so encrusted with dirt and I don't know what else that it should be burned for the safety of the public, and I couldn't say *anything* because they had more power in one eyelash than I had in my whole body. I was grimacing, looking down at the dirty sandals I carried, when an idea flashed in my head.

"Excuse me," I said, stepping forward. "You must have noticed that we were *both* walking side by side through this garden." *Be polite, Gauri.* "May I also have something to drink?"

The blue *yakshini* blinked and stared at me.

"I agree." Vikram grinned. "Everything you offer me, you must offer to my companion too."

"I don't think I want everything they offer you."

"One never knows until one tries."

I threw the sandals on the ground. "Would this be a fair trade? Shoes for a drink?"

The *yakshinis* recoiled, disgust written across their features as they stepped away from the shoes and disappeared.

"Come on," I said, grabbing the sandals. "Let's seek our deaths in this Tournament."

"Have I ever praised your eloquence?"

"No. But you have my leave to start at any time."

We walked through a garden of ice where snow drifted slowly upward. A white tree pressed skeletal fingers against the sky. Around the edges of a winter pool, twelve men and twelve women with haggard faces and wasted limbs stroked their reflections.

A wall of gold roses parted at the end of the garden path. Standing at a podium, with her back to the entrance of an ornate palace, a tall, spindly *yakshini* eyed us. Gossamer wings slipped from her shoulder blades, fluttering in the windless air. Vikram placed the ruby before her and she smiled:

"The Lord of Alaka, Keeper of Treasures and King of Kings, sends his greetings and welcomes you to the Tournament of Wishes."

17

COLD HONEY, CAUGHT MAGIC

VIKRAM

In Ujijain, the council had been quick to teach him who he was. At first, they had showered him with little slights, so small that when he was younger, he hadn't even recognized them. But enough tiny sharp jabs can cut as deeply as any knife. When he was twelve years old, the council brought him into an amber room on the far side of the palace. The Emperor never visited this room, they told him.

"Secrets are very powerful, young prince," said one of the council members, a man with a curved nose and chipped emerald eyes. "They make you dance."

At the center of the room stood a dais for shadow puppets. This was his favorite part of every festival held on the grounds. He loved watching a story bloom to life with nothing more than bits of paper and sticks. A strong puppet wearing a crown danced onto the screen.

"This is a prince," said a council member.

Vikram had clapped his hands, delighted. "Like me?"

Silence.

"No," one said. "Not like you."

"When you do not have the right blood to rule, the burden becomes very heavy. . . ." said another council member.

A shadow puppet limped onto the screen, something heavy bowing and breaking its back. Vikram had frowned. This was not the story they usually played.

"You see, young prince, this is you should you take the burden of that crown. But we can help," they said. "We can make it so that you'll stand tall. Like the other puppet."

"But I . . . I am a real prince. Father says—"

"Whatever your father may say, he knows the most important secret about you, little prince. He knows you are not his blood. We know the truth too. And do you know what happens when a secret like that is no longer a secret?"

One of the council members grabbed his chin, jerking it toward the screen. The broken puppet crumpled.

"So you see, little prince?" sneered the council member. "We have a secret. Do you want to stand tall—" The strong puppet popped onto the screen. "—or not?"

Vikram had spent the rest of his life fighting that image. But the council had been right. Secrets did make people dance. And he had made it his calling to know every single secret there was about Ujijain, until he could hold them in his fist and force the people around him to dance. But it was never enough. His own secret mercilessly tugged his strings.

The moment he spoke his secret truth before the gate, his heart sank. He had expected that Gauri would fix him with the stare he'd grown up with all his life. But she didn't. Understanding filled her gaze, and the force of it knocked the wind out of his lungs. He hadn't realized, until then, how much it mattered that she didn't see him the way everyone else did. And when she parted with her own secret, he understood. Threads had strung them up and tugged on both of their limbs. All this time, they were both just trying to cut themselves free.

The attendant led them down a path of marble and honeycomb chambers. At the end of the hall, a group of Alaka's magical attendants gasped and whispered behind their hands.

"—so pleased, so pleased!"

"The Jewel of Bharata!" hissed one excitedly.

"Oh," huffed someone in disappointment. "I thought it was an *actual* jewel."

"And there's the Fox Prince! They're here!"

Vikram bit back a groan. He was getting tired of that nickname.

"This is the Small Council of Alaka," said the attendant. "We will be watching and reporting back to Lord Kubera."

They made their greetings. Vikram caught none of their names.

"Where are the other contestants?" he asked.

"Everyone inside Alaka during the Tournament of Wishes is a contestant."

"Even you?"

"Even me," said the attendant. "But the rules are different for Otherworldly beings. Human players are the only ones who can win or lose. The only thing we lose is time and we have plenty of it."

"So how do you win?" asked Gauri.

"No one really knows," said the attendant, dropping her voice to a conspiratorial whisper. "Even those who are judges don't quite know what the Lord of Treasures looks for. He simply asks us things. Like what color a person favored. Whether they were smiling. What color the sky turned when they laughed."

"Sounds irrational," said Gauri.

The attendant's face darkened. "Nothing he does is without reason even if we do not understand. But your tasks will be different," said the attendant. "You are human, after all. And that is the nature of the game. The Lord of Treasures believes that the quest for power is a thing of loneliness. The game reflects that."

"Loneliness?" repeated Gauri. "I thought we were fighting together."

"Of course," said the attendant. "The Lord of Treasures would never separate lovers. He is too devoted to his wife, the Lady of Prosperity and Wealth, the Kauveri River."

"Lovers?" said Gauri.

Vikram elbowed her. Several of the council members' expressions slid into suspicion.

"Are you not?" she asked, her voice sharpening. "That would change your ability to play as partners."

"Of course we are," said Vikram drily. "Do we not look wildly in love?"

"Not particularly."

"What's her favorite color?" asked a council member.

"The color of my eyes," said Vikram quickly.

"Yes," said Gauri woodenly. "They are so very . . . brown."

"And her favorite food?"

Vikram slipped his arm around Gauri's waist. She stiffened. "Council, is true love really so severe that you can measure it in questions about someone's preferences? Our love is the kind that can't be quantified."

A couple of people sighed. But the attendant's suspicion sharpened.

She frowned, glancing at a piece of parchment. That did not bode well. He caught Gauri's eye, one eyebrow half raised. What he saw in her face stopped him. She looked *furious*. But not with him. With what she was about to do. He didn't have time to think. She only turned her head to his, but he felt the movement pinch the world. The people at the edge of the room disappeared. She leaned forward, pulled him to her roughly and kissed him. . . .

The rational part of him knew this was a display for the attendant. But every other part of him couldn't care less. He threaded his fingers through her hair, pulling her closer. Her kiss burned in his bones. And maybe it was the magic of Alaka or maybe his mind was splintering from everything they'd gone through, but he would have sworn she tasted like cold honey and caught magic.

He drew back. Her eyes fluttered open. She looked shocked. This close, her eyes were black and endless. In that stolen moment, a strange thought drifted to him. When he lived in the ashram, reading poetry aloud was a common pastime. He had spent hours listening to how the pull of certain people would supposedly make the world stop. Now he knew it was wrong. The world hadn't stopped. The world had just started to churn and breathe and live.

Gauri cleared her throat and stepped out of his embrace. A mask of calm slid onto her face. She turned to the attendant and said:

"We prefer not to have an audience."

The attendant looked away, her whorled *yakshini* ears tipped in pink.

"This way to your rooms, please."

Songbirds filled their room. The walls rustled, a living thing thick with iridescent plumes. The softest musical notes bloomed in the air. Not *made* sounds from crafted instruments, but elusive harmonies—growling thunder and silver rain, bird chatter and tree sway.

"In these rooms, none will be enter but you. You need not worry about theft," she said. "The Lord of Treasures looks forward to welcoming you and relaying the rules of the Tournament this evening during the Opening Ceremony."

"When should we arrive?" asked Gauri.

"The floor will turn to fire, my lady. That will be your signal to leave the room and join him."

"And the Tournament? When does that start?"

The *yakshini* smiled slightly. "By now, you are seasoned players."

She left with a curt bow. The moment they were alone, Vikram felt as if the room was expanding to fit all that was left unsaid—the truths they had given to the Gate of Tongues, the kiss that he still tasted on his lips. He felt Gauri's gaze like a threshold opening up inside him. Once it was crossed, they could never go back to what they had once been.

"You blame yourself," she said softly.

A statement. Not a question.

"I used to," he said.

He had been seven years old. He hadn't even gone far enough to see that he had placed his shoe two steps away from a ravine. That "what if" would never cease to haunt him. But he knew that if he let it eat him from the inside out, he would be nothing but hollows and shadows. His mother wouldn't have wanted that for him.

"I understand," she said, slumping against the wall.

There was more she wanted to say. He could feel the words scrabbling at the clasps of her thoughts, eager to be known. Freed. But she stood there, stony-faced and impassive. And he remembered the girl he had glimpsed from the Grotto—the one who let her shoulders drop when no one looked, the one who fought every day when no one noticed. The one who had once hoped that the Night Bazaar traded on dreams. She deserved more than loneliness.

"You can't blame yourself," he said quietly. "I saw what he did." Her eyes narrowed, searching his face. "I saw it right before we ran through the Grotto of the Undead. . . ."

She looked away from him.

"Even if I had two lifetimes on the throne, it wouldn't be enough to make amends for the things I allowed to happen."

Vikram tightened his lips. He couldn't say that she had no choice, because she did. But they were impossible choices, death flanking either side. They were cruel and horrifying. That didn't mean they were damning.

"A queen with a conscience will always have a far more enduring legacy. Besides, anyone would have done the same. You knew that fighting him openly was an even greater risk, and so you tried to protect your people. There's no shame—"

"I don't want your pity," she bit out.

"Why not?" he asked. "Don't I have your pity? What's more pitiful than an orphan with delusions of a grand destiny?"

It felt freeing to say the words. And the truth was that he was not afraid of being seen for what he was. He was afraid of being seen as someone who could never be more.

"I wanted to change things," she said.

"Me too," said Vikram. "But I can't change Ujijain with an illusion of a title. And if that's all that's left for me, then I won't go back."

Her gaze widened. "Is it because of . . ." She trailed off, and Vikram knew that she had glimpsed his mother in his memories.

"Her name was Keertana," he said quietly. It had been years since he had spoken her name aloud. "She was a singer in the court. Ujijain forced her to leave when she got pregnant. We were going to try and return to the palace and beg for her position back in court when she slipped on the mountainside. She needed protection and had none. Land and title aren't the only things that make a person worthy. Ujijain has forgotten that. To the realm, its own people are little more than ways for others to become wealthy. I would do things differently."

This time when he looked at her, she flashed him the smallest of smiles. Vikram felt that he was treading strange new territory. Gauri was at once everything and nothing he expected.

"Is this camaraderie going to be a regular ordeal for us?" she joked. But he heard a yearning that echoed his own. Somehow as they'd stumbled together from one near-death incident to the next, he had found a connection. And he wasn't ready to let it go.

"Why not? We're friends of a kind, aren't we?"

"I suppose so."

A grin lifted his lips.

"So," Vikram continued, "I have your pity. And you have mine. Let's call it even. Friends?"

"Friends," she said uncertainly. "Does this mean you're going to stop irritating me on purpose?"

"Absolutely not," he said.

As he walked toward the baths, he heard Gauri call out:

"Just so you know, that kiss meant nothing."

He laughed. "You're acting as though you're my first kiss."

He neglected to tell her that his first kiss was—technically—to the guard who had passionately spun him around after mistaking him for a courtesan when he was fifteen and trying to sneak into the harem.

Like most first kisses, it left him with the sour taste of regret.

"You're not, Gauri," he said, grinning. "But you were certainly memorable."

18

THREE IS A VERY NICE NUMBER

GAURI

When Vikram left for the baths, I threw myself onto the bed. My muscles ached. I stared up at the ceiling, blinking once . . . twice . . . before sleep claimed me. I woke to Vikram inspecting himself in the mirror. His hair was still damp from the baths and slightly curled around his ears. He tugged on the sleeves of a dark blue jacket embroidered with delicate silver feathers. The cut on his jaw had left a pale scar, but it only drew attention to the lips that I had thoroughly kissed not too long ago. He glanced at me, his eyes glinting a little too knowingly. I was painfully aware of how disheveled I looked.

"I was thinking about what you said earlier," said Vikram. "What was it that you told the *yakshini* attendant? *We* prefer not to have an audience?"

He turned slowly around the room, as if marveling at its emptiness.

"I can't remember," I said, standing.

That was a lie. Of course I remembered. The memory pounced on me the moment I fell asleep. Fire painted my bones when I kissed him. In the back of my head, I'd felt the kind of drowsy hunger that lit up my thoughts when I first ate demon fruit. For more and less. For something impossible.

"Do you kick?"

I followed his gaze to the bed.

"Oh yes," I said. "And I sleep with silver talons attached to my heels."

"Sounds painful."

"I also bray like a donkey in my nightmares, drool oceans and have a tendency to sleep-punch."

"I sleep like the dead," said Vikram, nonchalantly. "I won't be bothered at all. Besides, I prefer sharing my bed with slightly feral women."

"I prefer not to share at all. The chaise is perfectly comfortable."

"Then you sleep there. I'll take the bed. I wouldn't want to offend your maidenly senses."

"We'll discuss this later," I said, sliding off the sheets. "I need to get ready."

In the bath chamber, stained-glass lanterns floated through the steam, while stone crocodiles opened their jaws and sprayed hot jets of water into the empty bath from the corners of the room. I sank into the sapphire pool. For a moment, I let myself watch the shards of light dance on the water's surface. But, as always, I got out before I became overly comfortable. Too much beauty and luxury proved dangerous. Plenty of Bharata's advisers had let lust for a rare bolt of silk or gem-encrusted necklace blind them to Skanda's grabs for power or corruption. Alaka's beauty had teeth. I wouldn't let any part of it ensnare me.

A few paces away from the baths stood an onyx wardrobe. I chose a dove gray *salwar kameez* with little diamonds sewn into the hems.

Cosmetics lined a small vanity to the right of the wardrobe. I rolled the small vials between my palms, warming up the oils. After murmuring a quick prayer for my harem mothers, I donned my armor, lining my eyes with kohl until they were dark as death and patting crushed rose petals on my lips until they were scarlet as blood. In a separate dresser, I found a small cache of knives. I took two and strapped them to my thighs. Just in case.

When I stepped outside, Vikram blinked a couple of times.

"You are surprisingly lovely."

"You are unsurprisingly insulting."

He smiled. And just as he did, the floor burst into cold flames. I tensed, nearly leaping onto the nearest table. Vikram, however, watched the flames with interest.

"Lord Kubera is ready for us," he said.

As we left the room, I bit down on my cheeks. I'd been so concentrated on getting to Alaka that I only now realized how little I knew of what to expect. In battle, strategy and body counts paved the way to victory. Magic turned the game inscrutable, so that you didn't know if the darkness ahead of you belonged to the night sky or the lightless black at the bottom of a monster's throat.

Outside our room, the palace had changed. The hallway was thick with the press of bodies and musky perfume unraveling in the air. Small fiery insects appeared before us, beckoning for us to follow.

"Are you our guides?" asked Vikram.

The glowing insects bobbed like a nodding head.

"Well, shine on, little stars."

The insects whirred, glowing a little brighter, like a blush. We walked after them and I dropped my voice to a whisper: "Are you trying to charm the insects?"

"Spoken like a true princess," he said, shaking his head. "Never paying attention to the little people."

"They're insects."

"*Magical* insects."

Out of habit, I scanned the hall, looking for anything suspect. In front of us, a mirror caught the light. I expected to see our reflections. But I didn't see myself. Or Vikram. I frowned. An unfamiliar being with horned wings and a gold mask frowned back.

Oh Gods.

The mirror had twisted our reflections. Vikram followed my gaze and laughed:

"Clever," he said.

"*Clever?*"

"I can admire the method and the result."

Vikram preened his new reflection. "How appropriate, they tinged yours red with blood."

"You should be saying how deceitful because now we can't tell who might be an enemy."

"That's the point though, isn't it?" returned Vikram. "We're all enemies in plain sight. Our enemies stare at us from the mirror. That was the announcement the attendant made in the beginning, remember? The quest for power and treasure is a solitary one. Who else is the true enemy in such a quest but ourselves?"

"True war isn't philosophical."

"All war is philosophical. That's why we call it war. Strip it of its paint and it's nothing more than murder."

"Aren't puppets supposed to have heads made of wood?"

"I'm not very good at being a puppet," said Vikram. "Hence, my desire to fling myself at a supernatural tournament and hurtle toward certain death."

"Sound logic."

"I wouldn't mind a crown made of wood though. I might throw it at people for entertainment."

I shook my head. "Why are you like this . . ."

He swept a mocking bow and together we walked down a vestibule lined with glass birds. The moment our feet hit the floor, the birds took flight. Darkness choked the end of the hall. We walked slowly, our only guides the fire-dipped insects. Vikram moved closer.

"In need of protection?"

"I prefer to stay beside the monster I know," he said.

At the end of the hall, dark gray rock reared up to meet us.

"I thought this was supposed to be a feast," I muttered. "Does he expect us to eat away the shadows?"

"Oh no, dearest. We are far too glutted on such things," said a silky voice.

The small hairs on my neck rose. Someone in the darkness clapped their hands. Light dripped like blood down the walls, thick and slow. I squinted. This was the kind of light that made you crave the dark. It was lurid and almost bruising, as bright as a sun but empty of warmth.

When the light dimmed, I could finally see what was in front of us: an empty table. At the end of it sat the Lord of Treasures and his consort, the Lady Kauveri. Kubera was the size of a child, with a generous belly, heavy lidded eyes. His smile was graceful. Radiant. But it was the kind of smile that belonged to power. Not joy. You could only smile like that if you possessed the kind of invincibility that let you sharpen your teeth on the world. Warning flared through me. Around his neck curled a golden mongoose. The creature yawned and an opal dropped from its mouth. Beside me, Vikram inhaled sharply. I shot him a look, but his gaze was fixed on the mongoose.

The Lady Kauveri smiled at us. She wore a sari of rushing water, and in her elaborate braids, small streams and pebbles, tortoises and crocodiles no larger than a thumbnail clambered through her hair. No immortal being betrayed any flaw, but there was something restless about her, a kind of anxious energy that belonged to someone expecting tragedy.

"Welcome, contestants," said Kauveri, sweeping her arm before the feast. "Please. Eat."

When we sat, a lavish feast appeared on the table. I eyed it suspiciously. There were fragrant *biryani* with saffron rice, hard-boiled eggs white as moonstones in a thick curry, apple and mint chutneys in glass bowls, globes of *gulab jamun* drenched in cardamom syrup and bright orange *jalebis* coiled like gold bangles.

All the while Kubera eyed us, his gaze growing wider. He watched intently as we reached for naan, broke it and dipped it into a bowl of curry. I couldn't afford to give offense. The moment I placed the food in my mouth, Kubera leapt from his throne.

"Finally! Our food has passed your lips! Now that guest and host hospitality has been satisfied, I may finally speak. You had us both so curious. At the edge of our thrones! As I knew you both would—"

"Patience, my love," cautioned Kauveri.

I exchanged a look with Vikram. What did he mean that we made him curious? Nerves pebbled my arms. The day we escaped Ujijain, I felt the Otherworld reaching for us. It *wanted* us. But maybe it wasn't the Otherworld that had wanted us so badly but Kubera himself. Why? Did he want the other contestants here just as badly or did he intend to use us for some purpose?

Kubera climbed down from his throne and circled us like a merchant examining his goods. He reached for my hand and I extended it with as much grace as I could muster.

Kubera clucked approvingly. He dropped my hand and leaned toward Vikram. "Ah, what a hungering heart you both have. Delightful. I suspect both of you will make excellent storytellers. And king and queen, no doubt. Then again, that depends on which one of you will be allowed to leave. And now you are wondering whether that means one of you will die. Not so! One of you may stay here forever. You could be my new throne. That man—" He glared at his golden throne, which was shaped like a human on all fours. "—has a perpetual lower-back ache and I can't stand hearing him groan on and on. The other option, of course, is death. Oh, and no. You may not use your wish to grant an exit to the other person."

I refused to let the shock show on my face. I knew that the invitation ruby was good for two entries only. But, like Vikram, I assumed that winning the Tournament meant both of us could leave. Not one or the other.

"We can't both return?" asked Vikram.

"Maybe! I don't know! I make up the rules as I go." Kubera grinned.

Kauveri rose from her throne and joined her husband in the middle of the room. Wherever she stepped, golden coins fell.

"Speaking of play, you came here to win a wish."

Kubera's eyes lit up. "Ah! Yes! Instructions. My apologies." He laughed. "This is the realm of desire and treasures. And I want to see what you think is treasure. Two trials. One sacrifice. Three things in total. Because three is a very nice number. Exquisitely simple, as are most things that lead you to the greatest happiness or the greatest discontent."

"Are we competing against the other contestants?"

"No. All the things that make us wish for something impossible are different. As are your trials. Everyone could win a wish. Or no one can. It is what it is."

"My lord," I said cautiously, "you mentioned sacrifice. What are we expected to give?"

"Nothing bodily, physical, animal or human."

"That means he has not decided yet," said Kauveri, smiling.

"And the details of our trial, my lord?" asked Vikram. "How much time—"

"*Time?*" Kubera laughed. "What is time in Alaka but a thing that comes and goes as it pleases? When a century wanes, even Time leaps back and forth in glee. The Tournament of Wishes is a place where all stories may renew or reinvent themselves." Kubera smiled and ice danced along my spine. "We have borrowed a moon for the Tournament to keep track of 'time.' It is a new moon tonight and when it is a new moon again, then 'time' is up!"

A month. We had a month for two trials and a sacrifice. That wasn't much, but if time worked differently in Alaka, maybe even that could be manipulated.

"What about in the human world?" asked Vikram.

I hadn't even thought of that. I couldn't imagine emerging fresh from victory only to see the ruins of a time that had forgotten us and moved on long ago.

"Clever prince," laughed Kubera. "Only a month of your fleet-footed human time."

"My lord, how do we . . . which is to say what exactly are you asking of us for this trial?" I asked. "Will we fight? Trade riddles—"

"You seek the wealth of a wish," said Kubera. "And how does anyone achieve wealth? Do they cut throats and slit the heavy bulges of a merchant's purse? Do they breed kindness like a plague and collect smiles instead of coins? What is it worth to them? Do as you will."

That answered absolutely nothing. How would our trials be judged? Everything that came out of Kubera's mouth was its own riddle. I'd felt this way before with Skanda every time he spoke around a lie. When I bargained with my brother, I had to know exactly what he wanted or the price I paid would be too great.

"May I ask you something, Your Majesty?"

Kubera tilted his head. "Yes, little jewel, go ahead."

"Why do you want us to compete in this Tournament? What do you win?"

"I win a story," said Kubera, smiling slowly. "And that treasure is infinite and will change and grow wings. The world is entering a new age. After this game, there will never again be a Tournament of Wishes. The Otherworld will close its portals. It will smile at the human realm, but nothing will pass its lips. Those who play our Tournament and live to tell the tale will let us breathe in that new age. With a tale, we will not simply exist as figures in stone temples, all our myths static and told and fixed. We will live. Passed between mouth and mind and memory."

Kauveri clapped her hands. "You sound so ominous, my love. I think you're overexcited." She spread her hands and a thin mirror of water pooled and widened between her palms. "The key to immortality is in creating a story that will outlive you. Each tale is its own key, hiding in plain sight beneath all the things we want and all the things that eat away at us."

A ruby flashed in the water mirror, glinting and bright as the invitation to the Tournament of Wishes.

"Your first task is to find one half of the key to immortality," said Kubera.

The image disappeared. I didn't know whether to bow or run, thank them or scream. Find a *key*? It wasn't even clear whether that was an actual *tangible* key or not. Kauveri reached forward and cupped my face. Her eyes flickered from smoky quartz to brackish brown, like a drained riverbed.

"We find you through your hearts, you know," she said softly, stroking my cheek. "So bright and earnest. I almost envy you, for there are so many things I would wish for." Her eyes flashed. "Or maybe I just wish to want as you do. Perhaps I shouldn't. Desire, after all, is such a poisonous thing."

She drew away her hand. Where she touched me, my skin felt icy and damp. Vikram's expression sharpened.

"Enjoy the amenities of the palace, dear contestants," said Kubera, his teeth unsettling and sharp in the bright room. "And please indulge in the festivities of our Opening Ceremony. On the new moon, we like all manner of enjoyment."

for the trials and sacrifice—the idea of a sacrifice made me shudder every time I thought of it—we might just be whittling away our time until the final days. Kubera wasn't an opponent, but he wasn't an ally either. He held the game in his hands. His excitement seared my memory. He *wanted* to play.

And so did I.

The music of the Opening Ceremony trembled through the ground. The same courtyard that we had walked through to get to the palace of Alaka seemed to have expanded and changed in a matter of hours. Three large feast tables stood to our right. Down the center path, a mass of silk erupted before our eyes—moon-pale wings shivered into existence, a slender neck arced into the night. Before us unfurled a tent in the shape of an enchanted swan, large as a small town, and pale as frost save for the blue star nestled at its breast. To our left, a large banyan tree cast its gnarled branches over the beings swaying and dancing beneath its limbs. Lights as delicate as spun sugar drifted through the lattice of the tree's fingers. Alaka's beauty felt unsettlingly precise, as if it had torn out one of my childhood daydreams and slipped it on like a mask. I didn't trust it. Even the air smelled shrewd. I caught a whiff of a blanket I'd kept since infancy and tensed. This magic was a dangerous seduction of comfort. We walked through the crowds swarming the courtyards—tall and short, slim and stout, fair and hideous. Some had wings; others glided above the ground, surveying the world.

"Plain sight," I said. "There's nothing plain about it."

We started with circling the feast tables, searching for any clues that might leap out at us. A vial of poisons? A cachet of rubies? Kubera's instructions were more or less useless. And on top of that, I had to keep my eyes and ears open for information about other exits from Alaka.

At the end of the first table hung a small sign that read: "A Feast of

Transformation—*if you take from us, you must trade your hurt.*" The table had nothing edible. There were glass amphorae of dried wings, a finger bone, a braided circlet of hair and a straw doll.

Floating orbs of ice hovered over the second table. A lace of piled snow rolled off the edges. Its sign—a pane of ice—read: "A Feast of Cold—*if you take from us, you must trade your warmth.*"

Silk-pressed singing birds hopped across the third table. Songs fell from their beaks. Its sign read: "A Feast of Song—*if you take from us, you must trade your thoughts.*"

"There's nothing here," I said. I grabbed Vikram's arm before he could get too distracted by the shiny bottles and headed down to Alaka's gardens.

Beneath the banyan tree, a disjointed and listless dance had begun. Forest beings with bright green leaves for hair and vines twisting about their wrists leapt and swayed. I was watching them closely, wondering if I would recognize anything from Kubera's task, when a whispered hush broke over the crowd.

"They're back," whispered one of the Otherworldly beings beside us.

"Who? Oh!" returned its friend. "I hadn't realized they'd even won at the last Tournament."

I turned to see who they were talking about and found three young women moving solemnly beneath the banyan tree. A ragged blue ribbon hung around each of their necks. They walked strangely, as if their limbs bore the memory of movement but not the instinct. I glanced at the ground and bit back a shudder. No shadow moved over the ground.

"If the Nameless are here, then the Serpent King must be here too."

The other being laughed. "I can't imagine the Lady Kauveri liking that at all."

"If it wasn't the last Tournament, he would never have been allowed."

The Nameless drifted away from us, disappearing straight into the banyan tree. I watched the empty spot where they had stood and turned the new names over in my head. Who was the Serpent King?

Vikram touched my arm, shaking his head. Nothing here. The only thing left to explore was the giant tent. A line had already formed, sprawling out across the grounds and even winding its way between pools.

Voices flew at us from every direction.

"The Lord of Treasures has hired them!"

"But the line is already—"

"—surely one of them will be available."

"—the tent, over there."

A slow wind stirred the swan tent, and smoke poured out from the top. The crowd cheered. Tendrils of smoke shot into the air, taking the shape of a winged beast and a glittering serpent, a tree strung with lights and even a flickering crown. At the end, the smoke gathered into the hazy silhouette of a woman. The shape folded into a star and the color deepened from gray to blue. A blue star. Just like the one that was on the throat of every *vishakanya*.

Vikram grabbed my hand, his eyes shining in excitement. "That's it. The first half of the key has to be inside the poisonous courtesans' tent. It's the only thing that would make sense. The *vanaras* said the same in the Night Bazaar. Remember?"

"Not really. If you recall, I was fighting the urge to eat you at the time."

He grimaced. "Right. Well. It fits with what Kubera said anyway— *all the things we want and all the things that eat away at us.* At first I thought when he said 'us' that it included you and me. But a *vishakanya* has a different effect on Otherworldly beings. She shows them desires. Maybe that's what he meant!"

Vikram was so excited he couldn't decide between tenting his fingers together or making small shuffling movements between his feet.

"Could you not . . ." I started.

But he was already pulling me down the line and straight to the tent. Half of the people who had been waiting patiently in line turned and glared. At the entrance, shadow tigers prowled, snapping and growling. One of the beasts cut his eyes to us. It blinked, and then threw its head back.

"Are you so eager to end your life, dear mortals?"

This was an excellent start.

"No—" said Vikram.

"Then why do you seek entrance here?"

"Can we not go into—"

The tiger roared at us: "ONLY *VISHAKANYAS* MAY ENTER WITHOUT THE LINE. AND ONLY *YAKSHAS* AND *YAK-SHINIS* MAY STAND IN LINE. NO HUMANS."

Air gusted from the creature's mouth. The wind forced us backward and we retreated to the end of the line. Vikram paced furiously.

"How are we going to get inside when we're clearly not *vishakanyas?*" he muttered, tugging at his hair. He stopped, his brow creasing in thought. "Or maybe we just have to look like them."

I stopped pacing. "What?"

He glanced back toward the feast tables and started walking. I jogged to keep pace.

"I think I heard you say that we should look like *vishakanyas.*"

"You heard right. It's not my first choice. I'd rather not dress like a courtesan again—"

"Wait. *Again?*"

His face colored.

"The Feast of Transformation may have something for us," he mused.

"I'm still listening for the part where you explain why you dressed like a courtesan in the first place."

Vikram braced his elbows over the Feast of Transformation, fingers hovering over the bottles. He held up a bottle containing a scrap of a woman's sari and a pot of cosmetics.

"I hope this is more rewarding than last time," he muttered.

The Feast of Transformation demanded a trade of hurt. The moment I grabbed a vial, I felt ghostly fingers carding through my memories, searching for a kernel of pain. It wasn't hard to find. I felt a sharp tug behind my heart, the sound of a memory unclasping and rising to the surface of my thoughts. And then: Nothing. The memory faded. I looked down at my garb and found myself dressed in a rather revealing outfit studded with emeralds. A translucent veil draped down from my head. I looked unrecognizable in the mirror propped against the Feast of Transformation table. Thanks to glamour, my hair was now long and silver, my eyes were the color of quartz and I was taller and more willowy than I'd ever been without magic.

Beside me, I heard a sharp intake of breath. The magic of the Feast of Transformation had disguised Vikram as a short and shapely woman with a riot of copper hair. The only thing that looked the same was the sly smile he flashed when he inspected himself in the mirror.

"I look good," he said, examining himself from multiple angles. He shifted from one foot to the next. "This is horrifically itchy. Why do women wear this miserable garment?"

"I don't think that was our choice."

"Oh."

I laughed. "I can't think of many men that would glamour themselves as a woman."

He notched his chin a little higher. "This is just a form. In the older tales, a god made himself an enchantress just to trick a horde of demons. And the most famous warrior of the age became a eunuch for a year. *I* can have the form of a *vishakanya* for a night to win a wish."

I clapped. He bowed. And we headed down to the *vishakanyas'* tent. Before we reached the entrance, I pulled him to one side.

"What is it?"

"Assuming we get inside, you need to be prepared for a fight." I hiked up the dress. Vikram colored and immediately turned away.

"*What are you doing?*" he hissed.

I unhooked one of my thigh straps and handed it to him along with the small knife I had tucked inside it earlier.

"Where do I put this?" he muttered, patting his rather generous-looking hips.

"A real *vishakanya* wouldn't need one at all. Remember? Conceal it."

Groaning, he reluctantly strapped the knife to his ankle.

At the entrance of the tent, I gathered my courage. The line of people stared at us longingly. I hated being stared at like this, as if I were just a means of satisfying someone. Vikram looked indignant and folded his arms over his chest. The beast swung its head around:

"NO TRESPASSER—" it started, and then stopped, tilting its head.

Here goes.

"Since when am I a trespasser?" I demanded, sneering.

The shadow tiger shrank back, lifting its paw. "I did not—"

I raised a dismissive hand. "In what universe do you imagine that I am interested in recitations of your deficiencies?"

The beast's brow furrowed; its ears lay flat against its skull. "I did not mean to make a mistake."

Vikram—who had not lost his deep voice—wisely decided to keep his mouth shut and settled for a fierce glare.

"And I did not mean to find myself interrogated. *Move aside.*"

My heart was beating violently. One false move, and the charade would be ruined.

"My apologies," said the creature and stepped aside.

I murmured a quick prayer before lifting the gossamer veils and entering the warm dark of the tent. No lamps illuminated the interior, but small lights were sewn into the silk, winking like hesitant stars. Incense painted the air with bright notes of sandalwood and orange blossom. Something reflective covered every surface that wasn't already occupied by one of the Otherworldly patrons. We stepped inside carefully, searching around the corner for any sign of a *vishakanya*. Vikram went on his tiptoes to whisper in my ear:

"Just because we look like *vishakanyas* does not mean we are one. If they touch us, we die."

I patted my thigh where the other knife was securely strapped. The tops of Vikram's ears turned red.

"I haven't forgotten," I whispered back.

We moved quickly down the hall, scanning for any sign of Kubera's key or a ruby. But so far there was nothing. Unease prickled in the back of my head. If this wasn't the right place, then we had to get out fast. There was no telling how long the effects of the Feast of Transformation would last. At least a dozen patrons sat inside, their heads tipped back to stare at their desires twisting in the mirrors above them. I followed the structure of the mirrors overhead. They were all linked, held up by some kind of net.

Another hall, concealed from the patrons and courtesans, forked from the entrance. I stepped inside first, listening for any impatient footfalls or rasping breaths. Nothing. I scanned the walls. A mirror hovered above me.

For the second time that day, the mirror didn't reflect me. But it didn't show the glamour I wore either. The mirror showed my heart. *Bharata*. I saw a pewter sky blanketing the watchtowers, salt stacked in perfect wheels in the merchants' quarter, bonfires spraying ruby splinters into the air. I saw my people dancing, cheeks ruddy from laughing. I saw legends hanging off the trees like fruit, ripe for the taking and devouring, ready to be shared among friends and family. I saw every reason to return home.

My eyelids drooped. Maybe if I closed my eyes, the images in the mirror would shatter and become a reality—

"Gauri!" hissed Vikram.

My eyes flew open. I tried to move forward, but I couldn't. Fine silken ropes had fallen from the mirror and worked their way around my arms and legs, pinning me in place. Vikram, too, was trapped. Anyone with a foul sense of humor and a sharp knife could walk through the hall and kill us where we stood. It was only by sheer luck that the hallway was abandoned.

"I've heard of being trapped by your desires, but this is ridiculous," he grumbled.

"How long did you look at the mirror?" I asked.

"I only glanced at it."

I reached for the dagger on my thigh, but it slid out of the sheath, clattering to the ground. Biting back a hiss, I tried throwing all my weight backward and then forward, trying to untangle my limbs from the ropes. The iridescent ropes shone a little brighter, coy as a smile.

"How do you rid yourself of desire?" I mused. "It's not like I can magically become a different species."

Vikram paused. "That's it! Look back into the mirror—"

"Absolutely not. That's what got us trapped the first time."

"And maybe it can free us too."

I watched as he looked into the mirror. At one point, he turned a furious shade of red. Then, the silken ropes crumpled around him. He crept toward me, picking up the fallen knife and sawing at the silken bonds. The threads didn't even fray.

"How did you do that?" I asked.

"I just let go," he said, shrugging. "I looked at the desires and I told myself I didn't want them. Then they freed me. Try it."

I tried. I tried to pretend that I didn't want the images anymore. But I couldn't. I saw myself kneeling in a square of sunlight in Bharata's gardens, wrist-deep in earth as I dug a home for a rosebush. I craved for that belonging, the kind that knits happiness to your heart so it never wanders too far out of sight.

Blinking, I tore myself from the image. The silken ropes had grown in number and strength. But I also saw something else . . . *paint* had dropped onto the rope. I looked up at Vikram. The glamour of a woman's body was already fading. He had grown taller. The tight curls had begun to relax and lose their copper sheen.

"What is tying you down?" he demanded.

They would catch us—maybe even kill us—if I couldn't free myself. What was holding me back? Home, Nalini, vengeance, the throne. So many things tugged at me. It was different for Vikram. He wasn't driven by desire for the throne of Ujjijain. He was driven by the belief that it should be his. Somehow he could separate that. I couldn't. But maybe . . . maybe I could look beyond it?

I stared back into the mirror. This time, I tried to focus on the space between the images as they changed. There, in that undefined nexus . . . that was my real desire. The mirror couldn't show me the thing that pushed me toward that half-key to immortality because it was more. It was unquantifiable. A sylph with no face. It went beyond my need for vengeance or saving Nalini because it was the hunt for a legacy. It looked like nothing and everything. I blinked and the mirror shattered. The silken ropes crumpled.

I gathered them quickly before they could loudly *thunk* onto the floor. The moment I pushed the ropes to one side of the hall, Vikram shot me a warning glance and we both raced down the hall to where a gossamer screen separated one room from the next. Vikram reached for it, but I knocked his hand back. I squinted, gesturing for the dagger. Was someone standing on the other side? I stared for a moment longer, but no shadow moved behind the screen. I nodded, sheathing the dagger, as Vikram pulled back the curtain. There, lodged into the silk as if someone had punched it into place, was a glittering ruby.

"That's it!" he said. "It has to be."

I swept another glance around the room, careful to avoid the ceiling when I caught the gilded shine of a hundred mirrors overhead. No sign of disturbance to the pristine cushions. Nothing knocked aside in haste. A hall hugged one side of the room, curved out of sight. I stared a moment longer, but no shadow flickered on the wall's other side. Satisfied, I nodded to Vikram, who started walking to the ruby. Something shone in the facets of the jewel—a table surrounded by diners. Ice spangled the air around the stone. The cold of it formed a fist around my heart.

"Give me a lift," said Vikram. "Maybe I can tear this thing out with the knife—"

I had layered my palms together to give him a lift when I noticed something:

Silence.

When we had first stepped inside, the *vishakanyas'* tent had been full of low murmurs, whispered encouragements and even the occasional moans. I crouched, skimming my thigh for the dagger slung around my leg. A low sigh and a crumpling sound broke the silence. Vikram had slumped to the ground. The copper of his disguised hair had darkened. His limbs lengthened and the barest trace of stubble began to shadow his shifting face.

Panic raced through me. Before I could touch him, a low laugh echoed from the opposite side of the room. Eleven *vishakanyas* stepped from the shadows. They had been waiting. Invisible.

"What did you do to him?"

I heard a small gasp beside me and turned to see a beautiful *vishakanya* materialize in the air. She cowered away from Vikram. Her hand was still outstretched. Had she touched him?

The effects of the Feast of Transformation had vanished. Vikram lay in his original jacket and trousers. His face was pale, and sweat beaded on his skin. Things that were once eye-level fell little by little. The borrowed height from the Feast of Transformation had disappeared and I had returned to my original size and shape.

"A man!" gasped the *vishakanya*. She did not run to the others pressed in the dark corners of the room. Instead, she stared at me.

"Don't you dare touch him," I hissed, brandishing the knife.

I ran through what I knew about *vishakanyas*. Every inch of their skin was deadly. But they bled and died just like any mortal. At least, that's what Maya's stories always said. I just had to get past the skin.

The *vishakanya* sank into the corner, suddenly timid. "I only brushed against him for a moment . . . nothing that would kill him, I swear."

"He is not for any of you," I said loudly, swinging the knife at the rest of the gathered poisonous courtesans. I stepped protectively over Vikram's body. "We only came here for the ruby. That's all. Let us take it and leave, and no one will be harmed."

"And if we don't want you to leave?" asked one.

Her movements held all the terrible grace of a nightmare.

"You both came here willingly," she taunted. "To know us. To see us. To take from us."

Twelve to one, I repeated in my head. If this were a normal fight, maybe I'd have a chance. But unlike any fight, the very touch of my opponents' skin could kill me. I tore part of my *salwar kameez* and wrapped my bare arms.

The *vishakanya* shrugged. "Admirable, but futile."

"I'm warning you—" I started, but the words awakened something in the *vishakanya*. She was no longer smiling. No longer wheedling.

"No, girl," she said, as cold as glass. "I'm warning *you*. That human boy is now mine."

"He was never—"

"He is in our tent. He is not protesting. Therefore, he is ours. And now that he is mine, you should know that I am not someone to steal from. You see, girl, we like humans. Human desires are nothing like the desires of *yakshas* and *yakshinis*. Yours are a treat. There's something different about human desire. How damp it is. The way it gloms on to your nightmares and silvers your hearts with a rime of frost. You will carry that desire, ripping up the earth at its seams if it means you can have what you want."

"It's destructive," said the *vishakanya*.

"It's beautiful," chimed another.

"And we will have it," said another.

"So don't take my toys, girl."

And then she lunged straight for me.

20

OF RUBIES AND SISTERS
AASHA

If Aasha wanted, she could reach out and touch the human girl. Kill her. But if she did that, the questions brimming inside her would go unanswered. Already, they felt out of control, as if they'd grown thorns and would soon cut her apart. *Who could I have been? What life could I have called my own?* That urgency to know made her feign a headache earlier and wait, crouched and cramped and invisible, in a corner of the tent where the Lord of Treasures had hidden a ruby. He had visited the tent in the afternoon, informing her sisters that a pair of human contestants might come searching for the jewel. If the humans failed, they were fair prey for the *vishakanyas*.

Aasha had hoped to get to the humans first. She had planned to negotiate with them: answers to her questions about the human world in return for letting them escape with the ruby.

But her sisters had been faster.

Now there was no chance of conversation. Her sisters licked their lips hungrily. As one, the *vishakanyas* lunged. Hands darted for the girl's ankles as she leapt for higher ground. Aasha pressed herself farther into the corner. Beside her, the man stirred. Her touch had imparted a snare of sleep. Not death. Some of her sisters used the technique as a mercy killing. Aasha used it to avoid killing altogether.

Her sisters knocked over the table the girl had jumped on, slamming her backward. The girl leapt to the ground, slashing her knife across the air and catching one of her sister's arms.

"Next time I'll aim for your face," said the human girl. "Give us that ruby. I have no desire to injure you."

But Aasha's sisters only laughed and laughed. Wariness prickled through Aasha. They had plenty of desires to eat in Alaka. Maybe it would be easier to let the girl go and forget this business.

The human girl turned her face to the ceiling, her eyes darting across the hundred mirrors knitted together. An eerie grin lit up her face. Her sisters pressed closer. The girl leapt, her fingers outstretched as she clawed for the golden tether anchored to one of the walls. Swiftly, the girl sank her knife into the rope that bound together all the mirrors.

"Now that I have your attention—" said the girl, stabbing the rope. "You may have noticed that while I may not be able to kill each of you in one movement, the mirrors can."

Her sisters shrank a little closer to the ground. Aasha started inching along the walls, trying to get to them. The human girl swung her body, and the mirrors swayed dangerously to her rhythm, listing and groaning against their confines.

"I can do it little by little," said the girl, sawing delicately at the rope. She raised her knife: "Or I can start hacking."

Fear gripped her. If her sisters were injured, how would they feed? They'd wither to nothing. Aasha's fear turned thin and cold, slipping in the space between her thoughts and numbing her nerves. She changed direction and ran to the girl.

"Stop! Don't hurt my sisters, please," said Aasha. "I'll do anything!"

Something in the girl's gaze relented. Mercy flickered across her features for only an instant. The next moment, her eyes hardened.

"Anything?"

Aasha nodded tightly.

The girl turned her gaze to the rest of the room. "Leave."

All of her sisters but one disappeared into the shadows.

"You're a good opponent," said her sister, eyeing the girl with admiration. "You'd make an even better *vishakanya* should you seek a new outlet for your talents."

The girl let go of the rope, dropping to the floor with her fingers splayed against the ground. She stood up, and bowed.

"My duties have already been claimed for this lifetime," said the girl respectfully.

"Then perhaps in the next."

Pity and gratitude flashed in her sister's eyes. Aasha trembled. What had she gotten herself into? She only wanted to ask the humans of their lives. Now she was beholden to them. The idea of the mortal lands enchanted her, but humans were cunning and spiteful. The girl bent to check the boy's pulse. Satisfied, she stood up and tore the ruby straight out of the tent. She tucked it and her knife somewhere in the depths of her skirt.

"What's your name?" she asked.

Aasha blinked. She hadn't imagined the girl would speak to her this way. Even the *yakshas* and *yakshinis* only opened their mouths to make demands. *Give me something miraculous. Give me what I want.* This girl was asking. Her voice wasn't kind, but it wasn't cruel either. She stumbled to find her breath.

"Aasha."

"I'm Gauri," said the girl. She prodded at the man on the ground with her toe. "How much longer will he be unconscious? Will there be any lasting damage?"

"He will be awake at dawn. His mind should be fully intact."

The girl let out a sigh and dragged her arm across her brow. "You offered to help us, and what we need most is information. Do you know of a way out of Alaka?"

Aasha had forgotten how the rules were different for humans. For the Otherworldly beings, they could leave whenever they pleased. But if they left the game early, they forfeited a wish.

"If you have not been granted permission from Lord Kubera, then you must seek permission from his consort, the Lady Kauveri."

The girl smirked. "She said nothing when she heard that only one of us could leave, so I imagine her permission has not been granted."

"Then you must give her something she wants."

She raised an eyebrow. "What would a goddess want? More resplendence? The simple pleasures of a mortal existence, like wrinkles? Age spots?"

Aasha hesitated. Whenever the *yakshas* and *yakshinis* visited the tent, they brought bits of gossip with them. Some of which, she knew, should be ignored. But not helping the human girl could harm her sisters. She refused to let that happen. Besides . . . there was something she had heard. A rumor that kept the same shape no matter who told it. That in itself was a feat. So often, the beings of the Otherworld hated telling the truth, not because they preferred deceit, but because they preferred the taste of a decadent rumor on their tongue to the dull and brittle flavor of a truth.

"Not an object," said Aasha carefully. "It is said there is something she wants from someone. And he is in Alaka."

"Who?"

"The Serpent King."

21

THE GLASS GARDEN

GAURI

I was out of breath by the time I finally made it back to our chambers. Dragging Vikram along hadn't even been the most difficult part of getting him to the room. It was wading through a sea of intrigued Otherworldly beings. A couple of *yakshinis* tried to buy him from me. Some of the offers included a voice that would lull a thunderstorm to sleep and the skin-dress of a crocodile. They refused to believe me when I said he wasn't worth it. At one point, a *rakshasa* clapped me on the back, shouting, "Excellent find, human girl! Start around the spine. Always the best cut of meat." I had no idea what to say, so I said thank you. It only occurred to me after I was tugging Vikram halfway up the stairs that perhaps I should have said, "I don't eat people."

It had been a long day.

My thoughts tripped over one another. I'd made plans for Aasha to meet us tomorrow at high noon, but that left far too many unknowns. She could be giving us the wrong information about the Serpent King or selling us to some unnamed enemy. And even if we had a lead for discovering an exit out of Alaka, it only mattered if we survived and won the Tournament of Wishes. I shuddered. One day in Alaka, and magic had forced me outside myself. I was walking into battle without a helmet. Nothing to protect us except the flimsy trust I'd placed in a stranger and that most terrible of poisons: hope. Even now, I could feel hope seeping and settling under my skin. Growing. What shape would it take? Wings? Like something set free. Or mushrooms? Like something birthed in decay.

The half-key thrummed and burned in my pocket. Throwing open the doors, I dropped Vikram to the floor and stowed the key on a table near the bed. Outside, dawn had begun to braid the sky with gold, trussing up what was left of night. Bone-deep exhaustion weighed my body. I threw down a pillow and blanket for Vikram, clambered into bed and fell asleep within moments.

The problem with having a room full of songbirds was that the room was full of songbirds. I'd barely gotten any sleep before twittering and rustling feathers roused me into waking. I propped myself up on one elbow and stared at the room. The walls shivered, light dancing over the iridescent green feathers. Vikram was lounging in one of the chairs—already dressed and impeccably groomed—and tossing the ruby key in the air like a ball. He caught my eye and grinned.

"They say morning light reveals a woman's true nature. My condolences to your future consort."

"It's too early in the morning for bloodshed," I groaned, gathering an armful of pillows and burying my face in them. "Also . . . good thinking about the transformation."

Vikram's eyes widened. "What's this? Praise from Her Beastliness in the morning? Are you under a curse that makes you friendly before noon? If so, how do we make it permanent?"

I threw a pillow at his face. He tilted his head, dodging it with the barest amount of energy required.

"In all honesty, we got that first key together," he said. "We both thought of the riddle. Although I did have the brilliant transformation idea."

I threw another pillow at him. "I fought a horde of poisonous women to make sure we could keep the key."

"I wasn't conscious for that part."

"How convenient."

"I try."

"We did have some good fortune though," I said, telling him about the bargain with Aasha and our plans to meet with her later. Unlike me, he didn't even seem wary about meeting with the *vishakanya*, and when I confronted him about it, he shrugged.

"The world moves to the tune of logic, even if it wears the face of chaos. Maybe it was supposed to happen this way," he said, tossing the ruby between his hands. "At the very least, Aasha is part of the Otherworld and probably knows a great deal more about its power structure than we do. Meeting with her just might point us in the right direction and, wait, why are you scratching at your skin?"

"Your optimism is making me itchy," I grumbled, heading for the baths. "You're welcome, by the way, for dragging you back here. I had a couple offers to sell you and almost considered it."

"Intriguing. For how much?"

"A bag of gold, the ability to make thunderstorms go to sleep. Something else. Five goats?"

"Just *five* goats? I'm worth at least ten. Plus a cow."

I rolled my eyes and headed to the bath chamber. After I bathed, I threw my hair into a hasty braid and entered the room to find Vikram pacing and studying a length of parchment.

"What's that?"

"The Lord of Treasures sent us a letter. He offers his congratulations on solving the first trial and says that the second trial will take place at the full moon right after the celebration of Jhulan Purnima."

A familiar twinge of panic plucked at my heart. Jhulan Purnima was a festival that celebrated the soul bond of the sacred lovers, Krishna and Radha. Radha was more than just the deity Krishna's consort. She was the manifestation of his life energy. His very soul. Before Skanda had spread the rumor that I had taken a vow of chastity, the Council of Bharata used the festival to try and force me to accept a proposal of marriage from one prince or king or another. They claimed a proposal accepted on the day of Jhulan Purnima meant a lifetime of love.

I rejected every offer.

If I became queen, a strong alliance of marriage would be a key political move. I wouldn't base that decision on something as fickle and slippery as love.

"Jhulan Purnima would be the perfect time to ambush someone. Everyone would be drowsy or intoxicated—"

"Gauri," said Vikram, half indulgent and half stern. "It's a sacred holiday. Besides, the world is not always trying to attack you."

"I just want to be prepared. If you prepare for the world attacking you, then at least half the time it doesn't win."

"Spoken like a true queen."

"What? How so?"

"Only royalty is perpetually paranoid."

"I'm *prepared*. Not paranoid."

I knew from experience that paranoid was a moment's difference from prepared. The former closed your eyes and the latter opened them. The problem was that sometimes the difference announced itself only in hindsight. I twisted the ends of my *salwar kameez*, Nalini's heartbroken face fracturing behind my eyes.

"As you wish."

"Careful with that word," I warned, before glancing outside. "There's some time before we need to meet with Aasha."

"Excellent. At least we have some free time—"

"No such thing as free time. We need to explore the palace grounds," I said. "We don't know what the next trial will be so we might as well be prepared with potential arenas—"

"I was talking about food!" cut in Vikram. "Don't you want to eat?"

"We can eat as we explore."

Vikram grumbled. After safeguarding the half-key, we left the chambers and headed downstairs. A sizable crowd milled around the main entrance. A pair of human twins walked past us, hand in hand. Mango pulp smeared their faces and Vikram stared after them enviously. In a mirror's reflection, our faces stared back at us. Completely unaltered. Today, apparently, Lord Kubera had seen no reason for us to hide our true faces.

A long ivory table ran down the length of the hall. Plates of cut fruit, savory *uttapam*, crispy potato *sago* and crystal cups full of steaming masala *chai* covered the entire table. Down the line, I saw the three women who went by the Nameless eyeing the foods. Only one of them carried a plate.

Vikram caught their eye, ignoring me when I shook my head. Aasha hadn't said what the Lady Kauveri wanted with the Serpent King, but I remembered hearing the Serpent King's name in connection with the Nameless. What did they want with him?

The Nameless walked to us, slow and sedate.

"Not hungry?" asked Vikram with his usual brightness.

"This is not for us," said one. "We cannot eat this food anymore."

"It is for her," said the second. "Our sister."

"Our missing limb," said the third with a sad smile. "She loved *uttapam.*"

Vikram started to say something, but the Nameless walked off without another word. I laughed.

"If it lessens the sting of your rejection any less, I'm quite certain the demon on the other side of the room wanted to buy you for five goats. Shall I make introductions?"

"A sense of humor," he said. "I couldn't be more pleased with this transformation. Sometimes I think damp stones are more conversational than you."

He smiled. A true smile. I knew his smirks. His half-grins. Even halfhearted and lopsided upturns of his mouth. This smile was different. It was soft and unguarded. And it softened me in return. I had put that smile on his face and I felt strangely territorial about it. I wanted to keep it.

We set off down one of the five main halls, food in hand. The main hall ended at a set of doors that opened into the courtyard where the Opening Ceremony festivities had taken place. The first three halls led to nothing except elaborate pools. Vikram swore that the statues had a tendency to jump from one place to the next, but that didn't tell us anything. Down the fourth hall was a room marked with an engraved golden sign:

The glass garden

Curious, we stepped into the glass garden. The moment I pushed the door, familiarity rushed over me. The air felt balmy, spring sliding into the rainy season. It was my favorite time of the year in Bharata, where the clouds dragged rain-heavy bellies across the sky and the land swelled, as if making room for the torrential rains. Above us, stars pinned up the night, and thunderheads glided around the edges of the room before disappearing to dance in a different land's midnight. But what was most miraculous was the garden itself. Every flower and shrub was carved of crystal. And yet it *swayed*. A living, breathing thing of glass and quartz, magic and memory. The garden seemed lifted from my memory of the old lawns in Bharata. Before he died, my father was known for his gardens. Out of spite, Skanda salted the land and built a fountain over the grounds after his death. But I never forgot them. Maya and I used to play there. Once, I even found a slipper that I thought belonged to an *apsara* dancer.

"I know this place," I breathed.

"That's—" Vikram started and then stopped. "I was going to say *impossible*, but I'm trying to retire that word from my vocabulary for the rest of our time in Alaka. How?"

"My father built a garden just like this."

We walked through the garden and I reached out, letting my fingers graze crystal vines and quartz lilies. Every touch felt like a word of whispered encouragement.

"I love gardens," I said.

"You do?"

I nodded. "I love watching things grow. I know that sounds strange for someone who was raised in war."

He eyed me. "It's not strange at all. Why wouldn't you hunger for life if you've only been surrounded by death? If you could grow *anything* in your garden, what would it be?"

"Swords."

He snorted. "I should've guessed."

"Swords are very time-consuming to have commissioned. If I could pull them out of the ground with perfect balance and a sharp tip, I'd be happy and so would my blacksmiths. I'd also try to grow *gulab jamun*," I said. Nothing was better than those warm syrup-drenched sweets. "I just want to pluck it off trees and eat it on the spot."

"Vicious and sweet," said Vikram, shaking his head. "Beastly girl."

"You like me, don't lie," I teased.

"I couldn't lie if I tried," he said quietly.

At the end of the walkway was a small note written on an ivory plaque:

All things can grow again.

Each word was a layer of light. They slid into place inside me, gathering dimension and brightness until the words had reshaped, refocused and returned my hopes. I closed my eyes, and I almost *felt* my sister beside me, her hands steadying my shoulders, her dusk-dark eyes brimming with worry. When we left the garden, I carried the light of those words with me.

In the fifth and final hall, empty birdcages twisted down from a gold ceiling to form a sparkling lattice. Each cage door swung open, poised like a jaw fit for snapping. At the end of the darkened hall, a flurry of wings ripped the silence. We had walked closer, following the sound of frenzied, beating wings, when I grabbed Vikram. Someone was waiting at the end of the hall.

Kubera.

He sat cross-legged on the floor. I scanned the room, but he was alone. His head tilted up as he watched the birds above him. I stepped backward, angling for a quick exit.

"Hello, contestants," said the Lord of Treasures. "Would you not greet me?"

I dropped Vikram's arm. Together, we bowed. "We did not want to disturb you. You seemed pensive."

Kubera grinned. "Watching stories always makes me pensive."

I frowned. He was looking at *birds*. Admittedly, they were very strange birds. They slipped into new shapes as they flew, donning new colors with every swoop. It was impossible to keep track of each bird in that writhing mass of wings. Above me, I caught sight of a snowy bird with a crest of diamonds. Gold and bister feathers grew over the white. The feathers crumpled and contracted. In the next moment, the bird had turned into a sparrow. Kubera clapped, and the sound thundered in the darkened hall. Every bird stopped in midflight. Not even their wings twitched.

Kubera hummed and a single emerald hummingbird broke from away from the mass and dived for his palms. He gestured us closer.

"Each of those is a tale being told," said Kubera, pointing to the birds. "You see how they change in the telling? It reflects the tale. For example, this bird is your story with the *vishakanyas*."

He tossed the bird into the air, and the sudden hum of its wings sent a splash of images waving in the air—Vikram at the Feast of Transformation, the ruby sparkling in the tent.

"But this is just one story," said Kubera.

He snatched the hummingbird out of the air, whispered to it, bent its wings into a new shape and threw it aloft. Now, the bird had a tail like a peacock, the story twisted to show Aasha hiding in the hall beside the ruby, her fingers tracing the blue star at her throat and her eyes wide with want.

"You see," said Kubera. "Nothing is yours. Not even a story is yours, though you may lay claim to it with the teeth of your mind."

I watched as the bird spiraled over our heads. It kept changing the higher it flew, to the story of a patron who had bartered a year of his life just to see his dead mate through the *vishakanyas'* arts, only to be forced to flee when my fight with the *vishakanyas* drove him from the tent. I hadn't even considered the line of Otherworldly beings who had been waiting to visit the *vishakanyas*. I assumed they were all there seeking pleasure.

"Stories are boundless and infinite, ever-changing and elusive," said Kubera. "They are the truest treasure and therefore my dearest possessions. Each contestant grants the world a new tale, pours a little magic back into the earth. That's all that will remain once the world dons the clothes of a new age and the Otherworld seals its doors. You will see. If you survive."

"Even the ones who die?" I asked, sharpness creeping into my voice.

"What's a story without a bit of death?" said Kubera, grinning. "I've always loved tales of broken lovers who roam through countrysides singing their stories of woe and separation, their honey-sweet longing for the next life when they can suddenly be reunited. It makes other people happy, you see. It makes people grateful that it hasn't happened to them.

I like making people happy!" Kubera clapped his hands. "Well, I should not keep you. Enjoy the celebrations," he said. "And if you do nothing else, give me a tale worth telling. Worth keeping."

When we left, I turned his words over in my heart. Kubera might want to harvest a story out of our trials, but he'd let something slip: A story had no ownership. A story could break its bones, grow wings, soar out of reach and dive out of sight in the time it took just to draw breath. It meant we weren't walking a cut path. We carved it into existence with every step.

NO TOUCHING

AASHA

Aasha hadn't slept last night. Instead, she snuck off to sit at the end of a stone path that connected the courtesans' tent to a running stream. Bright green grass flanked the path, taunting her. Her fingers ached to feel the ground. Would grass feel hard and cold, like glass? Or would it yield like a gossamer thread, soft and fragile, before snapping abruptly beneath her palm? Experience stilled her hand. Any living thing she touched blackened and shriveled. She didn't even dare to dip her feet in the water out of fear for any hidden wildlife.

Aasha stood and walked back to the tent. Soon, she would have to meet Gauri and the human boy. Part of her thrilled to spend time in human company. Even last night, she couldn't tear her eyes away from Gauri. The way she was breathless and brittle and reckless. Aasha wanted to look like that. Like something alive.

Sometimes Aasha strained her memory to the days before the *vishakanyas* collected her, but all she could recall was a rain-washed field

and warm hands rubbing coconut oil into her scalp. Those wisps of the past told her nothing. The other part of Aasha felt nervous about meeting them. Even her sisters seemed worried. Since last night, they had been treating her like a glass doll.

"It can't be that bad," Aasha said, when one of her sisters tried, once more, to stop her from meeting Gauri. "We were once human after all, so—"

"Never say that in this tent," said one of her sisters. "We may bleed and birth the same way, but that is where the similarities end. We are different. Only we carry the Blessing in our veins. They do not."

After promising to keep their counsel, Aasha hurried to the banyan tree. She caught sight of them as she walked up the hill. Gauri stood tall and fierce. She held herself as if she were made of nothing but knife points, so sharp that Aasha cast a glance at her shadow, wondering if she had torn it to strips just by standing above it. Beside her stood the boy who had disguised himself as one of them. He was handsome, with a face and figure that some of her sisters would have wanted to touch regardless of his desires. He leaned against the banyan tree, easy and graceful, but with a keen brightness to his gaze, as if he could see more than most.

Gauri walked forward. "I was afraid you wouldn't show up."

"A being of the Otherworld always keeps their word."

Gauri only lifted an eyebrow. As if to say, *We'll see.* "This is Vikram." The boy flashed a smile.

Aasha sniffed the air cautiously, tasting their desires and searching for any threat to herself. But their desires had not been greedy or lust-filled. At least, not lust directed at her.

"You said there was something the Lady Kauveri wants from the Serpent King. What is it?"

"Venom."

Surprise flickered on Gauri's face. "Why would anyone want a *na-ga's* venom?"

Aasha had never been one for gossip. She'd always been the one at the edges of the room, listening to her louder and more excited sisters as they traded news from the Night Bazaar. It never seemed wise to talk about other people. But she had given her word to help the humans. And she felt rather proud of herself in that moment. No one wanted her killing or enchanting touch. They wanted information, and it cost her nothing to give. Even better, *she* had control over what information to divulge.

"It is said that whoever possesses the venom of the Serpent King can control him."

"Why would she want to control him?" asked Vikram.

Aasha was about to answer when Gauri cut in, her voice low and harsh—

"For vengeance. To retaliate for some wrong," she said. She looked at Aasha. "Am I correct?"

Aasha nodded. "They say he kidnapped the Lady Kauveri's sister and forced her into marriage. It wouldn't be the first time that a demon *naga* would do such a thing."

"Is he a demon?" asked Vikram.

"He's a descendant of the cruelest of all the demon *nagas*. Kaliya."

Gauri's expression darkened. "How do we get his venom?"

"I'm not sure," Aasha admitted. "But first you have to get access to his kingdom. There is a pool on the far side of the orchard that bears his crest and invitation."

If her sisters were here, they would have told her that she had done all she needed to and dragged her home. But Aasha lingered. The moment she returned, her world would fall back into its ordered chaos. She would keep her elbows tucked at her side when she walked so that nothing living brushed against her skin. Night after night, she would unspool a person's desire, slaking her hunger and trying to forget that the moment the beings left her arms, they would touch someone they loved, place food upon their tongue that would keep flavor and never turn to ash, maybe even sink their hands into the dirt simply because they could. *Not yet. Not yet.*

"I can take you?" she offered.

23

THE SERPENT KING'S INVITATION

GAURI

Aasha unnerved me. She stood too close. In war, the bulk of a soldier proved its own quiet threat. But Aasha wasn't taking up space to show that her presence was deadly. She stood and leaned toward us with a keen-eyed want. Not hunger. Not lust. I had seen both in the eyes of a *vishakanya*. This was something else. I didn't trust her want, whatever it was.

Before I could tell her no, Vikram drew me away.

"If you're going to tell me to trust her, this is a good time to remind you that you were knocked unconscious *by her* while we were nearly killed *by her sisters*."

"I'm not contesting that."

"Then why did you pull me aside?" I asked. "We can find this pool ourselves. She offered information in return for mercy. We've both kept our word. The end."

"Maybe she could be of more help," he said. "She knows this place far better than we do. And she wants something. Can't you see it in her eyes?"

"I can, which is why I don't think she should be trusted. What if she's just hungry?" I pointed at the two of us. "She can't help but want to touch us. And if she does that, we die."

"I can't help being irresistible."

"A *raksha* didn't even think you were worth ten goats and a cow."

He scowled. "Leading us to a pool doesn't place us in her immortal debt, Gauri. Sometime it's more efficient to trust people and ask for help."

"That sounds wonderfully efficient until the day you find a knife pressed against your throat."

"Have some faith."

"Between faith and distrust, which one is more likely to keep you alive?"

"And which one is more likely to let you experience living?"

I threw up my hands. "Why is everything so philosophical with you?"

He shrugged. "I like thinking."

"After she gets us to the Serpent King, that's it. We wish her well. The end."

Aasha was waiting for us when we returned. As we walked to her, the sunlight caught the underside of the leaves, illuminating her features into such heartbreaking loveliness that I found it hard to believe any man would welcome her into his bed without suspicion. But then I remembered the dumbstruck look on Vikram's face when he first saw Aasha. I would be lying if I said I didn't feel a flicker of envy. But envy did not make one lovelier. Mother Dhina had taught me that. Beauty, coveted though it was, could not outlive you. Only actions would. I never forgot that. In the harem, I might've disliked some girls for the ugliness in their hearts, but never for the beauty of their faces.

Aasha led us back through the courtyards. I expected strange glances like the ones from yesterday, but the Otherworld was too preoccupied in its own tasks. A horse with a translucent belly trotted past us. Between its ribs, pinpricks of light winked around a miniature alabaster city. The ground shuddered as a bull-aspect *raksha* dug a hole with its horns. Beside him, disembodied hands torn off at the wrists reached into the hole, tossing out dirt and carrying clumpy roots. The three feast tables from yesterday had nestled closer to the ground, their wooden legs tucked beneath them as if they were resting. The magic of Alaka felt tame. Even the air carried no fragrant seduction. No childhood memories nuzzled the back of my thoughts or tried to lull my heart from racing. All I could smell was damp, upturned earth and a trace of fruit on the wind.

When we left the feast tables, a hidden grove sprang into view. Dazzling trees sprawled in every direction, their limbs tall and spindly, reaching into the sky as if to etch their names onto the world. There were trees of gold and trees of bone. Trees where instruments swayed gently like musical fruit. Trees where letters were pinned to the trunk, scrawled in handwriting too distant to decipher.

I looked behind us, checking the perimeter for any sign of the Nameless. If they knew we had any clue where to find the Serpent King, they might have been spying on us. Or plotting something worse.

"What do you know about the Nameless?" I asked.

Aasha frowned. "I do not know of them. Then again, this is my first and last Tournament of Wishes. I am only newly one hundred."

"I hope to age half as well," said Vikram.

"Do they not live as long in the mortal lands?" asked Aasha.

"Well, not as long as that," I said. "Half the children of Bharata have no names because they have not lived long enough to prove that they can carry it well into adulthood."

"So you are very old then?"

I laughed. "I guess. I'm eighteen."

"A child," breathed Aasha, her eyes widening in wonder. "And your mate?"

The tops of Vikram's ears turned red. "Eighteen."

I immediately tried changing the subject. "I don't understand why Lord Kubera would even invite the Serpent King to the Tournament if the Lady Kauveri hates him so much."

Aasha only shrugged. "Any Otherworld being who played in a previous Tournament is always invited to play in the next game. Most of the Otherworld is invited, but some choose not to come because they know their presence will only inspire fear. The Lord of Treasures even invites the Dharma Raja and the Queen of Light. Can you imagine what would happen if they came?" She shuddered. "Nothing but chaos. Although I heard they sent a gift since they would not attend."

We walked in silence as Aasha stepped expertly around the strange groves. In the distance, water smoothed over rocks. Frost hung in the air, and a fine mist spilled over the tree roots.

"What do you eat?" asked Aasha suddenly. The question broke from her as if she could no longer fight the strength of it.

I eyed her. What if she wasn't staying close because she was angling to feed our desires or hurt us? What if she was just . . . curious?

"Fruits, vegetables—" I said.

"Sometimes a human if you have no choice," added Vikram.

Aasha looked startled.

"I read that somewhere," he said defensively.

"Don't tell her that!" I hissed, turning to Aasha. "It's not true."

ROSHANI CHOKSHI

She flashed a smile, but it looked more like a wince. "And you may leave from your home at any time?"

Longing filled her voice.

"Not anytime. It just depends what your responsibilities are and who you are."

Aasha nodded, but I could tell that answer had only created a thousand more questions. The longer we walked, the more the trees changed, tapering off into clumps of straggling saplings or growing sparse and skeletal. A pool of milky white water wound through the land like a slender ribbon. We followed it until we came to a still pond. Not even the trees kneeling around the water's edges cast a reflection. Enchantment burned in the air, creating pockets in the sky that peered into different worlds altogether.

"This is the entrance to his kingdom?" asked Vikram.

He stepped forward, leaning over the pool, and immediately jumped back.

"What is it?"

"There's writing in the water."

"That is the invitation of the Serpent King," said Aasha. "If you solve it, he will grant you an audience. Otherwise you must catch him when he chooses to surface."

Aasha and I joined Vikram beside the water's edge. Here, even the sky seemed different—gray and drained of color. Not a single cloud moved in the sky, and the light mist from earlier had thickened into smoky claws that scraped across the earth.

To one it is invisible
Yet be careful if you lose much
To some it is everything

A history to clutch
Though it is life, it cannot buy time
Speak wrong, and I will take it as mine

I groaned. "Another riddle?"

Vikram grinned and immediately tented his fingers together. Aasha looked fearful.

"I would not speak before this pool," she whispered. "If the Serpent King is in a foul mood, he may take even your musings as an answer. And you have only to look around you to see the result."

The mist folded back upon itself, revealing a boneyard on the opposite bank. I stepped back, my ears pricked for any sign of the water rippling or branches cracking around us. Nothing happened. I breathed a sigh of relief. I thought Vikram would be comforted too, but the boneyard had transfixed him. He refused to look anywhere else for a long while. Only when I tugged on his elbow did he step away from the water's edge. Once we were a safe distance away from the pool, Vikram folded his arms, gaze fixed on the ground.

"There were bones there," he said hoarsely. "People have died trying to get to the Serpent King."

"Maybe it's just a morbid decoration."

He whirled around to face me. "This is not a joke, Gauri."

I raised an eyebrow. "What's gotten into you?"

"Nothing," he said tersely and gave his hair a quick tug.

Aasha eyed us knowingly, but if she could somehow read his thoughts, she did not speak his secrets. As we walked back to Alaka's courtyard, the sun had begun to set. A crowd of raucous *yakshas* had gathered near the entrance of the groves. The moment they saw Aasha, a drowsy grin slid onto their faces.

"Come here, beauty," one of them sang. "Let us touch you."

Instead of threatening or maiming them, which is what I would have done in an instant, Aasha seemed to stumble. She shrank a little on herself. I glared at the *yakshas*, but I wasn't going to risk fighting with a magical being unless I had no choice. Instead, I walked to Aasha's other side. I was a flimsy barrier against magic, but it was better than nothing. Vikram stayed where he was.

"They won't attack you?" I asked.

"They might. It has happened before," she said quietly. "But for them to reap any pleasure from the desires I summon, I would have to want to touch them."

"Then there's no reason for them to attack you. Don't be scared."

I didn't know why my first instinct was to protect her. She was a thousand times deadlier than I'd ever be. But her face when she saw the *yakshas* tugged at my heart. I'd seen that expression whenever the harem eunuchs announced Skanda's visits. It was worse than fear. It was hopelessness. It warped a person's face—flattening their eyes, crimping their lips into grimly determined lines. I recognized it. And I hated it.

"That's not why I am scared," said Aasha. "They don't need to force me. They always know that I will want their desires just as badly as they want to be shown them." Aasha reached up and delicately traced the blue star at her throat. "I don't want to want their desires. But it is my sustenance. And they know it."

I shuddered. "That doesn't make it right."

"It is the way things are."

"It shouldn't be," said Vikram.

When we got to the banyan tree, a group of workers had already begun to assemble the *vishakanyas'* tent. This time, the tent resembled a peacock. Gold talons dug into the earth, and a tail the size of a village swept out as a grand carpet and entrance, speckled with sapphire and emerald. Silver and gold threaded through the false feathers, and the design of the bird's neck arched in a graceful welcome.

"Thank you for your help," said Vikram.

Aasha nodded. "My words are my honor."

She left afterward, disappearing down the hill and into some unseen quarters where the *vishakanyas* presumably took rest before entertaining the crowds of Alaka. I turned to Vikram. He had been quiet since he'd read the riddle of the Serpent King.

"Are you well?"

"Yes," he said, but his voice was biting and none too friendly. "Those bones . . . I just can't shake them from my head. I hadn't realized . . . that is to say I had forgotten about death."

"After all we've been through, you're just now becoming concerned about dying?" I almost wanted to laugh.

He lifted his gaze to mine. "It just feels different now."

Now it was my turn to fall silent. I stared around us. The setting sun had carved out the world into a landscape of gems. Hills red as garnets. Pools full of sapphire fire. And the people had also been transformed by the falling sun. Whatever light remained in the sky seemed to race eagerly to illuminate Vikram. If I hadn't known him, I would have thought he was some Otherworldly being who had come to try and steal something from me. Like my voice. Or the memory of my first kiss.

Or something far more precious.

"The risk matches the reward," I said, trying to keep my voice light.

"Gauri," he said softly. Too softly. As if my name were made of glass.

I stepped back and forced a smile. "Any more time with me, and you might truly lose your mind. Maybe we'll come up with the answer to the riddle faster if we take some time to think on our own," I said quickly. "I'll meet you here by nightfall."

Something in his gaze retreated.

"You're not going back to the Serpent King's pool, are you?"

"I haven't gotten this far into existence on stupidity."

He nodded and flashed a smile that didn't reach his eyes. "Don't start now."

I smirked, waved him off and stalked back in the direction of the groves. I had no intention of going to the pool, but I wanted to think alone, far away from where he could distract me. I couldn't shake the sound of my name on his lips. It slinked through my thoughts, spreading roots and thorns. Even though all he said was my name, a question had gathered form in his voice. As if . . . as if he was asking whether I would let him worry about me, and let him rest his fingers at the nape of my neck, and let him memorize my unimportant secrets that would never bring kingdoms to their knees but still pinned my soul in place. Away from him, I knew the right answer:

No.

Our situation was strange. We'd been thrown together in a competition for something we both desperately wanted. Needed. If we didn't win, what home would have us? I said I wanted to return to Bharata, but the Bharata I wanted—one with Nalini safe and my freedom secured—didn't exist without a victory. There was no future without victory. If we didn't win, we would be like ghosts: our forms held together by the sheer force of our unfulfilled wants, with nothing left of our lives but what had been and what could never be. In the face of that fear, maybe the mind couldn't help but scrape together feelings toward the only person we had a connection to. That was all it was. A consequence of survival.

I repeated this to myself as I marched toward the grove of magical trees. Every time I heard a sound behind me, I would turn, expecting Vikram. After the first couple of times, I realized I wasn't expecting him. I was looking for him. I shook my head and concentrated on the riddle.

To one it is invisible
Yet be careful if you lose much
To some it is everything
A history to clutch
Though it is life, it cannot buy time
Speak wrong, and I will take it as mine

My first guess was memory. But memory wasn't life. And my second thought was breath. But breath has nothing to do with history. I was so deep in my thoughts, turning the riddle over and pushing out the memory of Vikram's smile, that I almost didn't see the three people standing before me:

The Nameless.

24

A PLANTED HEART

GAURI

Y ou should not be here," they said.

I dug my heels into the ground. "Why not? Lord Kubera has not forbidden the contestants from entering this part of Alaka."

"We are honoring our lost sister," said the first, turning her gaze on me. She may have looked young—lovely, even—but her gaze held that flat heaviness of someone whose spirit was ancient. As one, the Nameless reached for the blue ribbons around their throats. Maya's necklace pressed against my skin. I tried to honor her, to live up to the stories she told me. But I'd failed.

"I'm not preventing you from honoring her. I was just walking around the groves."

"This grove is for her. Because of her. Because of us. Choose another."

I looked behind them to the bone white trees. When we walked past the grove earlier, I had dug my nails into my palm, fighting the urge to wander through this haunted grove. Something about it called to me. But what? No leaves sprouted from their ivory branches and no fruit graced their boughs. No earth covered the small grove; it was as if someone had shoved slivers of bone into ashes and called them trees, and the bones had forgotten how to be anything else.

"Queen Tara never liked visitors to her orchards anyway."

"Queen Tara?" I repeated incredulously. I knew that name. She was the missing queen of the *vanaras*, the one who had planted demon fruit and been cursed as a result.

"This is her grove."

Without warning, hunger coursed through my veins. I might not know what the tree of demon fruit looked like. But my blood recognized this place. The Nameless stepped backward, and one broke from the trio to place her hand against the bone white tree and rest her forehead to its bark.

"Planted of a sister's heart, unwillingly given," said the first.

"Fixed to the ground of a beloved's bone, unwillingly given," said the second.

"Watered by tears, unwillingly given," said the third.

Their words chilled me.

"And what of the demon fruit?" I asked.

The first, who had not removed her hand from the bark, stroked the tree. "The fruit lies in the heart of the tree. But it can only be taken by a man who has given away his heart. None else can take the fruit. And yet no man may eat of it."

"Why would you ever honor your sister's memory in a place like this?"

The Nameless smiled. "It is her heart that the Queen took. This is our sister's legacy. Our vengeance. This is the last Tournament. When we win, our sister will be honored forever."

I got away from them as fast as I could. I muttered something vaguely polite right before running to Vikram. I didn't care that it wasn't even nightfall yet. The words of the Nameless rang through my thoughts. My tongue felt thick and my mouth turned dry. I had *eaten* that fruit. I had eaten something grown from bones, heart and tears. Worse . . . I craved it. That bite of power. Of invincibility. Maybe the demon fruit brought a curse with it, but to me it felt like safety.

Vikram hadn't moved from the spot where I'd left him. Only now, his face was pale. And his hair was tousled, as if he had tugged at the strands one time too many.

"I figured out the riddle," he said. "The answer is blood."

It made sense. You could not see your own blood. If you lost too much, you died. Some people swore by their lineage. And blood was life, although having more of it wouldn't change the time of your death.

"I think he wants us to place some of our blood in the pool before he will let us enter."

My fingers trembled from my meeting with the Nameless. I clasped them together. I didn't want to die here. I didn't want to become like them, wandering through this palace and playing a game over and over, hoping for a different outcome. But I needed strength if I was going to win.

"I'll meet you by the pool at first light," I said.

"Where are you going?"

"To steal sleep and hope I don't remember the nightmares."

"On the night before possible death with all the food and festivities and dancing all around us, you want to go to sleep?"

"Celebrating as if it's your last night on earth generally makes for reckless mistakes the next day," I said, folding my arms.

"I solved the riddle. I demand a reward."

I narrowed my eyes. "What do you want?"

Vikram nodded to the revels taking place beneath the banyan tree. The music already made me feel heady with the frenzied drums and the musicians' lilting song of yearning and claiming. He stepped closer, to the point where I had to look up to meet his eyes. A vulpine grin crept onto his face. In that moment, he looked like mischief and midnight, like a temptation that always slipped away too fast and left you at once relieved and disappointed.

"I want one dance with you."

25

A TALISMAN OF TOUCH
VIKRAM

The bones had stood out too sharply. A little too knowingly. As if they had been waiting for him to find them. Maybe those bones belonged to someone like him. Someone who believed that magic meant they were destined for more. Maybe they believed it right until the moment they died.

Vikram wasn't so blinded by the idea of magic that he thought it was a toothless and beautiful thing. He knew it bit. But he hadn't imagined it could bite . . . them.

If he lost, what use would magic be? The life that waited for him in Ujijain was a husk of an existence. He couldn't return. And yet he no longer felt that glittering certainty that victory danced within reach. He felt . . . outside of himself. Grasping, once more, for that hope and belief.

And so he danced with Gauri not out of want, but out of necessity. In the ashram, pupils carried luck charms in their pockets or hid tiny figurines of deities all over their rooms. Vikram never understood that compulsion to hold what felt sacred. Now he did.

It was the connection people craved; the feeling that touch connected them to something beyond themselves. That was why he needed to dance with her. He craved that connection to the moment when magic had snapped his reality and showed him that his destiny as a puppet was only a path. Not a promise.

Before he met Gauri, he thought that the invitation to the Tournament of Wishes marked the entrance of magic into his life. But that moment was nothing more than what it served: an invitation. *Gauri* was the real beginning. He knew it the moment she flew toward him, lips pulled back in a snarl, eyes black as winter and just as unforgiving.

Vikram pulled Gauri to the revels. The air felt heavy and damp, as it always did during the rainy season. He drew her close until their bodies were flush. He wanted to memorize this, the way her leg pressed against his, the way strands of her hair got caught in the small buttons of his jacket. Even the way she glowered at him when he grinned. When he touched her, he didn't feel like some thread in a tale, pulled along without will. He was something that reached out and responded.

Gauri laughed when he stumbled through the movements of the dance.

"You are a discredit to your title, Vikram. Fox Prince, indeed," she said. "I've never seen a clumsier fox."

"What I lack in skill, I make up for in enthusiasm."

"Do you even know how to dance?"

"Not at all," he said, spinning her in a circle.

"I can tell. Were you lulled by the music?"

"The company."

"Now you're just trying to be sly and charming."

"I am a credit to my title, after all."

Twice, he had pulled her so close that her gaze threatened to eclipse his thoughts. When she danced, her eyes softened. No longer harsh and winter black, but vast and . . . not breathtaking, but breath-guzzling. Breath-devouring. This close, her eyes shone like fragments of night sky. If he looked closer, he wondered whether he'd see stars burst into life behind her lashes.

Twice, her lids dropped and her eyes traced his lips just as his traced hers. But he always pulled away in the end. He'd spent enough time with her to guess how she would interpret a kiss. She would see it as a reckless act of bravery, a thing to be done before death. It would have been a reckless act of bravery. But not for those reasons.

They danced until even the stars limped out of the sky. Only a few stragglers remained to watch the revels. A handful of hours were left between now and dawn. And at dawn, he knew that she would be up and ready to fight, so he led her away from the dance.

"Finally," she said. But he thought he heard faint disappointment in her voice.

When they trudged upstairs, he took the couch at the opposite side of the room without comment. Within moments, she was asleep. One arm flung over her stomach. One ankle tucked beneath her knee. He'd never seen anyone sleep in a knot, but Gauri made the pose look like the soul of slumber. He allowed himself a single moment to wonder what it would be like to know that warmth, to rest his cheek against her bare shoulder and trace what dreams fluttered beneath her eyelids. And then he closed his mind to her.

As he expected, Gauri was up with the dawn. She woke him up none too gently, but made up for it by shoving a cup of *chai* in one of his hands and a plate of *uttapam* in the other.

"Ready to die?"

He groaned. "I realize you're newly adjusting to a sense of humor, but have mercy."

"Not known for it."

He raised his glass to her. "It's never too late to start."

The world was gray and dark when they left their chambers and trudged through the grove. Gauri kept looking over her shoulder at a copse of skeletal-looking trees, one hand on the weapons belt slung around her waist. At the pool, Vikram held out his arm and Gauri quickly drew a knife across her forearm and then his. He didn't wince when the blood unfurled in the milky water, staining the riddle invitation scrawled across the pale surface. The water trembled. The pool sank into the earth, transforming into a set of sapphire staircases that formed a serpentine coil straight into darkness.

"Well done, mortals," called a voice from the depths.

26

THE SEVEN BRIDES
GAURI

I imagined that the Serpent King's lair would look like a snake's burrow—a hole in the ground littered with bone fragments, and shed skin boasting a phantom of its former brightness. But this subterranean palace was beautiful. At the bottom of the stairs, a large chamber sprawled out. Glassy stalactites spiraled from a cavernous ceiling flecked with bits of quartz and silver. A wave of still water covered with a thin piece of glass formed the floor.

At the bottom of the stairs, I grimaced. The stairs were the only entrance and exit. If we had to fight in the middle of the room, it strained an exit strategy. Even though the room was barren, the atmosphere felt strung taut. It felt . . . watched. I waited. In battle, I could sometimes guess when an enemy soldier would charge out of the dark. You could feel the air gather and release. As if it had guessed what was coming next and chose to step aside.

The dark unraveled:

Tail.

Torso.

Teeth.

"You came looking for a monster," said the Serpent King. "And now you have found one."

I wanted to take from this monster just as he had taken from the Lady Kauveri's sister. I wanted him to be as ugly as his actions, with mottled skin and yellowed fangs, a bloated brown tail attached to a puffy torso. But when I turned around, he was anything but hideous.

He was taller than any man I'd ever seen, but maybe that was because he had raised himself higher on his own serpent coil. His black hair was threaded with silver—not the dull silver that streaked hair as one aged, but *actual* silver. Aasha said he was descended of the demon *naga* Kaliya. But he was demonic only if you considered his beauty so severe that it bordered on sinister. The Serpent King moved toward us with a liquid grace before stopping and tilting his head. A knowing smirk turned his lips at the corners.

"You wish I weren't so beautiful," he said to me.

I frowned. "I—"

"You have nothing to fear," said the Serpent King, resting his gaze on Vikram. "My heart cannot be tempted from the one who possesses it."

He could read minds. Could he manipulate them? Or hypnotize? Perhaps that was how he seduced Kauveri's sister. My hand moved closer to the weapons belt slung around my waist. The Serpent King pulled his lips into a snarl and hissed. A cobra hood flared out behind his neck, as blue as the heart of a flame. His teeth lengthened into fangs. I braced my legs, preparing for an attack.

"That is what you think of me?" he said. "That I forced her hand? That I snatched her heart from her chest?"

Vikram moved to my side. The Serpent King turned sharply to Vikram, and his cobra hood flattened and disappeared.

"Wouldn't you agree, Fox Prince, that if you can be more than your blood then I can be more than mine?" He turned his gaze back to me. "You may play in the Tournament of Wishes, but you sleep in the Palace of Stories. Let me tell you a tale."

He moved forward, forcing us back a step.

"Once, there was a *naga* with demon blood in his veins who saw a beautiful girl singing by the river. He returned every day for a year to listen to her voice until her song ran through his veins instead of blood. He revealed the secret of his own venom in exchange for the magic of a mortal name just to share the same language with her. And once he could speak, he asked her to sing in his palace beneath the sea and promised her his whole heart, poisoned as it might be. She accepted."

The Serpent King's eyes softened. He moved forward again, pressing us back even farther.

"Let me tell you another tale," he said, so softly that it might have seemed meek. But I heard the tremor in his voice. It was barely restrained rage. "Once, there was a demon king who terrorized the river and poisoned it black until a god danced upon his head and banished him to the watery depths. The demon king learned his lesson. And he taught that lesson to every one of his descendants, down to the smallest hatchling, so that they would learn to ignore the poison threaded through their veins. His descendant fell in love with a river and the river loved him back. But no one had forgotten the deeds of his ancestors. And no one believed either him or the river who loved him."

Doubt fluttered at the back of my head. I thought back to those empty birdcages and the wings overhead, soaring and changing with every intersecting story. But Kauveri was the sister of the Serpent

King's wife. If the story wasn't true, then why would Aasha say that Kauveri wanted his venom? Kauveri's demand was proof of how she considered him: Untrustworthy. Out of control. Maybe she thought to free her sister from his clutches by using the venom. Maybe that was the only reason Kubera had invited him to the Tournament. I notched my chin higher as I stared down the Serpent King. I was ready to fight, but Vikram placed his hand on my arm:

"If you want us to believe you, let us speak to your mate."

Shame shot through me. What kind of person was I that I hadn't even thought to ask Kauveri's sister directly? My mind had instantly gone to punishment.

The Serpent King tilted his head. "We used to honor such requests. And do you know what we have received every time? Scorn. Ridicule. We refuse to be subjected to the doubts of others. My mate is the river Kapila," he said proudly. "She is stronger than every current and more powerful than the sea at its most ferocious. And yet she would have to listen—once more—to a hundred questions probing whether she was enchanted, stupefied, kidnapped and dragged down to the lair of a snake. I will not demean her so. And I will not let *you* demean her."

Vikram's hand ran down my spine. His eyes flashed in warning.

"Here's another story," hissed the Serpent King. By now, we were flush against the wall. "Once there was a demon king who stole away the beautiful river goddess and kept her as his prisoner until she was so weakened that she agreed to become his wife. That demon king would have had to break the ferocity of a river and all of her powers. And whatever pair of mortals decided to fight him would have to get through that. So which tale do you choose to believe? Don't think I don't know what you want. I could hear your thoughts screaming and calling for my venom the moment your feet hit the staircase."

"If you know that we're here for your venom then you know why we need it," said Vikram calmly. "We don't have a choice."

"Oh, but you do," said the Serpent King. "Choose which story to believe. A man in love or a man in lust? The wronged or the wrongful? You have the choice to believe my innocence and I will let you leave in peace. I will tell the Lord of Treasures what you have done and I will personally procure you an exit. Or you can choose to believe in the harm I caused. You can fight me for my venom, and if you win, I will give it to you. I, too, follow the rules of the Tournament. So what will it be? Once you choose, it cannot be undone. No matter how much all of our hearts may break beneath your choice."

The Serpent King moved backward, as if he were giving us privacy. But it made no difference, since he could read our minds anyway. The more I thought about Kauveri, the more I believed that he had done wrong. Why else would Kauveri want his venom? Even Aasha had seemed disgusted with him. More than that, this might be our only chance to secure an exit out of Alaka. Without this venom, it wouldn't even matter if we won the Tournament, because we didn't know which of us would be allowed to leave Alaka. My mind was decided. The Serpent King eyed me coldly, and then his gaze turned to Vikram. Vikram looked less decided, but his hand never once moved from the small of my back.

"I see," said the Serpent King. His voice was silky menace. "You wish to ask my wife for the truth behind our story? Then do so. As you chose which story of me to believe, choose her. But choose wrong, and your lives are forfeit."

I didn't understand what he meant until he moved to one side of the room. He flicked his tail against the glass floor, shattering it. Mist rose from the spider-thin cracks, pushing apart the fissures to make way for the seven women who rose out of the water. They were almost identical, but their manner of dress and jewelries varied. The Kapila River looked much like her sister, Kauveri. But there was a softness to her jaw compared to Kauveri's sharp edges. And where Kauveri's eyes had changed between the icy quartz of a river at dawn to the brackish brown of a river at dusk, Kapila's eyes remained a warm and constant blue.

"You have until the floor breaks," said the Serpent King, smiling. "Oh, and I would move quickly. Because the water beneath is poisonous."

I yanked Vikram away from a fissure that had begun to spider near his foot. Little cracks spread slowly from the holes in the floor where the seven women had sprung out of the water. I steadied my breath even as my palms began to sweat. Tread carefully. Choose carefully. That was all I could do.

"Did you believe him?" I asked under my breath.

"I don't know what to believe," said Vikram, scanning the line of seven women. "But if it was a chance to make sure that both of us would get out of here alive, I wasn't going to waste it."

The Serpent King watched us from his corner. The seven women stood in front of us, their faces nearly impassive. Vikram stepped carefully to the first of the seven women and I walked by his side.

"This one has longer hair?" he said.

"That doesn't tell us if she's his wife," I said. To each woman, I leaned close to her and said, "I'm going to get the venom to Kauveri. Help me and I can help you escape him."

But that changed nothing.

The first had a bright sparkling stone at the center of her forehead. The second wore a collar of scales. The third had a long emerald tail.

The fourth wore a dress of silver river fish. The fifth crossed her arms. The sixth rested her hand on her hip. The seventh had fangs.

We walked down the line, each step damning us a little further. The mist had begun to thicken the air. The women stood utterly still, but followed us with their eyes.

Vikram tented his fingers. Sweat beaded on his forehead. "It's all just a distraction."

I raised an eyebrow. "What do you mean?"

"The clothes, arm positions, everything. It's a trick. It doesn't tell us anything about which one is his real wife."

I pressed the heel of my hand against my eyes, as if that could somehow change the sight before me. I could almost imagine the Serpent King laughing in his corner.

"They won't respond to anything I say. I thought his real wife would have a reaction to him."

"You just gave me a brilliant idea," he whispered. "Give me your knife."

I raised my eyebrow. "If any of us is going to be using a knife, it should be me."

"Your aim is a little too good," he said. "Trust me."

I handed over the knife. The mist was rising fast. The floor creaked and splintered beneath us. Water lapped up the edges of the fragile sheet of glass we stood on, and the poisonous fumes stung the back of my throat. Our weight was too concentrated. All it would take was one good stomp to break the floor.

"Spread your legs," I shouted.

"Rather forward of you—"

"Distribute your weight or we're going to die."

He spread his legs, stabilizing the wobbling piece of the glass floor.

Holding the knife in one hand, he leaned down to whisper: "Watch their faces. Whoever is his true wife will have a reaction."

Vikram flung the dagger, aiming it at the space right above the Serpent King's head. The moment he loosed it, the sixth woman in line let out a scream.

"Her!" I pointed.

A furious roar lit up the caverns, shaking the stalactites. Whether it was pain at being stabbed or frustration at being caught, I didn't know. The mist was rising so fast that every surface turned slippery. Poison began to smoke and fume at the edges of my sandals, blackening them. My lungs burned and I choked back a cough.

"Run!" I shouted.

I leapt onto a slippery sheet of glass, barely keeping my balance as it careened violently to one side. I flung myself onto a new sheet, my body slamming into a piece that only just barely fit my frame. It spidered beneath me, threatening to crack. But I was quicker. I leapt from sheet to sheet, and was nearly at solid ground when I heard a shout behind me. I turned to see Vikram not far from me, his arms pinwheeling, feet shaky. He was going to fall. I didn't think twice about saving him. I reached out to grab him, using all my weight to push him to the shore. He tumbled, hitting the wall. I jumped to join him, but the unraveling threads of my *salwar kameez* snagged on a jagged edge of glass, yanking my body sideways. I slipped. Vikram reached just in time to pull me onto the floor, but not before a wave of water sloshed up my leg. I screamed. Spots of pain lit up behind my eyes. Poison sank its teeth past the silk of my pants, painting excruciating tendrils of fire across my calf and ankle.

I slumped against Vikram. He wrapped his arm around my waist, hauling me toward the staircase. I blinked. Fighting to stand. To push myself up and forward, but I couldn't. The Serpent King's tail lashed out, but he did not block our path. The woman who was his true wife had appeared at his side, her face buried in his chest. I looked into her face, fighting down the tremors skittering up and down my body. Vikram propped me into a stand. He was murmuring something, but I couldn't hear him. I only saw the Kapila River's face: shuttered and heartbroken as she sobbed in the arms of the Serpent King.

"What have you done?" she wept, staring at us. "Why couldn't you just believe us?"

We said nothing. What could we say? Vikram grimaced, turning from her. He half dragged, half carried me up the stairs. Pain seared my thoughts, but even through that haze I saw Kapila's tear-streaked face and watched the Serpent King brush away strands of her hair.

They loved each other.

The sickly pangs of victory shot through me. Or maybe it was the poison working through my leg. I couldn't feel it anymore. We had won this. We had an exit. And if freedom came with the price of guilt, maybe I was already so glutted on the emotion that the taste wouldn't register. I blinked, and Kapila's anguish burned in my vision.

I was wrong.

Guilt accretes. It builds and builds, whittling stairways and spires in the heart until a person can carry a city of hopelessness inside them. My guilt was building a universe.

Vikram was whispering. But his voice was coming from a thousand directions. When I stumbled, he picked me up. I didn't stop him.

At the top of the stairs, the Serpent King held out a blue vial.

"Now you know the truth," he said hoarsely. "But know this. Kauveri can banish or imprison me, but it will change nothing. You can tell her that if she cares so much for her sister she will not enjoy watching her waste away before her eyes."

My vision refused to focus. I set my jaw, my thoughts straining. I came to Alaka to free myself from guilt, not discover more. I would tell Kauveri what I'd seen even as I bartered our way out of here. I would make amends.

"Gauri?" called Vikram. His voice sounded faraway. "Gauri!"

I tried to focus on him, to push words from my mouth. But the pain had begun to eat into my bones. Darkness edged in from the corners of my vision right before it swallowed me whole.

A BROKEN SONG
VIKRAM

He had to believe that everything happened for a reason. In the ashram, he had pushed himself to run as fast as he could. The pupils joked that he had tucked a fistful of lightning into his sandals to aid him. Back then, Vikram thought he'd forced himself to run as fast as he could just to prove that he could. He was wrong.

It had all been practice for this moment.

Gauri's head bumped against his chest as he ran. She felt too light in his arms, as if the essence of her had already begun to slip and unspool. Her lips turned blue, and Vikram's heart slammed. *Not again*, he thought. Demanded. Prayed. *Not again*.

In his hand, the blue vial of the Serpent King's poison might as well have been a handful of blue flowers. Gauri's pale lips reminded him of another. Vikram blinked, and felt as if he were seven years old once more, toeing the edge of a rockslide. His mother crumpled in a heap at the bottom of the rocks. For an entire day and night, he had ordered her to

wake up. After that, he had hugged his knees to his chest, unable to speak because every word sharpened to a scream in his throat. He remembered the fan of his mother's hair beneath a boulder. White, writhing insects moving over her cut arms. Her neck bent strange, face angled to the light as if she were simply enjoying the sunshine. Only this time her lips were torn and blue.

Vikram hated fear. He hated how it fed on him and stripped away his comfortable blindness. Fear forced him to hold up the contents of his heart to the light. Once, he stood over a rockslide and beheld that fear: He would be untethered. Back then, his mother's love was a thread of unbroken light, a seam he coud follow through every moment of his life until he suddenly couldn't, leaving him to push through the dark, make out the shapes of his future in utter blindness. Now, when he clutched an unresponsive Gauri to his chest, fear forced him to see her. Only her. It felt silly to say that he couldn't bear to lose her. He never *had* her. She was not a thing to be possessed. But her entrance in his life had conjured light. And losing the light of her would plunge him into a darkness he'd never find his way out of.

Gauri was pale, damp with feverish sweat. Once the poisoned water had reached her bare skin, it had refused to leave. Heatless blue flames twisted and licked their way up her ankle, threatening to burn her alive without a single plume of smoke. Vikram's legs burned.

As far as he knew, there were no healers in Alaka. Even if there were, this wound belonged to poisoned magic. There was only one group of people he knew that spent their lives steeped in poison. But would they help them? He considered bringing her straight to the *vishakanyas'* tent, but it would be too easy for them to see her as wounded prey.

Instead, Vikram ran up the stairs to the chamber, out of breath and heart pounding. He placed Gauri on the bed. Her lips looked even bluer.

Sweat matted her hair. He brushed the strands out of her eyes, pulling a blanket over her body. Then he sprinted out of the room and straight to the tent.

At high noon, the tent hummed with lazy stupor. Some patrons stumbled out of the exit, blinking at the sunshine. No guard patrolled the entrance since there was no line. Vikram took a deep breath. Maybe this was the most foolish thing he'd ever done. There was no guarantee that the poisonous courtesans wouldn't harm him, especially since he brought himself willingly to their territory. Maybe he'd even die here and get poisoned himself, just as Gauri had. But he had to try.

He marched inside and found several *vishakanyas* lounging inside the tent. Two patrons sat with their heads lolled back as they stared at their desires twisting above them. One of the courtesans, a stunning woman with golden hair and dark eyes, stood up. Her eyes raked over him, lingering at his ripped pants and the nasty gash on his arm where the shattered glass fragments had cut him. Her pupils darkened in lust. Or maybe hunger. Or quite possibly both.

"I need to speak with one of your sisters immediately. Her name is Aasha. She knows me."

Her face changed. "Aasha? What do you want with her?"

"My—" He stumbled over the right words. "—partner in the Tournament has been gravely injured. She's going to die from poisoning if I don't get help."

"And you think one of us will part with our arts to care for a human?" she sneered.

More courtesans poured out from unseen parts of the tent until they had formed a small circle around him. At first they looked at him curiously, eyes widened in surprise. But slowly that surprised changed. Their pupils widened. Their lips parted. He was so anxious about getting back to Gauri that he hadn't even considered how that fierce desire would make him that much more appealing to them. They sniffed the air, cocking their heads sharply to one side as if pondering the fastest way to scrabble at his desires.

"Poison is not such a bad thing, princeling," she crooned. "Why don't you let her die? You can have all the glory for yourself. Maybe you can ask for the second wish that would have belonged to your partner? Perhaps you can ask to be immune to us." She stepped forward, hands outstretched in invitation. "We make excellent company."

Her smile widened. Vikram had stepped back, rolling onto his toes and ready to run out of the tent, when Aasha broke through the crowd.

"Aasha!" said the golden-haired *vishakanya*. She smiled. "This prince was just asking for your services."

"She's dying," he said hoarsely. "The poison from his waters has gotten to her. I need help."

Aasha's sisters murmured into her ear, tugging on her arm. He felt the moment sharpening to a knife's point. Everything balancing on her next words. She could doom them. But he hoped instead, and his hope roared inside him.

"Why don't you tell him that he should let this girl go and cure his sorrow in our arms?"

"Tell him the cure for the girl's poison is farther inside the tent," whispered another.

"He came here willingly," hissed a third. "So we may take him. The Lord of Treasures granted no protection to the humans if they came again."

Aasha bit her lip as she lifted her head. Vikram's heart sank. Her face was a death sentence.

"Where is she?" asked Aasha softly.

The others stared at her. Some in confusion. Some in shock. Others in hurt. Aasha turned to the golden-haired one and some silent conversation passed between them.

"I'll take you to her."

Together, they left the *vishakanyas'* tent behind. Only then did Vikram notice that Aasha was limping.

"What happened?" he asked.

"Oh. I . . . I fell."

He sensed she was lying, but he refused to press her.

"Why did you stay there for so long?" asked Aasha.

Vikram frowned. "We only left this morning."

"It is almost full moon," she said, shocked. "The Jhulan Purnima is the day after tomorrow."

Vikram's heart raced. Time ran differently in Alaka, but the Serpent King's kingdom did not belong to Alaka. Whatever time they had spent there had cost them days. After tomorrow, the second trial would begin. If Gauri wasn't ready to compete—or, worse, if she was *unable* to compete—all of this would have been for nothing. Helplessness gave way to a choked rage.

As gingerly as he could, he rushed Aasha up the steps to the room. Gauri hadn't moved from her position. But the flames had. They had spiraled from her ankle and now roped their way around the tops of her thighs. No heat burned from the flames, but the air crackled and snapped around Gauri's body. As if it had claimed her and refused to let her go.

Aasha leaned over her.

"Strange," she murmured.

Vikram paced over the floor, tugging at his hair. "What's strange? Can you fix it?"

"The poison in her skin," said Aasha. She looked up. "It's the same as mine."

"How is that possible?"

Aasha stared at the flames, her expression inscrutable. "I . . . I don't know. My sisters always said that we got our poison as a blessing from a goddess, but . . . but that doesn't seem to make any sense now."

He stopped walking. "What does that mean for Gauri?"

"It means that I can draw it out."

Vikram breathed a sigh of relief.

"But it also means that I can't counteract it. I can't control whether she will live or die. She'll have to fight it on her own. And if she lives, I don't know if the poison will have changed her."

Vikram slumped into a chair. "Just do whatever you can."

Aasha nodded, and bent her head over Gauri. He didn't look. Hours passed, and dawn lightened the sky. Aasha took a seat across from him, and her expression told him that she had done all she could. Now all they could do was wait.

Sometime in the night, Vikram sat beside her and watched the heatless blue flames gutter. They were dying. But so was she.

Magic might be vast, but right now, he felt it as a quiet hum in his chest. The enchantments that seemed greater than life had done them no favors. He turned, instead, to small, ordinary magic. The same magic that his mother had conjured each time his nightmares shot him out of sleep and left him breathless with fear. She used to fold him to her, rocking him back and forth and crooning a song. Vikram let go of reason.

He lowered his lips to her ear . . . and sang. Soft, broken words. He was no singer. But, he thought, thinking back to the sage's invitation so many nights ago, maybe it was about the sincerity. So he sang, forcing his heart into every lopsided tune. An unspoken summons and plea cropped up between the notes of his rusty voice:

Don't leave.

28

EATING POETRY

GAURI

I woke up to a burning sensation coursing through my leg. Pushing myself up one elbow, I looked around the room. The sky above me was flecked with stars and wispy violet clouds. How long had I been out? I groaned and tried to lift my leg. Nothing broken or sprained. Throwing back the covers, I saw only the usual expanse of bronze and unbroken skin. It was as if that poisoned water had never touched me.

"Gauri?"

Vikram rose out of a chair. Dark sleepless circles marked his eyes. "You're awake." He sat down on the bed beside me and reached for my hand. "We weren't sure you'd make it."

"We?"

A figure stood up from the other side of the room. The light washed over her. Aasha. She walked to me tentatively, her chin ducked as she looked at us through her lashes. Nalini moved the same way when she first came to Bharata. Hesitant. As if she thought the air would push back at her for not belonging. But then I remembered why I was lying down in a bed, pain shooting up my leg. I had chosen wrong after relying on Aasha's word. Kapila's crumpled face swam in my vision. From across the room, the vial of the Serpent King's venom caught the light.

"How do you feel?" asked Aasha. "You slept the whole day."

My hair had fallen in front of my face. Vikram leaned forward, raising his hand to brush away my hair. I turned my head, shoving the strands from my face, and he withdrew his hand as if stung.

"I'm in pain," I gritted out.

"Do you feel any different?"

I had drawn it away to show them the unbroken skin when something caught my eye. I thought I had no scar, but the poison had left something behind. A small blue star, no bigger than a thumbnail, was imprinted on the back of my calf.

Aasha saw it and sucked in her breath. "That is our mark."

A *vishakanya* mark was on me? My heart raced and I turned to Vikram. "You touched me. Do you feel any different?"

His eyes widened. "No. I don't feel a thing."

"Maybe it is just a scar from the poison?" offered Aasha. "I am sure it is nothing."

Bitterness stole into my throat. What was sureness and certainty? I used to hold on to certainty like a light inside me, hoping it would chase out the dark unknown. But certainty was a phantom strung together on hopes. It would lead you astray at the first chance.

"Are you?" I asked quietly. "Are you as sure as you were when you told us that the Serpent King had stolen Kauveri's sister? Or that she even wanted his venom in the first place?"

"Gauri . . ." said Vikram under his breath.

I knew that tone. It was a *stop while you're ahead* tone. I refused. There had been a chance to choose a path without bloodshed. Without hurt. And now that opportunity was gone. *Once you choose, it cannot be undone. No matter how much all of our hearts may break beneath your choice.* The problem with guilt was not how it attacks the present, but how it stained the past. Hindsight was a blemish on memory. Had I asked enough questions? Could I have figured out that I didn't have all the pieces I needed to make that decision? Could any of this have been avoided?

"The Serpent King didn't steal away his wife. Where did you get that information?"

Aasha stepped back, shocked. "I told you what I knew from my own sisters. All of the *yakshas* that serve the Lady Kauveri had said she wanted the Serpent King's venom. They told us this when they frequented our tent. I overheard many of them saying that the Lady Kauveri only wanted the poison because he had stolen away her sister. It was gossip, I admit, but it was all the information I had."

"Aasha saved your life, Gauri," said Vikram. "You can—"

"Did you save me out of guilt? Because you lied?" I asked, my voice rising. "Did you want the Kapila River hurt too? You knew that we would go down there and assume that he'd done something wrong because of what you told us. Maybe you did it out of spite. Maybe one of your sisters or even *you* were the Serpent King's scorned lover. Was that it?"

Vikram stood up abruptly. "You didn't make that decision by yourself. I believed her too. She gave us the best information she had. We had to make a choice. We did. That decision and responsibility is ours and ours *alone*."

"Oh, it's that easy, is it?"

"It is easy," said Vikram coolly. "You would see that if you took a moment to unclutter your mind from all your self-pity."

My cheeks grew hot. They were both standing and staring down at me. I felt caged. Small. Manipulated.

Aasha backed out of the room. "I didn't save you out of guilt. I . . . I only tried to help." She turned to Vikram. "I am glad she is safe. I must go."

She turned and fled the room, but not before I saw tears forming at the corners of her eyes and her limping gait. Every fight in me deflated. What was wrong with me?

"Are you satisfied?" shouted Vikram. "We were both worried about you. We both waited by your side. Aasha worked all day to try to get the poison out of your veins or manipulate it so that it wouldn't kill you. People *care* about you. You could have been grateful. Instead you spent the first moments of consciousness attacking everyone around you. Is this what you meant by surviving? You just blame and slash at everything around you because you can't control yourself?"

I stood up. The pain in my leg flared and dimmed. Pain or not, I owed Aasha my life. And I repaid her with cruel words. I had owed Nalini my life too and repaid her the same way: letting cold words chase her shadow into the night. My intentions might have been rooted in good, but they always grew thorns in the end.

"We deserved answers."

"What answer? She heard something. She told us. We acted on it, justifiably so, because we have no experience with Serpent Kings or their consorts who also happen to be actual rivers! Anyone would have done the same. You're just looking for someone to blame."

His words cut me. "Stop talking to me as if you could even understand anything I've gone through."

"Do you think you're the only person suffering?" he demanded. "I know you. I . . . I *saw you* in the Undead Grotto. In Bharata, you kept people alive even if it killed you a little every day. You made choices no one should have to make. *That* is the Gauri I respect." I flinched. "But this person? Now you're just looking for an escape."

The words hung between us. I wanted to yank them out of the air and retreat behind them, but I couldn't. Those words burrowed into my thoughts, bringing out a past I never wanted to revisit. In Bharata, surviving in Skanda's court meant knowing all the players and all the pieces and all the information. All that time, I only thought how those pieces affected me. I sank onto the bed, staring at the slightly mussed cushions where Aasha had kept her vigil. Vikram scrubbed a hand through his hair. He sat down at the edge of the bed, his spine straight and chin high. He didn't reach for me.

"Surviving isn't just about cutting out your heart and burning every feeling into ash," he said. "Sometimes it means taking whatever is thrown at you, beautiful or grotesque, poisonous or blissful, and carving out your life with the pieces you're given."

"Stop being wise."

He raised an eyebrow. "Then stop demanding wisdom."

Shame spread through me. I thought back to that last night in Bharata. I would never forget Nalini's tear-streaked face or the words I hurled at her. I never apologized when I had the chance. I wouldn't make the same mistake twice.

Leaving Vikram, I slipped out to the baths. As I dressed, I brushed my fingers against the strange blue star on my skin. It was small, almost smudged around the edges. Nothing at all like the ornate stamps branding the *vishakanyas'* throats. When I left the baths, Vikram was turning the vial of the Serpent King's venom in his hands.

"Tomorrow is Jhulan Purnima."

"What? That fast?"

He grimaced. "We lost time in the Serpent King's palace."

"Wonderful. Not even a day of rest before the next trial."

"It could be worse."

"Always optimistic," I said with a small shake of my head.

"Hope shapes the world."

"Or stains it so you don't know what it really looks like."

"Or that," he allowed.

"Rest," I said, when I saw him stare longingly at the bed. "I'll come back later tonight."

Outside, the courtyard had transformed. Delicate silver bells were strung through the trees. Snow dusted the air, and everything was silver and iridescent, pearl white or the barest touch of blush. Swings with braided lotuses for ropes hung from the trees, an homage to the sacred lovers who had spent so many afternoons with their heads bent as they swung side by side, flute music wreathing their limbs and their eyes brimming with the sight of each other's faces. The swings listed gently in the windless air, an invitation to sit and talk and fall in love.

I never wanted to fall in love. To me, love looked like pale light. Not lustrous enough to illuminate the world or dazzle one's eyes, but bright enough to fool you into thinking it might. In the harem, some of my mothers told me love was a decadent ambrosia, something to be sipped and savored. Others told me it was an open wound. One of the mothers—a slip of a woman who wouldn't survive her first pregnancy—had pulled me aside and told me something I never forgot: "Love is like Death without the guarantee of its arrival. Love may not come for you, but when it does it will be just as swift and ruthless as

Death and just as blind to your protestations. And just as Death will end one life and leave you with another, so will Love."

Her words terrified me. I would never feel that way about someone. I never wanted to.

Not too far from the *vishakanyas'* tent, I found Aasha sitting by a stream. She looked up when she saw me, any expression in her face instantly shuttering.

"May I sit with you?"

She nodded.

"Listen . . . I got lost in my head back there," I said. "And somewhere in between being horribly ungrateful and just plain horrible, I never thanked you. I owe you an apology. You have no reason to accept it, but I hope you will."

Aasha nodded. "I understand. And I forgive you."

My eyebrows shot up. "That's it? I was expecting you'd ask me to grovel or chase me away with a touch." I laughed. "You're a far better person than I am."

"Am I?" she asked. "A person, I mean? I started out as one. I started out like you."

Her question took me by surprise.

"Of course you're a person, Aasha," I said. "Humanity has nothing to do with what runs through your veins or shows up on your skin."

She closed her eyes, as if savoring the words. "Did you know that the Lord of Treasures had this stream commissioned especially for *vishakanyas*? He did it so that we would have a place to dip our feet into without worrying about killing any mortal thing in its waters. I found out only a day ago." She kicked her foot in the water, frowning. "I could have been doing this since the day we got here."

"Better a late discovery than none at all?"

"I suppose so." She shrugged. "There are some streams that run through our harem back home, but it's nothing like this . . . nothing under open skies."

"Where is home?"

Aasha looked away from me. "We are not permitted to say to those who are not *vishakanya*."

"Oh. Have you ever had another home?"

"I suppose I must have," she said. "But my sisters took me when I was four."

Anger flared through me. "How could they rip you from your family?"

"Don't say that," chastised Aasha gently. "They are my family. And I love them. As they love me. They meant to save me." My eyes widened. "A soothsayer had come to our village and declared that I would be a young widow. In my village, all widows must commit sati the moment her husband dies. They rescued me from a fate of burning alive with my husband's body. They even made sure my family would be well compensated. I hope my birth family loved well."

I watched her moving her foot in the water, something I could do a thousand times and never find reason to give thanks. "Would you leave the *vishakanyas*, if you could?"

She looked at me sharply. "I wouldn't be able to survive in your world. It's impossible. There's no way to feed on human desires without killing the human."

I noticed she hadn't answered me. Having a *vishakanya* mark didn't make me suddenly able to read desires, but Aasha's felt powerful enough. She wanted to know the world that had been denied to her. A vision of Nalini, alone in a dark cell in Bharata, bit into my thoughts. All this time, I had only thought about keeping her alive. What about beyond that? What about what she *wanted* for her life? Before the rebellion, Nalini had always asked me about returning home to her people. I always told her no because I knew she wasn't safe in Skanda's reign. But I wasn't any different from Aasha's sisters who had secured her life but given her no choice. Except now I couldn't even say that I had kept Nalini alive. Shame knotted my heart. When I returned to Bharata, I would make amends.

"You can ask me anything you like?" I said.

Maybe it was a flimsy offering, but it was all I had.

Aasha hesitated for only a moment. "Anything?"

I nodded.

Aasha pressed her brows together. "What does sweet taste like?"

"Uh . . ."

I stumbled. What was sweet to someone who didn't know flavor? I searched for the right words, trying to think of it differently. *See* it differently.

"It's like . . . like waking up and remembering a good dream. Like eating poetry."

Aasha closed her eyes. "That sounds good."

"It is."

"What about flowers?"

"Kinda like wet silk?"

She made a face.

"It's better than it sounds, I promise."

Aasha laughed. She asked me about dances and grass, bee stings and thorns.

She even asked about kissing and was disappointed when I explained that I didn't have nearly as much experience as she thought.

"Why not?" she demanded.

I choked. "What? That's . . . private."

"If there was a beautiful woman or a handsome man who wanted to kiss me, I would not hesitate. Especially if I wanted to kiss them too."

She gave me a very pointed gaze. I looked elsewhere. My gaze fell to the stream beneath us. Aasha had one leg submerged in the running stream, and the other drawn up to her chest. My eyes narrowed. Her position looked casual, but I'd sprained my ankle once in a fight and had to limp off to a pond just to bring down the swelling. Aasha wasn't relaxing. She was trying to heal.

"How did you get hurt?"

She looked to the water. "You may be glad of my assistance, but others are not. They say I should not have helped. Many will seethe in silence. Others will not be as silent."

"That's not an answer, Aasha."

"It is better than an answer," she said. "It is a warning."

I wasn't going to push her, but her words made me skittish. As far as I knew, no one could go into our rooms and steal what we'd won. But that didn't mean no one would try. And if someone had attacked Aasha, what was to stop them from coming after me or Vikram?

"I must go. My sisters will be anxious. I have been gone too long."

I stood up. "Thank you for your help, Aasha."

She smiled. "Thank you, Gauri, for your time and tales."

I trudged back toward the courtyard. In two days, our trials would begin. I was beginning to understand the Tournament of Wishes. Each step we took and every choice we made fashioned the tale that Kubera would keep from us. Whether we would survive to tell it ourselves was not his concern. He wanted to see what we thought, how our very will and ambition shaped the future. I was thoroughly mortal. My touch wasn't toxic. No magical abilities had ever revealed themselves to me no matter how much I wished for them. But I had a vast source of will. And will was an enchantment that no being could touch because I alone could wield it. That was power.

As I walked past the banyan tree, figures stepped out of the shadows. The Nameless.

The first one hissed. "You stole the Serpent King's venom. . . ."

The second one snarled. "That was not yours to take. We made the trade first. We bought his venom and enchantment with the cost of our own names. That venom was meant for us, as it has been for every Tournament."

I crossed my arms. "He has more. Go get your own."

The third looked off to the side. "He only gives one vial every hundred years. Those are his rules. This is the last Tournament. We need it."

The second spoke. "It is not the way of fairness—"

I laughed. "Fairness? Not even the gods promise fairness. This is a competition. We figured out the riddle. We fought. The end."

"Careful, girl," said the second. "You have no knowledge of the game you play. Everyone here has a story to tell. But some of us have more at stake. Some of us have magic in need of replenishing. And some of us will do whatever it takes to ensure that our wishes come to pass."

As one, they reached for the blue ribbons at their throats. Murmuring to themselves, the Nameless melded into the shadows. Silence draped over the courtyard. I felt as if the world had sewn up her secrets, gathering every bit of magic and hiding it elsewhere for tonight. No patrons formed lines outside the *vishakanyas'* tent. No Otherworldly beings partook in any revels or sampled the strange foods of the feast tables. I was alone.

When I got back to the room, I shook the snow out of my hair and stamped my feet. Vikram was slumped against the cushions, a book propped on his knee, a bandage wrapped around one arm and his shirt . . . not on him. An amber glow from several nearby lanterns threw his lean muscles into relief. From the training exercises and ends of battles, I'd seen plenty of men's bodies. There were some who made me wish I'd looked a little longer. And there were others whom my memory was still trying to purge. The Fox Prince didn't look anything like them. His skin was dark gold, unbroken and unscarred. His silky black hair looked wild. He didn't hold himself like a soldier, alert and tense. He was all languid elegance and knowing grins. Bracing his elbows on his knees, he leaned forward and looked at me, thoroughly amused.

"Well?"

I wrenched my gaze from him and stared at the vial instead. "On my way back, those Nameless women found me. They're furious because they want the venom."

"So do half the *yakshas* and *yakshinis*," he said, putting aside the book. "It's a competition. What did they expect?"

"That's what I said."

"What do they want with the venom anyway?" he mused, rubbing his jaw.

He reached once more for his book. Instead of his shirt.

"Did you run out of clothes?"

"No?" He looked down, as if just noticing that he was partially exposed. "I had to bandage some of the cuts I got after running back here."

"But you have your bandages on now."

"Astute as ever, Princess. Am I offending your maidenly senses again? Can I not luxuriate in a single evening without the threat of bodily injury?"

"Could you do it with more clothes?"

"Why does it matter to you?"

I threw up my hands. "What if I manifest *vishakanya* abilities and accidentally touch you and then you die or something?"

He leaned against the cushions. "Try it."

"Why would you openly invite death? You should be *scared* that I'd touch you."

"Quite the opposite." His eyes flashed. We stared at each other. Neither of us broke eye contact.

One . . .

Two . . .

Vikram burst out laughing. "Nothing? Still? One day I'll make you blush."

"Keep trying."

I rolled my eyes, ignoring that second of disorienting weightlessness, and walked over to the window overlooking the courtyard. A light frost coated the grounds of Alaka, and I saw where my footprints had formed divots in the earth. Tomorrow, the enchanted snow would steal away any evidence that I had ever walked there. What awaited me on the other side of Alaka was no different. Time would greedily lick up any step or imprint I tried to press into the world.

But for the first time, I wanted to believe in the things that outlasted us: the stories that came to life in a child's head, the fear of the dark, the hunger to live. Those were the footsteps that not even Time could discover and erase, because they lived far out of reach, in the song of blood coursing through veins and in the quiet threads that made up dreams. I wanted to hold the hope of those tales within me and follow it like a lure all the way back to myself.

29

TO SHARE YOUR SHADOW
GAURI

The morning of Jhulan Purnima dawned pink and cold. The air felt different from the way it did the day we left for the Serpent King's pool. Not crackling with magic, but taut as a drawn bowstring. As if the world hung in a balancing act, equally tugged by fire and ice, fervor and calm.

Vikram paced around restlessly. I rubbed the sleep from my eyes, watching him. Before I could say anything, he walked forward and placed a piece of parchment in my hand.

"He wants to see us."

Kubera. My heart sank.

"I'll get ready."

He nodded and then pointed to some breakfast items on the table beside me. "I went downstairs and got you some food. Everyone is . . . preoccupied today. And they're dressed in finery, so do with that what you will."

I raised an eyebrow. A terse and agitated Vikram in the morning? Had we switched bodies overnight? I looked down at myself. A blanket covered my body and a pillow rested beneath my head. I hadn't fallen asleep with either of those things. I was going to thank him, but he had begun to pace again. He kept patting the drawer with the half-key of immortality and, now, the Serpent King's venom.

"Did you say everyone is dressed in their finery?"

"Yes, but they're—" He hesitated, making a strange wheel with his hands. "—together. Of a kind. They dressed for someone obviously. So it doesn't matter what you wear. Honestly, you might as well go wearing that."

I was wearing a plain cotton spun *salwar kameez*, I had no makeup on and my hair was a ragged braid hanging down my back. Just because I'd been attacked, threatened, poisoned and deprived of an entire week did not mean it had to show on my face. I threw off the blanket, cast what I hoped was my most imperious face at Vikram and stalked off into the baths.

Today might be a holiday, but it was also the day before the second trial. Even if the Tournament had to skulk and sulk from the edges of the day, it was still there. The menace of it was a subtle beast, eyeing us sideways, and my armor needed to match it, so I turned to the stealth and power of beauty. In the harem, Mother Dhina never let me rush through the preparations of the day. Her advice was always the same: "Dress as if you are the mirror of your hopes, and the world will do its best to match you."

I selected the most beautiful dress I could find. The front was a cluster of intricate pearl beading and crystal thread. Around my neck, I had disguised Maya's sapphire pendant with a number of teardrop necklaces and silver chains. My cosmetics were just as elaborate. Pearl dusted on my cheeks. Lips and cheeks reddened. Eyes darkened. I stepped back and admired my talismans. I hadn't allowed myself this luxury in what felt like an eternity. I was fixing the slightest smudge on my cheek when I heard a violent knocking on the door.

"Are you waiting for the next full moon? You realize the Tournament will be done by then, yes?" called Vikram.

"Calm down."

"I am turning ancient."

I stepped outside. He opened his mouth to speak. Saw me. Closed it.

"Are you so ancient you've turned to stone?"

He straightened. "Are you planning to seduce your way into winning?"

"Envy doesn't suit you," I said lightly, stepping past him and taking the lead down the staircases.

He hurried after me. "Not envy. If I could seduce my way into winning, I would. In fact, I considered wearing your outfit, but chest hair lacks a certain feminine charm."

"You have far more obstacles to appearing charming than chest hair."

A number of small candles bloomed in front of us, winding their way through the graceful crowd. A guide from Kubera. No one turned to witness the small flames. But perhaps that was because each person was too distracted. We had to push our way through clasped hands, gripped waists, knots of lovers with lips buried into the hollows of necks and fingers skimming bare arms.

Walking on hot flames and polished knifepoints would have been far less uncomfortable than battling our way through enamored limbs. I knocked aside a couple of errant arms and tried to throw daggers from my eyes when a particularly amorous couple blocked a doorway.

"Honestly," I muttered.

Before long, we stood before the great double doors of a grand hall. Vikram moved to open the door. I steadied his hand. Last night we had talked about what to do with the Serpent King's vial. Assuming we saw Kubera or Kauveri today, did we hide that we had the venom or tell them immediately in the hopes of bargaining a second exit? We decided not to say anything. No one could begin to guess how the minds of the Otherworldly rulers worked. What if they made the second task that much harder once they found out we had the venom?

"Remember not to say anything," I murmured.

"I don't have a death wish."

We pushed open the doors and found a sparsely polished hall of gray stone. Nothing at all like the usual ornate embellishments. Kubera and Kauveri sat on opposite sides of a great swing that fell from the ceiling. Kubera wore a tailored *sherwani* of frosted blue and Kauveri wore a sari made of a frozen river where parchment-thin sheaves of ice floated across her garb. Around them, fragrant garlands of moon-bright lotuses, silk birds and shimmering ribbons arrayed the swing.

"Ah, you are alive!" said Kubera warmly. He patted his stomach.

Kauveri eyed us shrewdly.

Her sister's tearstained face caught hold of my thoughts. Did Kauveri know what we were hiding? What we knew? I looked closely at her. A river goddess had no flaws. At least nothing discernible to the mortal eye. Yet something felt muted about her, the kind of restrained energy of someone who was exhausted.

Beside me, Vikram forced a smile and bowed. "We are full of surprises, Lord Kubera."

Kubera grinned and bounced a little in his throne. "You certainly astounded me. I dearly wish to know where you disappeared to for a week! A new land, perhaps? Or even—"

Kauveri raised her hand. "Today is not for trials."

"But tomorrow is!" laughed Kubera.

"My lord, why did you ask to see us?"

"Curiosity, mostly. But also to remind you that the second trial starts tomorrow. You retrieved half the key to immortality after fighting through poisonous desires. What makes us outlast everything? The eternal is not solely a fight through desire. It is a fight through fear. I have never known fear, but I imagine it is like having no tongue to taste victory and filling your stomach with snow." Kubera shrugged, placed his chin in his hand and looked at us with an expression of pure boredom. "But perhaps the desire to see something through is half the battle."

I did not like how any of that sounded. A fight through fear? What did he think battling through a horde of poisonous courtesans was? A stroll through a tent? Vikram glared at me, and I tried to school my expression into a blank mask.

"Thank you," I said, bowing slightly.

Kauveri leaned forward, her eyes locking on to us. "Enjoy yourselves, dear champions. Alaka is yours to roam, yours to conquer. Sink your teeth into our gold. Lay waste to our palace. Perhaps find someone to share your shadow with by the end of the night because then the world is yours for the taking."

A mist rose out of the ground, washing over the pair. When the mist cleared moments later, they were gone. We were alone. Kauveri's last words rang starkly through my thoughts: This was a day for lovers and last pleasures before fear threatened to steal away everything. I clenched my jaw. The festival prodded at every thought I had tried to push far away from me. I was balancing on an edge: caught by what I shouldn't want and what I wanted anyway.

At the door, I turned around to find Vikram standing far closer to me than I imagined. Tall and lean, sly brown eyes shot through with gold. He *did* something to me.

I know you . . . I saw you.

In Bharata, I guarded myself. Weakness was a privilege. It divided you, snipped out your secrets and gave every sliver of power over you. I didn't have parts to spare. Bharata called me their Jewel, and maybe I was like one. Not sparkling or precious. But a cold thing wearing a hundred faces. Like facets on a gem. One for every person.

But Vikram had seen through every facet, holding me against the light as if I truly were translucent, and instead of making me feel as if I had been looked through and found wanting, I felt . . . seen. My eyes dropped to his hand. Even through the fugue of that poisonous sleep, I remembered his touch. Reverent and dream-soft. I remembered how he looked at me when I woke up, the way you behold the sacred—not with your eyes demure and half lidded, but with wide-open awe, gratitude and even a touch of greed because one sight will never be enough.

It was unburdening and freeing. And distracting. I only had to think of Arjun's betrayal and Nalini's imprisonment to remind myself why I was here. And why I wasn't.

"I plan on searching through Alaka's gardens and rooms," I said. "Maybe I'll find something about how to use the half-key that we have."

"I'll do the same," he said, folding his arms across his chest.

"I'd prefer to search alone."

His expression turned a shade colder. "I never said anything about wanting to join you."

Oh, I thought, feeling irrationally stung.

"In the evening, perhaps we can report back on what we've found. Unless, of course, you're otherwise occupied with the festivities."

Vikram's eyes narrowed. "The same goes for you. If I don't see you, I'll assume you are otherwise . . . occupied."

"Good."

"Good."

"Enjoy your night."

He smirked. "I will."

I spent the rest of the afternoon not analyzing what "I will" meant while I walked through Alaka's palace. If there was a secret arena or space where the next trial would take place, I had no luck finding it. Instead, everywhere I looked, love and companionship stared back at me. Everything had softened. A fine layer of frost iced the banyan tree. Frozen rain droplets clung to its limbs, diamond-bright and glistening. Tiny swings and wind chimes hung from its branches, so that the world was a thing of ice and music. A ghostly tent drifted across the grounds, shedding strange objects—an hourglass filled with pearls that drifted backward, crystal phials that danced over themselves and spilled music, miniature swans the size of thumbnails and horses made of enchanted rose petals that galloped through the trees.

I didn't resent the lovers all around me, but it was impossible to ignore that chasm opening inside me. I felt as if I were standing over it, my toes moments from the edge. Would it break or strengthen me to fall? In Bharata, there was no temptation to fall. Now I felt that quiet panic of knowing something was within reach and not knowing whether to snatch it or let it go.

In uselessly circling Alaka's grounds, I found myself staring at the *vishakanyas'* tent. No patrons stood in line. No guards flanked the entrance. And not a single plume of smoke rose out of the grand peacock tent. A small branch snapped behind me, followed by gentle footsteps that I instantly recognized.

"Here to join our ranks?"

Aasha stepped out of the trees carrying a bundle of twigs full of flowering branches.

"Maybe in my next life," I said. "What are you doing?"

"Experimenting," she said. "I realized the forest outside our tent was also immune to our touch, so I've been exploring. Look!" She dropped the branches and plucked a blossom off one of the ends. She pressed the blossom to her cheek and sighed. "It feels . . . better than silk. I wish this wasn't the last Tournament. I'll never have this chance again. What are you doing?"

"Trying to find some clues to the next trial."

She shot me a knowing gaze, and I knew she was sniffing out whatever desires I chose not to utter. I watched as she lifted a blossom from her cheek, eyeing it with narrowed eyes.

"Aasha, I would not—"

She stuffed the flower in her mouth. Her eyes widened. She spit it out, groaning. I couldn't help but start laughing, which made her laugh, and in no time we were doubled over in laughing fits.

She sighed. "Some experiments are, I admit, better than others."

"Why is no one lining up at the tent today?"

"Today is for true things," said Aasha, stroking the petals. "Not imitations. It is not so bad to have a break from patrons, but it does mean that the Tournament of Wishes is almost over. After Jhulan Purnima, the only thing left to celebrate is the Parade of Fables and then . . . and then there is nothing in my future but poison."

A pang of pity went through me. Aasha sighed.

"But it is worth it. I have done something I dreamed of."

I almost wished Aasha could come back to the human world, just to experience what she was and was not missing. I couldn't help but admire someone who wanted for nothing, but pursued knowledge out of curiosity and for the sheer love of learning. She was a lot like Nalini in that way, always moving and never quite satisfied. And just like Nalini, she was also trapped. The smile fell from my face.

"What did you say was after Jhulan Purnima?"

"The Parade of Fables," said Aasha. "It is when the Lord of Treasures showcases all the stories that have grown in his halls."

The story birds, I thought. Kubera loved his tales. He said it was because stories were the greatest treasure, but did he just want to collect them or was there something more?

"I wish to see it someday," said Aasha quietly. "But *vishakanyas* are never allowed inside the palace."

"Maybe one day you will?"

"Maybe," she allowed.

By now, evening touched the sky. Aasha left to be with her sisters and I was no closer to finding any hint for the next trial. Around me, song and dance filled the courtyard. I swept my eyes over Alaka's landscape. I kept expecting the Nameless to pour out of the shadows, but they had kept to themselves. With nowhere left to search in the courtyards, I headed for the magical orchards.

I'd never gone this deep into the orchards before. Everything was still. Quiet. The trees stood tall and solemn, with no wood for their bark, but ribbons of mirror all silver and tarnished. When I stepped back, the grove looked like the rib cage of some forgotten monster. Nothing left of its terror, but its winter bones and mirror teeth. No reflection shone in the mirror bark. Instead, the trees became something of a lens. They weren't transparent, but I could see *through* them to something hazy in the distance: pieces of a pewter sky through a lattice of trees. Energy hummed around the mirror trees, and I wondered whether they functioned like the Serpent King's portal pool. A bridge from one place to another.

Icy branches snapped behind me. *Vikram.* My whole body tensed and lightened at once. I . . . missed him. If this was the only day left, would I squander it on an austere and frigid existence? Or would I snatch it for what it was and figure out what it might become later?

"No beautiful woman should be alone on Jhulan Purnima," said someone softly.

My heart dropped. Not Vikram. I came face-to-face with a beautiful *yaksha.* He was dark and broad-shouldered. Amber sap ran through his hair and his eyes were a shifting and hypnotizing color of green and black.

"Who are you?"

He laughed. "The Guardian of the Orchards, both abandoned and tended. The trees told me they heard you. They like you, you know. You remind them of another. Why don't you let me escort you to the final rites of the evening? The festival is a celebration of so many things," he said in a voice like dark silk. "Things we do in the dark with only the night as witness. Things that if the day only knew would make the sky blush crimson at the sight."

"No. I was just leaving."

The *yaksha* appeared at my side in an instant.

"Tell me, beauty, are you the human who divested the Serpent King of his venom?"

He caught me around the arm. My hands immediately went to my dagger.

"Get your hand off of me."

"No reason to become hostile, beauty," laughed the *yaksha*. "I think we could make a trade. I want that venom. You can have whatever you like from me. I can be very generous."

He stroked my cheek. I spat in his face.

"No," I said sweetly, in case the spit dripping down his cheek was too subtle.

"I don't like being told no," said the *yaksha*.

"I don't like being touched without permission."

I spun out of his grasp. Roots spilled out from the *yaksha's* tunic, anchoring him to the ground. He laughed. The sound snapped my patience. I lunged, spinning the knives from the concealed belt at my hip, cutting at the roots tethering him in place. He snarled and fell back. Lust dampened his eyes and my whole body shuddered in disgust. I held my ground, not breaking eye contact.

Come closer. I dare you.

He dared.

I reached up to the branches sweeping overhead, pulled a handful back before letting go the moment he rushed toward me. He howled, clawing at his face. I moved forward, tackling him to the ground. I rolled him onto his back, kicking apart his knees and plunging my knife moments away from a place that would instantly kill his lust. For good.

"I didn't miss," I said. "Let me go, or risk tempting my aim."

I turned to go when I heard him growl.

"My turn," he hissed.

He threw his hands into the air, summoning a rustling cloak of moths. The ground disappeared. Everywhere I looked, moths with muted silver wings stole my vision. I crawled; panic tightened my skin.

His laugh filled my ears, and gripped my thoughts. I was out of my head. Out of my abilities. I couldn't fight his magic with strength.

"The trees want you, Princess," said his voice from everywhere. "You can grow a beautiful tree from that heart of yours. It's been so long for them. Not since Queen Tara ripped out a heart and watered it with her tears and sheltered it with her beloved's bones. I can teach you to live forever. I can teach you how to turn your vengeance into a fruit. I can teach you what it means to be invincible. All you have to do is give me the venom."

Moth wings whipped my face and tangled my hair. Before Alaka, I would have been tempted. Invincibility was all I had wanted when Ujijain had kept me in that cell month after month. But I'd tasted the fruit of vengeance. And it was narrow and sour. Not a story at all, but an ending. I deserved more.

"Never," I hissed.

The cloak of moths broke. Grabbing my dagger, I jumped to my feet and faced the *yaksha*. His eyes narrowed.

"You tire me," he said. "I will have what I want."

He glanced once at my dagger and it turned from metal to wood. I barely had a toy to protect myself from him. I steadied my breath, focusing on his weaknesses. The roots. Aim for them. Kick, rend, sever them with my hands and teeth if I had to. I was lunging, hands outstretched, when something bright and golden sailed through the air.

The orchard guardian jumped back just in time to avoid it. I thought the golden ball would splatter against the tree, but instead it sailed straight through the mirror bark. In the distance, I heard voices in a different forest. Even the *yaksha* frowned. The voices seemed to be coming from inside the tree. The small hairs at the back of my neck prickled. The people sounded too familiar.

They sounded just like me and Vikram.

But I didn't have time to process the eerie voices. Someone was crashing through the trees. I squinted into the dense net of branches. Whatever it was, it sounded like a deranged bull. I looked closer.

Not a deranged bull.

Not at all.

30

UNFASTENED WORLD

VIKRAM

Vikram was no stranger to finding weaknesses. It had been part of his talent as the Fox Prince of Ujijain. He survived by finding the threads that pulled people together, and stringing out their secrets, finding the holes . . . and pressing.

On one of his last visits home, he had scheduled a meeting with a high-ranking adviser in hopes of assisting on a city-planning project.

"And why would I allow you to participate in such a meeting, Your Highness?" sneered the adviser. "It is unnecessary for you to attend. We will handle those engagements when you sit upon the throne. There are better ways to spend your hours."

Vikram had walked in front of the adviser and tapped his fingers together.

"Perhaps I'll be inspired by the way you spend your hours," he had said. "Maybe I'll go to the dice tables. Your winnings, I've noticed, are controlled by just how little or how much you pay attention to the city representative's interests."

"How do you know that?" asked the adviser, paling.

"As it turns out, not everyone knows that I am merely to 'sit' upon the throne of Ujijain."

He let this information linger just to watch the adviser sweat.

"You have far too much time on your hands, Prince Vikramaditya."

"So change that," said Vikram. "Include me in the committees. Spend my time, and I may turn a blind eye on yours."

He was involved in seven committees that season.

But spending much of his time finding weaknesses meant that he could not ignore his own.

Jhulan Purnima threatened to unfasten him. Even the air turned intoxicating and sweet. It almost, thought Vikram, smelled like her. He had noticed that the other day, when he leaned down to murmur a broken song in her ear and plead with her to live. She had that sharp green fragrance that belonged to unopened flower blooms. Sun-warmed beauty on the cusp of bursting.

He hadn't even realized his weakness until that night, when those heatless flames licked their way through her bloodstream. What if she didn't live? At first, his mind refused to entertain the possibility of her death. But then he had carried her. He had held her limp, poisoned body against his chest, and felt her life unspooling. And he knew that the Tournament of Wishes had stopped being a game.

Since that night, he needed to tell her . . . something. But what? "Please don't die" sounded foolish. "You smell nice" sounded worse. He wasn't even sure what the right words were, but they sat on his tongue and made it impossible to speak around them. Before Alaka, he would have been content keeping whatever thorny not-feelings had reared up inside him. But Death commanded urgency. Death tore the skin off dreams and showed the bones underneath. And Vikram saw the bones now. When he closed his eyes, he saw Gauri's long-lashed gaze closing. And staying closed. He saw his own body crumpled by the shores of a pool not unlike the Serpent King's portal, turning to a skeleton for some ignorant prince to ponder or ignore.

Irritated, Vikram stalked through the revels and swiped a jeweled goblet from one of the floating crystal trays. He swirled the goblet, watching as the pale pink drink deepened from rose to garnet to winter black. The same shade as her eyes. He spilled the drink onto the ground.

Vikram stood far from the revels now, at the edge of the orchards. A low laugh resonated through the silent trees. It wasn't a laugh of camaraderie or love. It was a laugh of control.

Chasing the sound, he stepped into an orchard full of needle-thin bone white trees. Here, the snow and ice faded into soft ash. The grove possessed the undisturbed quality of cremation grounds. Grief dented the air, turning it so heavy and thick that he thought he could cut through it. His breath feathered into cold plumes as he crept forward, mindful of the strange trees.

Through a net of branches, he saw Gauri crawling along the orchard floor. Some distance before her stood a *yaksha* with amber hair. He held himself strangely, his legs ankle-deep in the ground, his face harsh and twisted. Vikram froze, mesmerized by the black blooming across the *yaksha*'s face, oil and fungus, roots dripping and dangling from nose and chin.

Something snapped. A howl from the *yaksha*. Gauri rising victorious. It wasn't until he saw that her hand gripped a wooden dagger that panic grabbed his heart in a fist. If she had her true dagger, she might turn them on him for daring to interrupt her victory. But this was not her usual flesh-and-blood opponent. Vikram glanced down and cursed. In Ujijain, he'd never had reason to carry weapons and so he never developed the habit. He was muscular, but that didn't matter in the face of magic.

However, he could run.

He could run *very* fast.

Time bore down on him. The *yaksha* stepped closer to Gauri. Running fast wouldn't make a difference if he couldn't distract the *yaksha*. He needed something. Something that would purchase a moment's distraction. Vikram bent down, sifting through the ash for a rock or a stick, and his hands hit the bark of the bone white tree. The tree quaked. With a lush sigh, the bark unfolded, splitting down the middle to reveal a perfectly golden apple at the center. Vikram didn't think twice. He reached in, grabbed the fruit, aimed it straight at the *yaksha* and threw. The fruit sailed through the air, burnished golden rind shining in the dim evening light. His aim, for once, was true. But the *yaksha* must have detected it. He stepped back, and the apple sailed through the bark as if the tree were made of water.

Not exactly what he expected, but he'd learned to accept stranger things. He didn't waste a moment. Vikram charged forward. Wind tore at his jacket. The ground blurred. Pale light spangled the mirror trees, but the light was terse and distant, like lightning pulsing behind a veil of clouds. Whatever roots had sewed the *yaksha* to the ground lifted in his desperation to move. But Vikram was faster. He slammed into him. The *yaksha* tipped sideways, arms flung back. Quartz-bright cobwebs spun out from his fingers, seeking purchase. Neck arched and eyes wide, the *yaksha* slipped sideways, crumpling to the ground. Vikram braced himself for a fall, but Gauri grabbed the collar of his jacket and righted him. He panted, his heart still thundering in his chest as the *yaksha* pushed himself onto his elbows and glared.

"Take her and be damned," he spat.

Gauri spun her wooden dagger between her fingers before taking aim at the *yaksha*. Vikram stepped out of her way.

"Take *this* and be damned," she said, releasing it. The dagger found its mark and promptly *thwacked* the *yaksha* on the head. He disappeared on the spot.

Gauri faced him. Her hair had come undone around her face. Somehow her eyes looked even blacker than normal, as if they'd captured the night sky in their gaze. He felt out of breath. But not from his sprint. Fire burned just beneath his skin. He cursed. What happened to always having a way with words? Words turned to ash in his mouth.

"Did you find anything useful—" he had started to say when she spoke over him:

"I was thinking about Kubera's warning. About desire. And how it's dangerous."

He stopped short.

"Yes," he said slowly. "It is." And then because he had to, because every splinter of him screamed that this moment could grow wings if his soul steered him true, he said, "To me, there is nothing more dangerous in this palace than you."

Now she looked at him. She didn't soften. Or smile. If anything, she had become a little of the ground on which they stood. Cold and lovely. But wonder poured out of her eyes. Wonder and something like . . . relief. And if he thought there was fire under his skin earlier, it was nothing compared to now. Now he had swallowed the sun. Now the world had stopped lurching forward and begun an impossible dance.

"I thought you were going to stay away from me," she said.

He looked at her, this princess who seemed so dangerously sharp that he might cut himself just brushing against her shadow.

"I don't know how."

He waited. He thought he could trace the space between them. It was delicate. Too delicate. A thing of silk and snow and filigreed gold. And nothing was real except her, and the exquisite brightness of her eyes, and the corner of her lips sweeping into a smile.

"Then don't."

31

A MEAL OF DESIRE

GAURI

Vikram's fingers laced through mine, and my skin flared at the contact. Within moments, we were out of the orchards. In the courtyard, the revels gathered us into the music. Enchantment abraded the dusk until there was only magic left to draw into our lungs. Not air. The music moved us to dance, and sent us spinning around one another as if our gazes were hooks and hinges, and our very dreams hung off of them. When the music relinquished us, we fell against one another. His gaze turned into a question, and mine formed an answer. Our shadows splayed onto the ground before us, guiding us through the revels and the lengthening dark, up the staircase and straight to our room.

I'd like to think I have a number of virtues. But patience has never been one of them. The moment the door closed, I caught his lips against mine. Swift and urgent. Our hands moved hungrily across each other. His fingers dug into my waist, pulling my hips to his.

At once, time was too fast and too slow and distance felt like an illusion we were trying to shatter. I pushed him against the door, tearing off his jacket. Vikram stood there, a tilt to his head as he let himself be appraised. The corded lines of his muscles caught the light, and my eyes roved from his broad shoulders down the lean, carved plane of his torso. I kissed him again. Slowly. As if the trial of tomorrow were an eternity away. We traded heartbeats until we kissed to one cadence, and I didn't know where we stopped and started. This was the reminder I needed, the hope that made me reject the *yaksha's* offer even as the memory of demon fruit sang through my veins. I didn't want to cut out my heart. I wanted to give it. Freely and without feeling as if it would be turned into a weapon against me. I wanted freedom to thaw me, to let it break the walls Skanda's rule had forced me to build. I wanted the privilege of weakness.

Vikram cupped the back of my neck, deepening our kiss. And I found . . . wonder. A new enchantment. This magic wasn't a flashy, many-splendored illusion. It was the kind of wonder discovered in the space between heartbeats and realized in the silk of fingers threading through hair. It was a magic coaxed and found, a tiny world no one could reach but us, and I wanted to revel in it for as long as I could. I kissed him on his cheeks, his lips, the underside of his chin. When I nipped at his chin, he groaned and I kissed that away too.

"Gauri," he said, his voice hoarse and wanting.

It was my name on his lips that stopped me. He spoke my name like a plea or a prayer, something to end or begin a life. Maybe he sensed my hesitation, because he lifted my hand to his lips, kissing my knuckles and the inside of my wrist. Whatever heat had twisted through my veins tightened to a knot in my belly.

If we lived through tomorrow . . . if we won the Tournament . . .

what did this mean? If I took away everything we were, it looked like a girl and a boy who had found something and wanted to see what it would grow into with more time. But I couldn't take away who I was or who he was. He was the Prince of Ujijain. One day, he would be the Emperor. And if we survived, those same hands wrapped tightly around my body would one day wield a great deal of power. Maybe they'd one day want power over me.

I stepped back. Vikram dropped his hands.

"Is something wrong?"

Yes. This. Us.

"No. I just . . . I need a moment," I said tightly.

I moved away from him and he caught my wrist.

"I'll wait for you here," he said softly. He looked at me intently. It was too dark to see the lines of gold threaded through his eyes, but I felt that I could see them anyway.

"I'll wait as long as I have to."

I leaned forward and kissed him. "I won't make you wait long."

"Have I inspired your rare and elusive mercy?"

"Something like that."

I ran into the baths, leaving him in the shadows. Bracing my hands on the basin, I stared at my reflection and sank my teeth into my cheeks as if looking a little more ferocious could somehow decide this strange battle warring inside me. I never dared to hope for someone who challenged and respected me, knew me at my worst and still coaxed out my best. And yet I had found that in the unlikeliest of places and most inconvenient of people. Wasn't that enough to fight for? Could I live with knowing that I'd left him standing in the shadows . . . waiting for me?

I couldn't. And that was all the answer I needed.

I splashed water onto my face, and smoothed down my hair. My heart thudded in my chest. I felt impatient and wary. Why hadn't I listened more closely to the harem wives' conversation? I'd always voluntarily lost my hearing, preferring to hide behind my hair. Blood and gore? I wouldn't blink. But intimacy? Baring yourself to someone else? Nothing horrified me more.

Outside, the night had begun to retreat. The stars were little more than muted jewels in the sky. I let a cautious wave of happiness run through me. And then I stepped outside.

But Vikram wasn't standing by the door where I had run off. And the bed wasn't disturbed. I frowned, looking toward the cushions and small seating area . . . but he wasn't there either. Cold licked up my spine as I moved closer to the door. Something wet and dark glistened on the floor. There, scrawled in a shaking hand, was a message in blood:

I could make a meal of this desire.
Couldn't you?

The second trial had begun.

32

A BELLYFUL OF SNOW

VIKRAM

The world ended not with a break, but in a blink.

One moment, her body had been a column of fire against his. The next, she had disappeared into the baths. He'd slumped against the door, breathless. His gaze, not knowing where to travel, had ventured to the sky beyond the window, where wispy clouds carried the scarlet stain of dawn. The sight had jolted him. That blink of awareness—*it's a new day*—flashed in his head. One blink later, and an empty, snowing hall filled his sight. His knees hit frozen dirt. Goose bumps pebbled his skin. He blinked. Breath knotted in his chest, leaving him gasping as his mind feverishly gathered scraps of observation—a kiss at the hollow of his throat, a shard of sky peeled back to reveal a new day. Snow in his eyes. A cold fire burning down to a new truth:

The second trial had started.

Cruel and swift.

His heart felt as if it was left dangling. He paused, pushing his fury out of the way. If he wanted to return to Gauri—and he *wanted*—he needed to focus. Vikram forced himself to a stand, racking his brains for Kubera's warning.

It is a fight through fear . . .

. . . it is like having no tongue to taste victory and filling your stomach with snow . . .

Above him, a net of cobwebs formed the sky. Silken threads laced together, spangled with frozen rain like diamonds. It would have been beautiful, but he could feel the cold down to the root of his teeth. The light from those suspended droplets was as harsh as a knifepoint, and the air tasted rusty and dry. Like blood and dust.

He took one step forward. Ice cracked beneath his feet. He shivered. Gauri had taken off his jacket, a thought that would have warmed him if not for the frost climbing over his shoulder. No sandals covered his feet. The frost burned. He took another step. A sound, like a slide of rocks, lit up the world. He looked up to see something encased in glass spinning before him. It was large, as tall and wide as him, and it was shaped like a chrysalis. Vikram cursed. He had no weapons. How could he win against fear if he couldn't *fight* it?

The chrysalis spun around to face him. It cracked down the middle, splitting with a clammy unclasping sound. There, standing in all his splendor, was his father, the Emperor Pururavas. Puru smiled, his face crinkling with warmth. Vikram stepped back, away from the illusion of his father.

"Son, you've done so well," said his father. "Merely speak and let me know that you want the throne and it is yours."

His father held out his hands and a miniature Council of Ujjijain nestled in his palms, staring up at Vikram expectantly.

Vikram opened his mouth, but not a single sound rose out of his throat. He was mute. He clawed at his skin, trying to scream. Trying to speak. Nothing but air whistled from his teeth.

"What's this?" asked his father, tilting his head. "Your tongue is your greatest weapon, Fox Prince. It is the thing you've shaped your life with. Will you not speak and claim your throne?"

Vikram looked up, shocked. His greatest fear taking shape in front of him—

He had no voice. No power.

Puru's face disappeared, replaced with the pet leopard's head. Blood flecked her muzzle. Flat animal eyes stared down at Vikram, full of taunting.

"Well," said the leopard with his father's voice. "You were always a weak thing. Now you can't speak. In that case—"

It lunged, tearing free of the glass confines.

Vikram ran.

Another fear sprang from the sky. Gauri. He skidded to a halt, heart wild with hope. But then he saw the ghostly shimmer of her skin. Another illusion. Vikram should have known. After his years spent manipulating the council, no two fears bore the same face. This was a fight they'd endure separately.

"It was so easy to fool you," she laughed. "I wanted a wish and now I have your heart and your empire. I wonder what it will be like to break both. Or maybe I'll show you some of that elusive mercy after all and cut you down where you stand. Speak, dear prince. Go ahead. Or I'll show you my famous mercy."

He tried. Over and over, he tried. But the words escaped him.

Gauri raised a sword high above her head. Vikram slipped where he stood, just barely avoiding the killing blade of his phantasm fear. He clambered to another stand, feeling the press of bodies all around him.

His mother hung in the air, spinning and sightless. A collar of frost circled her broken neck.

"I died for you," she said. "But you knew that, didn't you?"

He ducked, narrowly avoiding her swinging body. He took one step forward and her body dropped out of the air, this time shattering on the icy ground.

The body turned over, torn blue lips murmuring, "I died for you. And look at what you've become—"

He ran, icy wind tearing at his skin. His mother's body rose up, bent and twisting as she screamed:

"—I died for you and you became nothing but a human pet supping at the table of your betters, eager for scraps and trying to rut with an enemy princess who'd no sooner smile at you than she would snap your heart between her teeth." She lurched after him. "I didn't die for this. I want my life back. Speak, you dog. Show me my death was worth something or I'll take your life to get mine back."

Vikram ran.

His fears followed.

They walked with light steps, heavy gaits, swift and sly, pouring out of the shadows and unwinding from the cobwebs above him. They brushed his arm, tickled his throat, laughed at his bewilderment and pulled the ground beneath him. Vikram ran until he'd reached the end of the hall. His eyes scanned the end frantically. Looking for a door, a hole. Something. *Anything.*

He turned around to see the pupils and sages of the ashram, Gauri, his mother, his father, the council, Kubera, even himself, lowering their brows and staring down at him. Their eyes burned. Their mouths worked furiously. There was no escape from them. They took a step forward. Shadows spilled over the ground, reaching over him. A wall of inescapable fear hemmed him on all sides. This was it. He wanted to laugh. All this time, he had hoped that he was meant for more. He had fiercely *believed* it. And now he was staring at the truth, and the truth bore scimitars in its grin and flashed its eyes hungrily. Space squeezed out of the shadows. Vikram quieted his mind, concentrating. There was no direction to move except one:

Forward.

Through them.

He stood up. In his own mind, he stepped sideways. Shifting his thoughts. His fears were his own, weren't they? He'd spun them out from himself. He'd forged them from every hurt and fury. Fear was a reminder that even the insubstantial could kill. But insubstantial meant it had no shape. It couldn't be conquered or tamed or avoided. Only moved through, with force and will. Vikram crouched, his fingers splayed on the ground, his breath forming icicles in the air.

His fears bore down. Sharp. Hungry. He grinned.

I made you.

I own you.

He repeated the words like a mantra, until he found the strength to stand . . .

And run.

33

A FEAST OF FEAR

GAURI

P anic opened up like an ocean beneath me, but I wouldn't step over the edge. I wouldn't drown. This was magic. I should have known that when it was most beautiful, it was only silencing its blade. What I didn't know was that Kubera would have us fight the second trial without each other.

I focused on the dark between each of my racing heartbeats, finding that elusive calm and not letting go. This was war. Treat it as such.

The second trial was for the second half of the key of immortality. I didn't know whether the ruby was its own weapon, but I ran to the drawers, pulling it out anyway. Next, I circled the message on the floor. Vikram was no warrior, but he was far from weak. He should have been able to fight back. Or scream.

The fact that he'd done neither sat inside me like a cold stone.

I pushed open the door, half hoping for and half dreading a footprint or spot of blood. I found nothing. Downstairs, everything was still.

Nothing but silence and stone met my eye. I wanted to scream. I wanted to run into that demon grove, hack a fruit out of its tree and tear up the foundations of Alaka if that's what it would take to find Vikram.

I breathed deeply, stilling my heart. If I approached this like a heartsick fool, I would fail. Emotions could be sylphs lulling you to smash your head on the rocks. I closed my heart to every emotion except one: rage. Rage spiraled inside me, honing my thoughts. I bit down on my cheeks just as dawn sneered through the cut windows studding Alaka's halls. The air felt as sharp as a rebuke that taunted one thing over and over: *Time to play.*

I patted the daggers at my side.

Ready when you are.

A scraping, scuffling sound came from one of the chambers on the other side of the hall. I followed the sound, keeping close to the walls. We had explored this part of Alaka the other day and found nothing but a glass garden and a hall of stories. But Alaka was a riddle of whim and horror. It could do whatever it pleased.

A dim light shone at the end of the hall, casting waxen brightness over three glass doors. Light had never seemed threatening until now. This light didn't illuminate the other side, but it spared just enough glow to show me what covered the floor: blood.

In the middle of war, the mind and body either fused or fractured. I'd seen men fracture right before my eyes as some final horror—sometimes a delicate thing, like a wedding bangle trampled in waste, or sometimes a terrible thing, like a body at the mercy of carrion birds—broke them. I survived by forcing every emotion so far down that there were days afterward where I had to dig my nails into my palm and draw blood just to know I was there. In war, I knew only movement and stillness. Life and death.

As I walked, blood soaked my ankles, thick and warm. Rust and salt studded the air. Clenching my jaw, I walked forward. The blood didn't give like water. It clung. Every emotion that I had shoved deep inside me bubbled furiously to the surface. I closed my eyes, imagining the victory that I had to believe was waiting for me at the end of the hall.

One step.

When I closed my eyes, I didn't just see the throne of Bharata waiting for me or Nalini standing tall and free. I saw fingers tangled in my hair and a mouth made for grinning lowered to my skin.

Another step.

I felt a light within me that dimmed the world in comparison. That feeling pushed me forward—the hope for more, the promise of something better. Not just the quest for power, but the quest for hope.

I pressed my nose to the glass doors, trying to decipher the shapes behind them. In the middle of each door was a hollow where the ruby key would fit inside perfectly.

In the first: a table surrounded by a haze of figures. I pushed myself closer to the glass, but it was impossible to tell whether the figures at the table were even people.

In the second: a pool of murky water. I breathed in sharply. Floating across the surface, arms flung out and face down, was the figure of a man the same size and shape as Vikram.

In the third: my bedroom in Bharata. I could even smell the musk of my favorite perfume, sandalwood and sweet almond.

Instinct guided me to the second door and to the figure that had to be Vikram, but I hesitated. Instinct had been no friend of mine once magic entered my life. I thought of Vikram in the Crossroads, pleading with me to have a little more faith, to throw out the human reaction.

The blood-scrawled words drifted to me tauntingly: *I could make a meal of this desire. Couldn't you?*

Meal. I turned to the first door, with the table. One part of me screamed that it felt too easy. And the other part screamed: *Who cares?* I stood there, caught between my past self and my present. I wanted to be strong, but showing strength wasn't always about physical valor or even cunning. True strength sometimes demanded unstitching everything you knew. I unstitched myself. I turned myself blind to what I expected, and what I would have done had I never met Vikram or been forced to reckon with magic. I turned my back on the image of him floating facedown in the pool, ignoring how cowardice chased me.

I placed the ruby key into the door showing the dining table, and held my breath as the door absorbed the key and swung open. I stepped inside. The door swung shut behind me, plunging me into a darkness so thick I could feel it pressing against me. Had I chosen right?

Silently, I removed my daggers. Nothing charged at me. Nothing moved. In front of me, twelve starved and naked bodies hunched over a dining table. Each being hid its head beneath a piece of red cloth. The cloths were identical in color: crimson. Crimson as bloodlust in someone's soul, lustrous and visceral. This shade of red did not exist in the human world.

I took a step closer, but none of the diners moved. Their heads were bent over the table, hands flat against their thighs. They gave away nothing. Not even a tremor. No food appeared on the silver table, and yet I could hear and smell a feast.

A thirteenth diner appeared at the end of the table. He wore no silk to obscure his face. My heart dropped.

"Vikram?" I called softly.

But he didn't answer. He was staring straight ahead. A lace of frost spidered over his shoulder, as if he were freezing before my eyes. His chest didn't move. Was he even breathing?

I stepped forward, but a wall of air forced me back. My heart began to pound. Another blood-scrawled message seeped out of the ground like a wound:

We can eat first.

Or you can.

The message distorted and pooled across the floor. My mind started racing. Eat first? I stepped back out of the reach of the blood. Whatever invisible fence had blocked me from getting to Vikram shimmered into visibility: a thick wall of red. Nausea gripped my stomach. The wall repulsed me to the core. It looked . . . soft. The way rot corrupts a body and turns it into a stew of entrails. Or the way fruit left out too long puckers and collapses in upon itself. The blood on the floor reached my skin. I *felt* it. Not the texture, but the soul of it.

A vision flashed behind my eyes: bees buzzing near my ear. I swatted at it. I hated bees. I'd been stung once when I was seven and used to have nightmares of a whole hive chasing me deep into the forest where I'd never be able to find my way home. I jumped, moving away from the reach of blood. It seeped, finding my skin once more. This time I felt that I was standing over a tall cliff. A gray sea churned hungrily below me. Once more, I moved away from the blood.

I raised my dagger and plunged it into that soft wall. The wall burst, sending wet chunks of red all over me. I tried to reach through the gap and claw my way out, but the hole closed immediately. I felt a wet piece of the wall on my mouth. Disgusted, I dragged my hand across my face, but the nausea was so overwhelming, I gagged and some of that wall found its way past my teeth. The taste was bitter and metallic. I was clutching my stomach when I noticed something . . . a bit of the wall opened. And stayed open.

We can eat first.
Or you can.

Once more, the blood crept to my skin. I let it. This time I was prepared for the wave of fear that rushed over me . . . deeper this time. I saw myself riding triumphantly back to Bharata only to discover Nalini's funeral ceremony just past the gates. I opened my eyes, finally understanding the trial.

To get to the other side, I had to eat my fears.

Fear was no stranger to me. All my life, fear had been the hand on my back, steering me. Fear had cushioned my mind in wartime, sharpening my senses and keeping me a breath away from death. I narrowed my eyes, grabbing a fistful of the wall. It gave way with a sickening, unclasping sound. I closed my eyes. Chewed. Swallowed.

I wandered through the forest and found Maya's body. All those stories I had imagined for her, endings dancing out of sight where she wore a crown of stars and forgot how to grieve, shattered.

Another bite.

I fell in love with Vikram only to discover that love was a far better control than fear. His love and control would break me until I could not recognize myself.

The hole in the wall widened. Nearly wide enough to step through. My hands shook.

While I'd been eating fear, it had tasted me too. I felt like a bone licked clean. My memory lost focus. . . . Why was I raising my hand to this wall of flesh? What was so important on the other side? I didn't want to fight anymore. I wanted to curl around the cold, close my eyes. Ice knitted over my body. The blood pooled around me. Inescapable. Wave after wave of tiny fears assaulted me: spiders in my throat, holes opening up in the ground, doors that locked me inside where no one would hear me scream.

A final bite.

I bit down. Hard.

I would die here. And all of this—the magic and adventure, the terror and the hope—would be for nothing. I would be forgotten. My name would turn to ash in people's mouths. My efforts would not scratch a line into history. I would die here, not even remembering what I was chasing after anymore.

The wall opened.

I used to think fear either numbed or nudged. Now I knew fear did neither. Fear was a key that fit every person's hollow spaces—those things that kept us cold at night and that place where we retreated when no one was looking—and all it could do was unlock what was already there. Fear unlocked flames within me. I stepped through the wall and fear fell from my skin. One by one, the diners' heads were all facing me. Had they been facing my way before? Or somewhere else? I couldn't remember.

At the other side of the table, Vikram blinked. But still he said nothing. No warning sparked his eyes. No expression passed over his face. Behind him, a ruby glistened in the dim light. The final half of the key. If I went around the table, one of the six diners might reach out. Or all six. Jumping straight across was the least distance and maybe Vikram would snap out of whatever frozen enchantment had gripped him and be able to fight.

I had swung my legs onto the table, preparing to jump, when Vi-kram's head jolted back. His eyes widened in horror:

"No!"

The table shuddered. The diners woke. Slowly, the diners lifted their pale hands. The silk dropped from their faces. Their expressions turned empty and devouring. A low, guttural moan escaped their throats. I froze. They were all that was left when fear devoured a person, the stringy indigestible remains of bitterness and cravings.

At once, the table lengthened, stretching out like an arena. The diners clambered forward, pushing themselves onto the table on their ragged elbows. I ran, dodging the swipe of an emaciated hand. Vikram stood up in his chair, his lips pale and his eyes ringed white with terror. The ruby behind him dimmed and flared.

"Behind you!" I screamed. "Get the ruby!"

He ignored it. One of the diners lurched onto the table-turned-arena. It stood, tall and dark, dripping hunger. It loped toward me, its move-ments disjointed and horrific. It didn't run. It didn't have to. If it caught up to us, there would be no escape. The other eleven joined it.

Vikram ran to help me, and I tossed him one of the daggers. The diners encircled us. A mass of loping, fragmented bodies. They sniffed the air with noseless faces, the slashes of their mouths flung wide and gaping. They lunged. We parried, working seamlessly to stab, swerve out of the way, duck beneath their arms. The diners closed on us, some of them swatting at the air as if they could claw us out of existence. Hun-ger poured out of them. If I felt nauseous before, it was nothing com-pared to this. Their dried-out tongues reached out to taste what had long been denied: the world. Its nuances, colors like flavors dancing across the tongue. The taste of a kiss on someone's lips. Spice and air. Our breaths came in rushed, fast gasps. The ruby danced far out of reach. The diners advanced. Slower this time. As if they were preparing to savor the meal.

"Jump?" croaked Vikram.

"Together," I said.

He held out his hand, and I grabbed it tightly. Vikram scrabbled at the wall. The ruby came loose. Beneath us, the floor disappeared. His fingers slipped from mine. I prepared for a long fall, a terrible crash. But the endlessness sucked in its breath and made fools of us. We slammed into the floor. Vikram teetered backward and I caught him around the arm.

The diners had disappeared.

The silence had too.

Vikram slipped his hand into mine. His face looked pinched and I wondered what horrors and trials had kept him riveted to his seat, unable to move. We held on to each other. Our breath rasping. Hands shaking. The first trial had left me dizzy with victory. But this trial had wrung out my spirit. I looked up to find Kubera standing before us, clapping.

"Well done!" he said. "Excellent performance, contestants."

Not moving his arm from around my waist, Vikram threw the ruby at Kubera's feet.

Kubera smiled. "You have brought me an excellent treasure."

Our two trials required us to break free of fear and conquer desire. When Kubera told us that we were to find the key to immortality, I imagined something grand and coveted. Something that would make kings fall to their knees and even the gods would hide jealously. What we ended up with was everything and nothing like what I expected. Kubera took the ruby gently, reverently. He clasped both palms over the stone and when he opened his hands, a scarlet bird flew into the darkness. A story.

This was the key to immortality.

The thing that made kings quiver and deities distrustful:

Nothing but a tale.

34

A WHIFF OF SACRED

VIKRAM

V ikram had never been pious. He believed in the stories because he needed to, because he had to hope that if there was one place where he belonged it was in some celestial framework. He needed to know he wasn't some hiccup of fate. But for the first time, he felt a rush of something holy. There was a whiff of the sacred in all this darkness, a pulse that felt new and ancient. When he jumped into the dark and pried the ruby loose, calm had spiraled through him. Maybe he would never be anything more than a thread in the tapestry of fate. But he and Gauri had done something worthy of immortality's attention. No one could take that story from him.

The rational part of Vikram knew that he still had reason to be wary. Their host in the Tournament was still the fickle Lord of Treasures. But right then, he couldn't feel like anything but a story teetering on the verge of myth. He felt like someone who had vanquished odds, found someone who lit his dreams on fire and performed feats of magic without losing his life or limb. He felt . . . like a hero.

Kubera grinned before them, his expression wide and guileless.

"I was concerned you would not make it in time," he said. "Pockets of fear are their own lands. We can lose ourselves in them so often."

"In time for what?" asked Gauri. No formality. No deference. She added hastily: "Your Majesty."

She was trembling, her skin cold and clammy.

"The Tournament of Wishes is over," said Kubera. "Now we celebrate."

Kubera clapped his hands. Before, they had been standing in a darkened room. If the room had walls and floors, they were indistinguishable from one another. They simply merged into huge tracts of black shadows. But now, light pierced the darkness. A window unfolded, revealing an early evening sky.

"Fear takes away our sense of time," said Kubera. "That is why I saved it for last."

"Two trials and a sacrifice," said Gauri. "That was the bargain you struck with us."

Kubera nodded. Uneasiness seeped through Vikram. At first, he thought she was trembling with fear. But maybe it wasn't fear at all . . . maybe it was rage. He pressed his hand more firmly into her skin. She ignored him.

"What do we have left to give?" she demanded, her voice breaking.

Kubera's face split into a wide grin. "You'd be surprised."

"My lord, are you demanding our sacrifice at this very moment?" asked Vikram.

"Not at all. And I promise you that I will not ask for anything that wouldn't already be taken from you."

Vikram frowned, working through the words slowly. That did not bode well. Now that the initial victory had worn off, the trial had left him spent and cold. He hoped magic would make him feel chosen for something, remarkable in ways he hadn't realized. Instead, he discovered that magic hid her fangs behind fables. The stories of his childhood were not ways to live, but ways to see—a practiced blindness. And now he saw everything.

"All of the champions of the Tournament of Wishes will be present at tonight's festivities. You can tithe your sacrifice then. Return to your rooms. The evening's festivities will be a sight to behold."

"Champions?" repeated Vikram. "Does that mean . . . does that mean we've won?"

Kubera eyed him for a long while. A flush crept down Vikram's neck.

"Won?" repeated the Lord of Treasures. "What is a win?"

"I meant, my lord, have we each earned a wish?"

He waved his hand. "Oh! Wishes. Yes, yes. Pesky things. You may each have one," he said. "Although I'd not smile so quickly, Fox Prince. Have you thought about the wish? How you'd demand it, utter it, taste it? Because wishes have a tendency to take on lives of their own. Sometimes they'll do what you want. And sometimes they won't. Once, a hardworking artist known for his attention to detail and eye for color begged me for prosperity. I granted his wish because I am nothing if not kindness incarnate. And then I robbed his sight because I am nothing if not malevolence incarnate. The artist hanged himself. But he got what he wished for, did he not?"

"And you would do the same to us," said Gauri, accusingly.

"Maybe? I never quite know what I'll do until it's done!" said Kubera. "We shall see you tonight for the Parade of Fables."

He nodded his head, and turned on his heel.

Gauri called out to him. "What about the other contestants?"

Kubera stopped walking. He did not turn to face them as he said, "Oh, they woke up beneath trees or facedown in streams or perhaps not at all if they did not seem like appropriate vessels for stories. If you can't tell a good tale, you're of no use to me."

The shadows leapt up like a great bubble, covering them. Black swam in front of Vikram's eyes. In the next moment, they were both standing in their chamber. He looked at Gauri closely. There were circles beneath her eyes. The intricate *salwar kameez* was ripped and bloodstained. Her face looked pinched. Haunted. Without speaking, she pulled him close, wrapping her arms around his neck and kissing him deeply. His body reacted faster than his mind did. His hands gripped her waist. And they spent a few moments wound tightly together. But this kiss didn't feel like the one yesterday, where they had stepped into one another's arms with hesitation and nervous energy, enchantment softening the air and coaxing out unspoken dreams. This kiss felt tarnished. As if they were just trying to steal back something that was taken from them. It felt wrong. And for a moment, Vikram felt like the diners at the table of fear. Nothing more than a body reaching out for any feeling to shake off the cold.

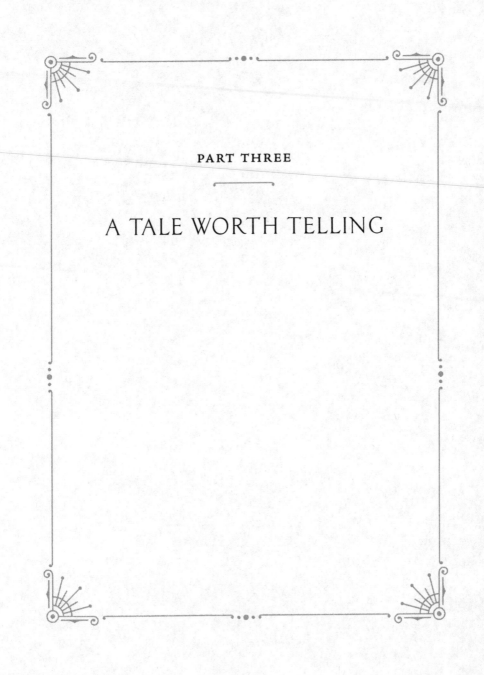

PART THREE

A TALE WORTH TELLING

35

A CROUCHING STORM

GAURI

Last year, Skanda and his war council had planned to lure and destroy an elite group of an enemy kingdom's army. I was the one who suggested that we plant Bharata's soldiers on either side of a river that ran through one of our mountain villages. Our scouts had seen the army camping just on the other side of the range. My plan was simple—take out their supplies, force them to cross the mountain for running water. Surround. Kill. Skanda liked the idea. A week before Bharata enacted my plan, I asked him when Bharata's messengers would return from informing the village to evacuate.

"I didn't tell the village to evacuate," he said, pouring himself a goblet of pale wine.

"But . . . they'll die."

"Don't you think it would be strange to the enemy if they ransacked an empty village? They'd wonder what had happened."

"Illnesses can claim whole villages at a time, brother. You could use that as an excuse," I said, trying to keep my voice from breaking. "Those are"—I bit back the word "my"—"*your* people. Your subjects. Your kingdom. Would you have them die?"

"If it means keeping the rest of my kingdom, then yes."

I couldn't allow that to happen. That night, I came up with a plan. All night, Nalini and I worked on a dose and capsule of poison. From a former visit to that village, I knew they made regular pilgrimages to a healing shrine beside a mountain geyser. I had visited it myself, wandering through the serene mists and taking rest in one of the numerous huts that surrounded the healing area. It was a large place. Large enough, perhaps, to shelter an entire village. I just had to get them there.

Harm to help, I murmured to myself, even as my fingers shook from arranging the poison capsules that would easily dissolve in liquid. Even as I knew that the village was in the midst of celebrating their harvest festival. All would drink from the ceremonial vat of malted honey barley. Children would take their first sips—life to life, from earth to blood—and lovers would shyly share their first cup, and husbands and wives would swallow deeply and savor the warmth of safety.

And I would have it poisoned.

Forced by the lack of supplies, the soldiers from the enemy kingdom arrived to a nearly empty village. *Nearly empty.* Some were too old to make it to the healing grounds. Some were with child. Some were children. Bharata's soldiers did as I had planned. They surrounded. They killed. Maybe a thousand lives were saved, but it was those few that haunted me. I felt every loss of life like a ghost curled inside my body, until I was so full of phantoms that they crowded my mouth and left no room for words. That whole week, I vomited every meal.

Harm to help. Harm to help. Harm to help.

Those ghosts would forever carry new fears . . . had I done enough, had I *been* enough. Fear meant not knowing where you started and ended because control was nothing but illusion. Alaka's feast of fears might not have devoured me, but it had sipped away my emotions.

Hollowed me.

When I drew Vikram to me, all I felt was cold. A cold that frosted over the very memory of warmth. He broke the kiss first. I stumbled away from him, disoriented.

"I don't want to be anyone's distraction," he said. He reached out to trace my cheek. "Not even yours."

"It was just a victory kiss," I said. My tongue felt dry. I stepped closer to him. "I can do better."

Vikram just looked at me, his gaze resting on my lips. And then he shook his head with a rueful smile.

"I have no doubt."

Vikram took my hand, guiding me to the baths and handing me fresh clothes that weren't crusted in blood. He ran a warm bath, turned around while I sank numbly into the water. He hummed a silly broken tune, scattering my thoughts. After I changed, he led me to the bed. I frowned, confused. But he didn't do anything except lean against the pillows, pull me to his chest and wrap his arms around me.

"Want to know a secret?" he asked.

I shuddered. Alaka had dredged up enough secrets.

"If it's a secret you want to give away, it doesn't sound that compelling."

"All right, if that's—"

"Tell me."

He laughed. "I sang to you when you were poisoned."

"No wonder I stayed unconscious for so long."

He flicked my ear. I swatted his hand.

"I'll tell you another," he said.

He told me ridiculous things. Like how when he was scrawny and fifteen, he'd dressed as a courtesan to sneak into the Ujijain harem only to get caught for looking too convincing. Or how he had trained one of his father's pet parrots to shriek obscenities at the palace priests. He didn't ask for any secrets in return. All he wanted, it seemed, was for me to laugh. And little by little, I realized I was smiling. The cold stopped gnawing at my heart. Little by little, I let myself feel. The feast of fears hadn't disappeared, but it had faded. We sat there for what felt like hours.

"Not quite what I expected of victory," he said, carding his fingers through my damp hair.

"How so?"

"Sadder, I guess."

"War feels like that," I said quietly.

"How do you get through it?"

I was silent for a moment. I'd seen horrifying battles. Sometimes I didn't know how I survived. Or even if I deserved to survive. The only way to face the next day was to change the story and live that new perspective. Sometimes the other horrors faded into dull silence. Sometimes they didn't. I told Vikram, and he nodded. Before, I would have thought he was agreeing out of politeness. But he understood this time, and I believed him.

"The tales we tell ourselves to sleep," he murmured.

I shivered and he held me tighter. "We're in a nightmare, not a story."

"That's not true," he said softly. "Here, I'll tell it to you. Once there was a beast princess and a fox prince—"

"*Beast princess?* That sounds awful, I—"

He shushed me. "—and they had to do all kinds of awful things.

Like talk to each other." I laughed. "And fight through memories that tried to lure them away, poisonous beauties and . . . fear." My chest tightened. "And they did all of this for freedom. One day, even if they couldn't see it now, it was going to be worth the pain."

We were both quiet. I toyed with my necklace. This was the first story anyone had told me since Maya left the harem. I'd almost forgotten the true power of a story . . . how it lulled you outside your thoughts, let you process the world in a way that was palatable. Not poisonous. Calm rushed through me.

"You forgot to mention the sacrifice," I said.

He shrugged. "It will be nothing. Kubera isn't going to take anything that wouldn't already be taken. If you think about it, it's not much of a sacrifice."

"How can you really believe that?"

"It helps when there are no other options."

I laughed. "Spoken like a true fox prince."

He frowned. "I wonder if they'll change my name to Fox King when I return."

"That doesn't sound nearly as intriguing."

"Perhaps I'll dedicate a royal committee to my new title. They can spend the day coming up with sycophantic titles and I'll become the dense king that believes them."

We laughed. Loudly. It wasn't even that funny, but we needed it and the sound of laughter seemed to sew back the dulled-down pieces of me. The feast of fears started feeling like a distant nightmare. Which meant that tomorrow pressed ever closer. What was I going to do when I finally returned to Bharata? What did this—laughing in the arms of the enemy prince—mean?

"What do you want after this, Vikram?"

His eyes widened. But when he opened his mouth to speak, the floor burst into flames. We got ready hurriedly. Right before we left, I went to the drawer that hid the Serpent King's venom and gently hid it inside a sewn-in pocket of my *salwar kameez*. We were so close to the end, I could almost taste the wish on my tongue. One step closer to Bharata. To Nalini.

"Gauri?" asked Vikram. He held out his arm. I took it.

The moment we walked outside, cold licked up my spine. I wasn't sure whether what I felt was some aftereffect from the feast of fear, but the atmosphere of Alaka was anything but festive.

It felt like a storm crouching over the sea, waiting for just the right moment to strike.

36

A DIFFERENT SONG

AASHA

S he couldn't stop staring at the invitation that had arrived in her chambers.

All champions are required to attend the Parade of Fables,
which will mark the conclusion of the Tournament of Wishes.
Upon conclusion, all wishes may be collected.
Arrive no later than sunset.

She was a winner in the Tournament of Wishes. She had *won a wish.*
. . . But how?

Her sisters danced around the tent.

"What are you going to wish for, Aasha?" exclaimed one. "Wish us a grander palace! With an elephant made of gemstones to carry us everywhere!"

"Lazy," scoffed one of her other sisters. "Wish for the ability to sing the weather into being. Then we could always have mild days or even snow when we wished it."

"Or wish for—"

"That's enough," said the eldest. The sisters fell silent. "Start preparing the tent. Once the Lord of Treasures has entertained the champions, every participant throughout Alaka will be storming the courtyard and begging for our time."

Another of her sisters shrugged. "Well done, Aasha!"

The moment they left, Aasha sank into her chair, folding her hands in her lap. A wish? She had never considered the possibility that there might be something she could finally decide for herself. All her life, she and her sisters had shared everything. It made sense that they would assume that even a wish won by one of them would be something to share. Guilt twisted through Aasha. She didn't want to share this.

Things had felt different, lately. She didn't even dress as she once had. Today, she wore a flower behind her ear. Most of her sisters thought it was little more than passing fancy, a curiosity that would fade the moment the Tournament ended because then she could no longer do such a thing. But her eldest sister hadn't stopped staring at her. As if she was finally seeing her.

"Don't listen to them," said the eldest. Aasha jolted upright in her seat. She hadn't realized anyone had been watching her. "That wish is yours. You earned it."

"I don't know what I did to win though."

Her sister smiled, but it was a sad and wistful smile, the kind that belongs to goodbyes.

"I know what you did," she said quietly. "You wanted. You acted on it. You were brave and kind and curious."

Aasha wasn't sure about being kind or brave, but she had certainly been curious. More and more, she had spent time out of the tent, pushing farther through the surrounding forests and not returning until she knew her presence would be missed. She couldn't help it. There was so much to see, so much to try to capture before they would have to leave. Just the other day she had found a shrub full of bright blue berries. Before, if she ever tried to eat anything other than the desires of the *yakshas* and *yakshinis* who visited her, she would end up with the taste of ash in her mouth and immediately vomit. But this time, the berries had stayed bright and plump in her palm. Blue as shards of the heavens. And when she chewed them, flavor burst behind her lips: syrupy and sweet. Small seeds lodged themselves in her teeth. It had taken forever to get them out, but she savored that anyway. Neither frustration nor flavor had ever accompanied the feeding of a *vishakanya*. There were no words or experiences to capture sweetness—it felt like an innocent memory, something stumbled upon and too easily forgotten. A smile, interrupted. Edible poetry, indeed. After that, she caught herself rolling her tongue across the roof of her mouth, hunting for every ghost of that flavor.

"I know where you've been, Aasha."

Her words didn't sound like an accusation, but Aasha flinched anyway. She wanted to be like her sisters: content. She wanted, so often, not to feel that she was the only person who desperately wished things were different. But she could not help who she was and she did not want to apologize any longer for her dreams.

"Go," said her sister. "I hear the Parade of Fables is quite a sight to behold. You can tell us all about it when you return."

"I wish you could come with me to the palace," said Aasha.

"Careful with your wishes, little sister."

Aasha blushed. "I wasn't thinking . . ."

"Unburden your mind, Aasha. We will miss you when you go," said her sister. She was staring at Aasha intently. Unspoken words sprouted between them. "Whenever you need us, we are here. Wherever you may be. And . . . whatever you might be."

She left. Now Aasha was well and truly alone. The room felt cramped. The weight of her decision had taken up all the space. In one short month, she had lived a far fuller life than she had in the past hundred years. A hungry desire to learn more, see more, *touch* more filled her until she found herself scrabbling at the blue star emblazoned on her throat. Desperate to throw it off.

Aasha readied herself. In the other rooms, she heard her sisters squabbling over lost cosmetics and borrowed outfits, arguing over the philosophical merits of one poem compared to another. Their love and gentle fights had been the music of her life for so long. But beyond the tent, a different song called her.

When she left, she kept looking behind her.

No *vishakanyas* were allowed in the palace proper. Aasha kept expecting someone to leap out of the shadows and tell her that she didn't belong. But everyone was preoccupied. She walked gingerly, her ankle still sore from the attack. Shuddering, Aasha looked around, but there was no sign of—

"Traitor to your kind," someone whispered.

"Besmirching our legacy."

"Ruining your sisters."

The Nameless stepped out of the shadows. Aasha trembled. The last time she saw them, they had chased her through the forest, screaming and demanding the vial of the Serpent King's poison. She ran so fast, she tripped over a log and twisted her ankle. Before her, they looked like vengeance poured into the form of three women. Desperation wearing skin.

"We will give you one last chance to aid us, sister," said the Nameless. "Take it from the humans and we will let you keep the Blessing. You would not want to force our hand."

Aasha's eyes widened. "The Blessing is not yours to take! I don't even know who you are."

The Nameless laughed. A terrible smile split their faces. Aasha fled into the palace, but she couldn't run fast enough to drown out the sound of their answer on the wind:

"We are you."

37

THE PARADE OF FABLES

GAURI

laka looked like the end of a story—calm and final. Every person smiled. Every scene looked serene. *Apsaras* danced on a podium of pressed wings. Tufts of light darted through the crowd, clinging to lacquered horns or gleaming tails. The air tasted like burnt sugar and jasmine, and felt like the end of a celebration where an exhausted evening was ready to push out the guests and embrace sleep. But I recoiled. It felt too . . . neat. I couldn't shake off the feeling of something unfinished and watching.

The crowd swelled. It was impossible to tell who was a contestant in the Tournament of Wishes and who was a champion on the verge of making a wish. In my pocket, I could feel the heat rising off the vial of the Serpent King's poison. I needed to speak with the Lady Kauveri before I made a wish. It wouldn't make a difference if I wished for my throne upon my return if I never had a chance to leave. If I could speak to her before the Parade of Fables, maybe I could convince her that the

Serpent King posed no harm to her sister. Maybe she would keep the vial of poison and not use it. I'd have my exit and my conscience cleansed too. Chance didn't favor me, but magic had at least taught me to believe in the impossible.

Beside me, Vikram inhaled sharply. "It's him."

I followed his gaze to the opposite side of the room, where the Serpent King stood with his bride. He appeared as a beautiful human man wearing long blue robes. His consort, the Kapila River, did not move from his side. She walked in front of him, almost guarding him.

"What are they doing here?"

Vikram shrugged. "It's the last day of the Tournament. Maybe everyone who was invited has to come?"

A *yakshini* appeared before us, holding out a crystal platter on which goblets full of sparkling liquid caught the light.

"Sweet memory?" asked the *yakshini*.

I reached for a goblet, and drank it in one swallow. The liquid was cold and fizzy on my tongue. A bright recollection lit up behind my eyes—climbing a guava tree with Maya and eating the tart fruit with a sprinkle of salt. Vikram was silent beside me, a misty look drifting across his face.

"Another?" asked the *yakshini*.

I set down my goblet. "No, thank you."

The *yakshini* bowed. Vikram swiped his arm across his mouth and stared a little resentfully at the retreating tray of goblets.

"If you wanted another sweet memory, you should have asked."

"I am not interested in recollections of the past," said Vikram, holding my gaze. "I have a future now. There's nothing sweeter than that."

I squeezed his hand.

"Welcome!" shouted Kubera.

The *apsaras* who had been entertaining the crowd stopped dancing, and moved to one side of a large podium where Kubera and Kauveri stood and surveyed the crowd. For tonight's festivities, Kubera wore scarlet robes. Kauveri's river sari boasted a pale blush to its waters. As if it were bloodied. "We hope you have enjoyed tonight's festivities. We know what you have waited anxiously to witness, and we dare not draw out the suspense any longer."

The light dimmed. A hearty applause broke out from the assembled guests. I snuck a glance at Kapila. I thought she'd stare reproachfully at her sister, Kauveri, but her expression held no hate. Only hurt. Disbelief. The same expression Nalini wore when I chased her away from me.

"Those who have been defeated in my Tournament shall now exit the realm of Alaka through the Parade of Fables," said Kubera. "Am I not the Lord of Wealth and Treasures? Am I not the King of Riches? I promised each of them that should they play, I would leave them richer." He stopped to smile widely. "And I did. Of a kind."

"I don't remember *us* getting that promise," murmured Vikram.

"What were we offered?"

"All our dreams or certain death."

"The risk and the reward are evenly matched."

He laughed. "Your sense of humor keeps confusing me."

"You'll grow accustomed to it."

He looked at me, a sly smile curving his lips. "With enough time, I could grow accustomed to anything with you."

At the end of the hall, a great banyan tree unfurled right behind Kauveri and Kubera. Small ghostly lights clung to the branches. A great rip had split the tree down the middle. A glowing path stretched from the ripped tree to a mirror at the end of the hall. Wind that belonged to another realm ghosted through the air, stirring the ends of my hair.

"Let the Parade of Fables begin," intoned Kubera.

A farmer walked out of the tree. With a lurch, I remembered where I'd seen him: kneeling on the lawns of Alaka, throwing rocks into a hole and cursing under his breath. He dropped to his knees in front of the crowd, doubling over and coughing. His hand clutched his stomach. Three of his fingers were pure gold.

Vikram stepped forward, as if to help him. I put out my hand to stop him. The farmer wasn't dying. He was trying to get rid of something lodged inside him.

The farmer coughed. A white bird freed itself from the cage of his stained teeth. *A story.* The story circled the farmer. Everyone looked up. A tale glittered in its wings—the farmer waking up facedown in a mangrove swamp and discovering his golden fingers. Perhaps he would sing songs about a palace beneath the tree roots and all would hear it and wonder. Perhaps he would cut off his fingers and never speak of what he had seen. *Perhaps, perhaps.* The story soared to Kubera, and the farmer stumbled through the mirror, leaving Alaka behind.

Next, an old woman clambered out of the tree. I looked closer. Not an old woman at all, but a young woman with pure silver hair. A story bird flew from her lips. Perhaps she would tell a trader that she had left her true hair somewhere in the boughs of an impossible tree where wishes budded from its sap at the new moon, and the trader would tell others and all would wonder. Perhaps she would hide from everyone and carve out her wrists in the fear that all would think she had lost her mind. *Perhaps, perhaps.* The story soared to Kubera.

Five, ten, maybe a hundred more stories clambered from the tree's hollow. I couldn't keep track. Above me, the caged white birds had already taken on different hues as they changed in the telling. Topaz and ocean blue, bleak grays and dusky emeralds. And then, the melody of

Alaka grew deeper. Fissures sprang up in the sound, as if it were a voice cracking from grief.

Bodies appeared on the floor. Bodies stacked one on top of another. No wounds marked the skin, but a smell rose from the center of the room—like wet mushrooms and dark earth. At some secret signal from Kubera, shadow beasts stalked out of the corners of the halls and fell upon the dead.

"Is this how they honor their dead?" I asked, clenching my teeth.

Vikram said nothing.

The beasts forced open the jaws of the dead. The scent of stale death filled the air. It reminded me of the battlefields. Even though the stench disgusted me, it was familiar . . . even welcome. I didn't revel in death, but I didn't hate it either. Death had raised me, like an older sibling. Amid death, I had found my bearings as a soldier. Surrounded by death, I had found my place as a leader. And so when the small white story birds tore themselves from the mouths of the deceased, I watched instead of cowered. And I wondered how long those stories had been trapped. Whether they stank of rot. Or whether they smelled like rain, free and unburdened.

As they flew out, the stories flashed in my head. I saw the bodies discovered at daybreak, the Otherworldly gashes that had split them in two. I saw astounded villagers picking up stray limbs. A jaw lying in the middle of a field. A grinning severed head. I saw villagers recoil from the horizon and warn against the monsters that stalked at midnight. *Perhaps, perhaps.* The stories soared to Kubera.

"Thank you, honored guests," said Kubera. "Thank you for the privilege of your voice. Thank you for feeding the magic."

He and Kauveri stepped down, disappearing into the audience. Quiet fell over the crowd. A *yaksha* attendant took Kubera's place on the podium. I stifled a gasp. It was the same *yaksha* who had cornered me on Jhulan Purnima. He surveyed the crowd.

"Champions of the Tournament of Wishes," he said loudly. "Kindly follow me."

The crowd turned restless. A surge of movement picked up, nearly blocking me from Vikram, but he caught hold of my arm and held fast. A shout lit up the room. I turned, not knowing what had called my attention, and saw that Aasha was running toward me.

"Gauri!"

The crowd of Otherworldly beings parted before her, some of them eyeing her with lust and others with vague disgust. She flew straight to me and Vikram, stopping just short of throwing her arms around both of us. Her eyes darted behind us. I followed her gaze, but there was nothing but a silk-covered wall.

"Aasha, what's wrong?" Vikram asked.

I had to stop myself from reaching out to grab her shoulders. She was shaking.

"They're coming," she whispered. "I tried my best to protect you from them. But they're after the poison—"

"What?" I demanded. "Who?"

"The Nameless," she breathed, her face paling. She stepped back. Her eyes narrowed as she searched the wall behind us. "They know you have the Serpent King's venom—"

Vikram's hand tightened on my arm. He held his dagger at the ready, hesitation tightening his face. He tried pulling me down the crowd, signaling for Aasha to join, but I was tired of fighting and being manipulated. Nothing was going to stand between me and that wish anymore. It was done. We had won.

"Let them try and get it," I said, old bravado sneaking into my voice.

"Just because you wear our mark does not make you invincible to the pain we can cause."

The Nameless stepped out of the shadows right next to Vikram. One fluid movement. In. Out. Inevitable from the very second I caught the metallic sheen winking in the dark.

"No!" screamed Aasha.

Beside me, I heard a grunt of pain. Vikram's hand tightened on mine to the point where I lost feeling in my fingers. I turned, catching him before he crumpled to the ground. I clutched his shoulders, trying to raise him up. Ice cut my thoughts. He . . . he wasn't supposed to fall. They were supposed to aim at me. Not him. Never him. His eyes went wide, lips paling. A hilt sunk into his back caught the light. My hand came away red. A thick stain . . . something dark . . . something that my mind refused to comprehend as blood spread across his shirt. I felt yanked open, hollowed in the space of a blink. Screams and fury and night rushed in to fill me. I fell to my knees.

"We don't need to touch you to harm you, girl."

38

DARK AS DUSK

GAURI

I always thought of silence as the absence of sound. But kneeling there—watching Vikram crumple to the ground, blood forming a red shadow beneath him—I thought I felt the world slump, begging silently for reprieve. Or maybe it was just me. This sight couldn't fit inside me. My heart refused to hold it. It unlocked. Broke. The sound of it made the silence scream.

Sharp gasps and murmurs crawled within reach of my hearing, but I shut out the sounds. The only thing I wanted to hear was Vikram's voice. Aasha crouched to his side, her fingers hovering over his hair and the growing bloodstain across his back. Tears slid down her cheeks. But she wouldn't touch him. Couldn't. Around us, the people of Alaka moved closer. I whirled on them, my dagger raised.

"Help him," I hissed. Then louder:

"Help him! What are you doing?"

A thousand glittering eyes met mine. No one moved. This was not their game.

The Nameless circled me.

The first sneered. "We tried to appeal to your heart, but you have none."

The second laughed. "We tried to appeal to your mind, but you have none."

The third smiled. "So we will take what is ours by force. The venom was our trade first. Our prize first. It is our legacy. Every hundred years, we fight for it. For the years between we sink into the ground, sleeping and waiting, our legacy growing. Did you really think you could take it from us?"

Aasha called my name. I looked over to see her holding the dagger that Vikram had dropped. She wielded it awkwardly, as if it might bite her at any turn. I thought she was going to throw it to me, but instead she walked to my side, her face grim.

The Nameless hissed. "This is the last Tournament, girl. If we don't take the venom, the poison will fade. You will fight your own? You will take this vengeance from your sisters?"

"No sister of mine would ever do this," said Aasha quietly. "My sisters don't call it vengeance. They call it a Blessing."

"So be it," said the Nameless as one.

They lunged, slashing the air. I clutched the poison in one hand, jumping out of the way. Aasha was a tiny wind beside me, a whirling living barrier. The crowd of Alaka formed a black crust around us, silent eyes tracking our every movement. Everywhere I turned, the Nameless unraveled from the shadows. I couldn't tell them apart. Even when my eyes cut away from one face to the next, no detail lingered. This was the price of vengeance, a slow obliteration of self until you were nothing but your hate. I roared, charging forward, swinging my arm to slice and cut. But the blade passed through them as if the knife didn't exist. They grinned.

One blink later, and the Nameless vanished. Catching my breath, I turned in a slow circle. Alaka stared back. Kubera and Kauveri floated above the crowd. Waiting. Aasha caught my eye, confusion spreading across her features. And then I realized what the Nameless had done. Pushed us to the shadows. They weren't trading spar for spar or punch for punch; they were trading light for dark.

I saw the shadow on my feet. I leapt out of the way, but a hand darted out, closing around my ankle. In that moment, I thought I could taste death on my tongue, all funerary ash and burning marigolds. I reached down, hacking violently—uselessly—at the wrist. The Nameless rolled out of the shadows. I lifted my blade. But it didn't matter. The smile on the Nameless was death. A pressure sank into my stomach. A blade. It didn't feel sharp. Just dull. They slid a hand across my waist.

"Ours now," they said, tugging the vial of the Serpent King's poison.

I sank to my knees, black edging my vision. In one fluid movement, the Nameless pulled the stopper from the vial of poison and drank it. Light fizzed across their skin. The blue ribbon each of them wore in tribute to their dead sister glowed and tightened into a knot at the hollow of each throat. My eyes sought Vikram. Someone had moved toward him. A beautiful woman wearing a crown of snow crouched beside his body. I was so cold. So empty. I looked back to the Nameless. The ribbons had transformed. A blue star unraveled at the hollow of each of their throats.

"Finally," they whispered.

I was weightless and empty.

I was gone.

When I opened my eyes, I was thrown over the back of some beast. It smelled of death. Not of rot and blood, but of closed doors and shuttered eyes. The beast whipped its tail, huffed and turned to look at me. A white horse. Almost beautiful, if not for the manic gleam in its eyes. I looked around me, but the landscape cut in and out, as if someone had taken a knife to this world and started hacking. Panic bit into my heart. Where did everyone go? Where was Vikram? And then a terrible thought wrenched through me.

"Am I alive?"

The horse laughed, and I nearly fell off in shock.

"What is alive anyway, but one shape telling another shape that it is there? By that logic, I am alive! And I do not think that I am. But I *do* think, so therefore . . . therefore something. Hm . . ."

The horse kept running.

"What's happening? Where am I?" I demanded. "Take me back to Alaka this instant!"

"A mortal thing making demands? Hmpf. The nerve. Must run in the blood." The horse grumbled. "It is most inconvenient that you are inedible. I do like to play with food."

The horse, if it could even be called that, stopped running before an ivory door that appeared in the middle of a wasteland. It tossed me off its back and nudged open the door with its nose.

"Where am I?" I said, digging my heels into the ground. I refused to move.

"Everywhere!" laughed the horse. "You're in the shadow of sleep. You're at the beginning and the end. You're treading the spit, sinew and gristle that makes a tale worth telling, girl thing."

"Who are you?"

The horse snorted. "Selfhood is a pesky thing. I left it ages ago."

It swung its head toward the door. "She won't be happy to see you," it said, with a touch of fondness. "But that is to be expected."

Not knowing what else to do, I stepped through the door and found myself in the throne room of a vast palace. The palace didn't feel like Alaka. The windows overlooked nothing but barren scrubland. The tiles beneath my feet pulsed like a heartbeat. I tried to look around me, but I couldn't even get my bearings. It was as though the room didn't want to be seen.

The door swung open. Two figures glided inside. I scrambled to my feet, my heart racing. I couldn't make out their features but I knew they weren't Kubera and Kauveri. The Raja wore a charcoal *sherwani* jacket. Dark, lustrous power curled off of him and he moved with an eerie grace. His queen walked beside him; starry wisps and coils of evening sky lit the space around her. And then she turned, and my heart stilled. My gaze traveled from the Queen's bare feet, where thunderheads danced around her ankles, past her arms, where lightning netted its way across her wrists, and to her eyes. Dark as dusk. I knew that the Queen's eyes tightened at the corners when she was nervous. I knew she preferred her room cold and her bed without blankets. I knew that her favorite fruit was guava and that she always ate it with salt.

I knew all these things because the Queen was Maya. Her eyes widened, first with shock and then with fury.

"What are you doing here?" she demanded.

The Raja moved to her side. Maya turned to him. There was no mistaking the glance that passed between them. Love. He looked at my sister as if she were wonders and miracles made flesh. And then he looked at me. I turned my head. The thought of meeting his eyes made me feel as if it were the last thing I'd ever do. He spoke and his voice was lush and dark:

"Forgive my manners, Princess, but I take no pleasure in our acquaintance, and would rather not meet you yet."

To anyone else, his words would reek of insolence. But I felt as if he had done me a great favor. I fumbled for my voice. "Perhaps another time."

At this, he smiled. "Inevitably."

He lifted Maya's hand to his lips and disappeared. It was just us. I wanted to cry, hug her, laugh. I wanted to tell her I looked for her in every constellation, not just ours. I wanted to tell her I was tired and scared. Maya smiled, holding out her arms to me.

"You've worked so hard, my Gauri," she said. "And I know that it has left your heart wounded and your soul raw. I can take away the hurt. I can erase it from your memory forever. Or you can return and I cannot tell you what will happen. I can only tell you that the choice is yours.

"Do you want to be brave?"

39

BELIEF WAS BREAD

VIKRAM

A woman crouched over him, snow falling from her hair. Her lips were as cold as salvation when they pressed to his cheek. A memory bloomed in his mind—he was laughing with Gauri, telling her how in Ujijain they gave their thanks in kisses. At her taunt, he kissed a boulder shaped like a woman.

For her greed, she is lost until a kiss falls upon her stony brow.

He knew the woman who sat beside him. Tara. The cursed queen of the *vanaras*.

That kiss. . . .

It had freed her.

His thoughts felt thick. Slow. Dimly, he remembered a knife parting bone from muscle. The sting of death. Tara reached for him, a glowing thread pulled taut between her fingers. Her expression was benevolent, full of gratitude.

"Is this a gift of Life?" he asked.

"Oh, Prince," she laughed. "Existence is the gift. Life is a choice."

Her hands moved over his eyes. He felt her carrying him, cradling him like a child. They moved past halls. Through doors. In a golden room, she lowered him to the ground, cold lips pressing just beneath his ear as she stamped his skin with one command:

Exist.

He opened his eyes, sucking in a lungful of air. He held on to it until it burned, until he knew without a doubt that it was his, his, his. Then he let it go. Callously. Breathlessly. When he looked up, he was on his knees before Kubera and Kauveri. He felt wild. Gauri. Where was she? But if there was anything or anyone outside of this room—a crowd, a sea, an embryo world not yet born—he could not see it. Kubera and Kauveri had shed their human glamour and become impossible to look at. Impossible to look away from.

He was a child and not a child. He was an eight-year-old crying into his pillow and scrabbling for meaning. He was a thirteen-year-old poring over myth and legend, assembling the clues for his future, holding his hopes so tightly within him that they had taken over his bones, his blood, his dreams. His hope was cold. Poisonous. Eclipsing. And he fed it anyway, the way someone feeds something out of habit simply because there is nothing else in their life worth growing.

All this time, he thought magic had chosen him. Maybe magic never chose. Maybe it had always been about the fit. A key latching into a hole. Maybe there had been just enough holes in him for magic to slip through and hook him like spurs into cloth.

Alaka had forced him to look in. Not out. And he had begun to borrow a little of Gauri's thoughts—her will was her weapon, and everything else was just cobwebs to cut through. Her loss was her own just as her victory was her own.

It terrified him.

Unstrung him.

And yet, he felt stronger. Belief was still bread, still warm and fill-ing. But Alaka had shifted it, pulled it out of sight, so that he could rely on nothing and no one but himself.

It was freedom.

"What more are you going to take from me?" demanded Vikram. "What sacrifice will you demand?"

Kubera merely tilted his head as his wife laughed behind her hand.

"I already took it, Fox Prince. I took the dreams you stored up until the day I came with an invitation. I took your faith every time you stared down death and wondered whether this was part of a plan for you. I took your resilience when you wondered whether the girl of your very soul was destined to die," said Kubera. "I told you I would take what you would already give. Am I not merciful?"

Vikram stood there, his heart a curious cross between hollow and heavy. He felt the ache of that sacrifice, the loss of that wonder replaced with wariness. "I thank you, Lord Kubera. But—"

"But you want to know why you were brought here?" offered Kauveri. "You want to know why my consort handpicked you and the Princess Gauri, even going so far as to disguise himself as a sage and even a *vetala*."

Vikram's head shot up. "The *vetala* too?"

He had guessed Kubera was the sage. The golden mongoose had given it away in their first meeting. Kubera grinned.

"Oh yes! But do not think that I had any hand in your success. I merely wanted to watch! And then, oh, perhaps I did feel a little attached to your soft hearts and your lingering looks. You were only bones and wanting. Exquisitely lovely."

"There's more to us than that," said Vikram.

"To be sure, Fox Prince, to be sure," said Kubera, waving a hand. "That was why I selected both of you."

The marble floor shifted, pale colors moving and sliding beneath its sudden translucence. Images flickered before him, stretched out like a hope not realized—an empire that looked a little like Bharata and a little like Ujijain. He felt the land beneath him, the bright and burning urgency of it to innovate and sink its teeth into history. It was a kingdom in the midst of creating its own legend, ushering in an age that had no room for magic. The strangest feeling was how possessive he felt. He knew it. He knew its libraries and buildings, its landscapes and temples. As if this land stretching beneath him was somehow . . . his.

"Soon," said Kauveri, "one will not be able to step into the Otherworld. We will seal our doors. Shut our portals. Live apart. These tales are not just pieces of magic. They are the foundations of legacy. We tried for years to find the right vessels. A lord and lady of the new era, so to speak. Two people who would break time because their stories would be timeless. We listened for hollow hearts and hungry smiles and guided them to our land only to watch them fail over and over. Until now."

Behind his eyes, Vikram saw the banks of the Serpent King's portal littered with bones. All of those who had been brought to Alaka possessed the same potential that he and Gauri had. But potential meant nothing in the face of willpower, and that was something no one could possess or preordain but him.

Kubera held out his hand. A small coin of light sat in his palm.

"You earned your wish."

40

THE GLASS HAND

GAURI

Do you want to be brave?

I heard the choice in Maya's words—

Do you want to start being brave?

I thought I had been brave. I had fought power wars with Skanda, defended my country, protected the people I loved. But that bravery required no choice. It was something I had to do. Living under Skanda's rule hadn't frightened me because I had expected his brand of horror and trained myself.

True terror came when a knife drew blood from Nalini's skin and Arjun stood in the gloaming of the throne room, silent and ruthless as my world went from an expected dose of horror to a long stretch of unknown tomorrows. That was the beginning of strength. At the threshold of strength and bravery stood hope. If I was going to be brave, it meant acknowledging that hope was not a promise. I wasn't returning for the hope of saving Vikram or even saving Bharata. I was returning for myself.

"Yes," I said. "I want to be brave."

As soon as I spoke, a tapestry to the side of the room lengthened. As if it were changing just because of my words. Maya smiled. I looked around us, but I couldn't get a sense of the surroundings.

"Where am I?"

Maya tilted her head. "Where would you like to be?"

"Home."

And so we were. We were sitting on the floor of Maya's old chambers in Bharata. Shades of deep violet painted the sky. Small clouds of fireflies drifted sleepily through the gardens. Maya pulled me into an embrace, resting her cheek on my head.

"Don't ever believe that I am not proud of you," she said. "I always am."

I clung to her and breathed in her scent. My sister always smelled like flowers that opened their blooms only to the moon.

"I missed you."

"I missed you too."

Outside, the sky changed. Deepening to night. And then, even the night began to lighten. A cold sense of loss worked its way through my limbs. I knew, somehow, that the moment the sky turned to dawn, Maya would leave. I wanted to ask where she was, *who* she was, but those questions kept being snatched off my tongue. As if I was not allowed to ask. Not to control me, but because those questions weren't important.

"Will you tell me a story, *didi*?" I asked.

Maya nodded. I curled against her, resting my head in her lap as I used to do. And she braided my hair as she used to do. The sun poured gold into the sky. I couldn't remember the details of the story Maya told me. But when she finished, I felt whole. Sometimes when you stare at a thing for too long, the moment you close your eyes, you can see the outline blurred in light. That's how my heart felt, clinging to a last image and letting it illuminate me.

"When will I see you again?" I asked.

"I don't want to know. It will always be too soon to me, and too far for you. But I promise when you visit, you will linger a little longer. You will sleep in my palace and dine at my table. I will show you my favorite room with all of its glass flowers, and I will hold your hand as we walk down the halls," said Maya. "You will always be my sister."

Consciousness crept back to me. Bit by bit. The sky outside our stolen hour changed. The floor disappeared. The last thing I felt was my sister's arms around me, warm and firm. I didn't know if I had dreamt the whole thing, but when I opened my eyes, heat surged through the sapphire pendant around my neck. I was kneeling before Kubera and Kauveri. Reality came back to me, first in wisps, before crashing into waves. *Vikram. Aasha.* Where were they? What happened to the Nameless? The last thing I remembered, they had drained the vial of the Serpent King's poison—my only bargaining tool to win an exit out of Alaka—and changed into . . . *vishakanyas.*

I looked around the room, searching for answers. But the crowd from the Otherworld had vanished. Nothing but polished floors and gleaming walls surrounded me.

"He is here. He is alive. And he is safe," said Kauveri, as if she heard my thoughts. "He is waiting for you."

"Which he seems quite accustomed to," added Kubera. "You will see him shortly."

"And Aasha?"

Kauveri lifted an eyebrow. "Have you grown to care for the *vishakanya?*"

I nodded.

"She is well, child."

Relief flooded me. I lifted my hand over my stomach, feeling for the wound inflicted by the Nameless when I stopped. *My hand.* It wasn't mine anymore. I raised my right hand to my face, blinking at the glass replica that moved and glinted as if it were flesh and blood. I stiffened my arm and watched the small muscles along my forearm tense. I thought about moving my fingers and the glass hand danced to my thoughts.

"Like it?" asked Kubera.

"You took my hand," I said breathlessly.

"It still works," said Kubera. "Although it will not pick up any weapons."

I reached for the dagger clasped at my hip. The glass hand felt no different from my other hand. A pulse ghosted through its cut-crystal shape. I could even feel the texture of my dress beneath my translucent fingers. But the moment my hand touched the dagger, the glass became . . . glass. Stiff and brittle. It hit the metal with a dull clink.

I tried again. *Clang.* I smashed my hand into the dagger, wanting it to shatter and getting nothing but a sore shoulder. My whole arm ached. The horror of my hand poured through me, slow and thick.

I couldn't fight.

I. Couldn't. Fight.

I shook my arm, trying to dislodge it. As if it were an insect. But the hand stayed. It *stayed.* The crystal caught the light. Held it. My throat tightened. Fighting was the last connection I had to Maya. Her stories made me brave. They made me see the world differently, fight for the world I wanted to see instead of the one I had. And my hand, even if it was only a part of that dream, had been...important. A flurry of goodbyes I'd never be able to utter choked me. I'd never know the weight of wielding both daggers at the same time. I'd never catch the scent of iron on my palm after a practice session. I wouldn't even have the chance to worry calluses at my hands, because the glass would never wrinkle.

"This is my sacrifice?" I asked, trying to keep my voice from shaking.

My skin felt tight with shock. Fighting was my solace, my grip on control that couldn't be taken from me. In Bharata, the battlegrounds were the only place where I could be myself. And Kubera had stolen that peace.

They nodded.

"But...but you said you would only take something that would *already* be taken from us. How would I already lose my hand?"

"You did not lose your hand."

I waved my hand. "Having lived with it for eighteen years, I can assure that it did not start off as glass."

"You did not lose your hand," repeated Kubera.

"You lost your sense of control," said Kauveri.

"How do you know I would have already lost that?" I demanded. I knew I sounded as petulant as a child, but I couldn't help it. This wasn't something I had been willing to give.

Kubera smiled, and I hated knowing that I had his pity.

"You began to lose your sense of control the moment you accepted magic into your life. You lost it when you lost your throne and jeopardized your best friend," said Kauveri. "You lost it when things repeatedly happened *to* you and you could do nothing but react. Your reactions still belong to you. It is not such a bad sacrifice to make, dear princess. You would have lost it anyway."

"And you did win a wish," said Kubera.

"What good is that without an exit?" I asked. I turned to Kauveri. "My lady, I know that—"

"I grant you an exit," she said smoothly.

I stared at her, dumbfounded. But the Nameless had stolen the vial of the Serpent King's poison.

"You think I wanted the poison because I yearned for control over my sister's husband?"

I nodded.

"No," she said. "After you exchange so many harsh words with the person that you love, sometimes it is impossible for them to trust you once more. The Serpent King's poison was supposed to be a gift of trust and faith. But you and I were both beaten to it. Only a deity could harness the ability to control him. I never sought to do that. I only sought to show her that I wouldn't. Sometimes the greatest power comes not from that which we do, but that which we do not. And I had my wish. You did me a great service, Gauri of Bharata."

I looked behind Kauveri to the small podium where the Kapila River and the Serpent King stood with their arms wrapped around one another, beaming in the direction of Kauveri.

"What does that mean for the Nameless?"

"They will continue to have the Blessing of *vishakanyas* for another hundred years. The Nameless thought they were fighting for the permanence of something. But nothing lasts forever. Eventually, the poison will fade."

"Your wish is yours," said Kubera.

Even though I knew we were still in Alaka, I couldn't sense the magic in the air. There was no curious weightlessness to the world, as if it were waiting to draw back its curtains and show me the wonder beneath the rot. The world stank only of death. Iron and salt and once-bright roses. Water strung through fish bones. I thought that the moment I'd won, my breath would catch and stars would pave my path. Instead, all I could think of was my own bone-weary exhaustion and the fact that I didn't know myself anymore.

"Be careful with your wish," said Kauveri. "Even a good wish may have its repercussions. A wish for rain to slake the parched throats of a field may turn to a flood that will steal away an entire village. A wish made from a wicked heart to maim another person may end up saving a thousand lives. I do not make those decisions."

After all this time, I realized that I didn't even know what I would wish for anymore. It had changed. I wanted my throne and I wanted Nalini's safety, but at what cost? My desires had trapped me. My fears had tried to devour me. If I acted on them, knowing how easily everything could turn against me, would I end up doing more harm than good?

"You don't have to make your wish now," said Kubera. "But when you return, remember to tell a good tale. Make up details! I do love that. Perhaps you can tell the world I was a giant! Or that I rode on the back of several eagles. Actually, no. I never liked heights."

"Was it all just a story for you to collect?"

Kubera tilted his head to one side. "It is impossible to collect a story. After all, the intersections of a tale and its consequences are far larger than you might ever imagine. May I tell you a tale?"

I nodded, and he spread his hands as the imagery on the floor shifted.

"Some tales that never end start with something as simple as an act of impulse and end with something as evil as an act of love."

41

A SELECTION OF BIRDS

A BIRD WITH BLUE FEATHERS

A courtesan dances before a group of kings.

Her heart is young, so full of light that no thorns have grown to puncture
*   her innocence.*

A king who had never heard "no" took notice. The courtesan fights. Loses.

Not because she was not brave.

But because bravery cannot buy breath when furious fingers wrap ribbons
*   around a throat.*

A BIRD WITH BONE FEATHERS

Grief wields a dangerous magic.

Three sisters sink into the shadows.

Their hands tremble over a broken courtesan's body on the floor.

Now she is dead.

But she was other things before: beloved, beautiful, sister.

Those things do not change.

They take the silk of her scarf—blue as veins—and tie it around their
    throats.

This is their shackle.

They trade the magic of their names for enchanted venom.

For vengeance.

And they act as all vengeance acts:

Blindly.

A BIRD WITH SCALE FEATHERS

A serpent prince slithers beside the riverbanks, caught on a song.

It lulls him from the winter waters.

Smitten, he longs to walk beside the singer, not crest over the waves where
    she sits.

He yearns to speak in her tongue.

A trade.

Legs for enchanted venom, language for vengeance.

He does not think twice.

The Kapila River regards him with pale eyes

So pale and bright, they rival unfinished stars

So clear and knowing, they see straight through his tainted blood

And into his heart

Where neither blood nor ichor fills his veins

Only her song.

A BIRD WITH GOLD FEATHERS

Blue-silk around their throat

Death at their touch

A group of kings slain
One villainous
The rest innocent
Killed not for their treachery
But their timing.
In a realm tucked in the Kalidas Mountains,
the vanara queen falls to her knees.
But a heart broken too sharply is like a glass flower dropped.
Sift through the pieces, and one can find a weapon.
She seeks vengeance, but none will champion her cause
And if she cannot find vengeance, then she must grow it.

A BIRD WITH NEEDLE FEATHERS

The world ends, not with a snap but with a sigh
A tether cut loose: before and after, beloved and bereaved, wishful and
     widowed
Rich loam for heartbreak.
Richer loam for demon fruit.
A body.
A bone.
A bounty of tears.
That is how the world ends
And curses begin.
Years pass
Names are dropped and picked up again
Kingdoms creep closer to the shadows, waiting.

And a queen turned to rock waits for a kiss.

42

HONEY-SPUN FLAMES
VIKRAM

He waited for her in the courtyard of Alaka. Now that the Tournament of Wishes was over, everyone had moved. The *vishakanyas'* tent stood empty, the enchanted silk pennants lay strewn across the grass. The orchards had been stripped of their fruit—no musical instruments or jeweled apples sparkled beneath dark branches. No *yakshas* or *yakshinis* floated by on gauzy wings or tossed horned heads in his direction.

The quiet was unsettling, but freeing. He had imagined victory a hundred ways. He thought he might ride golden elephants into the city. Or maybe appear in a shower of coins in the middle of a council meeting. Perhaps not the last idea, for fear of the golden coins smacking him in the head.

Before the Tournament of Wishes, he knew the shape of victory—wide and casting a shadow that seeped through the pages of history—but not the feel. The feel was something glittering and urgent pressing against his bones, pushing him to make space for a new version of himself. He didn't know how to accommodate this new Vikram, or the weightiness that came with having a former self and a new one.

Vikram had lost all sense of time as he stood before Kubera and Kauveri, watching as the stories undulated above him. Before he came to Alaka, he dared to hope that he was meant for something more. Now he dared to hope that he could shape that meaning for himself. All this time, he had expected that magic would stitch his future together. But all magic had done was show him how to stitch it together for himself.

He glanced at the enchanted document in his hand. Not even a wish was a solution. Although it was certainly a start.

"What do you wish for, Fox Prince?" Kubera had asked.

Before magic, the answer had seemed simple. He believed that the throne of Ujijain should be his and he thought that the magical tournament somehow validated that wish. But that was silly. All he had ever wanted was the potential in himself recognized. He couldn't magically shore up those deficiencies overnight. They needed to be earned, just as he needed to learn.

"I wish for others to see the potential in me."

Kubera had smiled. The next moment an enchanted document was neatly sealed in his hand.

"Show it to your council," he said. "And remember to tell a tale that is worthy of us."

Vikram smiled, holding the parchment close to his chest along with Kubera's other gift: a snake that constricted at the sound of a lie. He had named her Biju, for "Jewel," and spent most of the hour testing her lie-detecting abilities.

"I am the most handsome prince in the world," he said.

Biju constricted.

"Mind your manners, Biju. I'm the true heir of Ujijain now. Or something like that. Certainly not a puppet anymore."

Biju did not constrict. His heart leapt.

"I am the most handsome prince in Alaka?" he tried.

Constrict.

"I am the most handsome prince in the courtyard?"

She did not constrict. Vikram took a look around the garden, which confirmed that he was not only the lone prince, but also the only person in Alaka's courtyard. He frowned.

"Your sense of humor reminds me of someone else," he said. "She's also called a Jewel, but I don't think she can detect a lie."

Biju made no response except to slither around his neck and catch her tail in her mouth. He could have sworn he heard a resigned snake sigh. He turned to the entrance, his nerves dancing. Why wasn't she here yet? Had Kubera lied? Before, his belief would have been ironclad. But in a short month he'd learned something that would never leave him:

Doubt.

"Gauri is alive and unharmed," he whispered to the snake, praying that it wouldn't move.

He heard a soft laugh.

"Are you gossiping about me to a snake?"

Vikram froze. Gauri stood in the entrance. Tall and imperious, backlit by the sun as if she'd snatched a handful of its rays and decided it looked better on her than the sky. Gauri had a way of shoving out the elements, scaring away the air so that Vikram felt there wasn't enough for him to draw into his lungs.

"I would have gossiped to you about yourself, but you weren't around," he said, showing off Biju. Gauri looked at the truth-telling snake with a touch of envy. "Where were you? Walking the fine line between life and death?"

"As one does," she said, crossing her arms. "And you? Last time I saw you, you had a knife in your back."

"And last time I saw you, you had your arms around me."

Gauri looked exasperated. "Is that the only detail you remember? You were dying!"

"I was falling on the ground."

". . . To your death."

"To a questionable limbo of existence that was, admittedly, painful."

She laughed. And Vikram, who had never wanted for his life to slow down but only to move faster and faster to the next thing, found himself craving to live in this second. They stood there, watching one another. He felt as if he could sense her replaying everything that happened the night before the feast of fears. The smile froze on her face, now propped up out of habit rather than joy. As she reached to brush a strand of hair from her face, a handful of crystal caught the light and refracted it, nearly blinding him. He squinted against the sudden brightness before realizing that it wasn't a handful of crystal at all, but Gauri's hand.

"That's . . . new?" he said, pointing at her fingers.

Gauri's mouth formed a tight line. "It will be hard to forget the sacrifice I made." Pain sparked behind her eyes. "No glass limbs for you?"

He shook his head even as his heart thundered in his chest. Who was he to say that Alaka hadn't replaced some part of him with glass? Maybe it was his heart. Looking at Gauri, it felt far clearer than it ever had been. Like a shard of glass. Just as translucent. Just as easy to shatter.

"Before the Parade of Fables, you asked me what I wanted."

Gauri bit her lip. Waiting. He felt the words shuffling impatiently inside him. He tried practicing how to say them while he waited, but now that she was here, the light of her—brilliant and fierce—sent the words scattering as they tripped out of his throat.

"I want time with you," he blurted out. "I want time where we're not looking around our shoulders and wondering what's going to trap us." Had he taken a step closer, or had she? Or maybe the ground had leapt out of their way. "I want time where we're not running from or racing to anything but each other. I want time where holding you has nothing to do with trying to deceive anyone around us, celebrating a holiday or fending off the echoes of whatever horror just tried to kill us. Again. All I want is a day where there is nothing in it but you and me, and definitely desserts, but mostly—"

She grabbed him. He was already tilting toward her, and so when she grabbed a fistful of his jacket, he nearly went sprawling. Her lips met his. He lost his balance all over again. This close, she was intoxicating. All honey-spun flames and crackling lightning. He could taste the lingering in her kiss. The reluctance. And he knew, even before she broke away from him, that this was what she offered him. Not time, but a memory.

"Mostly that," he added with a weak laugh.

She rested her forehead against his chest. "I want that too."

Vikram waited, worrying the ends of her hair between his fingers. He wouldn't forget this.

"This place changed me," she said hoarsely. "I need to figure out who I am after all this. There are people waiting on me to take them out of chaos. I don't know how long that will take. I don't know how long it will be before I know who I am and what I need to do and . . . I need every part of myself for that fight." She looked up at him. "Especially my heart."

He knew what she would say, but hearing it didn't make it any better. Even bruised, he admired her. It was almost more than wanting her. He took in the dark silk of her hair and winter black of her eyes, memorizing her. And then he noticed something at her neck—a small curve of light resting right beneath the sapphire pendant she always wore. He frowned.

"Is that—"

She reached for her necklace, smiling. "I don't need it."

A wish. After all this, she didn't need it.

"I think sometimes the truest wish of all is not needing to make one," she said. "Besides, I think there's someone at home who needs it more than I do."

"What do you plan on doing, Gauri?" he asked, grinning. "Going to stroll through the gates of Bharata with nothing but a dagger?"

She reached into a small bag and pulled out a dagger he'd never seen. It was unnaturally blue, with a shimmering finish as if it were made of water.

"A gift from Lady Kauveri," she said. Gauri threw it to the ground, where it blossomed into a watery trident. "I think it's capable of making quite the entrance."

"You do like dramatic entrances."

"I can't help myself."

"If you need me—"

"I'll ask," she said, stowing away the dagger. "Will you do the same?"

He nodded. It took every thread of his discipline to pull away from her. The gates swung open. The moment he walked past them, Alaka would vanish. The empire of Ujjain would unravel before him. A wish could not carve out the future any more than believing in destiny could make you deserve it. He knew that now, and even if Alaka had cut out one belief, it had left him with a hundred new ones, each more powerful than the last.

"Vikram," called Gauri. He turned to her. "When I figure out . . . everything . . . I won't make you wait."

He laughed. "You said that last time."

And then he stepped through the gates.

43

RUSTLING FEATHERS

AASHA

Aasha traced the unmarked skin at her throat where a blue star once stained her neck. Closing her eyes, she searched herself for the memory of venom dancing through her veins, and the blue star bloomed beneath her fingers. She could control it now, and the ability to make that choice left her heady with power. The moment she made her wish, her life cleaved in two: before and after. Strange how it was nothing more than a handful of words that changed her life.

The Lord of Treasures was the one who coaxed the wish out of her. She had been crouching on the ground, her fingers stained with Vikram's blood, her whole body shivering with helplessness. Why couldn't she touch him and pull the knife from his back? Why couldn't she push Gauri out of harm's way? Her body was a prison.

"I knew it would be harder for you," the Lord of Treasures said from across the room.

Aasha remembered blinking through her tears and staring at the emptied room. The Otherworld was quick to lose interest. Once the humans slumped to the floor, the entertainment had ended. They had left for the courtyard grounds, goblets of happy memories sloshing onto the floor. Indifference painted the air stiff and brittle. Aasha had hated every moment that they left. She'd hated the moment where she had looked for Gauri and Vikram, only to see the outline of their bodies and not their actual selves. Had Alaka spirited away the dead so as not to ruin the palace decorations?

The Nameless laughed in a corner, blue stars shining on their throats. The knowledge that they were *vishakanyas* unsettled her. As the Lord of Treasures walked across the emptied floors and made his way to her, the Nameless had twirled in a circle and executed a clumsy bow in his direction.

"Another hundred years of magic are ours," they sang. "Our vengeance lives on."

"Yes," said the Lord of Treasures, and Aasha thought she heard an echo of sadness in his voice. "You've passed on your enchantments for another hundred years. Perhaps, one day, your vengeance will give way to freedom. Or perhaps you will always dance out of time, not quite ghosts and not quite beings, shedding a little more of your humanity every time."

"We do this for her," the Nameless said, pointing at Aasha and sneering. "We will do it again." They turned to Aasha. "You see, girl? We are you as you are us. We gave you and your sisters the gift of our blood and our legacy. Because of us, nothing can touch you. You should be thanking us, not mourning those things. They would not mourn you."

Aasha said nothing, and the Nameless only laughed and disappeared.

"You let them die," she said.

"I am not so cruel, child," said the Lord of Treasures, lifting her chin. "I merely let their choices play out as they will."

"What will happen to them?"

"That is not for either of us to decide," he said. "Here. Have a wish for yourself."

He held out his hand to show a wisp of light dancing at the center of his palm. A choice stretched out before her. The words of the Nameless rang in her ears: *nothing can touch you.* They were right. Knowledge and curiosity would never brush against her mind. She would only know an enclosure of silk and poison. She would know only the desires of others and nothing of her own. Magic was a bargain. In a hundred years, perhaps the *vishakanya* magic would ebb little by little, turning them human once more if they lived that long.

But Aasha was restless. The Tournament of Wishes had ignited a hunger in her own heart. Curiosity felt like a phantom limb, a part of her that had died and demanded resurrection. In the arms of her sisters, the world was so small she could cup it in her palms. That world had love and friendship. The Nameless were wrong. Vengeance wasn't their legacy. Only venom. Her sisters were proof. So many of them entered the *vishakanyas'* fold not for vengeance . . . but for freedom. They didn't even call their gift vengeance, but a Blessing. They made it their own.

With her knees folded beneath her, Aasha felt like a fledgling bird, half blind and all eager. She reached for the wispy wish, curling it between her fingers and bringing it to her lips. She uttered her wish without words—a wish for control and choice, for curiosity and courage. When she opened her eyes, the Lord of Treasures was gone. And so was her star.

Aasha had wandered through the courtyard, circling the *vishakanyas'* tent for most of the night until she summoned the courage to enter and reveal what she had done. She switched between her human and *vishakanya* self, bracing herself for disgust. But her sisters' embraces were nothing but warm, though they were careful to make sure they could touch her. They pressed their true names to her wrists, and enchanted bracelets sprouted around her arms: protection spells and keys between worlds, charms for beauty and wealth, for good health and better dreams.

That night, she slept in the forest, beneath the stars and on a bed of blossoms. The next day, she made her way to the gates of Alaka and she found a familiar silhouette waiting at the exit. Gauri stared at the gate as if her heart were on the other side. The moment she saw Aasha, she smiled widely before her gaze fell to the empty patch of skin at her neck.

"My wish came true," said Aasha.

"You wished to no longer be a *vishakanya?*"

She shook her head. "I wished to honor the heritage of my sisters and my own curiosity."

Aasha removed her hand, and the blue star flared onto her skin before disappearing.

"You can control it?" Gauri asked, wide-eyed.

"Perhaps it will be of use to me during my travels."

"Where will you go?"

"I haven't quite figured that out yet, but I think that's what I like most."

Gauri grinned. "I don't know where your travels will take you, but there will always be a home for you in Bharata. And plenty of food, so you won't have to try eating a flower again." Aasha laughed. "A room and a meal is the least I could offer. You saved our lives."

Aasha fell quiet. "Maybe you saved mine too." She held out her hand, but Gauri pushed it aside and drew her into a hug. "I wish you well, my friend."

"And I wish you will have no need of wishes."

Gauri stepped past the gates, her chin held high and eyes fixed on a world that Aasha couldn't see. Magic sparked through the air, sifting light through her skin until she looked like a held flame: incandescent and roaring. In a blink, she disappeared. Aasha smiled to herself and walked slowly to the gate. She looked over her shoulder, to the magic of golden spires piercing the sky, to the crumpled silk pennants of her sisters' tent and the rustling of feathers on the wings of unfinished stories. She walked forward.

This time, she didn't look back.

44

A TURNED HEART

GAURI

Midnight in Bharata.

Bharata looked the same. All that time that Ujijain had kept me locked up, I thought I'd come home to a collection of ruins. But I was far less critical to holding Bharata together than I thought I was. Only a month should have passed since my time in Alaka. One deep breath of air confirmed it. Monsoon season. Large thunderheads hovered over in the distance, their rain-heavy bellies waiting to snag on the mountain peaks.

I had imagined coming back to Bharata a hundred ways and a thousand times. I imagined riding at the head of an army. Pennants streaming. Flags flying so high that they looked like bloody dents formed by fingers raking the sky. I imagined clashing swords and brutal victory, terrible violence that seared memories and proved that no one could keep me from my throne. But Bharata didn't need bloodshed. And neither did I. What my country wanted and what I needed were the same. We didn't want to sing the song of war and blood, of power squabbles and viciousness. We wanted a new beginning.

The palace gates were shuttered like folded arms. Behind them, I heard the rustle of the sentinels' armor. Kauveri's gift burned in my bag, a snippet of magic from a roaring river and energy that was hungry for release. If my plan worked, I wouldn't have to fight. My glass hand caught the moonlight and I bit back a wince. I couldn't fight. This plan *had* to work.

"Who goes there?" called the main guard.

I cleared my throat and stood up a little straighter.

"The Princess Gauri of Bharata."

I could hear them shuffling behind the door, whispers growing into threats and hushed conversations. Seconds slid into minutes and the whispers grew into louder and louder threats.

"—let her in!"

"—a lie—"

"You know he won't allow—"

"—supposed to be—"

Alaka might have changed my perspective, but it had done *nothing* for my patience.

"*Open this gate and let me through,*" I said. "I am your princess and you are bound by honor and duty to obey me."

"What is the meaning of this?" demanded a voice I knew far too well. My body responded before my mind did, nausea gripping my stomach. Skanda.

"Your Majesty, the woman outside the gate says that she is Princess Gauri. Perhaps all these months that she has been lost, she has returned—"

"I have," I said loudly. I was surprised Skanda hadn't immediately spread a rumor that I was dead. But then again, Ujijain never had the chance to execute me. Skanda liked proof. I murmured a silent thanks to Vikram. "Dear brother, why don't you let me in?"

"We will not entertain these lies," said Skanda. "This woman is an imposter. She should be hanged on the spot. Guards!"

"But she sounds just like her," said a meek voice.

A murmur of agreement ran through the sentinels.

"No worries, brother," I said. "If you won't let me into the gate, I'll just go over it."

I smiled. I threw Kauveri's water dagger into the ground, and it grew into a trident forged from a river's mouth. Moonlight shone through the water, turning it silver and resplendent. The sound of rushing water lit up the air, shaking the ground with silent tremors. The trident trembled. Water pooled around my ankles, squeezing between the bottoms of my feet and the ground and rising like a controlled flood.

"What was that?" said someone behind the gate.

"Probably just the thunder," snapped Skanda.

Alaka taught me that the world was little more than a pulsing story that had no beginning and no ending. From the moment I set foot in Bharata, I was starting a story.

But why settle for a story, when I could start a legend?

I smiled, raising the trident into the air and smashing it into the ground. A thousand jetting streams of water rushed beneath my feet, bracketing my ankles and calves as they shot up and carried me with them. My stomach plummeted as the enchantment pushed me through the air. Up here, I couldn't even see the tops of the trees, but I was eye-level with the mountains and maybe if I reached high enough, I could peel a star out of the sky. Down below, the shouts of the guards barely reached my ears. I let myself hover above them, relishing the cold and sweet air of midnight, this moment of magic that teetered on the edge of breaking. I raised one of my legs, and the column of water followed suit, pouring over the gate. I raised my other leg for the final step over the gate. If I wanted, I could drown Skanda. But I refused to rule with blood on my hands. Even his. I closed my eyes, and the columns of water roaring beneath me collapsed gracefully until I shot down to the eye level of a dozen Bharata guards and my brother.

"Recognize me now?"

The guards dropped their weapons. Half of them prostrated themselves on the ground, muttering prayers beneath their breaths. The other half stared, jaws slack and eyes wide. It took every bit of strength not to gloat and scream. Skanda was the first to catch his thoughts.

"My heart is light to see you safe, my sister. And so . . . gifted from your travels," he said. "We have much to discuss. You there—" He snapped his fingers to a white-faced attendant. "—get her chambers ready and inform General Arjun that our princess has returned."

The attendant didn't move. I smiled. The attendant moved immediately. Skanda did not miss the exchange. His gaze narrowed.

"You returned despite great risk to life and limb," he said, his tone artificially admirable. "And with a fascinating trick to add to the country's arsenal of weapons. I am pleased."

We both knew that he wasn't talking about my life and limb. Nalini was the unspoken danger. But Skanda's words, despite their meaning, carried hope: I was *still* risking her life. She was alive. My greatest fear went unrealized. I had to fight down the urge to smile. Instead, I bowed my head. His gaze fell to my glass hand. I flexed it. I could already see how he was trying to twist the magic he'd seen:

Demon-touched.

Possessed.

A vector for evil.

But he wasn't the only one trained in storytelling anymore. I embraced my brother, even though I wanted to rip off my skin at his touch. As I walked along the corridors of Bharata, I kept looking out of the corner of my eye, waiting for someone to pounce out of the shadows. I wouldn't be able to fight them with a glass hand that *refused* to pick up a weapon.

I paced in the chambers, Kauveri's dagger strapped to my leg even as I bathed and changed out of the traveling clothes. After Alaka, every color looked dim.

Skanda refused to place me in the harem, claiming I would upset the women before he had a chance to explain my return. Coward. The last thing he wanted was every woman in the harem armed with the knowledge of magic and prepared to fight him.

Someone knocked at the door. I opened it, expecting to see an attendant. Arjun stared back at me. My throat tightened. Joy, hurt and fury shredded me all at once. This was the man who showed me what a brother was. He had carried me for half the day when I broke my leg. Split his desserts with me. Teased me out of bad moods and sobered me when I needed it. And yet, he'd stood by when Skanda had dragged Nalini to the throne room. He'd known my plans and betrayed me. He clenched his jaw, his gaze turning flinty.

"How could you come back after everything you did?" he demanded.

I felt as if the carpet had been pulled out from beneath me. I stood there, shocked.

"You put my life in danger. You put *Nalini's* life in danger," he hissed. Stepping forward. "How could you? And after all this, after we pleaded for Skanda not to kill you, *you come back?*"

Fury rose inside me.

"What are you talking about, Arjun?" I demanded. "How dare you even talk to me about Nalini's safety when you betrayed me at the moment when I needed you the most, when *Nalini* needed you the most?"

A shadow moved behind him. Useless as it was, I placed my glass hand on the other iron dagger strapped to my left arm. The shadow slipped into the room, and its owner slid into view:

Nalini.

I couldn't help myself. I tried to throw my arms around her, but she stepped away from me and *into Arjun's arms.* She didn't look as though she'd spent any time in a prison. I stared at them, my breath catching. What was happening?

"Nalini . . . it's me. . . . I came back for you."

"To do what? Make sure that she was dead even after we spared you?" returned Arjun.

"*Spared me?*"

They stepped into the room, closing the door.

"Talk to me, Nalini. Please. You have no idea what I fought through to get to you," I said, my whole body trembling.

Nalini stared at me as if I really were a stranger. She stared at me as if I were the enemy and not the victim. When I reached for her, she moved back a step. My heart split.

"Before you left, Skanda told me that he knew all about your rebellion," she said, not looking at me. "He said that it was to make sure that my father's lands would never pass to me—"

"I would never do that!" I protested.

"I asked you, Gauri," she said. "Don't you remember? I came to you and I demanded to know what would happen to me in your scheme of power?"

I remembered.

"*Why are you bringing that up?*" I said. "*You inheriting power only applies if you reach your eighteenth year. You're hardly in your sixteenth. A thousand and one things could happen between now and then. Focus on what we can control in the present.*"

Time froze. That was the same night I had confronted her in the garden. The same night I thought I heard Skanda's spies moving in the darkness.

"He showed us documents you'd written. . . ." said Nalini, her voice breaking.

The false documents. I closed my eyes. I had written those to protect what I was doing. I intended for them to fall into the "wrong hands," but my brother had done just that.

"You refused to speak to us, to tell us of your plans," said Arjun. "You shunned us, Gauri. And Skanda showed us the truth. He showed us how you wanted Nalini out of the way and proved what you've been doing with all your time."

I remembered Nalini falling to her knees, the knife pressed to her throat. Skanda's words—so carefully chosen—*I know what you want.* I thought . . . I thought he meant that I wanted her safe. But he'd performed to both sides.

How many times had Arjun begged to speak to me in private after I had rescued him? All this time, I had assumed he wanted to speak about what he had seen, the traumas that had held him captive. I didn't pay attention. It was too risky, too much of an open declaration that we were in league with one another. I told myself that I would be there for him as a friend later, that right now I could spare neither time nor security. The callousness that had saved me so often had destroyed me too.

"I begged Skanda to send you to an ashram where no one else could get hurt. I begged him to spare your life, even after everything you'd done to hurt us. Why did you come back?"

Before I left Alaka, I told Vikram I didn't know myself. Now I was staring at the depths of what that meant. *Heroine. Savior. Villain.* What were those words but different fistfuls of a tale that all depended on who was doing the telling? *You see, a story is not just a thing told to a child before sleep. A story is control.* I saw it now. Felt the talons of that truth scrape through me. I saw how I had laid down the bones of Skanda's story: a tale of a turned heart and insatiable greed.

"Skanda lied to you," I said, my voice breaking.

I sank to the floor, my head in my hands: one glass, one flesh. One translucent. One opaque. One that could wield a knife and one that could not. Past and present. Alaka had cut my life in half. When I looked forward, the hand that had been my horror became my hope: transparency. Nalini breathed sharply. Arjun tried to hold her back, but she crouched beside me, cradling the glass hand.

"What happened to you?"

I laughed. "I cannot even begin to tell you everything."

"Try," urged Nalini. "Arjun was sent to fetch you, but I couldn't . . . I had to see you . . ." She stopped, blinking back tears. "You know your brother will send another attendant soon."

I tried. I told them about what I had felt the day I emerged into the throne room to see the soldiers cut down and Arjun standing at Skanda's side. I told them about being thrown over the Ujijain border, my mouth gagged and my wrists bound; the months of silent torture while the empire decided what to do with me. I told them how Vikram changed everything, about the invitation to the Tournament of Wishes in the city of Alaka down to the moment where I earned escape. I didn't tell them about the wish though. Knowing Arjun, he would want a demonstration, and I couldn't risk giving away the last weapon I had. When Nalini held Kauveri's gift, her eyes narrowed from uncertainty to awe. Even Arjun stopped frowning to hold the dagger. The dagger shimmered in his hands, transforming into a trident of water. From where I sat, I could feel the rush of an invisible river, the magic of a powerful wave brimming through the room and roiling with energy.

"Why would I come back just to be killed?" I said when Arjun turned away from me. "This whole time I thought that *you* had turned on me. I don't know how else to prove—"

An attendant knocked at the door.

"General Arjun?"

My pulse raced. The attendant was knocking on *my* door. So why was he addressing Arjun? Arjun spoke through the door.

"I wasn't able to comply with the Raja Skanda's directive," he said. "Her travels have worn her and it seems that one of the servants gave her a sleeping draught to calm her nerves. Tell the Raja that I will escort her to the throne room."

"Very good, General."

Footsteps echoed and disappeared down the hall.

". . . He sent you here to kill me?" Arjun's mouth tightened to a cut, which was all the answer I needed.

"I wouldn't let him," said Nalini. "Not without seeing you. Or hearing why you did what . . . what we thought you did."

My heart leapt. "You believe me?"

Nalini held my gaze. "I don't know what to believe."

I reached for her hand, but Arjun stopped me.

"We need to go," he said tightly. "We can confront Skanda ourselves." He yanked me to my feet. "You have one chance to make me believe you. Otherwise, I'll follow through with the order."

And then he turned to Nalini, cupping her face between his palms and kissing her gently on the forehead. How blind had I been before now? All this time, I thought Arjun hadn't loved Nalini enough to protect her from Skanda. The truth was that he loved her so much that he had betrayed me. Nalini watched us as we walked to the door, her eyes never leaving my face.

"Thank you," I said when we started walking down the hall.

"For what?"

"For not killing me, for starters. And for keeping me safe when you didn't have to."

"I didn't do it for you."

"Arjun, I know how it looks. But we were like siblings—"

"Exactly," he said cuttingly. "We *were* like siblings. And then you changed. Skanda can set this record straight."

"Skanda is a liar. The things he's done and made me—"

"That's what you said before to make me pledge you soldiers. I did it because I trusted your word until you kept proving you weren't worth it. But did you ever once prove that he did everything you said?"

Weakness is a privilege.

I had never told him. I thought . . . I thought I was keeping myself safe. But sometimes weakness wore the face of strength, and sometimes strength wore the face of weakness.

"You may not believe me, but surely you've seen some of his deception ever since you became his second-in-command? Has nothing he's done convinced you that he might not be innocent?"

Arjun faltered. Skanda may be an expert storyteller, but even he couldn't keep up a ruse of innocence for too long. Pausing before the throne doors, Arjun fixed me with a dark look.

"Don't try anything."

I held up my hands in surrender. "I won't."

Inside the room, Skanda reclined against silk pillows. I scanned the room: no attendants. Not even a servant to answer his thousand insignificant needs. He looked as if he wanted this to be informal, but it felt calculated. On a glass tray stood goblets full of cold *thandai*. My mouth watered. I could smell the vetiver seeds and rose petals steeped in the milky drink.

"You used to drink this every time you came home from one skirmish or another," said Skanda, his voice swelling with mock brotherly pride.

I sat in front of him, mindful of Kauveri's dagger slung against my hip. I had placed it on the left side, hoping that Skanda would interpret it as a sign of peace and not a sign that my right hand refused to hold weapons. Arjun sank into the pillow next to Skanda, one hand protectively on his dagger.

"Now, now, Arjun, no need to be so aggressive. After all, the Princess Gauri has come back from a long and arduous trek. She was so weakened she could hardly stay awake." Skanda flashed a thin and oily smile. He held out cups of *thandai* to me and Arjun. I took mine gingerly, breathing in the spicy scent.

"May I see that dagger of yours, sister?"

"Later," I said. "I tire."

He smiled. "Of course. For now, let us drink to your health and your return."

I lifted the drink to my lips, but didn't sip the liquid until Skanda took a swig. I took a sip and bit back a grimace. Whoever made the drink had added far too much almond extract. Arjun downed his drink in one gulp.

"I am sorry that we had to have this meeting under such circumstances," said Skanda, with another small shake of his head.

The *thundai* tickled my throat. I coughed and drank some more. Warmth spread through my limbs. An itch burned right behind my calf.

"But you left me no choice."

Beside me, Arjun began to cough. He reached for a glass of water, but his trembling fingers knocked the glass aside. Skanda reached for something in the folds of his sleeve, drawing out a knot of leaves, which he chewed immediately. Arjun stared at him, wide-eyed and furious, clawing at his throat.

"What have you done to him?"

I grabbed Arjun, thumping his back. He began to shake. His face paled.

"You can't let him die, Skanda!" I screamed. "Give me the antidote!"

But Skanda didn't say anything. He just stared from me to the cup.

"Why are you still speaking?" he whispered.

The doors to the throne room crashed open. A swirl of silks and jangling silver clamored for volume over Arjun's violent coughing. Nalini whimpered. She reached for him, tilting his face to hers as she felt for the pulse at his neck. He convulsed. Sweat beaded his skin.

I lunged at Skanda, holding the dagger with my left hand to this throat. "I will let you live if you tell me how to save him."

Skanda pressed himself against the cushions, his fat face shining and his eyes widening in shock.

"He . . . he can't . . . I took the only antidote."

Shoving Skanda aside, I turned back around to Nalini and Arjun. She was crouched over him, her whole body shaking. Arjun lay in her lap, his lips parted and eyes staring blindly at the ceiling.

He was dead.

45

TO ECLIPSE

GAURI

Skanda turned to me. "Why aren't you dead?"

A vague burning sensation lit up my whole leg. And I knew, even without looking, that the small blue star from the poisoned waters of the Serpent King had saved my life. I thought of the accusation from the Nameless, the way they called me "marked." I couldn't kill someone with my touch, but somehow I had been granted immunity from poison.

"You killed him," whispered Nalini. "How could you?"

The screams had alerted the rest of the guards. One by one they filed into the throne room.

"The Raja Skanda has poisoned General Arjun," said Nalini, her voice strong but trembling.

"No!" screamed Skanda. "The Princess Gauri was the one behind it! She drank the poison and wasn't even harmed. It's unnatural! Seize her! You saw what she did outside the gates. She's a witch of some kind. It's not even her—"

"I can vouch for the Princess's innocence," said Nalini. Now her voice was pure steel.

I could hear the world holding its breath. The ultimate test of loyalty. Arjun had led the soldiers, given them reason time after time to trust him. Nalini was his wife, beloved by him as much as she was the soldiers. But Skanda was still the king. Then again, what is a king but someone that others say is such? He wore a crown. Just as I once did. But power is something you earn. Seduce. Maybe the circumstances of my birth gave me the skeleton of power, but it was up to me—my story, my voice—to put flesh on those bones and make that power live. Arjun knew that. Every day that I had known Arjun he had made himself worthy of power. Two guards stood behind Skanda. He looked up at them, furious. Expectant. A choice hung in the air: Which power to follow? They chose. Two of the guards pulled Skanda from his nest of cushions.

"Your Highness?" said one of the guards, turning to me.

Out of habit, I looked to my brother. But they weren't talking to him. They were talking to me.

I was queen.

For so long, the wants I had held in my heart—my kingdom wrested from Skanda's control, a reign secured with no bloodshed, Nalini alive and well—felt like seedlings of a future out of reach. Now those hopes grew roots inside me. I hadn't needed an army to reclaim my country. I hadn't even needed a wish. I had only needed to return and be honest.

I found my voice. "Take him to the prison cells and send a healer."

Skanda roared. "I am your kin! And you would kill me?"

46

TELLING A LIE

VIKRAM

The emerald snake tightened around Vikram's arm. He winced before patting the jeweled snake on the head.

"That's enough, Biju. You've proven your point."

Biju relented, flicking a forked diamond tongue at Vikram before sliding across his shoulders. Her tail gracefully swung from his neck to his shoulder. She bit the end, and immediately grew cold. Morning light glinted off her scales.

Unless she was detecting a lie, Biju preferred to live out her existence as a marvelous garland of polished emerald stones carved into the likeness of real snake scales. Sometimes she switched to sapphire. Once, she was even ruby. But green was her favorite color. Last week Vikram had called her "exceedingly predictable." She had responded by coiling into a vise around his arm. Her way of saying: *You tell a lie.*

Vikram started each of his mornings with a lie. And every day, it

I tilted my head, staring at this beast I shared blood with. "I'm not going to kill you."

He relaxed. "Then—"

"I am going to eclipse you," I said quietly. "I am going to bury your name in the dust, not with your death, but with my might. I am going to give you a fate worse than death, brother. I am going to erase you from memory."

They left, and Nalini stared at me, tears streaming down her face. "You know he's dead. Why summon a healer?"

I knelt beside Nalini and reached behind my neck for the clasp to my necklace. When I pulled it out, the unused wish glowed brightly. I closed my eyes, remembering Alaka as the images of the story birds whirled away into darkness.

"So will you make a wish?" asked Kauveri.

Beyond them, a river splashed diamonds into a bright gray sky. There was magic and hope in that space of sky and sea where a new tomorrow would haul itself into the world with the same sun and a changing moon, and all the secrets in its stars. I chose a new kind of bravery. One with a future I chose to earn, rather than demand.

"No."

Part of me almost uttered the wish I thought Nalini wanted. But I wasn't going to assume anymore. She deserved that chance and choice. When I looked at Nalini, Aasha's face loomed in my thoughts. The life she hungered after, the choices that had been denied. I closed my hand over the bright wish, and placed it in Nalini's palm.

"Here," I said. "I think it was always supposed to be yours."

"What is this, Gauri?" asked Nalini, opening her hands.

Light bathed her face, pouring gently over Arjun's unseeing eyes.

"A new beginning."

was the same lie. He would stand in front of his mirror and say, "Today, she is ready." And every day, Biju would tighten into a vise, which assured him that he should hope for no such thing.

Today, like every day for the past two full moons, had been no exception.

After returning from Alaka, he thought he had sated his hunger for wonder, but something still growled in need within him. He glanced out the window. Morning had barely touched Ujijain. Shadows hugged half of the city. Once the city bells rang out, he would begin his endless procession of meetings. It was a routine that gave him comfort. The meetings, the research, the debate. The fact that after all this time, his voice finally mattered. He had a purpose and a place. He even enjoyed complaining about his sore feet and his headaches, but suspected that the novelty would soon wear off.

Vikram set off for the Menagerie, but he had hardly walked five steps down the hall when a voice called out:

"Your Majesty!"

It took him a moment to realize he was being addressed. He was still getting used to his new title. "Emperor" tasted too weighty and bittersweet on his tongue. He stopped walking, allowing a fresh-faced courtier to catch up to him.

"May I walk in your shadow, Your Majesty?"

You used to run from it.

"Of course," he said, sweeping the air like an invitation. The courtier fell into step beside him.

"It was an honor to hear you speak at last week's assembly."

Oh, you were listening? When I saw your head thrown back and drool falling from your mouth, I thought otherwise. My sincerest apologies.

"I'm grateful you listened."

"I only wish that we had the opportunity to be enlightened by your intelligence earlier."

"I gave you multiple opportunities."

The color drained from the courtier's face. "Your Majesty, I did not mean to remind you of such . . . irresponsibility and ignorance from the council in the past."

Yourself included.

"But surely, Your Majesty, you saw how the council changed the day you returned. You astounded them. They were awed."

"Showing up with an Otherworldly treasure tends to do that."

Two full moons ago, he had returned to Ujijain and walked straight into a council meeting with nothing but the enchanted document in his hand and Biju around his neck. His wish had been for all who looked upon the document to recognize his potential, but it had the unpredicted benefit of allowing all who looked at the piece of parchment to see potential not just in Vikram, but also themselves. He told them about his travels in the Otherworld, demonstrating the truth with Biju. Little by little, his circumstances changed. Half the council credited Vikram's monthlong disappearance into the Otherworld as the reason he had risen to power and shrugged off the puppet ruler title. The other half credited themselves for finally noticing the Prince's "remarkable mind."

"I suppose you're right, Your Majesty," said the courtier. "However . . . I do believe that even without magic, they would have changed their mind. I've read your reports in the past, and you always provided the most creative solutions."

Vikram looked at the courtier a little more closely. "What's your name?"

"Chandresh."

"And who are you?"

Chandresh mulled over his response. "I was a fool of the highest pedigree before Your Majesty's return. I am the courtier who sleeps through most meetings. I'm also the courtier who provides the best feedback. I closely read the meeting's notes after."

Vikram grinned. "Intriguing. I would be interested in speaking to you after the meeting. Or your nap, as it were."

"I would be honored, Your Majesty."

The courtier bowed at the hip, and left him in the hall. Vikram watched him go, and a cautious happiness flooded him. Perhaps he was on his way to forging alliances within the empire. He was still learning how to navigate his way through politics now that the novelty of Kubera's gifts had worn off. The realm still murmured about the Otherworldly games where he had disappeared to for a month, but it was mostly rumor. Most believed he had returned to the ashram and observed the strictest of penances in order to succeed to the throne. Only the council—six men, half of whom wore the shadow of death and the other half of whom were so skilled in lying that not even their wives believed them—had seen his magical demonstration. Their word was the only one that counted. Once he had won their allegiance—or frightened it out of them, more like—he hadn't seen the need to continue impressing people with the enchanted document. The only thing he found indispensable was Biju. Conversations were far more efficient when lying was impossible.

Vikram stopped in front of the Menagerie and knocked twice. "Father?"

A growl echoed inside the room. "Come in!"

Vikram stepped through and quickly shut the door. The leopard, Urvashi, kept pushing her head against the wooden frame.

"I was thinking I might let her roam around the palace," said Pururavas, waddling to the door. "She's become so restless."

"Roam around the palace?"

"With a leash."

"With an armed guard."

Pururavas gasped. "Do you think someone would try to hurt her?"

Vikram stared. "Father, I think sometimes you are too innocent."

"But that is a yes to letting her roam?" said his father. "That decision falls to you."

"I'll consider it." Urvashi glared at him reproachfully. "Perhaps we could make her a new courtyard. Put things she can jump off of. She does have a tendency to climb." He pointed at the tables that had been stacked upon one another as a perch for the leopard.

Pururavas nodded approvingly. "I'm glad you thought to visit. There's something I wanted to discuss with you."

Vikram braced himself. He knew that his father's question could only be about one of two things . . . either Gauri or his marriage prospects.

"You fled with the Princess."

One out of two.

"I did. And she's not a princess anymore. She's the Queen of Bharata."

When he spoke the last words, pride glowed in his voice. He couldn't help it.

"And she was with you during this . . . tournament."

Pururavas couldn't make himself say any words about magic even though he had seen the wonders Vikram brought home.

"Yes, she was," said Vikram. And then his eyes narrowed. "You haven't been talking about this to anyone, have you, Father? Only you know she was with me."

"Of course not!" huffed Puru. "But since you've returned, Bharata has withdrawn their remaining military units from our borders. The letter from General Arjun came in only recently. We have done the same. I believe now it's just a matter of formalizing relations. The messengers we sent responded favorably. And the Bharata messengers sent to Ujijain have been nothing short of cordial. They even sent a gift last time, albeit a curious one."

Vikram bit down his grin. The gift had been a wooden crown with a small note: "for your entertainment." Some of his council had been inclined to believe that it was an insult, but Vikram understood.

I wouldn't mind a crown made of wood though. I might throw it at people for entertainment.

"Do you think it's because of your excursion with the Princess?"

"Once more, Father, she's not a princess but a queen. And I don't believe she would have found it wise to tell anyone that she, an unmarried princess at the time, spent weeks from her home with a prince and returned unengaged. But I did free her from her prisoner cell. I imagine that would have been reason enough to thaw our relations."

Freeing Gauri had been the only thorny comment when he returned to Ujijain. For the most part, he had convinced the council that freeing her had been a diplomatic strategy. For the most part, they had agreed. Once the delegates returned with positive reports, the rest of the council breathed a sigh of relief that they had stopped at imprisoning her.

"Then why not—"

Two out of two.

He lived this argument at least twelve times a day. One for every hour that the Emperor Pururavas was awake.

"Father, I know where you are going with this, and the answer is no."

Not quite. The answer wasn't no, so much as he hoped it was "not yet." She would come to him when she was ready. At least, he hoped she would.

Pururavas sniffed. "You spent a month with the girl, and you feel nothing? She is a powerful queen. Don't think that just because I spend all day in my Menagerie that I don't read those reports! She's ruled for hardly two moons, and already she is Queen Gauri the Great—"

"I read the reports, Father, I know what she's done."

Vikram smiled. He expected no less from her. In the short time that she'd been queen, she had changed the structure of power with the fractious tribes bordering Bharata by bestowing a title of governorship to Lady Nalini, the daughter of a powerful chieftain and wife of General Arjun. She'd also banned conscription into Bharata's army, reinforced the village militias so that the villages could defend themselves and commissioned new *gurukul* school systems throughout the kingdom.

"So why wouldn't you pursue anything with her? An alliance would be powerful indeed."

"I have my reasons."

"Pah! That is what I think of your reasons."

Vikram found the nearest chair and sank into it. His father could lecture him for hours before tiring himself out. While Pururavas began to pace the room, shouting about the necessity of marriage and heirs while his leopard doggedly guarded him, Vikram lifted Biju from his neck. He tried to restrain himself to asking only once a day, but today he couldn't help it:

"She is ready."

Vikram waited for the familiar tightening sensation around his arm. But for the first time, Biju didn't move.

47

UNSPENT DAYDREAMS

GAURI

The glass hand twitched. It always twitched whenever I stood in the weapons room. Sometimes I thought it was holding its breath, wondering when it was supposed to turn brittle and lifeless. My left arm ached, but I swung the practice sword through the air anyway, checking it for balance and weight. I wasn't as nimble as I used to be. But there was some advantage to training with the left hand. People always defended themselves from a right-handed attack. The left surprised them.

I liked being a surprise.

Outside, everything smelled fresh. Raw. My first edict as queen was to raze the garden and start anew. My reign would carry no memory of Skanda. I brought in new seeds from foreign cities that promised trees where the fruits were as bright as gems, with rinds dark purple and softest pink, and flesh that was sweeter than a dream. I even uncovered a secret among the gardeners: my father's garden hadn't been entirely ruined. The palace gardeners couldn't bear to see it destroyed, so they had preserved seeds and cuttings, and grown them in secret. Damask roses and sweet-limes, neem and almond tree saplings set down their roots in once-familiar earth. That garden was every hope for my reign. It was slivers of the past nestled alongside the present, silver roots tangled like histories that would one day eclipse the seeds from which they unfurled.

Concentrating on the weapons before me, I tried to take my glass hand by surprise and grip a practice sword. It turned brittle on contact, sending small waves of shock rolling through my arm. Wincing, I shook it out.

"Well played."

The glass hand settled back into liquid movement, although I couldn't help but think it felt a bit smug. Since I had returned, there hadn't been any need for me to wield a weapon. Ujijain's diplomats had arrived at Bharata no more than a week after Skanda named me queen and "retired" to a quiet life in an ashram. Together with my ambassadors, we'd begun constructing a treaty. I had even sent Vikram a gift. I spent the whole week waiting. Ridiculous daydreams kept sliding into my thoughts—that he would arrive disguised among his messengers, that he would burst through the doors and declare that he'd ridden on horseback the moment he saw my gift. But then my messengers came back. They confirmed he'd received it. And that was that. Disappointment curdled in my gut. I wanted to press them for details—did he smile, what kind of smile, were his fingers tented like always or were they at his side—but I didn't want to seem overeager in the face of rejection.

Every time Bharata's ambassadors returned, they carried new tales of the Emperor—his clever designs to reorganize the city, new ways of farming to maximize crops, even bits of his philosophical treatises that he'd begun to publish at the beginning of every lunar cycle.

"Gauri?"

I turned to see Arjun leaning in the doorway. He looked a little for-lorn, as he always did whenever Nalini had to return to her new gov-erning seat. She wouldn't be in Bharata for a while. After Nalini used the wish, I'd convinced Skanda—with a not entirely true tale—that it wasn't the only power I'd brought back from my travels. That, in addi-tion to Arjun and Nalini's fury, was enough reason for him to abdicate the throne and name me queen.

"Need a partner?" he asked, frowning at the practice sword in my left hand.

"How hopeless do I look?"

He laughed. My heart lightened. I hadn't heard Arjun laugh in what felt like centuries. Everything in Bharata was something to experience all over. I felt as if I I were relearning the friends that been my family. It was not unlike practicing with the sword in my hand, going through the movements that I had taken for granted. And like a new muscle, it ached.

We sparred for nearly an hour before a trumpet sounded, signaling the arrival of one of my courtiers. I dropped the practice sword and reached for the red silk glove. After that first night in Bharata, I limited the number of people who saw the glass hand. People hungered after what they didn't know and couldn't see, and I liked the enigma and mys-tery of it. My people made up their own tales, claiming that it was a mark of magic or a sign of transparency. They said that it would turn red whenever someone had a murderous thought and that when I looked into the glass palm, I could watch my citizens. I liked their stories far better than the truth.

"Your Majesty," called the courtier. "There is a woman who is knock-ing on the gates of Bharata demanding to see you."

Arjun touched his sword. "What did my men make of her? Does she seem like a threat to the Queen's life?"

"The men thought she . . ." The courtier trailed off, bright spots of color lighting up his cheeks.

I smiled. I knew who was at the gate.

A month later, Aasha leaned out the window, propping her chin in her palms and sighing loudly. In the second month of my reign, Aasha had showed up outside the city gates demanding that I fulfill my promise of a place in my palace. In the first week of her arrival, she'd foiled two assassination attempts simply by sniffing out the thoughts of whatever nobleman or noblewoman wished to meet with me.

"Can we go outside?" she asked. "This tires me."

Shock lit up half my attendants' faces. Aasha was one of the few people who never simpered. She didn't know how and didn't care to learn. Dismissing the attendants, I joined her on the balcony. The garden had grown lush and green in the three months since I'd pulled up the courtyard by the roots and started anew. I never walked along the paths. There were too many reminders tucked into the perfume of those blossoms. When I walked through the gardens, the reminder that something—someone—was missing from my life was impossible to ignore. I thought I saw him in every lean shadow splayed across the ground. I thought I heard him in every laughing fountain. When I came back to Bharata, it had been easier to push aside the ache of missing him, because I dedicated every moment to the restructuring of Bharata. But now I had settled into a rhythm. Every day looked a little more normal. I was even getting better at sparring with my left arm. Which meant there were too many moments where the absence of him gnawed at my heart.

"I know you're tired, but no, we can't go outside," I said. "I have papers to review."

Aasha frowned. "But you want to go outside."

Groaning, I covered my head with my hands, as if that would somehow stop my wants from betraying me.

"You also want to see him."

"Go away."

She leaned a little closer, sniffing me. "And you want food. Why do you always want food?"

"Please stop."

"Why don't you see him?"

"Because I'm busy!" I said, flicking a dead insect off the windowpane.

Aasha raised an eyebrow. "Lie."

"I will. Soon. I think," I hedged. "He never sent back a present after I gave him that crown."

Folding her arms, Aasha stared at me as if I had just announced that I was handing over the throne and taking up a new career in professional flicking-dead-insects-off-windowpanes.

"What is the word you taught me yesterday when I bit the rose that stung me?"

Yesterday, a handsome nobleman had left a scarlet rose for Aasha. She'd picked it up only for one of the thorns to prick her thumb. Growling, Aasha had bit the head off the rose. The nobleman ran in the other direction.

I sighed. "The word was 'petty.'"

"Ah. Yes. That is you."

What if the past two months of ruling had changed him and he was just happy with the gradual unthawing of the diplomatic relations and nothing else? Wouldn't he have sent some sign? Then again, I did say to stay away . . . but why would he stay away for *that* long? Wasn't the wooden crown a clear indication that I wanted to see him? I hated boys.

"What's that other word you like?" asked Aasha.

"I like a lot of words."

"True, but the word you use whenever you talk about someone for whom the desires in your mind turn to slow torture or a wish for their mouth to fall off their faces?"

"'Fool'?"

"Yes!" said Aasha brightly. "That is also you."

"You are the worst friend."

"That is not what your mind is saying."

"Stop reading it!"

Aasha rolled her eyes, and the blue star on her throat disappeared.

"Happy?" she asked.

"Yes."

"I do not need the Blessing to see that you are lying."

I was going to argue when the throne room doors were thrown back. I glanced at the sun, still high in the sky. Today, the Ujijain delegates wished to meet with me personally, but I hadn't been expecting their visit so soon.

Aasha pulled a silk head scarf over her face and around her neck just as the bright blue star glinted back into being. A group of Ujijain delegates entered the room, walking single-file and dressed in their finest crimson insignia. Aasha touched my shoulder: a sign that they came with no harm for me in their thoughts. But then her fingers tightened and her brows scrunched in alarm. Not a threat to my life. Something else. My thoughts flew to Vikram. Had something happened to him that the delegates knew and hadn't revealed immediately?

"Your Majesty," they said, bowing.

I walked back to my throne and sank into the seat.

"Welcome."

"Your Highness, Emperor Vikramaditya is pleased that your kingdom has been so gracious and amenable as we seek an alliance between our two realms. We wish to strengthen that bond."

My heart raced. I knew what a strengthened alliance between two kingdoms could be: a proposal of marriage.

"He hopes that you might be amenable to a discussion in four days' time when his official coronation takes place."

"Four days?" I repeated, frowning. He hadn't given me much time to travel. It took three days to travel to Ujijain. Unless he hadn't wanted to invite me. Or worse, unless he had forgotten until the last moment. I didn't know which pummeled my heart more.

The diplomat nodded. "He would be honored by your presence. Or by a delegation. Whichever Your Majesty sees fit to send. As our nations work together, we also hope that you will be in attendance for the Emperor's future wedding."

Now my heart froze. "Wedding? To whom?"

"His Majesty has yet to choose a bride."

"But there have been invitations for marriage discussions sent out to prospective brides?" I asked. I should have forced myself to keep quiet and not reveal so much obvious interest, but I couldn't help it.

"Yes," said the diplomat.

I let this information sit. Vikram was choosing a bride.

I was not on that list.

My first instinct was to refuse the invitation. That urge to latch up my heart flared inside me like an old wound. But I couldn't be scared. When I didn't talk to Nalini, I nearly wrecked our friendship. When I didn't listen to the Serpent King, I nearly destroyed his love.

I was scared to let go—scared to cough up that last bit of control and bare myself—but I was more terrified of what I'd lose if I never spoke up.

"I will be at the coronation," I said. Briefly, I sucked in my cheeks before flashing a terse smile at the diplomats. "Bharata is grateful for this personal invitation. We look forward to peace between our countries."

They bowed. I left.

I felt light-headed. Ever since I had returned from Alaka, marriage had hovered over me like a phantom. I heard the unspoken pressure in my council's demands and noticed the pile of gifts and letters from the eligible nobility. My council spoke of strong ties and advancing our history.

But I knew what I wanted.

I wanted a shadow curled around mine in the night. A hand that was never too far out of reach. I wanted someone who carried a secret light within them, so that I would never be in the dark. When I thought of that, I felt Vikram's fingers softly threading through my hair. I remembered how the feast of fears left my heart gaunt, how I had offered my own hollow body as a distraction. He hadn't accepted that. Instead, he had fed my starving heart with bright bursts of laughter and feather-light secrets. Until I ached, not from emptiness, but smiling.

Had he forgotten? Or . . . had it not mattered?

Aasha opened the door to my bedroom.

"Do you want me to come with you to Ujijain?" she asked.

I nodded. I would have asked Nalini to come too, but she was out of the capital.

"Perhaps you should pick out your attire? That always helped my sisters when they were nervous."

I nodded, pacing my room. I had brought some of Alaka back with me. The ceiling was painted with songbirds in midflight. Traces of gold foil hugged the paintings, so that when I went to sleep, the world above me was a shimmering thing tilting into magic. When I had it commissioned, I thought it would be a reminder of bonds formed through challenges. But the person I had wanted to remind never ended up spending a night beneath this ceiling.

"Perhaps blue?" suggested Aasha. "You don't want to steal too much attention from an emperor on his coronation."

You do like dramatic entrances.

I can't help myself.

I lifted my chin. "I'm wearing gold."

Aasha flashed a knowing smile. "As you command."

48

A WORLD IN WAIT

GAURI

For the next three days, we rode hard. The horses foamed at the mouth when we finally arrived. With only a night left before the coronation, there was no time for the usual political ceremony and veiled talks. My retinue and band of traveling soldiers had little more than a handful of hours to enter the palatial villa that Ujijain had prepared, take refreshments and prepare ourselves for the coronation.

I stood before a gilt mirror. I was moving slower than normal, as if my swollen heart had somehow weighed down my limbs when I wasn't looking. As I reached for the chest of cosmetics, I thought of Mother Dhina. She had died a month into my imprisonment with Ujijain. A small memorial waited for her spirit in the garden: a shrub of dusky roses with a water pipe buried beneath the roots. I stared at my reflection, biting down on my cheeks as I would for any battle. Contemplating my armor.

I darkened my eyes with kohl. Because sometimes my life felt framed by shadows, and yet I had changed how I looked at the world, and found beauty.

I rubbed a rose petal concoction on my lips and cheeks. Because I wanted my words, fanged as they might be, to wear the cover of sweetness.

I dusted crushed pearls over my collarbones and through my hair. Because I would be my own light. No matter what.

The golden sari clung to my figure, and I had draped the silks to cover my right hand. Before I left, I unclasped Maya's necklace. The sapphire slid off my neck, leaving me a little colder. I rubbed my fingers over the pendant, kissing it once. Maya cropped up less and less in my thoughts. Not because I didn't love my sister or didn't think of her, but because I no longer worried for her the way I once had. Sometimes I remembered a dream from Alaka—a white hall and a cold kingdom, a room where my sister waited with a sad smile. For whatever reason, the image gave me peace.

"I am ready," I announced to the empty room.

Ujjain had beautiful grounds. Not as lovely as Bharata's, I thought with a prickling sense of pride, but there was something beloved about the place. Ujjain's grounds celebrated its past and its present. Four statues of beautiful women adorned in the garb of empresses stood in the shade of gentle firs. Sapphire reflection pools lined the walk to the ceremonial pavilion where the coronation would take place. Everywhere, the scent of fresh marigolds and mint hung drowsily in the air. A sliver of gardens peeked out behind a veil of trees.

The crowd for Vikram's coronation was, as expected, huge. Diplomats and distinguished royal guests had poured in from every corner. Sweat stamped my palms. A nervous energy spiked through me. A servant offered me a quartz goblet and a pang lit up my chest. What were the chances they were serving bright memories?

"Your Majesty, we are so honored you chose to attend," said a diplomat at my elbow. "Would you mind accompanying me? The Emperor Vikramaditya has some time before the coronation and wished to meet with you alone and without either of your respective retinues."

We prefer not to have an audience.

I schooled my face into a blank mask. "Lead the way."

I think I lived and died a hundred times in the time it took to walk to the private garden path. Anger, fury, excitement and hurt raced through me. Every part of me felt gathered and strung taut. I kept imagining the words that would come out of his mouth, his gentle way of saying that Alaka had been an experience out of time that he never wished to repeat. Another thought, worse than anything, clawed at me . . . that I'd waited too long.

Here, the sounds of the coronation party never reached the trees. Everything was still. Silent.

"His Majesty is at the end of the garden walkway."

The courtier delivered a final bow before leaving me alone.

I'd never seen a garden like this. Most royal grounds favored sculpted lawns and elegant arrangements. This place felt like . . . whimsy. Above me, small moonstone thuribles were strung through the trees, an echo of the great banyan tree in Alaka where lights lit up the leaves and frost sleeved the branches. Small silk pennants dangled wind chimes through the thousands of branches. When the wind combed its fingers through the trees, music fell through the air.

I had always loved walking in gardens, but since returning to Bharata, I couldn't stand how the loneliness bared its teeth and announced itself at every turn. But here . . . here I felt a comfort rooted not in my senses, but in my soul. It was like recognizing one's bedroom in the dark. You didn't need sight to know it was yours.

Roses grew in colors I'd never seen—lush green and deepest blue. The fragrance moved like a song through the air, unhurried and haunting. Small tree saplings carved from mirrors were placed around the garden walkway, drinking in the light and casting its own illusion of reflections. Golden fruit sparkled beneath the branches of a tree. I peered closer, and saw that the golden fruits were ornaments. Not magic. Or maybe it was magic. What was magic anyway, but the world beheld by someone who chose to see it differently?

I walked faster. Sprouting from the dirt, the tops of swords sliced through flowering bushes. My breath caught.

If you could grow anything in your garden, what would it be?

Swords.

And there they were.

I took another step and looked up to see silver bowls hanging from the trees where the scent of syrupy *gulab jamun* clung to the air.

I just want to pluck it off the trees and eat it on the spot.

I remembered Vikram laughing when he heard that all I wanted to grow were sweets and swords. What had he called me—

"Beastly girl," he said. I looked up, realizing that the words had been supplied not by my mind but by the person standing a short distance away.

My heart leapt. I knew that if I looked at him immediately, my emotions would be plain on my face. So I looked at him in parts. First, his hands. Still steepled. Not quite as scholarly as they once appeared. A scar ornamented his left hand. Then, his shoulders. Ruling suited him. He held himself differently—his shoulders broad and thrown back, an emerald jacket clinging to his lean body. Biju, the snake, hung around his neck like a necklace. Finally, his face. His Otherworldly features remained the same. Handsome, maybe even unbearably so. There was the same tilt to his mouth, as if he were on the verge of grinning. He stood, half in shade and half in sun, mischief and temptation given form.

It was hard to look at him, as if I couldn't hold the sight all at once.

"What do you think?" he asked. "Does it look like the garden of your dreams, swords and all?"

"You did this for me?"

He nodded.

"But then why did the delegates tell me that you were—" I faltered, the words catching in my throat.

"Mostly to make you visit. I had to work on the timing too. I didn't want you to miss the event, but I also didn't want us stuck in an eternity of ceremonies for Bharata's first visit to Ujjijain," he said casually. "And I thought about going to Bharata, but I couldn't bring the garden to you and even if I did, I doubt your guards would have taken kindly to me stabbing swords all over the lawn—"

"You never said anything about the gift I sent you," I blurted out.

"The wooden crown?" he asked, picking it up from a table beside him. "It's my favorite toy. I have made good on my word and thrown it at people. Except the leopard seems to think it's a chew toy and that's—"

"*Why didn't you say anything about it?*"

He stared at me, his brows pressing together. "How was I supposed to know you wanted me to say something?"

"I give a gift. You give a gift back. That's how gift giving should work."

"That is *not* how gift giving works. You give a gift. I accept it."

"You could have said thank you."

"You made it very clear to me when I left Alaka that you needed time and space to figure out your reign and yourself," he said, his voice rising. "I didn't want to clutter your thoughts by inserting myself into them and reminding you, once more, that I was over here looking out windows and sighing like a heartsick fiend who just discovered tragic poetry."

I stared at him. "What?"

Vikram crossed his arms. "You think I string desserts and lights through trees because I have nothing better to do? I can't believe you have the nerve to be mad at me. I was doing what you wanted me to do and giving you space!"

"I didn't want that much space!"

"How was I supposed to know if you never told me?" he demanded, throwing his arms in the air.

"You would have known *if you responded to the fact that I sent you a present.*"

"It was a wooden crown."

"So you don't like it?"

"I never said that!" he grumbled.

My whole heart felt like a tangled ball of thread. At once, delight danced inside me because he had called himself a "heartsick fiend."

And yet, he had tricked me.

"You manipulated me here even though you didn't know how I felt—"

"I would *never* do that to you," he cut in fiercely. "I didn't manipulate. I encouraged. My council does want me to get married. I just thought that we'd grown so used to annoying one another that we might as well do that for the rest of my life and I would have preferred to ask you when you stood in front of me and not through a series of treaties! And I say the rest of my life, not *ours*, since this just confirms that you will be the death of me. And as for knowing how you felt, I knew because I asked."

He held up Biju.

"You told me to wait until you were ready. Day and night, I asked Biju. Day and night, she revealed that you weren't. Then, one day, I asked and she revealed that you were ready. I waited, Gauri." His eyes cut to mine and there was such fierce longing there that I felt it in my heart. "I waited day and night for you to say something the way I thought you would. You never did. I didn't want to wait for you anymore, so I asked Biju if you even felt the same way about me."

Biju flickered, turning from a necklace of jewels to an actual snake. She turned her head to watch me, flicking her forked tongue.

"Watch," he said, his voice low. "You feel the same way I do."

Biju didn't move. *Truth.*

"You were ready for us to see each other."

Truth.

"I love you."

Truth.

At that moment, the rest of the world slipped quietly out of sight. All I felt was the tug of something between us, a thread of a tale not yet finished. A beginning—or maybe it was an ending, or maybe there was no such thing as either—curled its fingers to me. Beckoning. I held out my arms to Biju and she slithered onto my shoulders before hanging from my neck and turning a deep shade of gold. Vikram tracked every movement with his eyes. His jaw clenched, face inscrutable.

"I believe you," I said.

Biju held still. *Truth.*

Vikram waited. A small muscle worked in his jaw. He was furious with waiting just as I was. And then I said the words I had known all along, the ones that haunted me as I slept and danced in my dreams as I woke.

"I love you."

Truth.

He didn't wait after that. He stepped forward, closing the space between us and pulling me into a kiss. We swayed there in that strange garden of sharp and decadent things, of ornaments that held the memory of magic but were remade with our own enchantment. He kissed me until the light moved slowly over the garden and even far away from the coronation ceremony, a murmur of confusion began to reach us.

"I wonder if this is what Kubera wanted," he murmured into my hair. "As an ending for us."

"Not an ending," I said, raising my head. "A beginning to our story."

Above us, something fluttered. I looked up and caught the edge of a scarlet wing. From here, I couldn't tell whether one of Kubera's story birds had followed us or whether it was just an ordinary bird hopping through the trees. But I did know that somewhere our story was taking flight. Maybe it had already traveled, from mouth and ear to mind and memory. And perhaps that in itself was the great secret—not just for legacy, but also for life. You could carry a story inside you and hold it up to the light when you needed it the most. You could peer through it, like a frame, and see how it changed your view when you looked out onto the world.

A new world awaited us outside the garden. A world with new dreams and worn hopes. A world waiting to be filled with stories that would spread pale roots over time until they became indistinguishable from history. Vikram held out his arm, and I took it.

Together, we walked into that new world.

GLOSSARY

Apsara: Celestial nymphs who danced in the kingdoms of the heavens.

Gurukul: A kind of residential school where pupils lived near their gurus (teachers).

Makara: A sea dragon commonly used as a vehicle for water deities and represented as guardians of a temple.

Raksha: A legendary kind of demon, not always entirely good or evil.

Vanara: Monkey-like beings with god-like powers who were created to fight battles in the ancient Indian epic, the *Ramayana*.

Vishakanya: A young woman fed on poison until her touch becomes toxic. Reputedly used as an assassin against powerful enemies in ancient India.